A Death in Canaan

Joan Barthel

A Death
in Canaan

Introduction by William Styron

Thomas Congdon Books
E. P. DUTTON AND CO., INC. | NEW YORK

Library of Congress Cataloging in Publication Data

Barthel, Joan.
A death in Canaan.
"Thomas Congdon books."
1. Murder—Connecticut—Canaan.   2. Gibbons,
Barbara, 1921-1973.   3. Reilly, Peter.   I. Title.
HV6534.C28B37   1976   364.1′523′097461
ISBN 0-525-08940-3   76-40240

Published simultaneously in Canada by Clarke, Irwin & Company
Limited, Toronto and Vancouver

For Jim and Anne.
Their book too.

Introduction
by
William Styron

Toward the end of Joan Barthel's excellent study of crime and justice, Judge John Speziale—the jurist who presided over Peter Reilly's trial and who later granted Peter a new trial—is quoted as saying: "The law is imperfect." As portrayed in this book, Judge Speziale appears an exemplary man of the law, as fair and compassionate a mediator as we have any right to expect in a system where all too many of his colleagues are mediocre or self-serving or simply crooked. Certainly his decision in favor of a retrial—an action in itself so extraordinary as to be nearly historic—was the product of a humane and civilized intellect. Judge Speziale is one of the truly attractive figures in this book, which, although it has many winning people among its dramatis personae, contains more than one deplorable actor. And the judge is of course right: the law *is* imperfect. His apprehension of this fact is a triumph over the ordinary and the expected (in how many prisons now languish other Peter Reillys, victims of the law's "imperfections" but lacking Peter's many salvaging angels?), and is woven into his most honorable decision to grant Peter a new trial. But though he doubtless spoke from the heart as well as the mind and with the best intentions, the judge has to be found guilty of an enormous understatement.

The law (and one must assume that a definition of the law includes the totality of its many arms, including the one known as law enforcement) is not merely imperfect, it is all too often a catastrophe. To the weak and the underprivileged the law in all of its manifestations is usually a punitive nightmare. Even in the abstract the law is an institution of chaotic inequity, administered so many times with such arrogant disdain for the most basic principles of justice and human decency as to make mild admissions of "imperfection" sound presumptuous. If it is true that the law is the best institution human beings have devised to mediate their own eternal discord, this must not obscure the fact that the law's power is too often invested in the hands of mortal men who are corrupt, or, if not corrupt, stupid, or if not stupid then devious or lazy, and all of them capable of the most grievous mischief. The case of Peter Reilly, and Joan Barthel's book, powerfully demonstrate this ever-present danger and the sleepless vigilance ordinary citizens must stead-fastly keep if the mechanism we have devised for our own protection does not from time to time try to destroy even the least of our children.

Naturally the foregoing implies, accurately, that I am convinced of Peter Reilly's innocence. I had begun to be convinced of at least the very strong possibility of his innocence when I first read Mrs. Barthel's article in the magazine *New Times* early in 1974. I happened on the article by sheerest chance, perhaps lured into reading it with more interest than I otherwise might have by the fact that the murder it described took place in Canaan, hardly an hour's drive away from my home in west-central Connecticut. (Is there not something reverberantly sinister, and indicative of the commonplaceness of atrocity in our time, that I should not until then have known about this vicious crime so close at hand and taking place only a few months before?) The Barthel article was a stark, forceful, searing piece, which in essence demonstrated how an eighteen-year-old boy, suspected by the police of murdering his mother, could be crudely yet subtly (and there is no contradiction in those terms) manipulated by law enforcement officers so as to cause him to make an incriminating, albeit fuzzy and ambiguous, statement of responsibility for the crime. What I read was shocking, although I did not find it a novel experience. I am not by nature a taker-up of causes but in the preceding twelve years I had enlisted myself in aiding two people whom I felt to be victims of the law. Unlike Peter, both of these persons were young black men.

In the earlier of these cases the issue was not guilt but rather the punishment. Ben Reid, convicted of murdering a woman in the black ghetto of Hartford, had been sentenced to die in Connecticut's electric chair. His was the classic case of the woebegone survivor of poverty and abandonment who, largely because of his disadvantaged or minority status, is the recipient of the state's most terrible revenge. I wrote an article about Ben Reid in a national magazine and was enormously gratified when I saw that the piece helped significantly in the successful movement by a lot of other indignant people to have Ben's life spared. The other case involved Tony Maynard, whom I had known through James Baldwin and who had been convicted and sentenced to a long term for allegedly killing a marine in Greenwich Village. I worked to help extricate Tony, believing that he was innocent, which he was—as indeed the law finally admitted by freeing him, but only after seven years of Tony's incarceration (among other unspeakable adversities he was badly injured as an innocent bystander in the cataclysm at Attica) and a series of retrials in which his devoted lawyers finally demonstrated the wretched police collusion, false and perjured evidence, shady deals on the part of the district attorney's office and other maggoty odds and ends of the law's "imperfection," which had caused his unjust imprisonment in the first place.

These experiences, then, led me to absorb the Barthel article in *New Times* with something akin to a shock of recognition; horrifying in what it revealed, the piece recapitulated much of the essence of the law's malfeasance that had created Tony Maynard's seven-year martyrdom. It should be noted at this moment, incidentally, that Mrs. Barthel's article was of absolutely crucial significance in the Reilly case, not only because it was the catalytic agent whereby the bulk of Peter's bail was raised, but because it so masterfully crystallized and made clear the sinister issues of the use of the lie detector and the extraction of a confession by the police, thereby making Peter's guilt at least problematical to all but the most obtuse reader. Precise and objective yet governed throughout, one felt, by a rigorous moral conscience, the article was a superb example of journalism at its most effective and powerful. (It was nearly inexcusable that this piece and its author received no mention in the otherwise praiseworthy report on the Reilly case published by *The New York Times* in 1975.) Given the power of the essay, then, I have wondered later why I so readily let Peter Reilly and his plight pass from my mind and my concern. I think it may have been because of the fact that since Peter was not black or even of any shade of tan he would somehow be exempt from that ultimate dungeon-bound ordeal that is overwhelmingly the lot of those who spring from minorities in America. But one need not even be a good Marxist to flinch at this misapprehension. The truth is simpler. Bad enough that Peter lived in a shacklike house with his "disreputable" mother; the critical part is this: *he was poor.* Fancy Peter, if you will, as an affluent day-student at Hotchkiss School only a few miles away, the mother murdered but in an ambience of coffee tables and wall-to-wall carpeting. It takes small imagination to envision the phalanx of horn-rimmed and button-down lawyers interposed immediately between Peter and Sergeant Kelly with his insufferable lie detector.

This detestable machine, the polygraph (the etymology of which shows that the word means "to write much," which is about all that can be said for it), is to my mind this book's chief villain, and the one from which Peter Reilly's most miserable griefs subsequently flowed. It is such an American device, such a perfect example of our blind belief in "scientism" and the efficacy of gadgets; and its performance in the hands of its operator—friendly, fatherly Sergeant Timothy Kelly, the mild collector of seashells—is also so American in the way it produces its benign but ruthless coercion. Like nearly all the law enforcement officers in this drama Sergeant Kelly is "nice"; it is as hard to conceive of him with a truncheon or a blackjack as with a volume of Proust. Plainly neither Kelly nor his colleague Lieutenant Shay, who was actively responsible for Peter's confession, are vicious men; they are merely undiscerningly obedient, totally devoid of that flexibility of mind we call imagination, and they both have a passionate faith in the machine. Kelly especially is an unquestioning votary. "We go strictly by the charts," he tells an exhausted boy. "And the charts say you hurt your mother last night."

In a society where everything sooner or later breaks down or goes haywire, where cars fall apart and ovens explode and vacuum cleaners expire through planned obsolescence (surely Kelly must have been victim, like us all, of the Toastmaster), there is something manic, even awesome, about the sergeant's pious belief in the infallibility of his polygraph. And so at a point in his ordeal Peter, tired, confused, only hours removed from the trauma of witnessing his mother's mutilated body, asks: "Have you ever been proven totally wrong? A person, just from nervousness, responds that way?" Kelly replies: "No, the polygraph can never be wrong, because it's only a recording instrument, reacting to you. It's the person interpreting it who could be wrong. But I haven't made that many mistakes in twelve years, in the thousands of people who sat here, Pete." Such mighty faith and assurances would have alone been enough to decisively wipe out a young man at the end of his tether. Add to this faith the presumed assumption of Peter's guilt on the part of the sergeant, and to this the outrageously tendentious nature of his questioning, and it is no wonder that a numb and bedraggled Peter was a setup for Lieutenant Shay, whose manner of extracting a confession from this troubled boy must be deemed a triumph of benevolent intimidation. Together the transcripts of the polygraph testimony and Peter's confession—much of which is recorded in this book—have to comprise another one of those depressing but instructive scandals that litter the annals of American justice.

Yet there is much more in the case of Peter Reilly, set down on these pages in rich detail, which makes it such a memorable and unique affair. What could be more harmoniously "American," in the best sense of that mangled word, than the spectacle of a New England village rising practically en masse to come to the support of one of their own young whom they felt to be betrayed and abandoned? Mrs. Barthel, who lived with this case month in and month out during the past few years, and who got to know well so many of Peter's friends and his surrogate "family," tells this part of the story with color, humor, and affection; and her feeling for the community life of a small town like Canaan— with its family ties and hostilities, its warmth and crankiness and crooked edges—gives both a depth and vivacity to her narrative; never is she lured into the purely sensational. As in every story of crime and justice, the major thrust of the drama derives from its central figures, and they are all here: not only the law's automata—the two "nice" cops whose dismal stratagems thrust Peter into his nightmare at the outset—but the judge, prosecutor and counsel for the defense. Regarding these personages, Mrs. Barthel's art most often and tellingly lies in her subtle selectivity—and her onlooker's silence. What she allows the State's Attorney, Mr. Bianchi, simply to utter with his own lips, for instance, says more about Mr. Bianchi and the savagery of a certain genus of prosecutorial mind than any amount of editorializing or speculative gloss. As for the fascinating aftermath of the trial—Arthur Miller's stubborn and deservedly celebrated detective work in company with the redoubtable Mr. Conway, the brilliantly executed labors of the new defense counsel, the discovery of fresh evidence that led to the order for another trial, and other matters—all of these bring to a climax an eccentric, tangled, significant and cautionary chronicle of the wrongdoing of the law and its belated redemption.

Joan Barthel's book would deserve our attention if for no other reason than that it focuses a bright light on the unconscionable methods, which the law, acting through its enforcement agencies, and because of its lust for punishment, uses to victimize the most helpless members of our society. And thus it once again shows the law's tragic and perdurable imperfection. It also reminds us that while judicial oppression undoubtedly falls the heaviest on those from minority groups, it will almost as surely hasten to afflict the poor and the "unrespectable," no matter what their color. But rather triumphantly, and perhaps most importantly, *A Death in Canaan* demonstrates the will of ordinary people, in their ever astonishing energy and determination, to see true justice prevail over the law's dereliction.

A Death in Canaan

PART ONE

1

When Barbara died, some of the news stories described her house as a little white cottage. The phrase made the place sound picturesque, as if it were one of the many charming cottages tucked into the northwestern corner of Connecticut, nestled against the mountains.

But the little house where Barbara and Peter lived was drab and boxy, set very close to the road. Once it had been a diner. It didn't nestle against the mountain, although the mountain was there, a rugged hulk behind the house. At night, especially, the setting was desolate and lonely.

On the north side of the house, stretching toward the town of Canaan, five miles away, there was a swamp with some scrubby evergreens, a few birches, and a billboard stuck in the marsh. On the south side, the owners of the property lived in a big old Colonial house that was only partly used, the rest of it closed off and musty. Past the big house, several houses were scattered down the road. There were no houses across the road, only a gas station. During the day, when Peter was in school, Barbara sometimes wandered over there, to have somebody to talk to. She was there talking when Peter came home from school on the day she died.

Although the house was small, it wasn't cozy, just cramped. There was one bedroom, ten by twelve feet, where Barbara and Peter slept in bunk beds. There were no table lamps in the bedroom, just a naked ceiling bulb, so Barbara put a clamp-on light by the top bunk for reading. She loved to read, especially mysteries. She went to the Falls Village Library regularly, two mornings a week, and when she died, she left two books overdue.

The front door of the house opened directly into the living room, also ten by twelve feet. A person coming through the front door could easily see the bunks in the bedroom just by looking to the right.

Beyond the bedroom was a bathroom, a closet, and a back door leading outside. To get to the bathroom or the back door, it was necessary to walk through the bedroom. The back door was kept locked, except when Barbara washed clothes in the bathtub and took them out to hang on the line, or when Peter took his bike out. Since Barbara rarely did laundry, and since Peter, once he got his driver's license, almost never rode his bike, the door stayed locked and unused. The night Barbara died, the door was unlocked and standing partly open.

As cramped and cluttered as the house always was, Peter was used to it. It was home. Peter was still a child, just turned twelve, when he and Barbara moved in. When she died, he was eighteen, legally a man, so he had spent some important years growing up in the little house. Besides, Peter was the kind of person who got used to things. He seemed to take life pretty much as it came. Barbara was a casual person, and Peter was too. "My mom never got uptight about anything," he said. "I got used to playing everything by ear. I think things work out best that way, myself. Things work out; they always do. Just give it time."

It never seemed to bother Peter, for example, that his last name was different from Barbara's.

"She just picked my name right out of the air," Peter explained. "I don't know who my father was, and I don't think anyone knows it. When I was old enough to understand, about fourteen, my mom told me what happened. She told me—this may shock you—she told me that she was raped in Van Cortland Park when she lived in New York. But she felt I should have my own name, so she picked a name she liked, and she said, 'Peter Anthony Reilly. That's what his name is going to be.'

"She got up so early in the morning," Peter marveled. "I need twelve hours sleep, but she'd be up at four-thirty or five, just as refreshed. Wide awake! First thing I'd hear, when I got up at a quarter to seven,

4

was Bob Steele on the radio, lots of old music and old jokes. That was too early in the morning for me, but my mom used to get out her pen and paper and write down the jokes and tell them to me when I got home from school. By then I was awake. I remember this one: Two caterpillars crossing the road. A butterfly goes over their heads. One caterpillar looks up and says, 'You'll never get *me* up in one of those things.'

"Sunday mornings, my mom would drive over to Mansfield's General Store. They had fresh-baked bread on Sunday morning, and she'd get *The New York Times* too. All Sunday afternoon she'd read *The New York Times*. She liked the Double-Crostic. She could do any kind of puzzles, upside down or rightside up. She was something else. She was reading better when she was five than I am now. She knew opera, you name it. She was terrific."

Barbara was casual about Peter's school work, so he was, too. But it bothered her, when he started high school, that he didn't like to read. "Let's just read one book," Barbara said to Peter. "I know you'll enjoy it." So she took him to the Falls Village Library and got *Tarzan of the Apes*. Sure enough, Peter was interested. "I read it and I thought, 'That was pretty good,' " Peter recalled. "So I began to read more. I could read a book a week and report on it pretty well. In Modern Literature you could read anything you wanted to, so I read James Bond, and I got eighty-five on it."

Once Barbara had got Peter off to school, she didn't have much to do. She hadn't worked for several years, since she was fired from her job at an insurance agency. Barbara always drank a lot, and after she stopped working, she drank more. She spent most of her time reading, and writing, and drinking. As time went on, Barbara seemed more and more adrift.

Usually Peter rode the school bus, but on the day Barbara died, he got a ride with two of his good friends, Geoffrey Madow and Paul Beligni. They rode home together, too. The three boys had been friends since the first day of their freshman year at Housatonic Valley Regional High School. When Barbara died, they were beginning their senior year together. They all had pretty much the same classes including Contemporary Problems. This year they were scheduled to study "Crime in Society."

Barbara was fifty-one when she died, but she always got along far better with Peter's teen-aged friends than with her own contemporaries, their parents. Paul Beligni often stayed overnight, and the summer before she died he stayed practically every night, sleeping on a piece of foam in the living room that he rolled up during the day and stuck into a corner. Paul used to shoot woodchucks in the backyard, using a twelve-gauge shotgun. Once he and Peter were fooling around with the gun in the living room and it went off, blasting away the top of a tall clock. Barbara just shrugged and said they were lucky it hadn't hit the red bowl.

One of her favorite pranks was to spot a car passing on the road, get the license number, then call the police and sob out a story, in a lisping, childish voice: "Oh a car has just run over my cat, and my cat fwew up in the air and it hit the tewephone pole and it came down again and now it's all smushed and dead—sob, sob—but I got the wicensepwate number. Oh, can't you pweath find the mean man who hit my cat?" She'd recite the number she'd written down, then stand in the doorway and, when the police car came by in screaming chase, she'd roar with laughter and pour herself another drink.

"I don't know that Barbara ever hurt anybody, but she could aggravate the devil out of a person," said Jean Beligni, Paul's mother, who was in Barbara's house only once, to bring back some laundry Jean had done as a favor for Peter. Doing the laundry was not one of Barbara's strengths. The night she died, the bedroom floor was strewn with dirty clothes.

When she felt like being aggravating, Barbara would sit outdoors and shout at passing cars. She liked to read outdoors, too; in the coldest weather she sat in the yard wrapped in a fur coat. She even read at night, under the floodlights that the landlord, Mr. Kruse, had put up for her. She was spontaneous, boisterous, and sometimes just silly, and the teen-agers loved it. Beyond the prankishness, they may have recognized and identified with an uncertainty in her, an indirection, that they sometimes felt themselves. What the boys may not have recognized was that in themselves this was a fact of adolescence, while in Barbara it was a permanent condition.

Barbara's most ambitious and successful prank involved an imaginary truffle hunt to be held on an estate in Sharon. She wrote a story about it and sent it to the *Lakeville Journal* just before presstime, so they wouldn't have time to check it out. On the day of the supposed hunt,

Peter recalled gleefully, "everybody you could think of was climbing Sharon Mountain, looking for that estate."

"If she'd been rich, you'd call her eccentric," said Father Paul Halovatch, curate of St. Joseph's in Canaan. "Around here, she was just an oddball."

Along with the very silly things, Barbara did some very serious things, as a woman adrift is apt to do. For a while, she had a black man living with her. Some teen-agers, peeking in the window one day, saw Barbara and the man naked, and the mother of one of Peter's classmates, who lived down the road, had to warn her son about going to Peter's. "Make yourself scarce," she told him.

Still, in her own way, Barbara looked out for Peter. In fact, her landlord's wife thought Barbara spoiled the boy. Once she drove out at night in a thick snowstorm to buy him some porkchops, because he'd had frankfurters for dinner the night before and didn't want them again.

And Peter looked out for Barbara. The week before she died he insisted on driving her to Sharon Hospital two days in a row for some tests she needed, because their car was in bad shape and he was afraid for her to drive it alone.

Peter was all Barbara had. Barbara was all Peter had. Perhaps that was why they yelled at one another. "They swore like truck drivers," a neighbor reminisced. "But they cared." At Christmastime 1971, Peter gave Barbara an electric portable typewriter that he bought with money he earned from playing guitar in a band. "She wanted a typewriter like I wanted a guitar," he explained. That spring, she'd given him an expensive amplifier. His birthday card said: *Did You Know I Was Put on This Earth to Bring Joy and Sunshine into Your Life? Love, Mom.*

Peter and Barbara. This is what it was all about. "You had to understand my mother," Peter would say, but hardly anybody did. "She was an enigma," said the Falls Village librarian, who saw her often. "She had a very keen mind, a lovely voice and enunciation, and a charming manner. But she looked like the dickens most of the time, and she was none too clean."

Barbara and Peter. Their last photograph was taken in the spring, a few months before Barbara died. The two of them are standing against the shed, near the house, where the landlord kept tools and barbed wire, and Peter kept parts for his car. Both Barbara and Peter are wearing dungarees and matching sweat shirts with striped sleeves. Barbara is rubbing the little finger and thumb of her left hand together, as she had a habit of doing. Peter is looking toward the house, and Barbara is looking at him. She is smiling.

Peter's friends called Barbara by her first name, or, sometimes, "Barbs." She didn't like the nickname "Babs"; her mother had called her that. She was born in Berlin on November 20, 1921, the only child of Hilda and Louis Gibbons. Her father was in the import-export business, and his work took him around the world. He and Hilda kept a house in England, and they were living there when Barbara started school at the Lady Bon House School in Manchester. Those were years of grace: a sweet-faced Barbara, with a pageboy cut and shiny bangs, wearing a white dancing dress and dancing shoes. A wide-eyed Barbara, chubby and adorable, playing shuffleboard on the S.S. *Baltic*. Barbara flanked by two Irish setters, Fifi and Wapsi, on the lawn of a house in Anglesey. Barbara on the boardwalk at West Beach in Bournemouth.

When Louis's company went out of business, the family came to the United States to live. Barbara told Peter that she brought with her a teddy bear bigger than she was. It was a remnant of affluence; in those Depression years, Hilda worked as a switchboard operator in a Manhattan office, and by 1940 the family had moved from a house in New Jersey to an apartment. Later they moved to the Bronx.

In her early teens, Barbara began showing signs of the naughty streak she never outgrew. At her school, which had Anne Morrow Lindbergh on its board, she was suspended for selling pictures of nudes. She was exhibiting her athletic streak, too—skiing at Big Bromley, playing tennis, swimming, and riding motor cycles. In the summer of 1940 she held Hilda on her shoulders for a snapshot at poolside, and then held a man—blond, grinning—on her shoulders too.

After high school, Barbara enrolled at New York University on Washington Square as a premed student. She had grown into a genuine beauty, with deep, dark eyes, thick black hair, full red lips, and an oval face. "She was very quiet, very beautiful," her cousin Vicky recalled. "She had thick eyelashes that made you sick with envy and naturally curly hair. She attracted lots of men—and women, too."

She didn't finish college. She left after two years, according to a form she once filled out for her welfare worker, because of financial problems and got a job at the Home Insurance Company in New York City. For several years Barbara edited the house paper and had a good time doing it. For a joke, she once proposed a "Strictly Personal" column with unusual entries—mentioning two employees, for example, "who have named their son, born November 1, 'Woody,' in memory of our annual outing at Bear Mountain." At the garden show, she wrote, there would be one special event: ALL CLASSES, ESPECIALLY PANSIES.

In 1950, Hilda and Louie bought a little red house on Johnson Road in Falls Village, Connecticut, an escape from New York's summer miseries. Later they lived there year round. Barbara stayed in the city. She had many friends there, most of them from the insurance company where she worked. Sometimes, when she went up to Connecticut to spend a weekend with her parents, she would take one of her closest friends, a lovely blonde woman whom Peter would come to know as his godmother, "Auntie B." Auntie B. worked at the insurance company too. She was the daughter of a rich family and probably was working only because she wanted to.

Peter was born in New York on March 2, 1955. Within the year, Barbara resigned her job and came to Falls Village to stay. The postmistress recalled very clearly when Barbara brought Peter to Connecticut. "She stepped off the train, held out a baby wrapped in a fuzzy blanket, and said, 'This is Peter Reilly.' And that was about as much as she ever said."

As Peter grew up, he came to love the house on Johnson Road. It was a wonderful place for people who liked the outdoors, as Barbara always had. When she died, and people all over town were talking about her, hardly anyone ever mentioned that—perhaps because her life was so unusual, so many of its details draped in mystery, that a simple, understandable quality such as liking the outdoors didn't seem worth noting. But it was important to Barbara, and so it became important to Peter and had something to do with the kind of person he was.

Even as a small boy, Peter would take his fishing line and wander off by himself to the lake. He could spend all the summer days in the shade of a pine, alone, his line idling in the water, the hot sun streaking the surface of the water with blurring light. There was a detachment about him even then, a fragile dreamy quality that may have had its source in those early days by the lake, in the house in the pine woods.

Barbara's father, Louie, was an outdoor person too, and Peter idolized him. He seemed the ideal father figure for a boy who had none. They hiked together, built feeders for the grosbeaks, and went canoeing, with Louie's hound splashing in the water. Peter went barefoot most of the time, and the pictures that survive these years show a regular Huck Finn, skinny and grinning, his hair cut short and his ears sticking out. He learned to swim when he was four. Barbara hadn't learned till she was fourteen and always regretted the time she lost. When she learned, though, she must have learned well, for she told Peter that when she was sixteen, she swam across the Hudson River, from New York to New Jersey, on a bet.

Most of the photographs dating back to the years on Johnson Road are marvelously serene: Hilda asleep in the sun, a *Saturday Evening Post* open on the grass beside her; Hilda and Louie laughing together, Louie holding a squirrel; Barbara seen from the back, walking down a country lane, disappearing into a leafy distance. Even though the reality of those years was far less idyllic, and although these lives eventually shattered, some of them past mending, the years on Johnson Road were good for Peter. At least, that is how he remembered them. Barbara liked to hike, and she cared about birds, so Peter did too. Even Hilda, who didn't get along with her daughter at all, was pleased by her fondness for nature. Hilda gave her a book of wild game birds inscribed: *To Barbara from Mother, Christmas 1956.*

"I can't give you much," Barbara once told Peter, "but I can always arrange things for you." His baby and toddler clothes came from New York, with labels from Lord & Taylor and Saks Fifth Avenue. When he started school, he was enrolled at Town Hill, a private school.

Barbara and her father drank a lot, and Hilda continually cursed them for it. "You had to feel sorry for Barbara," a neighbor pointed out. "Hilda had a vile temper, and it was hard to please her. She gave Barbara a bad time." When Peter was ten, Barbara and Peter moved out.

They lived for a while on Music Mountain, in a barn that was only partly renovated and usually cold, but Peter remembered only the good times there, too. He was going to school in Falls Village, and Barbara was working for the insurance agency in Cornwall. She kept in touch with people in New York, though, especially with Auntie B. For years the two women had exchanged notes and letters whenever they were apart. Barbara kept the letters. In the beginning, their tone was affec-

10

tionate, but later the tone was curt. Whatever the women's relationship had once been, it had cooled.

When Barbara brought Peter to the World's Fair, they stayed with Auntie B. Peter liked to sit in her chair at the dining table, stretching his foot to press the buzzer under the carpet. Auntie B.'s cook sent Peter cookies in the mail, and Auntie B. sent checks. At first these were mostly gifts at Christmas, and on birthdays, or checks for something special—but after Barbara was fired from her job and went on welfare, Auntie B.'s checks came regularly. They paid for some of the basics, and all of the extras: wine for Barbara, better food and shoes and shirts for Peter than welfare could provide. Sometimes Barbara bought things for herself, especially food—she liked pastrami, liverwurst on rye with mustard and onion, sliced pizza with everything on it, and beefsteak, sliced thin, which she ate raw with lots of oregano and pepper. But mostly Auntie B.'s money seemed to be spent for Peter.

Louie Gibbons never stopped drinking. One rainy night he skidded off the road, Route 126, and crashed into a telephone pole. Peter took his death hard, and insisted that either Louie had swerved to avoid hitting a deer or he'd just been very tired and had fallen asleep at the wheel. In the spring of 1967 Hilda went to a doctor in Lakeville, got a vaccination, and flew off to Switzerland. She never came back to Connecticut. She sent Peter a postcard from Basel, but she didn't write to Barbara. In fact, in the passport space for "In case of accident, notify:" she hadn't written her daughter's name at all. She'd written the name and address of Auntie B.

Once more Barbara and Peter moved, for the last time in her life. They rented the drab little place on Route 63, for which Barbara at first paid $35 a month, in cash. When she died, she was paying $55; she died two days before the rent was due.

For someone whose girlhood had been as careful as Barbara's, it seemed a pitiful place to live. The heating system consisted of one kerosene heater in the corner of the living room. The blue flowered linoleum was cracking, and curling up at the edges. The house was always cold, from late fall until late spring. Barbara wrote to her welfare worker that fuel was one of her biggest expenses, and that in order to save hot water, she took very few baths. Barbara explained that the electrical bill was very high because often she had to turn on

11

all the appliances she had, even the toaster and the iron, to warm the place. The clothing inventory Barbara submitted to welfare listed a skirt, a housedress, and a girdle, but no pajamas; because the house was so cold, she went to bed wearing her daytime clothes and slept in a sleeping bag.

For all its flaws, this house was home for Barbara and Peter. Although there were tensions between them, and sometimes Peter mentioned to friends that he'd like to move out, he never did. He'd say his mother needed him home, and he'd go back. They had some good times. Peter liked to work on model planes, and Barbara went to Mario's Barber Shop in Canaan and got him a straight razor with a black plastic handle, so he wouldn't cut his fingers when he worked. While Peter crafted balsa wood, or read car manuals, or played his guitar, Barbara listened to the radio and watched TV, read, and drank.

"She lived the way she liked livin'," Peter said, and in this little house on Route 63 Barbara could live precisely as she pleased. She could drink, and sing arias all night, and sit outdoors in the snow, reading under the floodlights. She could do whatever sad, doomed, compulsive things she wanted to do, or needed to do, and she didn't have to explain things that couldn't be explained anyway, perhaps not even to herself. She could diminish herself, even destroy herself, and while there were people to notice—"I watched her go downhill steadily," the owner of Bob's Clothing Store said gloomily—there was no one to stop her. In this drab little house, Barbara Gibbons had only herself to confront, and when she packed for the move, she kept out Hilda's book of wild birds and gave it to the Falls Village Library.

Peter was too thin, Barbara always said, nagging him to eat more, and by chance the school nurse weighed and measured him the day Barbara died. Peter Reilly weighed 121 pounds and was five seven, a slender boy with slightly crooked teeth, a nice smile, long hair, hazel eyes with sweeping lashes.

He skipped breakfast that day, as he always did, and dressed in blue jeans, his favorite dark brown braided leather belt, and a pair of Converse sneakers, tan with a black stripe, that he'd bought at Bob's Clothing Store just a week or two before. He wore a brown shirt from Bob's too. Paul Beligni, who worked there Friday nights and all day Saturdays, had one just like it.

The shirt had long sleeves; it was autumn, with a snap in the air. The sugar maples back of the house were beginning to flare, and mists swirled in the valley some mornings, hinting at winter on the way. Many people consider this the prettiest season in the northwest corner of Connecticut, in the Litchfield hills. The leaves are reflected in the Housatonic River, which meanders through the region like a strand of silver yarn.

The largest town in the area is North Canaan, and there is East Canaan, and South Canaan, which includes parts of Falls Village. But nearly everybody calls the area "Canaan," the name chosen by the settlers who worked their way up from Stamford in 1740 and named their town for the biblical land of milk and honey.

And once, the land surely prospered. The farms thrived and the valley's limestone and marble quarries swarmed with workers—the state capitol at Hartford was constructed of Canaan marble. A spacious inn, the Lawrence Tavern, was built; George Washington slept there, and so did Ethan Allen. Forty tons of iron a day were blasted out of the hills, much of it to be made into cannonballs. Altogether, it was a busy, lusty place; the general store in Falls Village stayed open all night, thirty clerks working three shifts.

Eventually, the trains stopped coming, and the tracks bristled with weeds. Nobody needed cannonballs anymore, and travelers to New York had to wait at Collins Diner for a bus. In Falls Village, the general store closed down, and the village seemed to lapse into rural sleep. In the twentieth century Canaan became a small-scale factory town. Two manufacturing plants moved in—Becton-Dickinson, where surgical instruments were made, and another small plant that made the little plastic packets called Wash 'n Dri.

Amid all the change, some things remained constant. The mountains still skimmed straight up, the South Canaan Congregational Church still stood small and white and proud, as it had for generations, across the street from the Kruses' house.

Fred and Helen Kruse, Barbara's landlords, had lived in the big white house since they came up from New York in 1946. Fred Kruse had bought land across the highway, too, and ran the gas station there.

For a while, after she was fired from her job in Cornwall, Barbara had worked at the gas station. When she filled out an application for the state-run Work Incentive Program (WIN) she wrote that her last

13

regular job was "Service Station Operator." Even after that, although the station was leased to various people, it remained a part of Barbara's life. One man who leased the place accused Barbara of stealing $50 from him, and Paul Beligni and Peter got even with him by way of an elaborate prank involving ammonia, dead fish, and an electric fan, on a 102-degree day. Barbara had the last word. "I might consider stealing fifty thousand dollars," she told the man, "but never fifty."

On the day Barbara died, she planned to drive into Canaan to do some shopping, although the car was in rotten shape—the transmission was almost entirely gone, and the only gear that would operate was fourth. But Barbara didn't want to trade it in. For all her shabby clothes, she liked being special, and the metallic blue Corvette that Auntie B. had paid for looked very sporty and special. Peter wanted a bigger car so he could carry around his musical equipment.

Barbara needed to buy a new wallet. About two weeks earlier, her old one had been stolen, with over a hundred dollars in it. She had reported the loss to the police. There was another old wallet in the drawer in the living room, with some old pictures and papers in it, but it was worn out. Barbara planned to drive into town and buy a new wallet at Bob's. She was expecting a check, too, and planned to stop by the bank.

So Geoff Madow picked up Peter for school; Peter didn't like the bus ride, slow and bumpy and roundabout. Geoff drove straight over Route 7, past Eddie Houston's Garage, where Peter's first car, a little red 1967 Triumph that Auntie B. had bought from a man in Vermont, was still sitting on blocks. Then Geoff made a sharp right, down the long driveway of Regional High. The driveway curved widely around the sprawling, handsome stone building. Steve Blass, the professional baseball player, was a graduate of Regional, and his autographed picture hung on the wall in the principal's office.

It was Friday, September 28, 1973.

Barbara did her errands. She went to Bob's Clothing Store and bought a new wallet, a folding, man's wallet, $7.50. She went to the bank, then across the street to the Falls Village market. When Barbara pulled out her wallet, the grocer noticed she was carrying a lot of money.

She didn't go by the library, which was open only two mornings a week. Whenever it was open, Barbara almost always appeared. The

14

librarian expected her. Even at 9:30 in the morning, Mrs. Kester remembered, you could usually smell liquor on Barbara's breath, though she wasn't what you would call under the influence, and in fact Mrs. Kester had invited her to come to tea at the library. Barbara never came. She didn't socialize much, at least not in that way. She had had an ulcer in 1969 and, a year later, a hysterectomy. She thought maybe she had cancer and was often depressed. She had mentioned suicide. Barbara didn't look at all, anymore, like the beautiful, healthy, robust young woman who'd once effortlessly held a grinning man on her shoulders. When she died, she weighed 115 pounds and, at just a little over five feet, she seemed frail.

When she got home from town Barbara probably did some reading, though no one can say for sure. Or writing. Some people suspected that she wrote for porno publications, but no one ever proved it. Mrs. Kester, who knew Barbara's reading habits so well, thought maybe she wrote mysteries, and after wondering about it for a while, she came right out, once, and asked her. "Do you write mysteries?" Barbara said no, but Mrs. Kester had her doubts, so she mentioned it to the postmistress. "Ruth, did Barbara Gibbons ever send anything out in big envelopes, like manuscripts?" The postmistress said she hadn't noticed.

Barbara had written some little fillers for magazines, though, and she wrote letters of all kinds, including one to *The New York Times,* challenging the grammar in an editorial. Herbert Matthews of the *Times* wrote back, acknowledging the error, and Barbara kept his letter for nearly ten years. When she died, it turned up in the assorted pieces of her life, along with a stack of Peter's report cards, showing him failing geometry; a glossy picture of an unidentified man with a lean, hollowed, cynical face, sitting on a tabletop, smoking a cigarette; a $30,000 flight insurance policy from Auntie B.'s trip to St. Croix, made out to Peter; a .38 caliber Smith & Wesson revolver; a gas mask; and warranties for Peter's amplifier and her Black & Decker electric drill. There was an itemized statement of hospital costs, in Barbara's handwriting: "$15.50 —me; $5.50—Peter," multiplied by eight days, plus $20.00 for anesthesia and $1.50 for the newborn's I.D. bracelet. One file of papers involved a running feud Barbara had had with Jacobs Garage in Falls Village, in which Jacobs had been represented by a lawyer in Canaan named Catherine Roraback.

There was also a picture of Auntie B., smiling demurely, looking

15

vaguely like Betty Grable, and one of Auntie B.'s father, a man so brilliant he'd been admitted to the New York bar a year before he finished law school. There were many letters from Auntie B., including one in which she'd threatened to stop sending checks after April 1 and suggested that Barbara get a job washing dishes. Barbara retorted that even if there were a place to wash dishes, she had only one pair of shoes, a pair of ostrich pumps. And she pointed out the irony in the date Auntie B. had given, All Fools Day.

Barbara had kept some of Hilda's letters, too. The two women never saw one another again. After Hilda returned from Switzerland, she went to Florida, where she had two sisters, and began writing letters to Barbara. Eventually she asked to come back, promising to give Peter money. Hilda had written other letters to other people, letters that Barbara called "poisonous" and claimed had cost her jobs. She told her Uncle Jim that Hilda's letters had made life so difficult that she might have to leave Falls Village. Even years before, Barbara complained, Hilda had always tampered with her private mail. Hilda died in Florida, two years before her daughter. Uncle Jim gave her clothes to Goodwill, except for her fur coat, which he sent to Barbara. Hilda left $7,352.22 when she died, but when the medical and legal bills were paid, there was only $2,854.60 left. She had willed it to Jim, but he sent Peter a check.

Among the letters and papers and fragments of her life that Barbara left behind was a questionnaire from welfare. She hadn't bothered to fill it out. The welfare people wanted to know:

What would you consider as your most pressing problem?
What can the average citizen expect from the police?
How can you prepare children for your absence?

At ten minutes past two, the students assembled on the lawn in front of the school and gave three cheers for the janitor, who was retiring. Then Peter got a lift home from Geoff Madow. When Geoff dropped Peter off, Barbara was over at the gas station. She and Peter were friends with the young man who ran the station, Ken Carter. He was a photographer, too, and had taken the picture of Barbara and Peter, back in the spring.

That afternoon, Barbara and Peter played a game of gin rummy. She showed him the new wallet she'd bought that day at Bob's. In an hour or so, Geoff came back, and he and Peter drove up to Great Barrington to see whether the Shopwell Market, where Geoff sometimes worked, needed him that weekend to work in the deli section. They didn't. Back at Geoff's house, he and Peter watched TV until dinnertime. The Madows asked Peter to join them at the table, but he stayed in the den.

After a while Geoff and Peter drove back to Peter's. When the boys arrived, Barbara was eating a TV dinner, but Peter said he wasn't hungry. Geoff sat outside in one of the chairs for a while, holding Barbara's cat in his lap, watching the sun set.

Peter and Geoff were going to a meeting at the Methodist Church in Canaan, a meeting to discuss the future of the Teen Center. In the *Lakeville Journal,* Joanne Mulhern, wife of State Trooper Jim Mulhern, had said there was very little adult support for the center, and she hoped people would come to the meeting. Joanne and Jim's son Michael was just a second-grader, but Joanne was interested in the status of teen-agers in the town. All summer long the center had been closed, and Joanne felt the young people needed something to do.

When Geoff and Peter left the house, each driving his own car, Barbara was watching the news, hollering back at Walter Cronkite. It was twenty minutes past seven. Less than three hours later, Barbara was dead.

2

Marion Madow was curled up on the sofa in the den, watching the Friday night movie, when the phone rang. Her mother was sitting at the opposite end of the sofa, with the dachshund nestled in her lap, the dog's shiny black nose sticking out from under the rainbow-colored afghan. Marion's sister, who had come up from New York for the weekend, was watching the movie, along with a family friend, a nurse.

Marion's husband, Mickey, had been watching television along with the others, but at 9:30, when the Mama Cass special ended and the CBS film, *Kelley's Heroes,* began, Mickey wandered out into the living room. He eased into the soft green armchair by the window, looking out onto the blackness of Canaan Mountain, and picked up the new copy of *Time.*

It had been a busy day, a busy week, and everyone was glad to relax. Marion had been up at 6:30 that morning, as usual, to make coffee, to put a load of clothes in the washer before she went to work, to get the rest of the household up and moving. Mickey got up without much prodding, but the boys liked to stay in bed in the morning till the last possible moment, and beyond.

When Arthur had graduated from Regional two years earlier, he'd had trouble finding a job, and Marion worried that Geoff would have trouble too. Jobs were scarce in Canaan. Many of the girls who graduated went to Hartford to work for one of the big insurance companies, or to New Haven to take up nursing. The boys could be hospital orderlies, or they could work for a construction company during the busy summer months and get laid off during the winter. Marion occasionally talked with her boys about their future, encouraging them to think about what they wanted to do. She thought Geoff, with his sense of humor, his gruff, good-humored voice, and his flair for words, would make a good radio announcer, and she was willing to send him to a broadcasting school to be trained.

As long as the boys had enough money for cigarettes and enough time to tinker with their cars, they seemed content. Almost every night they went down to the basement where they kept their musical equipment; Arthur played the electric guitar, Geoffrey took the drums, and when Peter Reilly came by, he played guitar too. One of the Madow cousins, Jamie, who lived down at the bottom of Locust Hill, often came by to sing. "He's got a scratchy voice," Peter would say jokingly, "but he's comin' along."

Sometimes Marion thought it really would have been better if she and Mickey had stayed in New York and raised their sons there. She felt Art and Geoff had missed something by being brought up in a country town.

Both Marion and Mickey were New Yorkers, and had lived in the city for a few years when they were newly married. Mickey was a salesman for a construction tool company then. "I broke the territory in West-chester," Mickey said proudly. They moved to Connecticut in 1950, so Mickey could work out of the home office.

The boys were born in Canaan. When Geoffrey, the younger boy, started school, Marion went back to work fulltime, as a bookkeeper at Mickey's office. Marion's father had died, and her mother Hanna took care of the boys and the house. She cooked big meals and grew plants— Swedish ivy, flowering cactus, and trailing philodendron. The boys called their grandmother Nanny, or Nan, and soon everybody else did too.

Marion and Mickey, and Mickey's brother Murray and his wife, Dorothy, were just about the only Jewish families in town. But they seemed to be accepted, especially Mickey. His real name was Meyer, but he was so jaunty and sociable that Mickey seemed a much better name. He became a junior vice-commander at the VFW, and he was always a star of the annual Variety Show. He volunteered for the ambulance corps, and once had his picture taken with Dr. Ernest Izumi, the Assistant Medical Examiner for Litchfield County.

Marion wasn't as outgoing as Mickey, but she joined the VFW Auxiliary. Canaan was an easy town for knowing people: Dr. Martin, the dentist; Mario, the barber; and John Bianchi, who had been appointed State's Attorney for Litchfield County, the prosecutor's job, in the summer of 1972. Before that, when he was in private practice, John Bianchi had handled Mickey and Marion's property sale, and he'd handled some matters for Barbara Gibbons, too. He knew about her problems. "Around here, people know when you part your hair," was a local saying. Sometimes that seemed like a good thing, sometimes not.

At the VFW Auxiliary, Marion got to know Joanne Mulhern, wife of the state trooper. Jim Mulhern was young. He had a fresh, boyish face, and he seemed especially friendly with young people. They seemed to trust him. One night Arthur Madow was in a car accident in Hudson, New York, and at two in the morning Jim Mulhern was the first person Arthur thought to call. Mulhern got out of bed and drove all the way to Hudson to help Arthur out. In midsummer 1973, the Madows put up new wallpaper in their dinette, a dark blue and red poppy print, and Jim Mulhern came over to help. Then, when Jim Mulhern put in a sidewalk at his house on Church Street, the Madow boys went over to help him. Peter Reilly and Paul Beligni helped too. Sometimes Peter stayed all night at the Madows', although he usually went home. Barbara was often depressed and drank too much, and although it felt good to be away from her, he always decided, sooner or later, that he ought to go back. Peter felt Barbara needed him. Besides, when he didn't come home, Barbara often would call up other people's houses, looking for him. It was easier just to go home. One night near the end of the summer, when Peter had been visiting the Madows and Marion drove him home, Nan went along for the ride. Barbara was sitting outside in the twilight; she'd been reading. Peter hopped out, and Barbara walked over to the car. Barbara knew Marion by sight, but she'd never met Nan, so Peter introduced them.

Nan motioned toward the house, small and squat, looking closed and even sinister in the gathering dusk, nothing but marsh and the mountain around, and looked at Barbara curiously. "Aren't you afraid to live out here?" Nan asked Barbara, who laughed and said she kept a gun in the house and was never afraid.

When the phone rang, Marion was close enough that she could reach out her hand and pick it up, still watching the TV screen. One of Kelley's men had just jumped up on the tank and yelled to his buddies that he wanted to go with them across the river to get the gold.

Geoffrey had just come in from the Teen Center meeting. He had picked up a bag of chocolate chip cookies in the kitchen and was walking into the den, taking a bite, as Marion spoke.

"Your Mom sick, Peter?" the others heard her say. "You call your doctor, and we'll be right there."

Marion hung up quickly. "Peter says he needs the ambulance," she said. "Something's happened to his mother." In the hallway between the den and the living room, Mickey was grabbing for his orange ambulance jacket with VFW in black letters on the back. Geoffrey dashed for the door. His car was out of gas, so he jumped into the little Toyota that belonged to their friend Fran Kaplan, a nurse. Marion, Mickey, and Fran took the Chevelle. By the time they got to the bottom of the hill, Geoffrey and the Toyota were out of sight.

At the four-way stop by the Arco station, Mickey made a quick left and drove faster. The ambulance was parked at Geer, the nursing home across from the VFW. When they got there the three of them jumped out of the car and ran to the ambulance. Within seconds they were back on Route 7, heading south.

Peter stood at the edge of the road, waiting. It was very dark. The floodlights that Barbara used to read by, at the corners of the house, were turned off. Peter hadn't turned them on because the switch was in the closet, in the rear room. He didn't want to go through the bedroom, so he waited in the dark. The gas station across the road was closed. The night was thick and black as Peter strained to see.

Then he saw the headlights of the Toyota, pinpoints of light that grew rounder and brighter as the little car hurtled down the long straight stretch of road. Geoffrey braked sharply and leaped out. He ran over to Peter.

"Where is she?" Geoff asked.

"She's in the bedroom," Peter said.

Geoff ran toward the house, with Peter just behind him. Geoff didn't wait at the door. He raced right in, into the living room, to the bedroom door. Then he stopped.

Barbara lay sprawled on the floor, a pool of blood around her neck. Her short black curly hair was soggy with blood. Her throat had been slashed and her vocal cords hung out. She was nearly beheaded.

In the light from the clamp-on reading lamp, Barbara's body shone whitely, the blood glaring around her. There were gaping cuts in her stomach. Three of her ribs were broken, and both her thighbones were broken too. Her legs were spread apart; she was nude. Her blue jeans and underpants lay beside her body, soaking wet. Barbara's left arm was lying flat, but her right arm was bent at the elbow, in an upraised position. Her right fist was clenched. Her nose was broken. Her eyes were blackened and staring open.

Geoff stared at Barbara. He turned and stared at Peter.

Peter looked blankly at Geoff. "Well, come on then," Peter said after a moment, his voice tight. "Let's go outside."

In the ambulance, Mickey was trying to get Sharon Hospital, but he couldn't get through, so he called Canaan barracks. They said they had sent the Falls Village ambulance as a backup and had dispatched a trooper.

"I know," Mickey said. "He's passing me right now."

Mickey swerved a little to let the approaching cruiser whiz by him, then speeded up, and pulled up to Peter's house just behind the trooper.

Bruce McCafferty, curly haired, blue-eyed, and boyish, the prototypical rookie cop, just ten months on the force, was working the four to midnight shift. He'd been traveling Route 44 near Furnace Hill Road, doing routine highway patrol, when he got the radio call from Trooper John Calkins at the barracks, who'd just heard from Sharon Hospital. The police got the call from the hospital at 9:58 P.M.

When the blue police car with its flashing lights came into view, Peter began jumping up and down, waving, motioning it into the yard. Trooper McCafferty got out and ran over to Peter and Geoffrey.

"Where is she?" McCafferty asked.

"She's in the bedroom," Peter said.

McCafferty hurried into the house. He knelt on one knee beside Barbara and felt her left wrist for a pulse, but couldn't find it. He went out to the car and radioed the barracks, to ask his supervisor to come. Then, as though he could not be sure of so dreadful a sight, he went back into the house. He looked at Barbara again, then he came outside and made a second radio call to the barracks.

"I have a possible one twenty-five," McCafferty said, giving the code number for a homicide.

"Are you kidding?" the other voice said. "Then you better seal off the house."

Peter and Geoffrey were pushing furniture around in the living room, making a path for the stretcher. One of them had knocked over the little portable heater. When McCafferty came back in, he told them to stop. Peter looked at him, then went over near the kitchen, as far away from the bedroom door as he could get. He sat on a chair at the edge of the kitchen doorway, near the kitchen cabinet with the brown leather pouch hanging from its side. There were three or four knives in the pouch, including a knife that Wayne Collier, one of Peter's friends, had given Barbara when she had complained that she didn't have a really good carving knife. That knife was in the pouch now, with part of the handle sticking out. The knife had a six-inch blade, or a little less, because its tip had been broken off.

Mickey came into the bedroom, knelt down, and felt for a pulse. Fran Kaplan felt for a pulse too. Then Mickey went out to the ambulance to get a blanket to put over Barbara.

From the doorway to the bedroom, Marion looked at Barbara, but she didn't go in. She could see blood spattered around the room, on some freshly ironed shirts hanging on the curtain rod. A green chair with brown wooden legs, in the corner of the bedroom, was spotted with blood. There was a gray steel tool chest near Barbara's foot. The back door was standing partly open.

Barbara lay flung across the floor, her feet pointing toward the doorway where Marion stood. Her head was turned toward her left. Her nose was pushed to one side; blood had oozed out of the nostrils and from her mouth. Marion noticed that the soles of her feet were filthy.

She turned away then and saw Peter sitting on the chair, near the kitchen. He was shivering. She went over and put her arms around him.

Peter looked up at Marion.

"Can I come home with you?" he asked.

"Yes, Peter," Marion said. "I'll yell at you, just like I yell at my boys, but you can come home with me."

"Did I do the right thing?" Peter asked.

"Yes, you did," Marion told him.

Peter wasn't wearing a jacket, only his long-sleeved brown knit shirt. He was still shivering and Marion asked Geoff to let Peter wear his coat. Geoff took off his beloved navy pea coat, the coat he wore nearly twelve months of the year, and Marion draped it around Peter's shoulders.

At nine minutes past ten, McCafferty's supervisor, Sgt. Percy Salley, arrived. He went into the bedroom and looked at Barbara, then he came back out into the living room, where Peter and Marion stood.

"Are you all right?" Sergeant Salley asked Peter.

"Yes, I'm all right," Peter said.

Sergeant Salley told Peter to open his shirt and hold out his hands. He examined Peter's chest and turned his hands over, the palms up, then down. Peter looked blank and, watching him, Marion realized that no one had told him his mother was dead.

Sergeant Salley went out to his cruiser, then, and called his own supervisor, Lt. James Shay, at his house on Silken Road in Granby. Shay directed Salley to get everybody out of the house. The sergeant walked back to the little crowd of people standing in the living room and told them to go outside. Peter got up from the chair and followed Marion across the room, to the front door. As he passed the bedroom door, he turned his head and looked. He saw the white sheet over Barbara, covering her head. He looked away and walked past, out of the house.

Now the darkness outside was sliced with the flashing lights of the police cars, lined up in front of the house like bright sentinels. Bruce McCafferty took Peter into the front seat of the cruiser, so he could make a statement. McCafferty turned on the overhead light and another light that had been installed in the front seat for reading. McCafferty took the statement on paper that had the constitutional rights printed on it. He gave the paper to Peter to read, then Peter put his initials after each of the five items.

1. You have a right to remain silent. If you talk, anything you say can and will be used against you in court.

2. You have the right to consult with a lawyer before you are questioned, and you may have him with you during questioning.
3. If you cannot afford a lawyer, one will be appointed for you, if you wish, before any questioning.
4. If you wish to answer questions, you have the right to stop answering questions at any time.
5. You may stop answering questions at any time if you wish to talk to a lawyer, and may have him with you during any further questioning.

Peter asked McCafferty if he was being accused of a crime. McCafferty said no.

McCafferty asked Peter if he had any idea who did it. Peter said no.

I, Peter A. Reilly, aged 18 (DOB 03/02/55) of Route 63, Falls Village, Connecticut, make the following voluntary statement: I went to Great Barrington, Massachusetts, with Geoffrey Madow this afternoon. Geoffrey had to check in to see if he was working this weekend. He works at Shopwell in Great Barrington. We left there between 3:00 and 3:30 P.M. When we left there we went to Geoffrey's house and watched TV. Geoffrey had dinner and we started to my house. We passed the ambulance by Deely Road. We figured it was going to pick up Geoffrey's uncle who has been having chest pains. After passing the ambulance we went to the Arco station located at the intersection of Route 7 and 44. Geoffrey bought $1 worth of gas and we went back to see where the ambulance was going. When we found it, it was by Locust Hill Road in East Canaan. We followed the ambulance to Norfolk, then turned around and went back to Geoffrey's house to see if it was his uncle. I waited in the car when Geoffrey went into the house. We left Geoffrey's house and went directly to my house. We arrived at my house around 6:45. I was late for dinner and apologized to my mother for being late. We both stayed at my house until 7:20 P.M. At this time we both left for the Teen Center in North Canaan. Geoffrey drove his car and I drove my mother's car. We got there around 7:30–7:35 P.M. and waited until about 7:50 P.M. for Father Paul to get there. We stayed there until about 9:30 P.M. I dropped John Sochocki off at his house located on the road to the dump. After dropping John off I came directly home. I arrived home between 9:50–9:55 P.M. I parked the car in front of the house and got out to fix a headlight. I got back in the car and shut it off. I got out and locked the car. I went inside and said, Mom, I'm home. My mother

25

didn't answer. I looked through the doorway and didn't see her in bed. I then saw her lying on the floor. She was having a problem breathing and she was gasping. I saw the blood at this time. I didn't touch my mother but went straight to the telephone and called Mickey Madow and told her that my mom was lying on the floor and was having trouble breathing and said that there was blood all over the place. Mrs. Madow told me to call my family doctor, that they would be right down. I then called information and asked for Dr. Bornemann in Canaan. I got the number and called him. I got Mrs. Bornemann and told her the situation. She told me Dr. Bornemann was out of town and that I should call the Sharon Hospital Emergency Room. I went outside and threw the charcoal grill out of the way. I then moved my car to the right side of the house. I then went to the driveway and waited for the police or ambulance. While I was waiting, Geoffrey Madow came and we both went in and looked at my mother. Then we went back outside to wait.

I have read the above and it is the truth.

Each of the four pages was signed Peter A. Reilly and witnessed by Trooper Bruce McCafferty, badge number 723.

At 11:10, Lieutenant Shay arrived, tall and square-jawed, the very image of a flinty detective on the trail of murder. Lieutenant Shay had worked out of Hartford in the detective division for nearly a dozen years and had been promoted to command Troop B in Canaan just four months before Barbara died. Since he'd taken over the Canaan command, this was his first homicide. He walked over to the cruiser and spoke to Peter. "Let me see your hands," the detective said. Peter held out his hands. The detective looked at them closely, then walked away from the cruiser, back toward the house.

Lieutenant Shay was not in uniform, and when he walked away, Peter turned to McCafferty, sitting behind the wheel.

"Who's that?" Peter asked. McCafferty told him that was the commander, Lieutenant Shay. "I'd like to become a state trooper," Peter told McCafferty. "I wonder what kind of marks you need to get in high school for that job?"

It was about 11:30 when McCafferty finished taking Peter's statement, and the scene, by now, was bustling. A police van had pulled up in front of the house, one of a line of police cars that rimmed the highway. Mickey could see that they didn't need the ambulance, so he drove it back to Geer, picked up the car, and drove back. Lieutenant Shay was annoyed that Mickey had covered Barbara with a blanket and told him so.

Other troopers had awakened the Kruses, in the big house next door, and told them about Barbara.

"She's a mess," one of them said to old Mr. Kruse, who stood in the back doorway. The Kruses said they had gone to bed around ten, as usual, after their usual hot cocoa. They'd seen Barbara outdoors reading, sometime during the evening, but after that they'd seen nothing, heard nothing.

Lieutenant Shay came back to the car and told Peter to come along with him. He took Peter to the back door of the Kruses' house, and into the kitchen, and told him to take off all his clothes.

"I have to go to the bathroom," Peter said. Lieutenant Shay waited in the kitchen while another trooper went into the bathroom with Peter.

Back in the kitchen, Lieutenant Shay again told Peter to strip, and when Peter had taken off all his clothes—the brown shirt, the Land-lubber jeans with the brown braided leather belt, his shoes and socks and underwear and was standing naked in the big, bright, chilly kitchen, Lieutenant Shay searched his body. The officer asked Peter to tell him briefly what had happened; Peter told him what he'd told Bruce McCafferty. Lieutenant Shay asked him about the rear door to the house; Peter told him that the door was generally kept closed. When Shay searched Peter, he found that one of his knuckles was red, but there was nothing else. After the search Peter was taken back to the cruiser.

Jim Mulhern got a call to report early for duty; there'd been a homicide. He had been here before, when Barbara had complained that she was getting harassing phone calls. Shay now gave him the job of visiting all the houses on the south end of Route 63. Mulhern started on his rounds, but first he went over to the cruiser and spoke to Peter. "If there's anything I can do, let me know," Jim Mulhern said.

Dr. Ernest Izumi, the county's assistant medical examiner, was in bed when he got the call at 11:15, but he dressed quickly and was at the house at 11:40. Dr. Izumi had a habit of blinking often, with a half-smile on his round face. He said hello to Mickey when he saw him. Dr. Izumi said he would prefer to wait for Dr. Gross, the Chief Medical Examiner, who had also been notified, but when the chief didn't arrive, Dr. Izumi decided he ought to go in.

In the bedroom, he stepped carefully. He took off the blanket that was covering Barbara and knelt down. There was no room between her right arm and the bunk bed, so he took her left pulse. He put his hands on Barbara's stomach to feel for body heat. Her stomach was still slightly warm. Her arm was not stiff; rigor mortis had not set in. But the wrist was cold. At 11:45 P.M., Dr. Ernest Izumi pronounced Barbara Gibbons DOS—dead on the scene.

Dr. Izumi didn't want to examine Barbara any further, or move her, until pictures had been taken. So he walked back and forth through the house, looking around. He noticed the light shining by the top bunk. He noticed that there was a sleeping bag on each bunk. The sleeping bag on the top bunk had the flap open; on the bottom bunk, that flap was closed.

The room was so cluttered that when Sgt. Richard Chapman, the photographer, arrived, he had a hard time taking pictures from all angles. He was an experienced man, twenty-three years on the force, but it still wasn't easy. The bunk bed was only seven feet from the opposite wall, and Barbara sprawled in most of that space. Sergeant Chapman took pictures of all the dirty laundry strewn around the room, too.

Trooper Walter Anderson, the artist, sketched the rooms quickly, marking what Lieutenant Shay said was a bloody footprint on the bedroom carpet, near Barbara's left foot. Sgt. Gerald Pennington, the fingerprint man from the crime lab at Bethany, dusted for prints with a gray powder. He found a print on the back door, the door that was standing open, and he took a picture of it.

Trooper Don Moran took the old wallet from a drawer in the living room. There was no money in it, or anywhere else in the house, except for sixteen cents that Lieutenant Shay found scattered on the floor. The wallet that Barbara had bought at Bob's Clothing Store that day was not found, and neither was the money from the check she'd cashed.

When Trooper Marius Venclauscas arrived, he began searching the house. He found the pouch of knives in the kitchen, including the knife with the broken tip. He was especially interested in that one, and he carved his initials on the brass part of the knife, in case he needed to identify it later. He found others—throwing knives and hunting knives, and an all-purpose knife that Barbara had seen advertised at the A&P. He found a knife for cutting tar paper and a kitchen knife that Peter used for working with model cars. He found several pairs of scissors and a large pair of clipping shears. Behind the living-room door, on the coat rack, he found a machete and an ice pick.

But it wasn't until much later, long after Peter was gone and Barbara had been taken away, that the police found the razor. It was a straight razor with a black plastic handle and a six-inch blade, the razor that Barbara got at Mario's Barber Shop for Peter to use when he worked with balsa wood. The razor was closed when the police found it. It was lying on the shelf in the living room, where it was always kept, in its usual place.

Mickey was just wandering around, waiting for Peter, when he saw Geoff being taken into a cruiser by Sergeant Salley. Mickey hurried over to the cruiser and got in, too. Salley said he was going to take a statement from Geoff, and Geoff looked at his dad. "They just searched me," he said.

"What do you mean, searched you?" Mickey demanded.

"They took me into the van and stripped me and searched me," Geoff said.

"Well, why didn't you call me?" Mickey said angrily, though he wasn't really angry at Geoff.

"Well, I didn't know what was going to happen," Geoff said.

Mickey got out of the car and went looking for Lieutenant Shay. "What the hell is going on here?" Mickey asked Shay.

"It was just something that had to be done," Lieutenant Shay said, in a businesslike, yet soothing kind of way.

Mickey looked at him. "Well, were you satisfied?" he asked.

"Yes," Lieutenant Shay said.

The night grew colder and longer, and still Peter sat in the cruiser. Not many people spoke to him. Eddie Dickinson, his neighbor and good friend, had come running down the road when he heard the news and had said something to him, not long after Peter got in the cruiser. Geoff, too, had something to say. Geoff had noticed that Peter had a blank expression on his face, and he hesitated to speak to him. But there was something he really needed to say, and finally he just went over to Peter and said it. He asked for his coat back.

Bill Dickinson, Ed's dad, approached the cruiser to speak to Peter. McCafferty waved him away. "You aren't allowed to talk to him," McCafferty said. Bill was surprised to hear it, but he didn't argue.

Bill wasn't worried yet.

Mickey told Marion to go home, that he would wait around and bring Peter back. Marion agreed. She said she'd open the sleep sofa in the den for Peter, and she would leave the porch light on.

Marion wasn't worried yet.

It was nearly two in the morning when Lieutenant Shay told Sergeant Salley to take Peter down to the barracks. By then Peter had been sitting in the cruiser for three hours. Mickey had told Sergeant Salley that he was waiting to take Peter home with him. He had told that to another trooper, too. When he heard that Peter was going down to the barracks, he said he would come along and wait for Peter there. Sergeant Salley said that wouldn't be necessary. "Go on home," he told Mickey. "We'll bring him back later on."

Mickey persisted. "As long as I'm here, I'll come down and wait for him," Mickey said. But the trooper persisted too. "You go on home," he said again. "We'll run him up when we're through."

Sergeant Salley got behind the wheel of the cruiser.

"How do you feel?" he asked Peter.

"I feel all right," Peter said.

The cruiser headed north on Route 7, leaving the murder house behind, with all the lights and bustle. The night closed in again, thick and black. Mickey watched the cruiser disappear down the long straight road, past the dark swamp, then he got into the Toyota and drove home.

Mickey wasn't worried yet.

The Connecticut State Police Barracks, Troop B, is a solid, square, red-brick building about a mile from the center of Canaan, right at the Massachusetts border. The town was very quiet at 2:00 A.M. when Sergeant Salley and Peter drove through.

Sergeant Salley took Peter into a big room. The room was used as a kitchen and lunchroom by the troopers, and there were a table and chairs in the center and several vending machines along the wall.

"Do you want a cup of coffee?" Sergeant Salley asked Peter.

"No thank you," Peter said. He never drank coffee. He was hungry, though. He hadn't eaten since lunch at school on Friday, more than fourteen hours before. He bought himself a candy bar from a vending machine and ate it, sitting at the table across from Sergeant Salley.

For a while he tried to make conversation. He told him a little about school and who his friends were. He said he was very interested in cars.

But as the morning dragged on, Peter yawned more and more often. He put his head down on the table, and finally he asked Sergeant Salley if he could lie down. "Not yet," Sergeant Salley said. "Wait a few more minutes. Lieutenant Shay will be here, and then you can get some sleep."

The lieutenant was still out at Barbara's, where the lights were all on, the scene still busy and hectic. When Sergeant Chapman had taken all his pictures, Dr. Izumi finally had a chance to examine Barbara further. He picked up the clothes near the body, the underpants inside the blue jeans. They were still wet. He took off her T-shirt, which was pushed up around her breasts, and her outer shirt, which was unbuttoned and partly off. He straightened out the fingers of her right hand and saw that something had pierced the palm all the way through. He tied plastic bags around Barbara's hands.

Mickey had just got into the house when the phone rang. It was a Corporal Logan, asking whether Mickey and Marion and Fran would mind coming down to the barracks in the morning to give statements.

"We're still up," Mickey said. "We might as well come on down now."

"No, no," the policeman said. "Tomorrow's soon enough. Get some sleep, and we'll see you in the morning."

"What about Peter Reilly?" Mickey asked. "Will he be finished soon?"

"In about half an hour, maybe three quarters of an hour," Corporal Logan said.

"Do you want me to come down and get him?" Mickey asked.

"No," said Corporal Logan. "We know where you live, Mick. We'll run him up to your house when we're finished."

Mickey hung up, and soon everybody went to bed. Marion had already opened the sleep sofa in the den; she left the porch light on. It was between 2:30 and 3:00 then, just about the time a policeman was knocking on the door of John Sochocki's house. Peter had driven John home after the Teen Center meeting, and the police wanted to talk to him down at the barracks. John was in bed, but the police didn't want to wait. Tomorrow wasn't soon enough.

It was after four in the morning when they took Barbara away. First they rolled her to the left and put a sheet on the floor under her. Then they rolled her to the right and put the rest of the sheet under her. In this way, four people could carry her out without touching her, simply by holding the four ends of the sheet. When they rolled her over, they saw slashes and puncture marks on her back. But they didn't know her legs were broken until several hours later, at Sharon Hospital, when her body was lifted to the autopsy table and Dr. Izumi heard a sound, the sound of grating bones.

"I have to go to the bathroom," Peter said once more. And again, a trooper went along into the bathroom with him. Back in the lunch-room, he put his head down on the table again, but still he couldn't sleep. He was very, very tired. He had sat in the cruiser out at the house for three hours, and now he sat in the barracks kitchen for four hours more, waiting for Lieutenant Shay.

Sergeant Salley left the room a few times, and when he came back in, after one of his trips out, he had a card in his hand. He told Peter he was going to read him this card, which listed his constitutional rights. "It is my responsibility to give it to you, and it is very much your responsibility to pay attention to it," Sergeant Salley said.

"Am I being charged with something?" Peter said.

"No," Sergeant Salley said. But he began to read the rights anyway. He was still reading when Lieutenant Shay walked in. It was about six in the morning.

Lieutenant Shay and Peter went upstairs then, to a small back room on the second floor, away from the street. The officer took out a constitutional rights card, too. The language was similar to the others, except that this form, which Lieutenant Shay asked Peter to sign, included a waiver as well.

"Does this mean I can't have a lawyer?" Peter asked.

"No," the lieutenant said. "It just means you are willing to talk to me without a lawyer."

Peter signed the warning form then, waiving his rights. In fact, he signed two of them. Then he began to talk.

He related the day, just as he'd told it to Bruce McCafferty in the cruiser and to Shay himself in the Kruses' kitchen. When he got to the part about Barbara lying on the floor, Lieutenant Shay was surprised that Peter didn't cry.

Peter and Barbara. This is what it kept coming back to. Although Lieutenant Shay asked Peter questions about school, and his cars, and whether he had any relatives in Connecticut or anyplace else, and whether he went out with girls, he talked mostly about Barbara. He asked Peter whether he'd ever had sexual relations with Barbara. Peter said he hadn't. Lieutenant Shay talked in such a probing way that finally Peter asked him some questions.

"Say, how many years of psychology have you had?" Peter asked.

Lieutenant Shay seemed taken aback, but he answered.

"Two years," he said.

"Am I a suspect?" Peter asked.

"Yes," Lieutenant Shay said.

"Then could I have a lie detector test?" Peter asked.

"That's a good idea," Lieutenant Shay told Peter. "I'll arrange it for you. Meantime, I think some sleep is in order."

They had been in the little room about an hour, maybe a little longer, starting about 6:30 in the morning. It was a quiet room, in the back of the barracks. It was a quiet Saturday morning. The window and the door were closed, only Peter and Lieutenant Shay in the room, ten by twelve feet, facing one another across a table. The entire conversation between the two of them, in this quiet little room, was recorded, but later, when people tried to listen to the tape, and many people did, they found it was far too garbled to make any sense.

Lieutenant Shay took Peter to one of the barracks bedrooms. There were two single beds, one of them all ready for Peter, with the top sheet turned down over a gray wool blanket. As he left, Lieutenant Shay took Peter's shoes.

Dr. Izumi was sleeping down the hall, in a room just like Peter's. He had left the house a little after five, but instead of going home, he had come to the barracks to get a few hours sleep before he did the autopsy on Barbara. Dr. Izumi's door was closed, but the door of Peter's room was open. A trooper sat on a chair in the hall, facing into the room, watching Peter.

Peter said later he couldn't seem to fall asleep. He turned over one way, then the other. He couldn't stop thinking about the night before, about things people had said. When he finally fell asleep, he dreamed. He dreamed that he hadn't gone to the Teen Center, that he'd stayed home, and that somebody came into the house. Peter dreamed about Barbara.

Just as he was falling asleep, the Madows were getting up. In the morning sunshine, the porch light was still on.

3

"Hey, Pete," Jim Mulhern said. "Wake up. Hey, Pete."

Peter came awake suddenly, with a start. For a few seconds he didn't remember where he was—a few, unfocused seconds when he didn't remember any of it. Then he remembered that something bad had happened, and he wanted Barbara. She always told him she would be there, if he needed her. Peter stared at Mulhern, then it all came back, a crash within his head. He'd been in bed about four hours. It was noon.

"Are you hungry?" Jim Mulhern asked. "Do you want something to eat or drink?"

"No thank you," Peter said. "I don't have any appetite."

"Well, come on then," Mulhern said. "We're going to Hartford now." That was where the polygraph tests were given.

"OK," Peter said. He got out of bed and put on his jeans and his belt. Mulhern had brought back his shoes, and he sat on the bed and put them on, too. They were the same clothes, the same shoes—brown knit shirt, Landlubber jeans, tan sneakers—that he had worn to school the day before; the same clothes he was wearing at the Teen Center meeting that night. Joanne Mulhern had seen him wearing those clothes at the meeting, and she saw him wearing them now. She had been asked to come down to look at Peter and she did. The police asked whether these were the same clothes Peter had been wearing the night before. "Yes," Joanne Mulhern said, and she signed a statement saying so.

Lieutenant Shay had told Mulhern not to discuss the case with Peter, so they talked, on the drive to Hartford, about all sorts of other things. Peter sat in the front seat, just the two of them in the car. They talked about TV commercials and about motorcycles. Barbara had always loved motorcycles. For stunt riding she preferred the big bikes, Peter recalled. She used to laugh and say that riding a little Honda was like riding a skateboard.

Police headquarters in Hartford is a sturdy, stone block of a building, across Washington Street from the courthouse, one fortress facing another. Jim Mulhern and Peter had made good time. They had left Canaan at 12:40 and got to Hartford at two o'clock. Lieutenant Shay arrived a little later in another car.

Peter asked to go to the men's room, where he washed his face and tried to brush through his hair with his hands. His hair was long and needed washing, and he felt a little scraggly. Mulhern took him upstairs, to a small room where a police officer was waiting, then Mulhern left. Peter didn't see him again for quite a while.

Cpl. Jack Schneider was short and brisk, with a crew cut. He seemed interested and friendly.

"Pete, you know why you're up here, don't you?" Corporal Schneider asked.

"I guess I'm here just to confirm my statement," Peter said.

"Right," Corporal Schneider said. "That's the reason you're here."

Schneider explained to Peter that Sgt. Tim Kelly would be doing the actual testing. "He's reading all the reports over, so he'll know what he's talking about when you and him get together in the polygraph room," Schneider said.

"Right," Peter said.

Schneider gave him a form that said he was taking the test voluntarily. Peter signed it and wrote the time. It was 2:40 P.M. "This is confidential information," Schneider told Peter. "It stays here. Everything that we do today, or any forms we make out, remain here.

"What do your friends call you?" Schneider asked, in a friendly tone. "Do they call you Pete?"

"Either that, or Petey," said Peter.

"I'll call you Pete," Schneider said. "Most of my friends I call Pete."

36

He asked Peter where he lived, and where he was born, and when. "Somewhere in New York City," Peter said. "On March 2, 1955."

"What nationality are you?" Schneider asked.

"English, I think," Peter said. "And German. English and German."

"Basically the same thing that I am," Schneider said. "What's your religion?"

"I have none," Peter said.

"You have none?" Schneider repeated.

"No, I've never been baptized," Peter said.

"You've never been baptized?" Schneider repeated again. He paused. "You ever think about it? Do you believe in the Supreme Being?"

"Well, I believe there's got to be someone, someplace, always has been and always will be," Peter said vaguely.

"OK, good," Schneider said. "You own a car, Pete?"

"Well, it's my mom's car," Peter said. "It's in her name. A 1968 Corvette."

"You lived with your mother. Was it just you and your mother?" Schneider asked. Peter said yes. "Any idea who you'll be living with now?" Schneider asked.

Peter named Jean Beligni. "She told me, if anything ever happens, to come right to them, if I ever need help, if I ever need a place to stay. So that's what I'm going to do."

"Now, Pete, have you ever been in a mental institution?" Schneider asked. "Treated by a psychiatrist or psychologist?"

"Not that I know of," Peter said, then he thought of something. "Lieutenant—what's his name—yeah, Shay—he told me he had a couple years of psychology. That's the only thing I ever had to do with it. That was in the last twenty-four hours."

"OK," Schneider said. He established that Peter wasn't on drugs and hadn't been smoking marijuana.

"Did they give you any kind of medication to calm you down?" Schneider asked.

"No," Peter said. "I've been very level-headed about it."

"You are," Schneider agreed.

"I figure I would save my tears for later," Peter said. "This is more important."

Schneider was about finished. "If you have any questions about the polygraph, I'll be glad to answer them," he said.

"You're the only person who has been straightforward with me the last twenty-four hours," Peter said. "I've been drilled and drilled and drilled, and gone over and gone over, you know?"

The polygraph room was quiet. It was a pleasant room twelve by fourteen feet, in soft colors—yellow acoustical tile, a green carpet. The polygraph machine was built into a desk. Corporal Schneider motioned to the chair beside it, a straight-backed chair with a leather seat and wooden arms that could be adjusted up or down.

"Sit right here," Schneider said. "That's what we call the seat of honor."

Peter sat down. Schneider told him to roll up his sleeve and flex his muscle. "That's good. Right there," Schneider said. He tied a rubber cuff around Peter's arm, a Childs Cardio-Cuff, but he didn't tighten it yet. It was attached by a tube to a stainless-steel pen. Schneider explained the apparatus that measured blood pressure, heartbeat, pulse. "That's very important," Schneider said, "because that's the only muscle in your body you can't control."

"Right," Peter said.

"There are three things we can say here today," Schneider said. "You told us the truth. Or you didn't tell us the truth. Or there's some mental or physical problem, and we can't test you. If there's some reason we can't test you, we'll test you some other time. As long as you want to. OK?"

"Right," Peter said.

When Peter was ready, the apparatus set up, Corporal Schneider told him he was going to get Sergeant Kelly. The corporal looked at Peter as he left the room.

"Just relax," the officer said.

Peter sat straight up in the seat of honor, waiting.

Marion Madow knew that Peter was going to Hartford for a polygraph test. Jim Mulhern had told her when she went down to the barracks a little before nine o'clock Saturday morning. She was a little surprised, but she thought it was just routine, just a little delay until Peter came home with her. She knew Jim Mulhern. Her sons knew him. So did Peter. They all knew him, and they trusted him.

She gave Mulhern a statement about what she had seen and done the evening before, beginning with Peter's phone call. Then she went home, to start her weekend chores. She did the weekly food shopping on Saturday, a big job with a family of five. And now there were six. Everybody was pleased that Peter was coming to stay with them. Nan couldn't get over how thin he was. "Oh, I'm going to fatten him up," she had said, with a smile.

Sgt. Timothy Kelly was a big, strong-looking man—six feet, 220 pounds, a brown belt in judo. He had a bristling gray crew cut, and his eyes were keen behind black-rimmed glasses. Tim Kelly had been a member of the Connecticut State Police for twenty-one years, stationed all that time in Hartford. He was chief of the polygraph division, with four men working for him. But this was his last season in Hartford. In the spring he planned to retire to Fort Myers, Florida, where he was going to do private polygraph work and collect seashells. He was a big man, with a big voice, but his voice wasn't gruff or rough. It was deep, but surprisingly soft.

K: Pete, how are you?
P: OK. And you?
K: Good. Tim Kelly is my name. Sergeant Kelly of the state police.
P: Pleased to meet you.
K: Know why you're here, Pete?
P: Well, I guess, to determine whether the things in my statement are true.
K: Right. Now, last night you gave a statement up in Canaan. They told you your constitutional rights. Now I've got to go through the same thing again. This is a new day. I'm a new person, OK?
P: OK.
K: You have a right to remain silent. If you talk to the police, anything you say can and will be used against you. You have the right to consult with an attorney before you're questioned and may have him present during any questioning. If you cannot afford an attorney, one will be appointed for you. If you wish to answer questions you can stop answering questions at any time. In other words, Pete, you can leave here anytime you want. You just say, 'Hey, Tim, I want to go home, let me take the equipment off.' And you can go home. Fair enough?

P: Right.

K: OK. You may stop answering questions at any time, if you wish to talk to an attorney you may have him with you during any further questioning. Understand that?

P: Mm-hm.

K: OK. Now read it to yourself again, Pete, put your initials down the side and sign it at the bottom. If there's anything there you don't understand, just speak up and I'll explain it to you, OK?

P: After I leave here will I be able to go and try to make the arrangements for myself?

K: Oh sure.

P: Because I've been all tied up and haven't had a chance to speak to anyone about what I'm going to do.

K: What time did you leave the house yesterday?

P: When I finally went out for the evening?

K: Yeah, what time was it?

P: Approximately twenty after seven. And I got to Canaan around . . .

K: Not too fast, now. We're going to go over this whole thing. I want your mind completely clear.

P: Well, this is the most calm I've been.

K: You and I are going to talk here, man to man. I want no yelling, no screaming, OK?

P: OK.

K: When you were leaving, how was your mother dressed? Do you recall?

P: I think she had a white T-shirt on with a blue shirt over it, unbuttoned. A pair of jeans and sandals. She was sitting at the living-room table, eating a TV dinner. She was watching the news on TV, seven to seven-thirty, the national news. I left at seven-twenty. Geoff Madow was with me. We're good friends.

K: Was Geoff in the house? Did he meet your mother?

P: Yes. He already gave a statement.

K: You left in your Corvette, right?

P: I was in my Corvette. Geoff drove his car because he didn't have enough gas to drive me home and then go home.

K: Is there anything wrong with your car, or is it in pretty good shape?

40

P: It's in fairly decent shape. The transmission is a little rattly.

K: My brother-in-law has a Corvette, but for me it's too small a car. Every time I get in and out of it, I crack my head.

P: There's a lot of leg room, though.

K: Oh yeah. Well, how are the lights and the rest of the equipment?

P: Well, everything is fine except one headlight. You have to get out and jiggle it while the car's running. There's something messed up in the vacuum. Plus I have oversized tires, and it weaves a little bit, it gets away from you, so I don't drive that fast.

K: OK. So, you went to their meeting. Now tell me what happened.

P: Around nine-thirty, nine-thirty-five, I decided to leave, and this kid, John Sochocki, asked me for a ride home. So I dropped him off at his house, and then I went straight home.

K: Now tell me exactly what happened.

P: I pulled in the yard. I had to find a level spot to park because my emergency brake wasn't working. I got out and jiggled the light down, then I got back in, shut it off, put it in gear, and locked it up. I walked in the front door. The screen door was open, on the catch, and also the inside door wasn't quite closed. I walked in and I yelled, "Mom, I'm home!" There was no answer, so I figured she probably fell asleep. I looked in the bedroom, up at her bed. We were very limited on space, so we had bunk beds. When I wasn't home, she always slept in the top bunk.

K: Oh, I see.

P: I looked up, and I didn't see her. I turned, like I'd seen her, because I'm so used to it, and I turned around again, and found she wasn't there, and I looked down, and there she was on the bedroom floor.

K: Now, tell me exactly how she was.

P: She had a T-shirt on, and it was kind of pushed up to here. Nothing else on. I think she might have had that blue shirt on, but I don't remember. There was blood all over the place, around the chin and the throat and on the carpet around her. She was breathing, and she was having trouble breathing, but she was breathing, and she was unconscious, her eyes were closed, and she didn't respond to me when I yelled to her. She didn't seem to be bleeding anymore, but there was blood all over the place.

K: All right.

P: Ah, what's his name, the lieutenant?

K: Shay.

P: Shay. He told me that my first reaction should have been to go directly to her to see how she was. But my first reaction was to hit the phone. He said there might have been something a little wrong, but I was afraid to touch her for some reason. Mysterious reason. So I called the Madows. They're on the VFW ambulance squad. Mrs. Madow said they'd be right down. Then she told me to call my family doctor. So I hung up and dialed information, one-four-one-one, and then I called and I got the number for Dr. Bornemann, and then I called there. His wife told me Dr. Bornemann was on vacation. She said call the Sharon Hospital emergency room. So I hung up and dialed information again and got Sharon Hospital. I dialed there, and they connected me with the emergency room. They asked me whether she was still breathing, and I went in and looked, and at that point she'd almost stopped breathing. I came back and told them, and they asked if I knew anything about artificial respiration. I told them I didn't. They said they'd contact the state police. I said I already contacted an ambulance.

K: What did you do then?

P: I walked out the door. I *ran*. There was a hibachi by the door. I threw it out of the way so it wouldn't be in the way of the ambulance. Then I got in the car and pulled it around to the side of the house. I shut off the car, then I went to put the headlights on, and I thought no, it would kill the battery. So I left the emergency flashers on, and I stood in the front yard. Then I saw this little car coming out of nowhere, a Toyota, and Geoff was driving it, going like a bat out of hell. He pulled in the yard, and we both went in the house and looked at her.

K: What did Geoff say?

P: He said it looked like somebody raped her. Maybe I said it. But I think he said it.

K: I was just wondering what his reaction was when he saw all the blood.

P: He just turned pale. I was already like a ghost. We went back out and stood in the front yard. By the time Geoff got there it had been seven or eight minutes, I think. Maybe five. Then, a couple minutes later, the cruiser pulled in, and the ambulance was right behind it.

K: Well, what do you think happened there?

P: I honestly don't know. My mom used to get very depressed. She told me that sometimes she felt suicidal, but that she didn't have the guts to go through with it.

K: Do you think your mother committed suicide?

P: I don't know. I don't know the facts on what actually happened to her.

K: Do you recall her being all wet?

P: No. But the police officer showed me the pair of pants and asked me if they were mine or hers. He told me they were wet. I saw they weren't bell-bottoms, so I knew they were hers, plus she had the cuffs rolled up.

K: And they were soaking wet. And her shirt was wet.

P: I didn't notice that her shirt was wet.

K: Yeah, it was when they examined her. Any idea how she got all wet?

P: I can't understand it. Did they check the bathtub or anything? I don't know what they did down there.

K: Do you have any suspicions as to who would hurt your mother like that?

P: I told them about [name deleted], who's an alcoholic. I don't suspect him, but as far as I know, an alcoholic will do anything.

K: Or somebody that has a mental problem. A person might have a mental problem and do something that they're sorry for, afterwards. They've taken a life, but they can't help themselves.

P: Right.

K: Things just snap, and suddenly, a few hours later, they're back to normal again.

P: Like a split personality.

K: Right. When was the last time you saw [the alcoholic]?

P: Last time I saw him was, at least two years ago.

K: Has your mother heard from him recently?

P: We had phone calls last week. Tuesday or Wednesday. Then on Thursday and Friday last week I had to drive her to Sharon Hospital for tests. My mom was the lousiest driver there was.

43

K: Most women are.

P: But she wouldn't admit it. Besides, the way the car moved, she wasn't that strong in her arms. If the car weaved, she might not have been able to pull out of it.

K: Other than [the alcoholic], you have no other suspicions?

P: Well, I gave the name of [name deleted] but he left this area five years ago. He went to California.

K: So you have no real strong suspicions?

P: No.

K: And you never touched your mother?

P: I never touched her. I know it was kind of odd that I didn't, but I know I didn't.

K: I understand there was a lot of blood.

P: There was, and that's what scared me.

K: Where was that coming from? Could you tell?

P: I couldn't tell.

K: If I ask you this question on the polygraph: Do you know for sure who hurt your mother? What would you answer?

P: No.

K: Pete, I'm not trying to trick you.

P: Even if you are, it's for the better.

K: Well, I'm not, in no way, trying to trick you.

P: Right. I understand that.

K: That's why we'll talk these questions over to make sure that you understand. If you don't, we'll change them. Now, the next question: Last night, do you know for sure who hurt your mother?

P: No.

K: Last night, did you hurt your mother?

P: No.

K: Now, they had to take her into the hospital and examine her.

P: They performed an autopsy, right?

K: Right. She had two broken legs.

P: She *did*? I didn't know her legs were broken.

K: Just above the knees. So it looks like she had to be hit with something. I broke my leg playing football, but that's a different situation. I'm sure your mother doesn't play football.

P: Could she have fallen out of the top bunk? But I still don't think she'd break both legs. I've fallen out, and I never got hurt except bruises.

K: If I ask you on the polygraph: Do you know how your mother's legs were broken?

P: No.

K: The only way you would know would be if you were there and saw this happen.

P: Right.

K: You said before, Pete, that you didn't talk to your mother other than the yell as you came in. If I ask you on the polygraph: Last night, did you talk to your mother when you came home? Carry on a conversation?

P: No.

K: If I ask you on the polygraph: Do you know how your mother's clothes got wet?

P: No.

K: You gave a statement to the police last night. Is the statement you made the truth?

P: Yes.

K: Now, whoever did this, there's no doubt, deliberately hurt your mother. You say she talked about suicide. She certainly couldn't . . .

P: Break both legs, then commit suicide.

K: Right. Right. So, if I ask you this question on the polygraph: Did you ever deliberately hurt someone in your life?

P: No.

K: From what the fellows say, you got along fairly well with your mother, right?

P: We had arguments. We'd swear up and down at one another.

K: This is a normal thing. I argue with my wife. Everybody gets into arguments. But I don't know if you're involved in what happened there last night or not. That's why you're here. If I could read your brain, I'd be a millionaire, and I wouldn't be sitting here. That's why I have this. It reads your brain for me.

P: Does that actually read my brain?

K: Definitely. Definitely. And if you've told me the truth, this is what your brain is going to tell me.

45

C. 2

P: Will this stand up to protect me?

K: Right. Right.

P: Good. That's the reason I came to take it. For protection.

K: Last year I talked to a colored boy here, twenty-one years old, who four other colored people accused of committing a murder. They said they seen him come down the street, pull a gun out of his belt, and popped this other colored guy. These people picked him out of a lineup. Individually they said, that's him. They gave sworn statements. He sat right where you're sitting now, and when I finished testing him, I got the New Haven police, and I said, you got the wrong guy. Two months later I talked to the actual man who committed the crime. He sat right where you're sitting now. That's how the polygraph works. If you're honest with me, that's all we need, OK?

P: Let's go.

K: We don't rush here, Pete. We take our time. We have no place to go. Now, to get back to the questions. If you committed this thing last night, if you hurt your mother, it would be a rather shameful thing, right?

P: Right.

K: You've never done anything that you're really ashamed of, have you?

P: Can you guarantee this won't go out of this room?

K: Absolutely. Right here. You and I.

P: I got involved with a homosexual. I was afraid of the guy, because he was a brown belt in Judo.

K: Did he commit an act on you, or did he make you commit an act on him?

P: Neither, really. Nothing really happened. But he tried.

K: You're afraid someone's going to say you're a homosexual?

P: Right. And if you check my background, if you saw the girls I go out with, it's ridiculous.

K: No problem. I think everybody is approached at least once by a homosexual. That's not shameful.

P: Well, it's something I was really ashamed of.

K: All right. All right. Let me put it this way: Besides what we have just talked about, have you done anything else you're really ashamed of?

P: I don't know whether I told you that I smoked pot. Not all the time. Every three months, something like that. I'm not ashamed of that, except the shamefulness that I lied to my mom, saying I didn't.

K: What I'm interested in is if you're lying to me about last night, that would be shameful, wouldn't it?

P: Yeah. But it would be ridiculous for me to come down and volunteer for this test if I was lying.

K: Let me say something, Pete. I've had people here who have committed serious things. As serious as this. They needed help. It wasn't a vicious thing they did. They just couldn't help themselves. I've had people actually come in here and take this test because they knew they were guilty but they didn't know how to tell somebody. They were looking for help. Maybe you're looking for somebody to help you.

P: What do you mean?

K: Say you did this thing last night. Say you hurt your mother. Maybe you want the polygraph to help you.

P: If I had any doubts, I would see a doctor.

K: Well, if I feel there's something wrong, this is what we would do for you. Get a doctor. A lot of times, people don't know they need help. And the test says they need help. It's amazing but true.

P: Right.

K: Now, I'll ask you some real easy questions on the test. Were you born in the United States? Do you live in Connecticut? Are you wearing a brown shirt? Is your first name Peter?

P: Yes.

K: I'm going to go across the hall and make one phone call. I want to write these up on a form so I can read them intelligently. Then we'll go through them two or three times on the polygraph. If you broke an arm and you went to a doctor, he wouldn't take one X ray. He would take several before he set your arm. I do the same thing with the questions. I compare one to the other. Now, is there anything you want to ask me?

P: I just want to understand how it works.

K: It works on your heart. That's your conscience. All we're trying to do is arrive at the truth. And the truth will be on that tape.

The polygraph, the "lie box," has been used in the United States, in one form or another, since before the turn of the century. But it came to be widely used only in the last few decades. In the mid-1960s, about seven hundred polygraph tests a day were being given in government offices and in private places. In 1965 the House Government Operations Committee, alarmed by widespread use of the machine, made a study and reached the conclusion that "There is no 'lie detector,' neither machine nor human. People have been deceived by a myth that a metal box in the hands of an investigator can detect truth or falsehood." Even J. Edgar Hoover, who was about as interested in law and order as anybody, said the device was incapable of "absolute judgments," and said the term "lie detector" was "a complete misnomer."

The machine itself can vary from the $12.95 model, virtually a toy, to the sophisticated models used by most police departments. The high-priced brands measure pulse rate, blood pressure, and breathing, as well as the galvanic skin responses, and cost two or three thousand dollars. Even these models can be considered a bargain, though, considering the results obtained. According to Richard Arther, a private polygraph examiner in New York City, almost fifty percent of the persons examined by a police polygraph examiner are lying.

Three types of questions are used in a polygraph session.

There is the irrelevant question. "Were you born in Kentucky?" The response to the irrelevant question is considered a person's normal response.

There is the control question, unrelated to the matter being investigated, but in the same area. In the case of theft, "Have you ever stolen anything?" is a control qusetion.

And there is the relevant question. "Did you steal the rubies?" A response greater than the normal response, when the relevant question is asked, is said to denote a lie.

In a book he wrote about scientific crime investigation, Mr. Arther pointed out that a person can learn to operate a polygraph machine in one day, just as a three-year-old child can learn to use a television set in one day. But that does not make the person a polygraph expert, any more than it makes the toddler an engineer. Mr. Arther, who teaches a class in polygraph testing, explained that the accuracy of the device depends on a blend of "natural ability, proper training, adequate experience, and personal integrity" of the examiner. Even so, he admits that

"A conscientious, full-time examiner properly doing his job will probably average one error a year."

One of Mr. Arther's former polygraph students was Sgt. Tim Kelly of the Connecticut State Police.

Peter was interested in the apparatus. "What does the whole unit cost?" he asked.

"You're an inquisitive little guy, aren't you?" Sergeant Kelly said. "It costs about two thousand dollars. It's the best one made. Are you a mechanic at heart?"

"Yes," Peter said. "I love taking things apart and finding out how things work."

"Well, don't take this apart," Kelly said. "Now, Pete, sit up nice and straight for me. Sit as quietly as you can, without moving, as I ask you the questions."

"Do you want me to speak out loud?" Peter asked.

"Oh, yes," Kelly said. "You're going to answer yes or no. Now I'll tune in on your emotions, and I'll tell you when the test starts and when it ends."

He tightened the cuff around Peter's arm. "It will be snug, and your arm may get slightly red, but I guarantee it won't fall off," Kelly said. "Now, the test is about to begin."

K: You were born in the United States?
P: Yes.
K: Right now do you live in Connecticut?
P: Yes.
K: Last night do you know for sure how your mother got hurt?
P: No.
K: Are you wearing a brown shirt?
P: Yes.
K: Last night did *you* hurt your mother?
P: No.
K: Did you ever deliberately hurt someone in your life?
P: No.
K: Is your first name Peter?
P: Yes.
K: Do you know how your mother's legs were broken?

P: No.

K: Last night did you talk to your mother when you came home?

P: No.

K: Do you know how your mother's clothes got wet?

P: No.

K: Besides what we've talked about, have you done anything else you're ashamed of?

P: No.

K: Is the statement you made to the police the truth?

P: Yes.

K: Sit quietly for ten seconds.

P: All done?

K: Yes.

P: How'd I do?

K: You're very cooperative, let me put it that way.

P: What do you mean?

K: Well, that was just a warm-up, to show you you're not going to get electrocuted.

P: How does it look?

K: What do you mean?

P: Does it look like I was lying to you?

K: That wouldn't be fair for me to say. You're nervous. Did any of these questions bother you?

P: Well, whether I harmed my mother or not.

K: Why?

P: Well, that question . . . they told me up at the barracks yesterday that—how some people don't realize—all of a sudden, fly off the handle for a split second . . .

K: Right.

P: . . . and it leaves a blank spot in their memory.

K: Right. This will help bring it out.

P: Well, I thought about that last night, and I thought and I thought and I thought, and I said no, I couldn't have done it, I couldn't have done it, you know. And now, when you ask me the question . . .

K: Peter, let me say this one thing.

P: . . . that's what I think of.

K: If you did it, this is probably how it could have happened.

P: What do you mean?

K: Bango, just like this. All right?

P: Right.

K: Just looking at you, Peter, you don't look like a violent person to me at all.

P: I'm not.

K: I've met a hell of a lot of people in my life. Now, if you did it, it was a split-second thing that you did. You lost your head. Who knows why? Maybe you and your mother had an argument, and one thing led to another, and she attacked you. *I* don't know. It could have been an accident with her last night, right?

P: Right.

K: I want you to review for me those questions. I want to make sure you're paying attention.

P: You asked me what color my shirt was. You asked me if I harmed my mother. You asked me if I had anything to be ashamed of. You asked me—let's see, I haven't been to bed in almost thirty hours. I can't remember anything else.

K: Didn't you get any sleep this morning?

P: I got a little. A couple hours. Maybe it was more than I realize.

K: Now, I'm going to have Jack come in and make you lie. If he can pick out where you are deliberately lying, then we know we are getting proper recordings from you. Regardless of how simple a lie, your body rebels. If you don't rebel to the simple little lie, we'll just say, today is not Pete's day to take a polygraph test.

P: It's the best time to give it to me, after a crisis, isn't it?

K: We'll see.

Sergeant Kelly left the room again, and Corporal Schneider came back. He asked Peter to pick a card, any card, and he would try to guess which one. Peter was to lie, and Schneider would try to spot the lie on the polygraph.

Corporal Schneider and Peter ran through the little test twice. Schneider said he spotted the lie readily both times.

"That's great," he said. "You're a textbook reactor. When you tell a lie, you go right to the top of my chart. Any amateur can pick out where you lied. This is great for us; we'll have no trouble here today."

Peter seemed pleased. "I'm perfect," he said.

"You're perfect," Schneider repeated. "Now, I'll get hold of Tim. One or two more tests, then he'll have the answer. You know the answer now. He'll tell you exactly what the answer is when he's finished. OK?"

"Will do," Peter said cheerfully.

Alone for a moment, Peter coughed loudly. Then Kelly was back.

"I'm a textbook reactor," Peter said, still sounding pleased.

"Look at this," Kelly said. "Right off the paper, practically. Now we'll go through these questions a couple times and we'll have the answer. Your brain will tell me."

Again he pumped air into the cuff, tightening it on Peter's arm. "All you have to do is answer me truthfully. Now, the test is about to begin." Sergeant Kelly asked the same twelve questions he'd asked before, in the same order. Peter gave the same yes and no one-word answers. Then the second polygraph test was over, and the sergeant again instructed Peter to "Sit quietly for ten seconds."

P: Did I hit any peak or anything?

K: Oh, you're popping along there OK.

P: Am I lying that you can tell?

K: I think I have the answer, but I want to make absolutely sure. I'm going to mix the questions up. I think I have the answer here but I want to double-check. Keep looking straight ahead. I may repeat some questions more than once this time, Pete. This is the procedure on this last test. This test is about to begin.
Is your first name Peter?

P: Yes.

K: Did you ever deliberately hurt somebody?

P: No.

K: Last night did you hurt your mother?

P: No.

K: Right now do you live in Connecticut?

P: Yes.

K: Do you know how your mother's legs were broken?

P: No.

K: Besides what we've talked about, have you done anything else that you're ashamed of?

P: No.

K: When you came home last night, did you talk to your mother?
P: No.
K: Last night do you know for sure who hurt your mother?
P: No.
K: Did you ever deliberately hurt somebody?
P: No.
K: Last night did you hurt your mother?
P: No.
K: Besides what we've talked about, have you done anything else that you're ashamed of?
P: No.
K: Do you have a clear recollection of what happened last night?
P: Yes.
K: Is there any doubt in your mind, Pete?
P: Can you stop the test?
K: OK.
P: I didn't understand that last question.
K: I think we've got a little problem here, Peter.
P: That last question . . .
K: I was just trying to probe your subconscious.
P: But I wasn't sure whether you meant what happened to her, or whether I knew who did it to her and everything.

In Sergeant Kelly's office, near the polygraph room, the reel of recording tape ran out. Corporal Schneider, who was operating the tape recorder, changed tapes quickly. In the same room were Lieutenant Shay and Trooper Mulhern, watching Peter through the one-way mirror.

Several other state policemen were working on the case full time already. Peter had told the police he had relatives in Florida, and in New Jersey, so the police called both places during the day on Saturday. The first family member to be told was Barbara's Aunt Stephanie, one of the Florida relatives. Aunt Steffie was eighty and ailing when Barbara died. She had always liked her niece and had given her a platinum ring with three diamond chips, which Barbara wore until she died, and it couldn't be found.

After the police called Aunt Steffie, they called Barbara's cousin June. It was about 3:00 or 3:30 on Saturday afternoon when June got the call at her house in suburban New Jersey. Trooper Toomey said he was calling to notify her that Barbara Gibbons had been murdered.

"Oh," said June. "Oh, give me a minute. Please, just give me a minute to think."

June hadn't seen Barbara for seven years, since Louie Gibbons's funeral. She was younger than Barbara, but she had a teen-aged son of her own, and while she stood holding the phone, trying to comprehend Barbara's murder, she thought of Barbara's son. He was only eleven when June had seen him last.

"There's a boy, Peter," June said to the policeman. "I don't want him in the house by himself. Where is he? Is he there?"

"He's not here," the policeman said.

"Oh, try to find him," June said. "Please find him for me."

When June's husband got home, he called Canaan. "Where could the boy have gone?" he asked the policeman. "We don't know," the policeman said.

June had called her sister Vicky in upstate New York, and Vicky's husband John made calls to Connecticut, too, asking for Peter. John was told, "He's assisting the police."

On the second floor of the police headquarters in Hartford, Corporal Schneider turned on the machine and a new tape began.

K: Well, I think we got a little problem here, Pete.
P: What do you mean?
K: About hurting your mother last night.
P: I didn't do it.
K: You're giving me a reaction. Do you have any doubt in your mind?
P: Can you reword the question in any way?
K: Which question?
P: About hurting my mother. We went over, and over, and over it, you know what I mean? When he told me I could have flown off the handle, I gave it a lot of consideration. But I don't think I did.
K: But you're not sure, are you?
P: That's right. Well, I could have.
K: I think you possibly did. I don't think you're a vicious person. I think you and your mother had some kind of argument.

P: What about the question that says, did I speak to my mother?

K: That's bothering you too. You whipped out on that question.

P: What bothers me is my yelling to my mom. When you ask me that question, that's the first thing I think of.

K: But I explained to you what I meant by that.

P: Right.

K: When I ask you how her legs were broken, you react to that. Did you hurt her? Do you know who hurt her? We go back to this test, see. Then we go back to the last test, same thing again. Look what happened to you here this time when I said: Last night, did you hurt your mother? That's why I started asking you: Do you recollect everything that happened last night? Look at this reaction. See?

P: Is that a no or yes?

K: You said yes. But, the way you reacted shows me——

P: I was unsure. That's the question——
     You were unsure as to what happened in that house last night, aren't you? You're unsure as to what——

P: What I did?

K: Yes.

P: I'm sure what I did.

K: Then why did you say here a moment ago you're not sure if you hurt your mother last night?

P: Wait a second, you got me confused now.

K: No. I'm not trying to, Pete. But you said a moment ago that you had doubt in your mind if you flew off the handle last night and you don't recollect.

P: It doesn't seem like me. I've never flown off the handle.

K: There's always the first time.

P: It still doesn't seem like me, because I remember coming in the yard, and I remember driving home, and I remember walking straight in that door from——

K: Pete, we're missing the boat. Now, from what I read in the reports, your mother likes to walk around at night, in the yard or something.

P: She likes to sit in the front yard and read.

K: Now is there a possibility that you came in that yard like a bat out of hell last night and you hit your mother?

P: No.

K: And you become frightened and you said, "Holy Christ, what do I do now?"

P: No, I'm positive.

K: Accidents can happen.

P: Right.

K: And probably you're so ashamed to admit that this happened that you set it up to look like something real violent happened in the house.

P: I see what—

K: This is a possibility.

P: —you mean. But it wouldn't have been like me. Honestly, if I had hit my mom, the first thing I would have done was call the ambulance.

K: All right. But, what if your mother was dead after you hit her? This would scare the shit out of anybody.

P: But, I also said on the report that she was breathing.

K: Right. But maybe she died shortly afterwards. You see?

P: I don't recall doing it. They can check the car.

K: I'm just talking to you. From what I'm seeing here, I think you got doubts as to what happened last night. Don't you?

P: I've got doubt because I don't understand what happened.

K: Are you afraid that you did this thing?

P: Well, yes, of course I am. That's natural.

K: Is there any reason where you've had a lapse of memory before?

P: No, no.

K: For any reason in the past?

P: No. None. Absolutely none, except once when I tied on a bender.

K: Well, you certainly weren't drunk last night.

P: No.

K: No. The police officer said that. You're not sure, are you?

P: What do you mean?

K: In your mind, if you hurt your mother last night.

P: I'm not sure. It scares me a little bit. You know what I mean?

K: I think you need a little help. If you and I talk this out about last night . . .

P: With the polygraph or without it?

K: Without it. Just man to man. You tell me what happened.

P: I drove home about forty, and I distinctly remember that because there was a car in front of me I thought was a cruiser. I walked in the front door. Both doors were not quite closed all the way. I yelled, "Mom, I'm home." There was no answer. I looked up at the bed, the bed light was on and the bed was turned down. I did a double take, because first I figured I'd seen her, because I'm so used to her being up there, then I looked down and I saw her on the floor. There was some blood, and her T-shirt was pulled up. I remember she had no pants on. My first reaction was like, oh my God. As he said, I should have gone to her. But I went to the phone.

K: What I'm talking about, Pete, is, do you have any recollection as to how she got hurt?

P: No. I absolutely do not.

K: Are there any blank areas? Could you have had an argument with your mother last night and not realized it?

P: No. I don't know. I'm not the one to say.

K: You were there, Peter. I see things here that I don't like. On the question about hurting your mother, you gave me quite a reaction to that.

P: I know it.

K: If something happened, let's get it ironed out so we can see what we can salvage out of this thing.

P: I don't understand you.

K: I think you hit your mother, from what I'm seeing here.

P: I don't.

K: Then why the reaction?

P: I don't know. Maybe it's just nervousness. I mean, my mom *did* die.

K: All right. I'll buy that.

P: That's why I'd like to come in and take another test, rather than go by this one.

K: You said you're not sure if you hurt your mother last night. Why aren't you sure?

P: If I had a lapse of memory, I wouldn't remember. What I say I did, I'm absolutely sure of. If I had a lapse of memory, that's what I'm not sure of. Do you understand what I mean?

K: Do you think you had a lapse of memory?

P: No.

K: That's what I'm trying to get at here, Peter. I don't know if you did or not. This is why I'm asking you these questions. Because you do give me a certain amount of response when I ask you, did you hurt your mother? See this one . . .

P: How about on the first one, when you first ran the test?

K: First test? We normally don't look at that. Right here, about your mother, you give me a reaction there. Your heartbeat changes right then. Exactly like your heartbeat changes on the number. We go into this test there. Right there you get the same type of change in your heartbeat when I asked, did you hurt your mother last night? Now on this test, there's a little bit there, and a great amount here, the last time. A *great* amount. Then I asked you, do you recollect everything that happened last night?

P: That was the question I said I did not understand.

K: The doubt.

P: Yes.

K: You answered yes. Then I said, is there any doubt in your mind? And you hesitated and, as you said, you didn't understand what I meant. And that's when I stopped. But that's the reason I asked you that at the end. Because I don't think you recollect everything that happened.

P: Everything I say I mean. If I don't, it's not my fault. I'm not doing it on purpose.

K: Is there any possibility, Peter, you're covering up for somebody?

P: No, no. Absolutely none.

K: Did anybody ever say you might need a doctor?

P: No.

K: I'm going to take these across the hall. I want Jack to look at them. If he feels the way I do, maybe we'll give you another test.

P: Now?

K: No, not today.

P: Good. But if I did it, and I didn't realize it, there's got to be some clue in the house.

K: I've got this clue here. This is a recording of your mind.

P: But there has to be something in that house, someplace. If I did it. Or whoever did it. There's got to be something, somehow, somewhere.

K: Right. Right.

P: They must have found something by now.

K: They're working on it, Pete. I'm not in contact with them up there. I'm only a little cog in the big wheel.

P: Have you ever been proven totally wrong? A person, just from nervousness, responds that way?

K: No, the polygraph can never be wrong, because it's only a recording instrument, recording from you. It's the person interpreting it who could be wrong. But I haven't made that many mistakes in twelve years, in the thousands of people who sat here, Pete.

P: That's right.

K: Is there any doubt in your mind, right now, that you hurt your mother last night?

P: The test is giving me doubt right now. Disregarding the test, I still don't think I hurt my mother.

K: But you have a doubt, don't you?

P: Yes. I've been drilled and drilled and drilled.

K: Did I drill you?

P: No.

K: OK.

P: I don't know. The doubts—like, when they tell me——

K: What? Tell you what?

P: I'm trying to think of what he did say. I know he told me something. I'm losing all memory now because I'm getting tired. But he did tell me that I could have forgotten. That really shook me.

K: I want my partner to look at these.

P: Could I go out and have a cigarette?

K: In about two minutes. OK?

P: Two minutes. OK.

K: I just want to have him look at them, and then I think we'll get you out of here. I don't want to keep you here anymore. I've been looking at your eyes, and they're sort of sinking down.

P: What's going to happen? Am I still going to be staying up at the barracks again, or are they going to let me go?

K: Well, where could you stay?

P: I've got two families—the Madows, they already offered, and——

K: Well, we'll have to take that up with the investigators. I'll be right back.

The other family Peter meant was the Beligni family.

Jean and Aldo Beligni, their teen-aged sons Ricky and Paul, and their seven-year-old daughter Gina, lived on Furnace Hill Road in East Canaan, not far from the Madows on Locust Hill Road. The Beligni and Madow boys were friends. But their parents had little in common, and until Barbara died, they had never been in one another's houses.

The Belignis were thoroughly hometown people. Jean was a brisk, take-charge person. She had short hair with bangs, blue eyes that saw just about everything there was to see, and a habit of saying whatever was on her mind. She had studied nursing, but after she married and had children, she stayed home and kept the books for Aldo's well-drilling business. Jean was born a Speziale, one of the best-regarded and best-known families in their corner of Connecticut. The family prestige didn't have anything to do with money, though some Speziales acquired it. It had more to do with roots and character, cousins and politics. Jean's father Sam had been the town barber, a man so well-liked he was called "Sam Special." When Sam's funeral procession went through town, all the shopkeepers along Main Street turned off their lights. Another Speziale, Jean's cousin John, who lived in Torrington, became a lawyer, and then was appointed a Superior Court judge.

Aldo had been born in the house on Furnace Hill Road and expected to die there too. Not that Aldo talked much about dying. In fact, he was an enormously cheerful man, with bright brown eyes and a way about him that suggested, somehow, that everything was going to be all right. He was an old-fashioned man who didn't drink or smoke and wouldn't even keep liquor in the house, because of the boys. He had had to drop out of school at age sixteen, but he never stopped reading. Philosophy was his favorite subject, and Kant was his favorite philosopher. But the most remarkable thing about Aldo was not that he was a philosophical well driller, but that for such a sturdy, old-fashioned, hardworking, churchgoing man, he was so popular with the teen-agers, with his sons and their friends. "The most terrible lesson I'm learning in Contemporary Problems is that my father is always right," Ricky Beligni said. Peter Reilly liked Aldo a lot.

K: Did you know your mother made a phone call last night? About nine-thirty, to Dr. Lavallo. She was discussing her condition—liver, or something . . .

P: I hadn't heard whether the test came through.

K: She called him at nine-thirty, which puts you home at almost the exact same time.

P: That was when I left the Teen Center. I'm positive.

K: I'm talking approximate. From what the doctor says, she was all alone when she called him, the way she was talking.

P: How did she sound, did he say?

K: No. Pete, I think you got a problem. And Jack feels the same way. We go strictly by the charts. And the charts say you hurt your mother last night.

P: The thing is, I don't remember it.

K: The charts don't say that, Pete. Did she have some fatal disease? Maybe what happened here was a mercy thing. Maybe she asked you to do something to her.

P: No.

K: They've found out you left the Teen Center before nine-thirty. Your mother hadn't been dead that long.

P: She hadn't?

K: She talked to the doctor about nine-thirty. That leaves a very short time, Pete. If you say you didn't do it, the person who did it would have had to be there when you arrived home.

P: They told me they found the back door open. As much as I remember—and I think I remember all of it, I *believe* I remember all of it, I never went past the bedroom door, so I couldn't get to the back door.

K: Maybe your mother left it open. But I think you got something on your mind, Peter, and you just don't know how to come out with it.

P: Would that show you what I'm actually thinking right now?

K: That shows me from your heart that you hurt your mother last night. How, I don't know.

P: I don't know either.

K: I'm trying to figure this out. If you came roaring into the yard, a Corvette is a car you go like hell with. My brother-in-law has one, and I know how he drives it. You come flying in with that

61

damned thing, and you went over her with the car, and you panicked.

P: I didn't, though. I don't remember it.

K: Then why does the lie chart say you did?

P: I don't know. I can't give you a definite answer.

K: You don't know for sure if you did this thing, do you?

P: I don't. No, I don't.

K: Why?

P: Well, your chart says I did. I still say I didn't.

K: You're not sure, are you? Let's go over this thing again. Maybe we can bring it out of your subconscious, then we can get this straightened out and see what we can salvage out of this mess. You don't look like a violent person. Maybe, spur of the moment. Now, have you ever hit your mother in the past?

P: Yes. Three months ago. It had something to do with fixing the car. I threw a flashlight. I didn't mean to throw it hard. It was a metal flashlight and it caught her on the shin.

K: Did you throw it deliberately?

P: Yes. Spur of the moment. But I realized I had done it and apologized for it.

K: This thing is so violent. Maybe you don't want to remember.

P: You've lost me now.

K: The last time you hit your mother you hit her lightly. This time when you lost your temper it wasn't just a little bit. She is now dead. Maybe you're so ashamed of this thing . . .

P: What about that question where you asked me about being ashamed?

K: Not very much reaction. The big one is hurting her. I think this is possibly the whole thing here. It wasn't a deliberate thing. Something happened between you and your mother, and one thing led to another, and someway, you accidentally hurt her seriously.

P: But how?

K: I don't know, Peter. You were there; I wasn't.

P: I wouldn't mind so much if they could prove I did it. But there's a doubt in my mind. I know consciously I didn't do it. Subconsciously, who knows?

K: I think you're trying to eradicate it and not let your conscience say you did it.

P: Would it definitely be me? Could it have been someone else?

K: No way. From these reactions.

P: Now I'm afraid, because I was so sure I didn't do it, you know what I mean? I want to go back to school. I don't have any place to go.

K: This isn't the end of the world. As long as you don't get it straightened out in your mind, you'll never have a day of peace.

P: I gotta get it straightened out right now.

K: Right. Once we do that, we're halfway home. There's no doubt in my mind from these charts you did it. But why and how?

P: That's what I don't know. If I did it, I don't remember it. What I told you is exactly how I remember it. Is there any way they can kind of pound it out of me?

K: Peter!

P: Well, not pound it out of me, but dig deeper into me.

K: This is what we're trying to do here. And I think you can give me the answer if you want to. I think you're so ashamed, that if you tell me, you don't know what I'm going to say to you. You're so damned ashamed of last night that you're trying to just block it out of your mind. You just feel that by sitting here and denying it and denying it and denying it, that it's going to go away.

P: I'm not purposely denying it. If I did it, I wish I knew I'd done it. I'd be more than happy to admit it if I knew it. If I could remember it. But I don't remember it.

K: How are we going to solve this? What's your suggestion?

P: I don't know. Another test would help. Find out what they found in the house. The thing is, I don't want to go into a mental hospital. I don't want to leave the people I know. I don't want to leave the band; we're starting to go professional.

K: Is that what's worrying you, Peter? That you'll have to go into a mental hospital?

P: The thing is, if I did it, I don't remember. I don't want to go into a mental hospital. I don't mind a session with a psychiatrist once a week, but I want to stay in the school I'm going to. But I'm stuck. I'm hung up. I don't remember.

K: My charts say you remember this right now.

P: But I don't. Can you fire this thing up and ask me again?

K: No. I have enough now. I think our problem is that you don't want to remember. You're afraid of what's going to happen to you if you tell me the whole truth.

P: I can't understand it. If it meant bringing my mother back right now, I don't remember it.

K: You said three months ago you fired a flashlight at her. Have you done anything more serious? Tried to choke her, or hit her in the face?

P: No, no. Absolutely not.

K: So how do you think we're going to resolve this, Pete?

P: We got to keep drilling at it. But I'd like to get some sleep.

K: Do you want me to start yelling at you?

P: No.

K: Would you come back here and talk to me again?

P: I'll be happy to come back anytime you want me to. If you want me to see a psychiatrist, except I don't have any money now.

K: That's why I keep talking to you now. I think you almost remember.

P: I don't know. I still don't remember anything. There's space in there now.

K: Sit there and close your eyes and just relate your story again from the time you arrive in the yard with the Corvette.

P: OK. I drive in the yard. Shut off the car. I remember shaking down the headlight. I put it in gear. Locked it up. I went in and yelled, "Mom, I'm home." I looked up at the bed.

K: Was the bed messed up, or just turned down?

P: There was a sleeping bag on top of the blanket. She had the sleeping bag open. The bed lamp was on. I thought I saw her, you know what I mean? Then I did a double take.

K: See what I mean?

P: That's what could mess me up.

K: This is probably where you flipped over. You probably *did* see your mother there. And the next thing, you see your mother on the floor. This is our gray area. You feel you saw her standing there.

P: No, lying in bed.

K: Oh, all right. Lying in bed.

P: But I still don't remember.

K: Would she have had the light on? Does she normally go to bed so early?

P: As soon as the news is over, and it got too cold outside to read, she'd go to bed and read. Usually when she went to bed she wore all her clothes. It wasn't all that fancy as far as cleanliness went.

K: Maybe this is the problem. Your friends' houses are nice and clean. You come home to a dirty house.

P: That doesn't bother me that much.

K: Maybe this turns you on. You know?

P: I wish I could go out and have that cigarette now.

K: I got a couple here. Let me get an ashtray.

P: If I did do it, why don't I remember it?

K: Because you mind is trying to——

P: Block it out. I don't think I'm any dummy.

K: Oh no. I don't think you're a dummy. I think something happened, and you're so goddamned ashamed, you're afraid to come out with it.

P: Do you think I'm deliberately lying to you?

K: Yeah, I do.

P: I don't.

K: I feel you could tell me right now exactly how your mother died. The way I read the report, something violent had to occur between you and her.

P: It had to happen between her and I?

K: Especially with the broken legs. She had to be hit with something, right? Or it could be a complete goddamn accident and you hit her with your car. Maybe with this ailment she had, she had fallen down, and you hit her with the car, and you panicked.

P: Are my footprints going into the bedroom there?

K: I understand they have some in blood.

P: Blood? In my shoe marks?

K: Well, this takes a while to check out. This isn't magic.

P: When I fell asleep this morning, I dreamed I hadn't gone to the Teen Center, I stayed home, and somebody came into the house, and I was trying to protect her. I don't remember that clearly either, but I want to find out. I'm more than willing to come back and take another test because if I did it, I want to know I did it.

K: I think you know now. I think you're afraid.

P: I'm not. All my fears are gone. If I was afraid, I'd start crying.

K: You know what I think, Pete? You're afraid we're going to lock you up someplace and throw away the key. This isn't going to happen. You're a decent-living guy. You're not a criminal. You did a crazy thing. I've done crazy things. Probably when I was your age I did crazier things than you've done. Screwing around, you know? I'm not going to sit here and tell you that I'm an angel. I'd be lyin' to you. The people in the area think you're a decent guy. This is our problem. You're such a decent guy and this is such a shameful thing. What your friends would think of you . . .

P: Well, that does bother me. Could it be that I've totally put it out of my memory?

K: RIGHT! This is our problem. Once we get this out in the open and get you the proper help, it will be over with.

P: Would truth serum help? Sodium pentothal?

K: This is better. I think right now, Pete, you're ashamed of the thing and you're afraid you'd go into a mental hospital. Let me speak from experience. I've known people who have gone into a mental hospital. They keep them, depending on who they are, in classes together. It's just like going to school. It's not like in the movies, where you're in a cage and people stare at you.

P: It would be coming back and facing people I knew.

K: We had a girl here one time, about eight years ago. She was seventeen. Probably she's twenty-five today. She had a hang-up, she was going around burning down all her relations' homes. Aunts, uncles, cousins. She sat right where you're sitting now. Exact same chair. That's the same chair we had eight years ago. Not the same polygraph, but the same chair. And she gave us reactions like this. She denied it for, oh, I don't know how long. I kept talking to her like I'm talking to you. Finally she admitted it. She thought the world hated her. Especially her relations. OK? We got her out of here. They put her in a mental hospital for three and a half months. She's a normal person today. Married, with a family. We still get Christmas cards from her, and she signs— I'm not going to tell you her name, it's none of your business—she signs it, and underneath she puts, Thanks. We know what she means.

P: Did she realize she was doing it?

K: Yes. Fortunately, nobody was ever in the house. She used to do it when they were away. But she gave me the same thing you're

66

giving me now. Finally she told me. We got her the help, and she's a normal person today. As simple as that.

P: I *want* to tell you I did it now. But I'm still not sure I *did* do it.

K: Look, you're afraid. Nobody's going to hate you.

P: The part that really bothers me is the band. That's my *life*.

K: Three months out of your life. That's not a very long time. It's not the end of the world.

P: It seems as though it is, though. She's gone.

4

Barbara was chilled at the Sharon Hospital morgue for a while on Saturday, until Dr. Izumi arrived for the autopsy. There were very few murder victims brought into Sharon Hospital and Dr. Izumi kept thinking of Barbara as a patient.

He cut out Barbara's heart and put it on a scale. It weighed 280 grams. He cut out both her kidneys and weighed them, too. He took a sample of her blood, using a syringe. He pushed a little metallic probe through the wound in the palm of her right hand, and it came out the back. He pulled out some of Barbara's pubic hairs, and hairs from her arm and head, and turned them over to Trooper Venclauscas, who put them in plastic containers. Sergeant Chapman, who had taken pictures of Barbara at the house, came to the autopsy too. He took nineteen colored slides. The autopsy took a long time, more than six hours. It began while Peter was sleeping at the barracks and continued through midafternoon, while Peter was driving to Hartford with Jim Mulhern, and then, in the seat of honor, talking with Sergeant Kelly. Talking about Barbara.

K: There's nothing we can do about your mother now, right? You're only eighteen, right? You got a long way to go in this world. We can concentrate on *you,* get you straightened out, so this thing that happened here will disappear. But if you don't talk about it it's not going to disappear and you're going to keep sliding down into a deeper hole. Right now you're at the point of this hole. You haven't dropped in yet.

P: I've sometimes wondered if I'm mentally right.

K: Let's see where we go from here. What instrument do you play in the band?

P: Guitar. If I had to give up the band, I'd have no outlook on life anymore.

K: Three months out of your life isn't going to hurt you.

P: Missing band practice . . .

K: First we gotta straighten Peter out. If you don't get straightened out you're gonna screw up the band worse. You're gonna be strumming away some night and you're going to be off-key.

P: My outlook on life now is a big question mark.

K: I think this is why this thing happened. I think you're mixed up.

P: I *know* I'm mixed up now.

K: You're a little mixed up upstairs. I'm not saying you're nuts, don't get me wrong. You're confused. Now, you went in the house and saw your mother. Lying in bed or standing there?

P: Lying in bed. It seemed, you know, like a double take.

K: Possibly she said something to you. "You son of a bitch, where ya been all night?" And you went off the handle.

P: She was always calling up after me. I didn't get the freedom of being eighteen.

K: Eighteen, you're a man, according to the law. You're a free man, you can vote, you can drink, you can do anything you want. Your mother wouldn't let you go, huh?

P: No. You know, the apron strings. Actually, I think my mother could have used help herself. There's a record in my family of mental problems. My mom had an aunt who hung herself. My grandfather had a drinking problem. That's why I don't like to drink so much.

K: Is this what happened: You came home and because, as you said, you're tied to your mother's apron strings, she flew off the handle and went at you or something and you had to protect yourself?

P: It's still not coming through. I still can't remember and I want to.

K: This could be the whole thing. She could have went at you, and this is strictly a self-defense thing where you had to protect yourself. Do you follow me?

P: But I'd still have a problem. I mean, self-defense goes just so far.

K: But this is where you went off the handle. You lost complete control of your mind and your body.

P: I wish I hadn't gone home last night. I wish I'd stayed at the Teen Center.

K: We can't change that.

P: If it hadn't happened last night, do you think it would have happened some other time?

K: Possibly. . . . We have to think of the future. You got a long way to go in the future. I wish I had as long as you.

P: Could I make an appointment with a psychiatrist?

K: They'll arrange it for you, the fellows that are investigating. But first of all, we gotta know: Do we have a cold-blooded killer sitting here, or do we have a guy with a problem that needs to be straightened out?

P: You don't have a cold-blooded killer sitting here.

K: Then we have a guy with a problem. Now, tell me the problem, and we'll get you home so you can get some sleep, and Monday morning you talk to a doctor. You know, very few doctors work on Sunday.

P: Very few doctors *work*.

K: That's why I said Monday. Pete, I know people, and you certainly aren't a killer, all right? We gotta find out what it is. We have to get it out in the open. What did she say to you when you came in the house?

P: The only answer I can think of would be from another night, when she might give me hell. "You're late, why are you late?" Something like that.

K: Was she mad at you last night? She flew off the handle at you?

P: I can't think of any reason.

K: Why don't I let you sit here for a couple of minutes and meditate by yourself?

P: I'm so damned exhausted.

K: Yeah, but I think it's all coming out now. I might be confusing you. I'm just gonna walk out now. You just meditate there.

P: I'm just gonna fall asleep.

K: No you won't. I bet you won't fall asleep.

Kelly left. OOOHHH! Peter said loudly. A little later, Kelly returned.

K: I just called the investigators up in Canaan and from what I'm learning now I think I have a reason why it happened. They've talked to your friends. Every one of them said that your mother was always on your back. I think this is probably the whole thing. Last night you came in the house, she started buggin' you again. Am I right?

P: I would say you're right, but I don't remember doing the things that happened. I believe I did it, now.

K: I know that you know that you did it, but I feel you're afraid to come out and say it. I have no reason to hurt you, but I have reason to help you. I get more pleasure out of helping somebody, I want you to know that. I think you want to tell me, but you're ashamed to tell me.

P: But do I realize I'm ashamed?

K: Yes, you do. You tried to wash your mother off. That's why her clothes were all wet. You were ashamed.

P: I don't remember that, though. Can you give me any more information about what they found up there?

K: No. I told you what they learned. They learned your mother was constantly on your back, constantly nagging you, constantly after you. That's what I just learned on the phone. Last night you came home—you're a man—she started nagging and bitching and moaning and you lost control.

P: It seems like that's what would have happened, but I don't remember it happening.

K: Peter, you still don't trust me. What I want you to do is to tell me how it happened and then you're home free. You're halfway through the battle.

P: I do trust you. But I have to say things to myself, too. I don't know what to say to myself to get these things out of me.

K: If you trust me, tell me how you did it and I promise that we're on the uphill swing. I can understand you doing something like this, if she was constantly on ya. This could happen to anybody. This is just like a prisoner being tortured. The prisoners of war— these are whole Americans. They beat them down and beat them down and they finally say anything they want to hear, and they give out secrets, but they're still good Americans. It's the same situation here. Your mother kept nagging and nagging and finally you lost your self-control and you ended the nagging. It's exactly like I said—a prisoner being captured. You were captured by your mother. She wouldn't liberate you. She treated you like a little kid, but the law says you're a grown man. You've been nagged so badly; that phone call told me how she treated you. Am I right, Pete?

P: You're right. Something's coming.

K: Come on Pete, tell me. I told you the truth. Now I want to hear the truth from you.

P: Somewhere in my head a straight razor sticks in.

K: OK. What did you do with the straight razor?

P: It's not that I had it. It's because there was a straight razor in the house.

K: All right.

P: And, when I looked for it, it was gone.

K: When was this?

P: This was last night and I thought—and I asked one of the police officers if it was there because they said there were some cuts or something. I asked if they looked like they could have been done with a straight razor or razor or something. They said they didn't know yet.

K: Did she hit you first or did you hit her first? I think she hit you first. Am I right? She wasn't feeling good, she called the doctor, and she was pissed off because you weren't there.

P: I don't think she hit me, though. But I don't think I have the power to break somebody's legs.

K: When you're in a state like this, you become powerful. The adrenaline. You become twice, three times your normal strength under a stress situation, and I think what we had there last night was a stress situation. We know she was upset because she called the doctor.

P: Maybe she wanted to go to Sharon Hospital and was upset because I had the car. That seems like a good reason. Sir, do you suppose I could get something to drink?

K: Sure. Would you like a soda?

P: Can I get a Coke?

K: I'll have Jack go down and get some.

P: Do you think I could have anything to eat, too?

K: There's nothing to eat here. I'm getting a little hungry myself. But I think we should iron this thing out before we leave. You wouldn't be able to eat with this thing prying on your mind, you know what I mean?

P: I feel hungry, then I feel like there's a pit in my stomach.

K: Must be Jack with the sodas.

J: Anything else, Tim?

K: No, that's good, Jack.

This could be the whole thing. If we put a dinner in front of you, you wouldn't be able to eat it. Once we get this out you're going to eat like you've never eaten before.

P: I been losing weight. I been missing meals.

K: You can tell me how you think it happened. An argument?

P: I could have got mad on the way home, maybe. The way the car was running, or something. I probably would have confronted her with the fact that she's got to get a new car. And from there, I'm blank. But whatever it is, it's got to do with her being in bed. Doesn't it?

K: Did she get up and throw the book at you?

P: No. As a matter of fact, the book was on the table in the living room. Tell me something. Will I remember this? Will I remember all the details?

K: A little bit. Yeah.

P: There was a bicycle—in the bedroom—near the wall. The way to get it in and out was through the back door, and they said the back door was open.

K: Were you going for a bike ride?

P: In the middle of the night? Not this kid. I haven't been on a bicycle in so long, not since I got my license.

K: Tell me. You just thought of something. I can almost read it on your forehead.

P: I'm just thinking of how tired I am.

K: Once you get this out you'll be able to sleep for a week because your conscience will be free.

P: When I get this out will I be totally cured? I feel so free now, like things that have had hold of me are letting go. It started last night when I started to fill out statements.

K: Right. Because you don't have any more nagging, that's why.

P: But the first thing I thought of, when I woke up, was that they were really giving me a rough time and I had to call my mom to help because if I ever got in trouble she'd be right there. And then I realized what happened.

K: OK.

P: Gotta keep digging. Gotta dig. Gotta keep pushing. I believe I did it.

K: I *know* you did it.

As Peter Reilly and Sergeant Kelly were talking, it was nearly dinnertime in Canaan. Mickey Madow had spent the day at an ambulance drill in Goshen. When he came home and found that Peter still wasn't back, he decided not to call the barracks again. Instead, he went over to see what was going on. It was just six o'clock when he talked with Sergeant Salley, who told him that Peter was cooperating with the investigation. But Mickey was worried now. "Does Peter need a lawyer?" Mickey later remembered asking Sergeant Salley. "No," the officer said. "Not at this point."

At that point, Lieutenant Shay made a phone call from Hartford to Canaan barracks. He told an aide to find the public defender.

And at that point, Joe O'Brien of the *Hartford Courant* was closing his story of the murder. He called the barracks and asked whether they had any suspects in custody. The police said they did not.

Back in the polygraph room, Peter Reilly was telling Sergeant Kelly he thought he did it, and Sergeant Kelly was telling Peter Reilly he *knew* he did it, so there was a certain irony, a melancholy coincidence, in the timing of these conversations and calls. Eventually though, there was such an accumulation of ironies in the Peter Reilly affair that one irony, more or less, scarcely seemed to matter.

K: Right now what you and I are trying to do is iron this thing out so we can get rid of this problem.

P: I wanted to take that test because I believe I didn't do it.

K: No. You want this to come out.

P: I remember something about her really bitching. I remember cigarettes on the table. I picked one up and lit it, but I don't know when it was.

K: Was it the last cigarette in the house?

P: No.

K: As I said, when I made that phone call and they told me what she did to you—calling your friends up and all this kind of crap—then I realized what happened. That's when I realized we had a problem, OK?

P: Maybe I'm imagining it. But it seems to be coming out. Me yelling, "leave me alone."

K: Now what happened?

P: I don't know.

K: Let me ask you a very personal question. Have you ever had relations with your mother?

P: No. I was asked that yesterday. I remember her having relations with another man, though.

K: I heard about that. We won't go into that.

P: When I was little, we were superclose. Once she started having relations with this other guy, it started going downhill. If something like that ever happened to me again . . .

K: No, I don't think this would happen to you again. But we gotta get it out. If we don't, man, you got a problem. The thing is, you got to tell me.

P: It's got something to do with cars. She harped at me a lot about that model T. Get that junk out of here.

K: So last night was the night. I don't think you planned anything.

P: Oh no.

K: This was no premeditated thing. I think you just had it right up to here, and it snapped, and you did it. It's as simple as that.

P: The thing that bothers me, what right I had to take her life?

K: I don't think you realized what you were doing.

P: I know. But I still can't—I still can't—

K: All right, Peter, I agree with you.

P: I'm hung up for words right now.

K: I agree with you one hundred percent. But it has happened. We cannot change that. You're not the first guy and you won't be the last guy . . .

P: The whole thing I'm worrying about is jail.

K: Peter, don't worry about things like that.

P: That's not going to help, throwing me in jail.

K: Damn right it's not going to help, throwing you in jail. I've said that for many years. I'm the guy that says, "This guy needs some help from a doctor." And they'll take my word for this. They'll get you help with a doctor.

P: I spoke to Mrs. Beligni last week about could I move up there? And she said no, because my mom would be calling up constantly. Everybody I know has a really nice home.

K: I think this is what's bothering you, Pete.

P: Should I keep going?

K: Yes, go right ahead.

P: I never had my own car. I had my mom's. Every time I tried to do something for myself . . . made a deal, tried something . . . even if I came out on top . . . she'd say I was a dope.

K: That's terrible.

P: But now that she is gone, I think about going to these friends of mine—and it's fantastic. When I'm there I'm like another son. The thing is, now I don't want to go there. I don't have any apron strings.

K: Now you're emancipated. You're a man. You're eighteen.

P: I wanted to move out, and everybody told me, "Don't leave your mother all alone."

K: I think you should have, Pete. It unties the apron strings.

P: I didn't move out because I wanted to go to school. I don't think people had the right to tell me not to move out.

K: From what you've told me so far, I think you should have.

P: I always thought I should.

K: Now we have the reason, we have to know how. Let's get this out, then we'll get you some nice dinner once we get this out in the open. What was the hassle about when you got home?

P: I don't remember. But I got the feeling like I was hitting her. I remember using this arm. But I don't have any marks on it.

K: Not necessary to have marks.

P: Maybe I do. I do have red knuckles. One red knuckle.

K: Of course, that ring would protect your hand, anyway. Keep going now. We know why. Because of all this hassling and shit you've been taking for the past couple of years . . .

P: I got a feeling it is going to come out.

K: I know it is.

P: After it's out, I want to try making it on my own—before I go to any psychiatrist—because I don't think I was responsible for my actions last night.

K: I don't either. I don't think you're a vicious man.

P: I've never been given a second chance at anything.

K: You'll get your second chance. If we don't get this out in the open, there's no second chance.

P: Gotta find out.

K: All right. You remember hitting her, right? How does the straight razor come in?

P: I don't know. We got it for model airplanes.

K: I have one myself. I build boat models.

P: A couple of times my friends would say, let's go out, and I'd say, I think I'll stay home and work on my model. Once I spent twenty dollars on wood and glue. She yelled, and she's the one that started me. I love building models. There's something about building things like that, you feel you're accomplishing something. I'm in the middle of a Newport.

K: The one I'm building is very complicated—a revolutionary war ship. It was built in Massachusetts, the U.S.S. *Rattlesnake*. Someday I'll get it done. It's relaxing.

P: I like to build the fuselage the most. I had the Newport out, a Newport spy plane, out on the table a couple of days and she yelled at me for having it out. She threatened to throw it in the garbage.

K: Peter, you had a real problem with your home life.

P: I did. I hated being home. I'd go to my friends' house for a week or two, then I'd miss home. I'd go home, and I'd be there for an hour, and I'd hate it all over again. I'd miss my mom, but once I was back, I had to go out. And I kept getting harped on about a job. All my friends work. I don't work. I quit a job washing dishes. She said she could handle the job.

K: She was really on you, wasn't she?

P: Constantly. Could I have a cigarette?

K: Sure. What was she on you for last night, Pete? Huh? What was it all about? That made you go this far and get so upset? It had to be something really drastic to have you lose your cool this badly?

P: I don't know. But violence is coming into it now. With the straight razor, slashing and stuff. But not much. One thing toward her throat. I may be imagining it. And shaking her up a lot.

K: Slashing at her throat with the straight razor?

P: Yeah.

K: How about her legs? What kind of a vision do we get there?

P: I don't want to remember that because I'm going to get sick if I do. Something like that makes me sick anyway. And to think I did it.

K: Did you step on her legs or something? While she was on the floor? And jump up and down?

P: I could have.

K: Or did you hit her?

P: That sounds possible.

K: Or did you hit her with something?

P: No, if I hit her with something, it probably would have been my guitar, and no matter what I did, I'd have never used my guitar.

K: I don't blame you. Can you remember stomping her legs?

P: You say it, then I imagine I'm doing it.

K: You're not imagining anything. I think the truth is starting to come out. You want it out. You want that second chance.

P: The thing that bothers me is people saying, he murdered his mother.

K: Murder is premeditated. I don't think this was. You just kept slashing and kicking and hitting and it was too late. You lost all your composure because of all the build-up over the past year or two, and all this came out at one time. I don't think you *murdered* anybody.

P: But other people will look at it that way.

K: Let's talk turkey. Let's get it out.

P: I think I walked in the door, and she said something. . . . Whether she threatened to break my guitar—not allow me to use the car . . .

K: Where did you get the straight razor?

P: Probably on the kitchen table. But when I asked the police officer, he said they didn't find one. Maybe I threw it, either over to the gas station or behind the barn. Because whenever I wanted to get rid of something, that's where I threw it. One time I threw some pot behind the gas station, once, a bottle of booze.

K: So where did you cut her with this razor?

P: The throat is the only thing I can think of.

K: More than once?

P: Once.

K:. Anyplace else?

P: Not that I can think of.

K: How about the water? Did you try to clean her up?

P: Yeah, but wouldn't I have been out of breath if I carried her in?

K: From where?

P: From the bathroom.

K: Maybe you did it right there on the floor and tried to clean her up. I don't know, Peter. I wasn't there. You were there. If this is true, it shows that you're sorry for what happened.

P: I *am* sorry for what happened.

K: I know you are.

P: Do you think we could quit now? So I could get some sleep? I think I'm saying things that I don't mean to say.

K: Oh no. You're telling me the truth now. You told me about slashing her throat with a straight razor. I'll have to see if this is true or not. Now, how did we break the legs? How do you think it happened?

P: Jumping up and down. If it was me.

K: Oh, Pete. You know it was you.

P: What would you do if something came up where it turned out that it absolutely wasn't me?

K: I'd apologize to you. But this isn't going to happen. Now, we've got to get it out. If I was there, I could help you. But I wasn't there. This is the next day. Now I'm trying to help. Did she come at you with something last night? Was she going to beat you up?

P: No, she was smaller than me.

K: How about the water?

P: Something about swimming registers, almost like a pond. It seems that with her clothes off I was trying to clean her up. Maybe I thought it would make it all better.

K: Is this why you put the water on her?

P: Things aren't clear, you know? I remember thinking, Oh my God, when I saw her lyin' there. But I don't remember whether that's when I came home and saw her.

K: You've tried to blank it out of your mind. That's why you thought you came home and found her. But you can't blank it out. Now your mind is going to be relieved of it. You got a second life now.

P: But the one thing that bothers me is, what right I had to take her life? That's something I'll never be able to get over. Is there any way, when all this is over, that it could be wiped out of my head?

K: I don't know. It's possible. How do you think you broke her legs?

P: Jumping up and down.

K: Yeah? When she was on the floor?

P: Yeah.

K: OK. Where was she when you first came in the house? In the living room or what?

P: No. It would seem to me she was in her bed.

K: Oh. Did she get out of bed?

P: The fact that her book was on the table means that she could have gotten out of the bed and put her book on the table and then we started yelling—

K: Ya.

P: —screaming and everything started happening.

K: Right. Is this how you think it went?

P: Yeah.

K: Where did you keep this razor?

P: Probably on the table in the living room.

K: Right where you were arguing.

P: So I'd have just reached out for it. Or she reached out for it and came after me.

K: That's what I asked you before . . . you remember slashing at her throat?

P: I think I remember.

K: You told me you did remember it.

P: But if I did it, wouldn't there be some marks on me? Wouldn't I have been wet if I tried to clean her down?

K: I don't know. I wasn't there. I don't know how you tried to clean her down. Maybe you dried your hands very carefully. Did you change your clothes?

P: Mine? No. I wore these clothes to school yesterday. I've had them on since it happened. She always used to harp at me about my clothes.

K: I used to wear dungarees myself, bell-bottoms, twenty-five years ago when I was in the navy. Now we have to get this straightened out.

P: I think it's pretty well straightened out now.

K: You think the razor's behind the barn? Or behind the gas station?

P: Those are the two places I could think of. I wish I wasn't so tired because things come into my head and go right out again. What time is it?

K: Six-thirty.

P: I keep thinking I gotta be home, so my mom doesn't miss me.

K: What else, Peter? Did you take her pants off?

P: I don't think so. I really don't think so. That just doesn't register, but her pants were off. Maybe she didn't have clothes on when I got there.

K: Run through the whole picture again.

P: I walked in the door. I looked up. Let's say she's in bed.

K: All right.

P: She gets out of bed. We start arguing.

K: You think it was the car, or what?

P: I don't know. I don't think that's important, though.

K: Just another goddamned argument. A continuous one.

P: Yeah. Either she picked up the razor, or I did. She may have come toward me, and I would have taken it away from her and then gone after her with it. I remember slashing, and if I had, she may have fallen right back over. If there are any other injuries, I don't remember. But even if I do remember slashing at her throat, that's all I really have to remember. Because I remember doing the damage.

K: Now, the legs.

P: I think I could have jumped up and down on her. I don't know if there were any ribs broken.

K: I don't know.

81

P: Maybe I could have kicked her.

K: Do you remember kicking her?

P: No. I never had a real fight, but I always told myself in a real fight, I'm not going to fight clean. You fight to win. Right?

K: Right. Maybe we should let you talk to the investigator, this last part we just talked about.

P: I don't want to get thrown in a cell.

K: We'll see what we can arrange. I'm not going to lie to you, Peter. I just work here, you see? I want you to tell these people what you just told me.

P: Do you have any records of this? Have you been tape recording me?

K: No. I got my tape right here. That's all I need. That's you. That's your conscience.

Peter was right when he told Sergeant Kelly "there's got to be some clue in the house." A little past noon on Saturday, when the sun was bright and the house didn't seem nearly as eerie as it had in the darkness, Trooper Don Moran found the straight razor Barbara had got Peter from Mario's Barber Shop, the razor he said he used to slash her throat. It wasn't thrown behind the barn, or behind the gas station. It was lying on the third shelf in the living room, the odds-and-ends shelf. The usual place.

Peter felt a little better across the hall in the interview room than he had in the polygraph room. It was no larger, but the window was open to the early evening breeze, the furnishings were comfortable. There was a leather couch along one wall, a desk, and a leather armchair by the desk, rather like a doctor's office. Peter was sitting in the leather armchair when Sergeant Kelly came in with Lieutenant Shay.

S: Hi ya, Pete.

P: Hi.
   Well, it really looks like I did it. The thing is I must have flown off the handle. I'm kind of pooped, you can tell him what I told you about how much I got nagged.

K: His mother's been on his back, Jimmy, for the past couple years. Nag this, nag that . . .

P: Every day.

K: He said he came home last night and she started . . .

P: I said that we argued about something but I didn't know what. Remember I said I had a double take at the bed and then the floor? What I must have done was walk in and actually see my mom in the bed and then that's when everything went blank. And, what happened was—'cause the reading light was on— she must have come out into the living room 'cause her book was on the table. And, we got in an argument about something. But I remember picking up the straight razor off the thing. I think it was the straight razor that I used. And, uh, I slashed for her throat. I remember when she was on the floor that I jumped up and down on her.

K: Well, maybe the lieutenant can clarify this. Were there any bruises, Jim?

S: Yeah. You say that you used a straight razor?

P: Yes.

S: What did you do with it?

P: I don't know. I think I either threw it behind the gas station or over the barn.

S: What about a knife, Pete? Remember using a knife?

P: I don't, but a straight razor thing registers.

S: And a knife, Pete.

P: Maybe. Could you give me the details?

S: I think you know the details.

P: I'm not absolutely sure of it, though. I mean, everything hasn't come out yet. . . . When you checked my shoes, did you find anything wrong?

S: Well, they're still checking.

P: What did they find at the autopsy?

S: They're still checking that.

P: The only thing that bothers me, I'm afraid my friends will find out what I did.

S: Well, Peter, I told you at the onset of our conversation this morning that I think anybody that knows you realizes . . .

K: I'll be right back, Jim.

P: What trouble I had.

S: What you were up against with your mother for the past sixteen years of your life record, and I don't think anybody is going to hold it against you, Peter . . . more than likely, before this is all over, you will receive psychiatric treatment. There are many forms of therapy—outpatient clinics, all kinds of possibilities, Peter. I'm going to tell you right now. We know by time now, when your mother became deceased—when she died—you were in the house. We know that. We can prove that. So, this is academic. I want you to understand that this is the best for you. I want you now to sit back there and recite for me what happened. I know this may be painful to you . . .

P: It is.

S: You're tired and I'm tired. We on the State Police are not your enemies.

P: I know.

S: We don't find happiness in other people's misfortune. If we can help you, and I know we can help you, we will help you.

P: Before I start going over it, I've got to have someone to turn to.

S: Now, Peter, you've got us to turn to.

P: Right.

S: You don't have any parents.

P: Well, I mean I want one particular person who's on my side, to help me. I don't mean a lawyer, I mean someone like an adult. A father, a mother or something.

S: Is there anybody here that you trust? Do you trust Trooper Mulhern?

P: Yes, absolutely.

S: All right. Would you be willing to sit down with Trooper Mulhern and trust him enough to tell him in detail what happened? From beginning to end, what happened.

P: Well, I trust you that much, and I also trust . . .

S: Sergeant Kelly?

P: I don't know. The man who gave me the test. I feel so guilty about it, you know.

S: Once you get this thing straightened out, and I mean *out,* you will realize that perhaps what motivated this action on your part was years of unhappiness, of deprivation, of embarrassment, of a mixed feeling towards your mother. And you're not as guilty and you're not as responsible as you perhaps think you are now.

P: I've got to get this out in the open so I can see what happened. And say, it's done, I've done it, I've got to live with it. And I could start again now.

S: A very astute observation. . . . So, let's make a start, Pete. Let's get this thing out.

P: Yes. Well, are you gonna write it down now?

S: Yes. OK?

P: Um . . . I got home, I went in the house.

S: OK.

P: I did yell, "Hey, Mom, I'm home."

S: OK.

P: And there was no answer. She may have been asleep and I may have shaken her to wake her up or something when I was home, I don't know. So, she was definitely in bed. The bed lamp was on and uh, the—what-do-you-call-it was open. The sleeping bag or something. So, I think she came out to the living room. Her book was on the table. We must have argued about something. I don't know what. There were several things we could have argued about. We could have argued about the fact that I wanted to get rid of the Corvette and she didn't. We could have argued about the fact that I wanted to get a Vega wagon so I could transfer my amplifier on it.

S: Mm.

P: Because my amplifier—half of it would fit in the Corvette. And she—I remember other times she said, "Oh, you're just getting a station wagon so you can transport everybody's stuff around." Really harping on me.

S: Yeah, could be. Have you ever felt close enough to someone that you could really trust them?

P: No.

S: That you really liked?

P: Nope . . . yes, excuse me. I do have someone that I could speak to like that. That would be Aldo Beligni.

S: Let's you and I try something. You try to feel about me . . .

P: Like a father?

S: Like somebody who's really interested in you, and then . . .

85

P: Well, I do already. That's why I come out with all this.

S: OK. Now when you say that you don't know what you argued about, you said you were beginning to trust me.

P: I said it and I do feel it. What do you mean?

S: You know what you argued about.

P: Well, no, I don't.

S: Peter, I'm saying to you that you are obviously a bright person.

P: I don't know. Am I? Do I seem to be?

S: Yes, you are. A bright person. So far.

P: Oh! I know what it was. And it slipped my mind again. I remember saying something about "leave me alone, leave me alone." My mom was really harping on me about everything.

S: What were you arguing about?

P: Must have been something—something that—maybe because—well, that wouldn't be it. That wouldn't tie in, um, because I'd come home and maybe she was drunk, I don't know—did the autopsy come up with a blood report?

S: Oh, it will, yes.

P: Where is she now?

S: She's over the hospital.

P: At Sharon?

S: Yeah. Now, why don't you just try this. Try and believe in somebody. Believe that we're not out to hurt you.

P: Well, the thing is, every time I try to I always get fucked over.

S: Yeah. But, you know, if you don't try to trust somebody, somewhere along the way, there's no hope here.

P: Yeah, I know I've got to trust someone. That's why I trust Mr. Beligni. Because he's the only man I've ever met that never tried to burn somebody in a deal. He's a well driller and one of the things he does—he charges half price for a dry hole. He's the only person I've ever met who's totally honest. I think maybe if I got involved in some religion it might help me too.

S: Would you like to be like Mr. Beligni?

P: Yes. Because he's a very honest man. I can't stand someone who lies. I didn't realize I was lying on that lie detector . . . I mean, when I was doing it I didn't realize it, until you started probing. You're really busting your ass trying to help me right now and I really appreciate it. Just—if I could get something written down that says I wasn't gonna go to jail or something, and I wasn't gonna go into a psycho ward or a mental institution, it wouldn't be so bad. But those are the two things that I'm scared of.

S: Let's say that you need institutional care, for a period of time. This will be a determination that I wouldn't make and that you wouldn't make.

P: Well, what I'm saying is, I don't think I need the treatment now. Now that she's gone, all those things, all the tension and the pulling and the things on my nerves. Everything's letting up and I feel free again. I feel like—reborn. I feel like I'm starting all over again, and I want a chance.

S: All right. The first step . . .

P: Is to break it down.

S: Is to break this down. To get it out. And then let us put the wheels in motion. Why don't you try to trust me?

P: Well, OK. Where'd I leave off?

S: We left off at the beginning. We haven't got started yet. We've been here three days and we haven't got started yet.

P: Three days?

S: Two days.

P: Holy Christ! We have.

S: But you've had some sleep. I haven't had any.

P: Well actually I've been up nearly as long as you.

S: But you had about six hours sleep I didn't have.

P: Did I get six hours sleep? It went by just like *that*.

S: Peter, put your trust in somebody. We'll start from the beginning again. Trust me. Tell me what happened. Let me put the wheels in motion. I promise you I'm not going to hurt you.

P: I understand that now.

S: I don't want to see you hurt. Mr. Mulhern doesn't want to see you hurt.

P: No, I like Jim. I really like him.

S: All right. Let's take the bull by the horns. Trust people.

P: OK.

S: All right.

P: Right on the level now.

S: Right on the level.

P: I think I did it.

S: Don't be afraid to say, "I did it."

P: But I'm incriminating myself by saying I did.

S: We have, right now, without any word out of your mouth, proof positive.

P: That I did it?

S: That you did it.

P: So, OK, then I may as well say I did it.

S: And by so doing, we take the first step towards getting you the kind of help you need.

P: You know what one of the things—before I get into it—would have helped?

S: What?

P: When I was younger. When I was fourteen or fifteen, is if I had one of these Big Brother outfits.

S: You know what would have helped, Pete?

P: A father.

S: A decent home, a decent mother and father. That's what would have really helped.

P: I don't think my mom was that indecent.

S: No.

P: I think she did a good job for what she was doing. I think she really tried. But, last year or two she told me that at this point she wasn't putting her all into taking care of me like she used to. When I have children, I want them to have a good family, a good home, the things they want.

S: That you never had.

P: Well, I had everything I ever wanted mainly.

S: You haven't had love.

P: I haven't had the love . . .

S: Right.

P: I'm hitting the nail over the head now.

S: I want you to tell me the truth.

P: Is my name gonna be put in the newspapers and everything?

S: No, no, no.

P: I mean will people find out what I've done?

S: We don't run newspapers, Pete, but we have an obligation to take every step possible to see that people like you aren't crucified in the paper.

P: Will I end up going on trial or something?

S: Let's put it this way. You'll end up getting the help that you need.

P: Yeah, but I mean am I actually gonna end up going into a court?

S: You will go to court. You'll be arraigned.

P: I mean, will there be like twelve . . .

S: No.

P: . . . men there?

S: This is a question I can't answer. If it's decided that you are in need of psychiatric help and you're not fit to stand trial because you didn't understand the nature of what you were doing.

P: Am I under arrest now?

S: No.

P: Will I have a record or will it be considered a mental thing?

S: This is a decision that will be made by the State's Attorney. We have nothing to do with this. But I will say this, Peter, I think it's obvious to everyone concerned here that the direction your case should take is for treatment.

P: Yeah. But I'll put my foot down right now that I just can't go out of society for three months or something. Or leave my school.

S: Suppose it's the only way you can get help?

P: Oh, if it was the only way, I'd do it. In a state hospital, would I still be going to school?

S: You're asking me questions that I really can't answer. I'm a police-man, and I really can't answer your question. I know basically what they do. They treat people. And, I suppose they have pro-visions for young people going to school. But you're asking me questions about different things I can't answer because it's not within my—it's not within the purview or scope of my duties. What is the primary interest to me is, number one: As it stands right now, we know and we feel that we can prove that you were responsible for what happened last night. Just by virtue of the time sequence here, we know you were in that house at a certain time and we know your mother died at a certain time, and the two identify. OK?

P: What do you mean? Do you think I killed my mother?

S: I know you killed your mother.

P: I mean, do you think I kicked and beat on her until she was dead?

S: As I said, Pete, I know that your mother died at your hands.

P: In my hands?

S: *At* your hands.

P: Because of me.

S: Right. Now what we do now is to seek the help you need. We do that first by establishing a trust between you and I. All you got to do is get over the mistrust. You've got to trust someone. I think you ought to trust me.

P: But still, should I really come out and say something that I'm not sure?

K: Peter, I think you're sure.

S: Pete, you're sure.

P: No, I'm not. I mean I'm sure of what you've shown me that I did it, but what I'm not sure of is how I did it.

S: Pete, if you don't begin to trust me, you're never going to receive the kind of help that you need, because you've got a problem.

P: Um, could you give me an idea when it could be arranged for me to see a psychiatrist? I mean, I want to go soon as possible.

S: Well, the sooner that you and I sit down here and have our talk the sooner you'll see a psychiatrist. Now, why don't you start and just try to trust us enough to put your future in our hands. We won't hurt you.

P: OK. I walked into the house. I yelled, "Mom, I'm home." Now maybe she did answer me and maybe she didn't. And, I looked and I know I saw her. And, the double take was when I saw her on the floor. So, should I say I did it now? That I did do it?

S: Peter, you did.

P: I mean everything's not too clear. Things are still getting clearer. Things are clearing up, you know what I mean?

S: As you trust us more, if you do, things will clear up.

P: Well, it's hard for me to say I did take the razor . . .

S: It's hard for you to trust us.

P: OK. And, I'm not sure whether she—well, she must have gotten out of bed. I don't remember that, but she must have because the book ended up in the kitchen—uh, the living room. So, we argued about something, which I still haven't been able to narrow down. Most likely, and in my head, it is about the car. Because of how much I needed a station wagon. And, whether she pushed me or she picked up the razor or what—came after me, I took it away from her or what, I don't know. I remember slashing toward her throat and—let me see—things are getting lost now. And, at that point I'm not too clear on how her clothes got wet. Whether I took her—whether I cleaned her up on the floor or what. Or whether she—you know, they were wet when I got home or what. Or—which I—you know, I doubt. And, then I remember seeing her on the floor and that was the second half of the double take.

S: You remember the knife?

P: There may have been a knife but I don't recollect it as well. Why do you ask about a knife?

S: Well, Pete, you know there was a knife.

P: I mean, was there a knife mark?

S: Pete, you know very well why I won't answer that question. 'Cause you're not being honest. You're being dishonest with me. You're trying to maneuver me and trick me into telling you facts that you already know. I know the facts.

P: Well, if you would give me some hints . . .

S: No, Pete, it's not necessary for us to give you hints. You know the facts as well as I know the facts.

P: But I don't.

S: And, you know as long as you play these headgames with me, you're not trusting me. You know, I'm going to tell you something and I'm telling you this from my heart. Until you begin to trust people, especially people like me that work for the state of Connecticut and are responsible for handling these situations, you're not gonna get the help; you're not gonna reach the goals or objectives that you have laid out for yourself.

P: Well, I'll go right in there on the polygraph—the polygraph machine again.

S: Pete, you're playing headgames again.

P: No, no, no, no . . .

S: Sure you are. You're playing headgames with me, Pete. You've been playing headgames with us here for two days. You know it and I know it.

P: I don't know it.

S: Listen to me for a second. I know for a fact you been kicked around. I know a lot about your background. Although you may think that my objective is to put you behind bars and hurt you or

91

bury you someplace, you're wrong. If I can help you, if I can help any citizen, especially any young boy or girl, that's what I get paid for. OK? Playing headgames with me here, showing your mistrust in me, is not doing a thing for you. Because you see, Pete, I know what happened last night almost as well as you know what happened last night. And, I'm telling you honestly, and I'm telling you this looking you right in your eyes, that the only way you're gonna have a prayer of straightening yourself out is to play it straight with us and we'll play it straight with you.

P: I'm trying. I'll go in on the polygraph machine if you'll ask me if I know this.

S: Pete, you've been on the polygraph test.

P: But that part of the question wasn't asked.

S: Pete, let me tell you something. I've sat in the other room and watched hundreds of these polygraph tests. OK? And, for once you got to realize that if we're gonna get anyplace you've got to break down and trust me.

P: I know it.

S: OK.

P: But I wish I knew.

S: Well, I'm *telling* you, Pete.

P: I want to know, that's it.

S: Pete, sit down and relax and give yourself a minute. All right. Your mother's dead. Now this could be the best thing that ever happened to you. OK? If it is, let it happen.

P: Well, it happened.

S: All right. But let the freedom that you speak about happen.

P: I'm really trying. I'm trying as hard as I can.

S: I know you're trying, but you're so afraid that we're gonna hurt you.

P: I don't feel afraid. I feel very calm, except that I'm getting irritable because everyone's telling me I'm playing games. And I don't mean to play games.

S: Tell me about the knife, Pete.

P: I don't know anything about a knife. What's the difference between my saying something about a razor or saying something about a knife? Either way I'm still saying that I did it, right? If maybe I made a mistake about the razor, then maybe I did, but I don't remember that knife. If I did, I'd say it. That's what I'm trying to put across. I don't remember a knife.

S: How did you—how did your mother's clothes get wet?

P: That's what we were talking about, and I wasn't sure, but I may have tried to wash her down and clean her up or something.

S: Where?

P: I don't know. That's blank.

S: Why?

P: I don't know. Maybe I don't want to remember it. I don't know. I still got to keep pounding it till it all comes out. I know that.

S: Why don't you remember?

P: I'm trying hard as I can. I mean, it's bad enough realizing and finding that my mom's dead, but, finding that I did it makes it even worse.

S: How many times did you cut your mom?

P: Once is all I can remember. Slashing at her throat. That's all. I remember jumping on her.

S: Do you remember cutting her any other place?

P: No.

S: Do you remember when you got mad, at the door—the machete?

P: I was—that was something when I got mad that night—and, uh— I was trying to sleep—it was three o'clock in the morning and she was singing opera just to make me mad.

S: Yes.

P: At the top of her voice. I'd close the door and she'd open it and I'd close it and lock it and she'd sing all the louder . . . I picked up the machete and I just put it through the door and the handle just slid down. And, she stopped. I just got so furious, you know. I just blew my cool then and I remember doing that.

S: Well, you blew your cool then when you hit the door with the machete. Was that similar to what happened last night?

P: No. It was different. Then she was just trying to make me mad, you know what I mean? Last night she wasn't trying to make me mad, she was doing it and she wasn't realizing how much she was doing it.

S: Mm-hm.

P: And, I just must have gone off the handle. Trying to get ahead and, every time I'd start to get ahead someone puts me down.

I wanted this Vega and she'd say, you know, "Oh, gee, that piece of junk! Every time you pick out a car, you know, it's a piece of crap." That has to be what I flew off the handle about, because that is the main, the very most up-to-date issue at our house, was about a car.

S: Now that you know that you were responsible for your mother's death, do you feel a great sense of guilt?

P: I feel guilty to the extent that no matter what she did, she shouldn't of had to give up her life to pay for the things she did to me.

S: Don't you think your mother took your life?

P: Not always. She didn't cut it off like that.

S: She might as well have.

P: Why do you say that?

S: Well, are you happy?

P: No.

S: Have you ever been happy?

P: I can't actually say I ever have been. I'm always being questioned about what's going to happen.

S: Do you think you have a—you had a normal relationship with people?

P: Mm-hm. I'm very level-headed about that. I knew I didn't have the greatest, you know, homelife. But, like when I was at somebody else's house—like when I lived with my grandparents, I learned all my manners and everything. I don't know whether you noticed how I always excuse myself and apologize for saying things . . .

S: . . . trust people?

P: Well, the thing is nobody's ever given me a reason to.

S: So, your relationship with people is not normal, is it?

P: No, I guess not. There are very few people I trust.

S: Don't you think maybe your mother was taking your life in a sense?

P: Yeah, but you see, she didn't stop it. I still got another chance. I can still rehabilitate. I can still start again.

S: Well, you can't even trust me. You can't trust me for five minutes.

P: Well, what do you mean? I don't understand this. I mean I'll always say everything that I can think of but I can't think anymore. Everything is so messed up. Nobody's giving me a chance to think about it. They give me maybe five minutes or two minutes but they don't let me sleep on it. They don't let me, you know, be alone or just sit down. They don't talk about what really built up to it, why I didn't like my homelife.

S: All right.

P: You know my mom had a boyfriend, which is something I was ashamed of. And, let me see . . . I always had the things that I wanted but I never had the things I needed. You agreeing with me there? I mean the physical things that were given to me I could always have. But, if I wanted love or something or someone show affection toward me, it wasn't there. And, I always felt kind of left out. Know what I mean?

S: Yeah.

P: That's one of the things that I just faced up to right now, which I really hadn't thought about too much. Things are going together a lot now. Everything is fitting together. Most of the background of it. I know my godmother had that kind of love for me.

S: How do you know?

P: She always wants to do things for me. She always wants to help me. Anything. She wanted to put me through college. It could be some other kid, you know? But it's me. And whenever I need something she can stretch things to help me. Always has. And, I know she's not physically showing me the affection but it's the best she could at a hundred miles away. If I wanted something she came through with it. My mom always says, "I'm doing for you, I'm taking care of you. I don't give you much," she said, "but I try to arrange things for you."

Barbara had arranged things for Peter with some success for eighteen years, from his baby clothes from Saks Fifth Avenue to the Converse sneakers and $15 shirt he was wearing the day she died. He had fine musical equipment—they had the Corvette. Auntie B. paid for the extra insurance that covered Peter as the driver.

The checks from Auntie B. stopped, though, when Barbara died. The police said they tried to reach her, the day after the murder. They called her at her house, and they tried a Teletype request to the New York police. But they couldn't find her that day, just as they couldn't find the public defender for Peter on Saturday either. They said they tried his office, and his home, and even a restaurant where somebody thought he might be having dinner, but they just didn't seem to have any luck.

S: I can understand . . . why you did what you did.

P: I hope you can because I can't. I can understand why I did it but I can't understand, you know, how I flew off the handle just like that. That's the thing I don't understand 'cause I don't have the background in that type of thing anyway.

S: Well, were you treated like a human being?

P: No.

S: You've been treated like an animal.

P: Yeah. I've been given my food and I've been given my place, but I've never been shown any affection.

S: And you acted like an animal last night.

P: But I still . . .

S: Do you think this is unique? Don't you think this happens every day of the week?

P: It happens all over the place.

S: Right. You know, if you could learn to trust . . .

P: I don't think I'm crazy. I don't know whether you think so, I don't.

S: Of course you're not crazy. But suppose I tell you you're ill.

P: Yes. It's something that snapped in me.

S: You got a problem.

P: I got a problem.

S: You got a problem.

P: Right. The problem was I was never shown the proper love and affection that parents should give.

S: Now, your problem is not insoluble.

P: What do you mean, insoluble?

S: It's not beyond repair. It's not beyond help.

P: I feel new again. I feel like I've just woken up to a new world.

S: Well, your problems are serious.

P: But don't you think that now that she's off my back . . . what I think is I've got to find somebody that can show me the affection that . . .

S: You got my help, Pete.

P: Right.

S: Now you got to start. And you can start right now.

P: I've tried as much as I could, but nobody's helping me out with what I'm supposed to say. They're not helping me out with what they found down there. You can't give me any hints?

S: You know I can't give you any hints. I'm asking you to trust me.

P: I trust you, but you're not giving me the help I need.

S: If you trust me, Pete—you hear what I said? If you trust me— listen now and listen and feel. If you trust me, I'll see that you get the help you need.

P: You personally?

S: Yeah.

P: I've got to find something. Are you married?

S: Yes.

P: Any kids?

S: Six.

P: Six! How old?

S: They run from a year and a half to twelve.

P: It was a dream, but I was hoping I could find someone. Like maybe you'd be willing to help me.

S: Maybe.

P: Anything, 'cause nobody really . . .

S: Go ahead, cry. Go ahead, cry, go ahead, come on . . .

P: Nobody's really right there to help me, never.

S: I know it. Maybe I can get you some help. Why don't you cry? You know you've been trying to cry for two days.

P: Yeah, I have.

S: Sure you have.

P: I haven't cried, till I found someone to turn to.

S: Crying, you know, is a very normal and very healthy function. I'm going to tell you something, Pete. You may find it hard to believe.

P: What?

S: I don't feel sorry for your mother, I feel sorry for you. 'Cause you've been a victim for years.

P: I'm not a victim again now though, am I?

S: No.

P: Can you, ah—where do you live?

97

S: I live in Granby, Connecticut.

P: Is there any chance that someone will take me in, you or someone?

S: Sure there's a chance.

P: God, I'll do anything. Work around the house, chores, anything. I'd love to do it.

S: You've got a big problem.

P: Mm-hm.

S: And, you got to straighten it out first, Pete. Now, I can sit here and lie to you and bullshit you. I'm not going to. You got a big problem and that's got to be straightened out first.

P: I realize now, I definitely did do what happened to my mother last night. But, the thing that I don't realize is the exact steps that I took doing it. They're the things that I'm foggy about. But, I think the main thing is that I am waking up to the fact that I did do it. I'm not afraid to admit it now.

S: Let me tell you something. People have the wrong idea about death. People think that when someone dies, that's the end of them.

P: I've sat down and I've thought about that. What it's gonna be like to die. Whether everything—like the basic part of your body, you know, if your head hurts or . . . There's got to be something that survives.

S: Your spirit, your soul.

P: Right. But my mom was atheist. And since she was atheist, I was never given a chance to believe in something. Now, I'm getting my own views on it.

S: Good.

P: I'm starting to do things for myself. We had a thing in Contemporary Problems, just last week . . . I got a sheet that you're supposed to fill out, and then I was supposed to take it back to school. It asks how you brought up your child. How old he was when he was weaned, how old your child was when toilet trained. Ah, when you show affection to your child, do you just say "that's good" and give him a pat on the head. And, that was what I've been going through. If I did something good, it was "OK, Pete, move on."

S: You know that if a baby's born and it doesn't receive handling, it dies.

P: I didn't know that it would die. But I know it feels rejected.

S: You know that children that come from orphanages as opposed to children who come from normal families do not achieve academically—do not succeed in later life, socially. Just by virtue of the fact that they don't receive the attention or receive the love that they should from their parents.

P: I didn't receive all the love that I should have received.

S: You perhaps got maybe one little hundredth of what you should have gotten. What you needed.

P: That's right.

S: You know, you don't need money to be happy.

P: I know it.

S: How many families do you know—families who don't have any money but they're happy?

P: The families that I always go to their homes.

S: Sure.

P: That's why I love hanging out around there. That's why they like to take me, because I enjoy the way they get along.

S: Mm.

P: And, I don't know, I started dressing this year, for school, better because I noticed Paul dresses very well. He works in a clothing store also. So he dresses very well and I like the way he dresses, you know, that's the way people . . .

S: Is Paul your age?

P: Paul's seventeen, I'm eighteen. And, we're like that. We'd do anything for one another.

S: Yeah, right.

P: And, oh—where was I?—Mrs. Beligni said that out of all the kids that ever went up there, I was the only kid that really associated, and all the other kids that came around, they always had to do something and they weren't content with just sitting around the house and enjoying it.

S: You should have had it.

P: And it's because I didn't have it and I missed it. That's why I like it up there.

S: That's obvious.

P: And Madows also. Because it's not just the way they get along. I'm sure they have family arguments and the parents and the

99

kids argue back and forth, that's normal. They are gonna have a disagreement.

S: Do you think it was too much to expect?

P: I never expected that from my mom.

S: But was it too much to expect?

P: What do you mean?

S: Well, was it too much for you to expect this kind of relationship with your mother and father?

P: No, I think that's normal.

S: Sure.

P: That's the basis of having a family.

S: Well, this is the basis of your problem. This is what I've been trying to tell you for the last hour. Now, if you let us, we'll help you. We don't want to see you go down the drain. What the hell good would it do me to see you go down the drain?

P: Wouldn't do you any good. I'm not going to allow myself to go down the drain. I've already put my mind to it.

S: Right. If you'd really put your mind to it.

P: I could never give up no matter how hard it is, I always try to get it. Just like when I quit smoking. I was really smoking but I stopped because there was this girl that I cared about and she doesn't want to smoke and every time she started telling me I smoked too much, I stopped. She's the type of person—when my mom has the funeral, she's gonna be there.

S: Let's do something.

P: I really want to. I really want to try. Can you give me a chance to get it gradual? Because, you know, I've never had it. It's something I've got to get used to.

S: Are you hungry?

P: Yes.

5

Joanne Mulhern called Marion early Saturday evening.

"Jim isn't here," Marion told her. "He hasn't brought Peter back from Hartford yet."

Joanne was concerned. "Jim hasn't had any sleep," she said. "I'm afraid for him to drive when he hasn't had sleep." She told Marion that she'd seen Peter at the baracks.

"How did he look?" Marion asked.

"He looked a little dazed," Joanne said. "He was just putting on his belt. They asked me whether those were the same clothes he had on last night."

"Were they the same clothes?" Marion asked.

"Yes, they were the same clothes," Joanne Mulhern said.

They were still the same clothes, in the interview room at Hartford, when Jim Mulhern came in with food.

M: Ham and cheese. Can you eat that?
P: Yep.
M: Cupcakes.
P: Thank you very much.
M: What's happening?

P: Oh, I'm messed up.

M: You're messed up?

P: But it's getting all together and I'm just seeing why everything happened.

M: What do you mean, why everything happened?

P: Well, I mean, the way I was brought up.

M: Why, what happened?

P: Well, it turned out I did it.

M: You killed your mother? How did you do that?

P: Well, we haven't really gotten into it. We've been digging and digging and digging and Lieutenant . . . what's his name?

M: Shay.

P: Shay. I keep thinking . . . from some TV show. Want half of this, Jim?

M: No. I've already ate downstairs. Why did you do it?

P: The whole situation was that I flew off the handle. We must of had an argument 'cause everything showed up on the polygraph. So, ah, the reason behind it was the way I'd been brought up. I never had the love that I should have had. The basics. You know what I mean?

M: Yeah.

P: And that's what it all built up to.

M: And it terminated in this, killing your mother?

P: Mm-hm.

M: What did you argue over?

P: We're still trying to take it apart. But there's a time lapse in there. And we finally found a blank spot I couldn't remember and that's when we got into it.

M: What was the argument?

P: It had something to do with the car.

M: The Corvette?

P: Mm. To have traded it in, most likely. I'm not positive. I'm really gonna have to think this one out. I want to go back down to the house. Just to be in the surroundings of the place, you know, maybe it will give me a little push.

M: Why you did it?

P: Right. I feel terrible about it, of course.

M: Well, it's an awful shock.

P: I know. You knew me, and you wouldn't expect me to do something like that.

M: In other words you blew up, and you lost control. Is that what you're saying?

P: Something just snapped with all the tension and everything, you know. I mean not having this and always having her on my back and always calling up for me, and always saying you can't use the car, you can't use the car and everything's my fault when it starts breaking down, and I always pick out duds for cars, and stuff like that. And everything builds up. And saying I make bad deals when I swap things for something. Trading in something. It all built up and it finally broke last night.

M: Well, just what happened?

P: Well, I remember using—I say it's the straight razor that I used and I slashed my mother's throat with it. And that came in out of nowhere. And I remember, I think, jumping up and down on her. I'm pretty sure.

M: You say a straight razor. You mean a straight razor like a barber uses when he shaves your hair?

P: Yes. I know, what did I have one of those for? Model airplanes. My mom picked it up from Mario in Canaan.

M: I never even knew that you built them. I thought you were a fisherman.

P: Oh, I'm a Jack-of-all-trades, master of none. I do a little bit of everything. Models, old cars, records, music. Music is my big thing though. Like music?

M: What did you do, do it as soon as you came home from the Youth Center?

P: When I looked at the bed she was in bed, and when I looked down she was on the floor. And in between those two things was a lapse of time. That's what we're digging into.

M: Did you cut her throat?

P: That's right. I can remember it, yes.

M: What did you do with the razor?

P: I don't know. I think I threw it. And if I'd thrown it, there were only two places that I would have thrown it that I'd know. One would be behind the gas station and the other would be over that red barn by the house.

M: The gas station across the street?

P: Yes. If I used the razor. That's something that pops into my head.

M: Did she scream or anything?

P: I don't remember.

M: Well, I knew you were having trouble with your car but didn't know that you were thinking—you mentioned quite awhile back that you were thinking about trading it in for a van or wagon . . .

P: A Vega wagon or something.

M: Plus the fact that she calls up the Madows and Belignis and all over looking for you.

P: I never got any real affection from her. I never knew what it was really like to grow up normally.

M: So in other words, even though you loved her there was a conflict there between you.

P: Yeah. That's something I didn't realize. Something you never had you don't miss.

M: Well, you got a problem. Something's wrong.

P: Something's wrong.

M: Have you ever fought with her before?

P: We've had arguments. I threw a flashlight at her once, underhand, just quick loss of temper and hit her in the shin.

M: Did you get any blood or anything on you when you cut her?

P: That's what I don't understand. There's nothing on me. I'm still wearing the same clothes. I can't understand that.

M: Well, they look like new pants. Are they?

P: No, they've been through the washing machine, once.

Lieutenant Shay had been listening and watching through the one-way mirror. He came back into the room where Peter and Jim Mulhern were talking. Shay sounded tired.

S: All right. It's getting late. You're tired, we're tired. We're going to reduce what you said to writing. We're gonna try to cover what you told us. How you came home, how you came in the house and you said, "Ma, are you there?" and the fact that you had words, and you're not sure what they were about, but it was something about a car. Now, did she come after you, do you recall?

P: I don't recall.

S: But you recall cutting her throat with a straight razor?

P: It's hard to say. I think I recall doing it. I mean, I imagine myself doing it. It's coming out of the back of my head. But I'm not absolutely positive of anything.

S: Peter, you spent an hour here talking about trust and you said to us repeatedly that you were responsible for your mother's death. Now the last hour you said this emphatically at least two-dozen times. You told us a half-dozen times that you cut your mother with a straight razor.

P: I said I thought I did.

S: No, you said you did. You didn't say you thought you did, you said you did. OK. Now, all I want to do now is reduce this to writing.

M: Look, Pete, it doesn't make that much difference whether you say it orally or whether it's reduced to writing. It's just a question of logistics for us.

P: Well, I'm still not positive that I did it.

M: You just told me that you did it.

P: I told you that I've been drilled so much that it seems like I did it. And the chances are that I did do it. That's what it's boiling down to. But, I'm not positive.

S: Get it down on paper, Jim, and we'll go from there. You know, Peter, obviously what you're doing is playing headgames. You said here for the last two hours—at least two-dozen times—that you are responsible for your mother's—for what happened to your mother.

P: Yeah, I know I said it. But, everyone is saying that everything shows that I did do it.

S: Here you go playing headgames again. I told you that we got you locked into the house at a time between nine-thirty and ten minutes to ten and I told you that we got your mother on the phone with the doctor at nine-thirty. So, when your mother died you were in the house. We can prove this.

P: I already said that when she died I was in the house.

S: All right. So, if she died when you were in the house and there were only the two of you there, somebody is responsible for the other's death. The other is you, Pete.

105

P: Wait a minute. My original statement, when I walked in the house, she was already lying . . .

S: You made a statement to the effect that she was in bed, she got out and advanced on you and that you . . .

P: I said I was not sure that she advanced on me.

S: You didn't say may have, Pete. You're playing headgames again.

P: No, I'm not. I know what I said there. I said I wasn't sure if she advanced on me or whether we just argued or what. Or whether she came after me with something or what.

Peter was never a scholar. He was not interested in most of his school subjects, and his report cards reflected that. He was especially not interested in geometry. "Peter gave up a long time ago," his geometry teacher wrote in May, the year Barbara died. He was a dreadful speller. Besides music, his best subject was United States history. His school grades, all in all, were barely passing. To pass from junior to senior at Regional, a student needed sixty-five credits, minimum. Peter had sixty-seven.

But as he had told Sergeant Kelly, he was no dummy. He had a quick and clever mind, when he chose to use it. Beyond the lack of interest in schoolwork, beyond his own remoteness, he was aware. When Peter told Lieutenant Shay, after five or six hours of intensive questioning, "I know what I said there," he did know. He had a mental resilience, an ability to sort things out, to anticipate, that most observers never suspected.

Barbara had known, though, ever since she had taught Peter to play chess, when he was eight. They played two games together, and after that he beat her all the time. He wasn't a brilliant player, just better. "I could never think more than two or three moves ahead," Peter explained, "but she could never go more than one or two."

M: Is there a report in here to write this down on?

S: Yeah, in the drawer.

P: I don't know what to do, Jim. I'm still not positive any of that happened. The only things I'm positive about are when I walked in and I saw her on the floor. My original statement was the only thing I was positive about . . .

M: Well, this is what I'm going to do. I'm going to take a statement and you tell me just what you just told me here a few minutes ago.

P: Now wait a second. Can this be used against me now? The statement?

M: Oh, yes.

P: Then why should I say something that I'm not sure of if it can be used against me?

M: Well, this is what I'm saying. I'll take the statement. You give it to me and I'll write it up.

P: Mm. In the statement, can we say that I'm not sure of . . .

M: Yeah, whatever you tell me I'll put onto here.

P: The whole statement that I make, I'm not sure of.

M: This will be included in here.

P: OK. But the entire statement that I make, I'm not sure of.

M: Now you're eighteen, right?

P: Mm-hm. Will I stay at the barracks again tonight?

M: I don't really know. All right. Today's Saturday . . .

P: Twenty-ninth.

M: No, this is Thursday evening when this happened . . .

P: Friday evening.

M: That's the Methodist Church, right?

P: Mm-hm.

M: Now, what time did you leave the meeting?

P: I think around nine-thirty or nine-thirty-five.

M: Returned home, right?

P: Mm-hm. I dropped off John Sochocki first.

M: OK, you arrived home. What time was that?

P: Around nine-fifty to nine-fifty-five. You know, Jim, after what I said, I honestly don't think I did this.

M: This is something you're going to have to make up your mind about.

P: I really don't think I did it. Because as I remember, when I turned around after seeing her both times, the clock hadn't moved.

M: What clock hadn't moved?

P: 'Cause the first thing I did was look at the clock when I came in. And when I turned back around after I saw her on the floor it was still the same time.

M: Well, what time did the clock say when you first looked at it?

P: It was either ten of or five of. Either one or the other.

M: Well, it can't be one or the other.

S: How you doing, Jim?

P: I'd say five of ten.

M: Well let me get this now. You arrived at your house about nine-fifty to nine-fifty-five. Take it from there. What happened?

P: Well, I shut off the car, and I jiggled the headlight. . . . No matter what that test says in there, something I just remembered is after I found my mom on the floor I looked at the clock again, and it hadn't moved.

M: You shut off the car. Then what?

P: Then I went inside and the first thing I do is yell, "Hey, mom, I'm home," and I looked at the clock.

M: Which door did you go in?

P: The front door.

M: And you yelled what?

P: "Hey, mom, I'm home," or something to that effect.

M: All right. Go on.

P: There was no answer, so I looked in and saw her by the bed.

M: To the left or to the right?

P: To the right. Can you stop for a second after you finish with this line?

M: Go ahead, say whatever you want to say.

P: Everything that I've been saying, it's almost like I'm making it up. I'm not sure about it.

S: Now look. Now listen. You've been playing headgames with us now for too long a period. Now, I told you once before when you and I were talking here that we have definitely established that you were in that house when your mother was killed. OK, now look. There are many things that we can do to make this thing a very difficult process for you. You realize that?

P: Yes.

S: All right. Now, I've tried very hard to be understanding and I've tried very hard to get across to you that we're not out to hurt you. We're out to treat you as a decent human being. But, I've been fooling around here for a lot of hours with you and I'm getting tired. I don't want you to treat me like some kind of a jerk.

P: I'm not.

S: Now, you sit there and you tell me that you're responsible for your mother's death and you say it twelve or fifteen times. I tried to treat you like a human being. I tried to be understanding, but it seems you've had such a rough upbringing that you reject every offer that we've made to be kind to you. Now you're trying to treat us like muck. I've been out of bed—I missed two days sleep. And I just can't fool around with you forever. Now you said here fifteen times in the last two hours that you were responsible for your mother's death, that you cut her throat with a razor, that you threw the razor either over the barn or over the gas station yard. You've indicated that you jumped on your mother's legs and that you jumped on her. These remarks, although they were solicited from you, were reported back very accurate and very astute comments on what actually happened there.

P: Right.

S: OK. Now, I don't want you to play any more headgames with us. And if you want to play this way we'll take you and we'll lock you up and treat you like an animal. Now, you're eighteen years old, I realize you've had a hell of a rough time in your life but sooner or later you're going to have to face this. You're going to face life and you're going to have to face what you've done. And I think it's about time that you sat up in that chair and you faced us like a man and you realize that trying to talk to two state policemen like they're two goddamn idiots, it's not gonna work. Now, you are here because you are responsible for the death of your mother. I am not sitting in judgment of you. I am not saying it was right or wrong. It is a death that we must investigate.

P: Mm-hm. I understand that.

S: Then let's stop the nonsense and let's get going here. Our design is not to hurt you. Our design is to help you. We know what your life has been like. We know what your mother's reputation is. We know a lot more than you give us credit for. I'm not even saying that you were wrong doing what you did. But, you've got to take hold of yourself and you've got to get yourself some help. OK?

P: Right.

S. Now, let's get the problem solved. I don't want to see you in prison. That's not what I get paid for. I don't get paid by the number of people I put in jail. Neither does he. And neither does Sergeant Kelly or Sergeant Schneider. Or anybody on our whole state police department. Now somebody is dead. You are responsible, we know. We can prove it with extrinsic evidence. Now we're telling you that we are offering you our hand, take it. Do I make sense to you?

P: You say you can prove it?

S: Yes, we can prove it.

P: Wait a minute.

S: Just a minute, Peter. I told you that I'm not going to play head-games.

P: I'm not.

S: When two people are in a room and there's a third person outside that witnesses those two people in a room, and one is dead and the police should establish that death occurred at a certain time and the third party puts the second party in the room, the second party is responsible for murder. That's common sense.

P: Right.

S: That's rules of evidence. Now, your mother called the doctor at nine-thirty. You called the hospital at ten minutes of ten. We can place your mother's death in that fifteen-minute period. That means you and her were there alone. Now, if you think you can beat that you're crazy. And, if you're going to act like a hardened criminal, John Dillinger, try to beat the police, you're nuts. So just sit there like a man and understand that you're not gonna go to the gas chamber or you're not gonna go to life imprisonment. You're going to be treated. You're going to be put into a hospital where you get care. Why? Because you have to.

P: Am I going to be put in a hospital?

S: Yes, you are. Now, let's stop the headgames and maneuvering here. I'm not going to give you the details of the murder. You know the details and so do I. I'm telling you if you cooperate with us, stop kidding around with us, fooling around with us, we will do right by you. And that's no kidding and that's no con job to get you to give a statement. That's just plain simple truth. Now shall we proceed?

P: Mm-hm. I looked to the right into the bedroom. OK. First I thought I saw my mother in bed and then I saw her on the floor.

M: Which bed was she in?

P: Top bunk.

M: What was she doing on the floor?

P: What do you mean what was she doing there? That was the double take. Right there.

S: Pete . . .

M: Look, Pete, let me explain something to you. What the lieutenant is telling—I don't know what he knows. He knows a hell of a lot more than I do because he's in charge of this investigation.

P: Right.

M: He told me that you were responsible for her death.

P: Right.

M: What the lieutenant is trying to tell you, you will be charged. This is a formality. You'll be charged with murder. But there's extenuating circumstances here. The only one that can give us the answer to these questions is you, yourself.

P: Mm-hm.

M: We have enough from what he tells me and from what he says here, apparently, to prove you guilty of murder in the state of Connecticut.

P: Mm-hm.

M: But if there's a problem here, something is wrong. You're going to have to go see a psychiatrist. You may have to spend time in a hospital. In fact, it's a good possibility that you will spend time in a hospital. It may be a week, it may be a month, it may be three months. But there's no sense, if you are responsible for her death, sitting here telling us you don't know what's going on.

S: Now there's no such thing as a double take. There's no double take. You're not a camera. You're a human being.

P: But, what I mean by double take is I looked once and I thought I saw her in bed and I looked again and saw her on the floor.

S: No, you looked once and you saw her in bed. You have good eyesight. You're not a camera. You don't double take. This is a maneuver.

P: What I mean is, in between the time that I saw her in bed and on the floor, it seemed like a split second. So it was a blackout in my memory there. That's what I've been trying to draw all these facts from, all these things about the razor and stuff. They're coming back. Now, the man in there who gave me the thing on the polygraph told me that after I had done what I done, that I was ashamed of it and what I was doing was I was rejecting it from my memory. And that's what I wanted to explain about that in the statement.

S: Do you remember cutting your mother's throat?

P: I remember going like that by my mother's throat. That's one of the things that came back.

S: Do you remember cutting your mother?

P: Just at her throat.

S: You remember seeing blood?

P: Yes.

S: On her throat?

P: No, 'cause when I saw her on the floor I had come back into normality again and I've already blanked out what happened. And I didn't realize what had happened at that point.

S: Do you remember jumping on your mother's stomach and legs?

P: Yes.

S: Do you remember cutting your mother's abdomen?

P: No.

S: Do you remember doing anything else to your mother?

P: No. There were things in there that I was not positive about.

M: Well, I'll take this as such and put that he don't recall . . .

S: Now, wait a minute now. Just a minute. You recall cutting your mother's throat?

P: Yes.

S: You recall seeing blood on your mother's throat?

P: No.

S: You just said you did!

P: I said I recall seeing blood on my mother. First I said I saw her in bed, next I said I saw her on the floor. When I saw her on the floor was when I saw the blood.

112

S: Where did you see the blood?

P: On—it was on her chest and her T-shirt was rolled up to about——

S: When did you say that you pushed the T-shirt up over her chest?

P: I didn't say that. I never said anything about the T-shirt. I said I saw it pushed up like that.

S: Did you push it up over her breasts?

P: I don't remember. I'm not playing games now, I'm being as honest as I possibly can with you.

S: Mm. Did you take her pants off?

P: That I don't know. I may have tried to wash her down.

S: Why did you try to wash her down?

P: Because of the embarrassment of what I'd done.

S: What did you try to wash off?

P: Blood, I guess.

S: What do you mean, blood, you guess? Did you try to wash off blood?

P: Well, what else would I want to wash off?

S: I don't know. I'm asking you, blood? What part of the body did you wash?

P: That I don't know.

S: How did you wash it?

P: That I don't know. I don't remember taking her pants off.

S: Well, how did you wash her if you didn't take her pants off?

P: I don't know. The pants were wet though.

S: Do you remember taking her panties off?

P: No, I don't.

S: The pants were wet or you wet the pants?

P: The pants were wet, the police officer showed me.

S: Now never mind the police officer. I'm asking you, from your own experience. Were the pants wet?

P: I don't even remember the pants from my own experience.

S: Well, you just said that you took the pants off to wash the blood off your mother, didn't you?

P: I said I must have washed the blood off my mother. I didn't say I remembered taking the pants off her to do it.

S: Where'd you get the water?

P: That I don't know either.

S: Were you in the bathroom at any time?
P: I don't know.
S: Did you take her panties off?
P: That I don't know. That's all blank to me.
S: Did you have blanks before in your life?
P: No.
S: Pete, why should I believe that you have blanks now?
P: I don't know.

Eddie Dickinson, Peter's friend, asked his mother on Saturday afternoon if he could go to the barracks to try to see Peter. She told him he'd better not. "Peter's closer to the Madows and the Belignis than to us," she told Eddie. "I don't think we should interfere."

Marie Dickinson was worried, though. Her family lived just down the road from the Gibbons' house, on Route 63, and all day Saturday they could see police searching the area, in and out of the house, digging up the septic tank, raking through the fallen leaves at the side of the road. Once her husband went out and spoke to one of the troopers.

"Where is Peter now, do you know?" Bill asked.

"No, I don't know," the trooper said.

Marie called the barracks. "We're not through with him yet," somebody told her. When she called several more times, the answer was the same. Marie thought maybe they just didn't want to give out information on the phone, and she told Bill she could understand that. Finally, Saturday night, she told Eddie he could go down.

Eddie drove down and saw the man at the front desk, Trooper Calkins.

"Can I see Peter?" Eddie asked.

"Sure, you can see Peter," Trooper Calkins said. He paused, then he smiled. "Only Peter isn't here."

"My God, what's going on?" Marie asked Bill, when Eddie reported back. "Where could he be?"

With so many people calling and asking, messages zigzagging and overlapping, some confusion was bound to occur. And some troopers—perhaps the trooper to whom Bill spoke, the man raking leaves—really didn't know where Peter was. But there also seemed to be more involved than confusion and not knowing. When Barbara's cousin had asked whether anybody in the area was looking out for Peter—"Doesn't anybody care?"—she'd been told nobody had been asking for him, nobody cared.

By Saturday night, Marie Dickinson was badly upset. "What do you suppose is going on?" she asked Bill again. "It's as though Peter has just walked off the edge of the earth."

S: You definitely remember coming into the house and seeing your mother on the top, and you definitely remember cutting your mother's throat with a straight razor, and you definitely remember seeing blood on her throat when she was lying on the floor.

P: Yes.

S: Do you remember noticing that her throat was cut when she was lying on the floor?

P: No.

S: Did you notice the cut in her abdomen when she was lying on the floor?

P: No, I didn't.

S: Did you notice the condition of her T-shirt when she was lying on the floor?

P: I noticed it was rolled up.

S: OK.

Now, get what he says in the statement. He came into the house, he looked and saw his mother in the cot. Then saw her on the floor. Then he cut—he remembers cutting his mother's throat with a straight razor. That he remembers seeing blood on his mother's throat while she was lying on the floor.

P: Yes.

S: And you were jumping on your mother's legs and stomach.

P: Well, wait a minute before you write anything. I remember the blood on my mother's throat but I remember that clearly from my original statement. The blood.

S: How many straight razors do you own?

P: One.

S: Now, you remember slashing once at your mother's throat with a straight razor, right?

P: Right.

S: Are we through playing headgames now, Pete?

P: No more headgames.

115

S: Look, if we can help you—and we can help you—we will help you.

P: OK. That I understand. That's why I'm doing this now. Jim, when this goes to court will it be considered temporary insanity?

M: I don't know, Pete.

P: After having this on my record is there any chance I can still get on the state police?

M: All depends on what happens.
That was with the straight razor you used for the airplanes?

P: Mm-hm.

M: Where was that razor?

P: It was on the living-room table.

M: You jumped on your mother's legs?

P: Mm-hm.

M: What else do you remember? Also remember jumping on—let's see—remember slashing at my mother's throat with a straight razor I used for model airplanes. This was on the living-room table. I also remember jumping on my mother's legs.

P: That's really just about it. Because I'm not sure about washing her off.

M: Did you say something about kicking her or something?

P: I don't think so.

M: All right. How about blood?

P: OK. Do you have that in there—the area where it seems like a lapse in time? Know what I mean?

M: No, not here.

P: Well, that would be next. Could you put little quotes in between the part from where I was slashing my mother's throat to where I jumped on her legs? You know, so you can tell that section is the stuff I—that I'm digging up.

M: All right.

P: Now, the next—from here on in it's ah—I saw blood on her ah, on her ah, chest and on her throat and face. And I think it was on her T-shirt too. And the T-shirt was rolled up.

M: Saw blood on her face—

P: And throat.

M: —and blood on her T-shirt?

116

P: Mm-hm. I think. I'm pretty sure.

M: And the shirt you say was rolled up?

P: Yeah, rolled up to the bottom of her breast about.

M: All right. Then what?

P: Then I went to the phone and from there on in it's the same as my original statement.

M: OK. Pete, read it over for me please.

P: Sign here?

M: Sign right beside—want to lean on this?

P: No, this is OK.

M: OK. I want you to do something else here.

P: Want me to initial.

M: Here. I want you to initial up here and over here.

P: I've got more initials written down now.

M: Well, this is for protection. This is so later nobody can say that I added anything or deleted anything out of it. Now, down here at the bottom.

P: Here?

M: Yes. All right. Now, I want you to sign this page here.

P: Are we leaving yet or can I speak to the lieutenant, possibly alone again? Before we leave?

M: Let me just check to make sure I don't have any mistakes here. You want to speak to Lieutenant Shay by himself?

P: Mm-hm.

M: OK.

P: Getting chilly now, isn't it?

M: Yeah, it's probably cool when you get outside and you don't have a jacket, do you?

P: No. I'll survive. Can I have another cigarette, Jim?

M: You need a match?

P: I've got some.

M: Throw this in the trash. Hey, Lieutenant!

P: Well, I just stated it there and I signed it.

S: Pardon me?

P: I've done it and I've signed it. And, now I want to speak to you about some kind of psychiatric help. When you and I spoke man to man you said you'd help me. . . . Is there any possible way

I could possibly live with your family if you had the room? *If* you had the room. I wouldn't want to impose, and I know my godmother would pay my way.

S: Well, it would be a rather unusual turn of events.

P: I've taken a liking to you, a kind of father image, and I trust you. And I know you're gonna do as much for me as you possibly can.

S: Peter, I will do as much for you as I can. I have some friends in the psychiatric field. One fellow in particular I have in mind I would like you to talk with. Um, a psychiatrist that I think might be just what the doctor ordered.

P: I would like to live with a family, like a complete family for a while anyway. When I was at Belignis, they treated me just like they did the rest of the kids. And that's what I enjoyed.

S: Pete, let me read this statement.

Lieutenant Shay left. Sergeant Kelly returned.

K: How's it going, Pete?

P: OK.

K: Gonna eat your sandwich?

P: I've been taking a bite here and a bite there.

K: Oh, Pete, I've just read your statement. Something's still wrong here, Peter.

P: Those are the things that I'm positive about. I don't want to say something that I'm not sure of.

K: What things aren't you positive? Remember, you and I were talking and we were talking about your mother's legs. Remember?

P: Yes.

K: What did you do to her legs?

P: I jumped on them.

K: And what else did you do? What's really burning inside of you that you don't want to tell us about, that you did to your mother?

P: I'm not sure. I know it sounds like I'm giving you the run . . .

K: No. What do you think you did?

P: Did I—I think I raped her.

K: OK. Why do you say that?

P: I mean that's what it seems like I did. That's what everything looks like I did.

K: You mean you raped her with your penis or what?

P: I don't know.

K: Well, what do you think?

P: What do you mean, what do I think?

K: Well, I called up Canaan and I know a few more facts now.

P: Such as?

K: Well, I want to hear them from you. OK? What else did you do to your mother?

P: The things that I don't know—they're blank areas.

K: What do you possibly think you did?

P: I don't know exactly what I did.

K: Was your mother drunk or what?

P: That I don't remember at all.

K: You told me before she's an alcoholic.

P: Yeah, I believe she was an alcoholic. She wouldn't admit it.

K: Most of them won't.

P: Well, I know that. People don't like to admit that they're addicted to something like that.

K: Right. That's the problem here with you, Pete. You don't want to admit to what you did. You're just thinking everybody will think you're really sick. You know?

P: Well, I realize what I've done. I'll admit to doing it. But, it's just I don't remember the facts of doing it. I don't remember every detail.

K: What's the worst thing you did to your mother?

P: I did cut her throat.

K: The next worst thing?

P: The jumping up and down on her.

K: The next worst thing?

P: I don't know. That's about the only two things I put in the statement, I think.

K: I know what you put in the statement. I just read it.

P: The other thing was seeing the blood. And possibly if I raped her, 'cause that would be even above cutting her throat. But, I don't know that I did that. I mean I don't remember doing it. But, I must have done it.

K: Why?

119

P: That is the worst thing. I mean, since I was there.

K: You did rape her?

P: Well, I don't know. I don't know whether I did or not.

K: I don't think you did.

P: You don't?

K: No.

P: Well, what did the thing tell you?

K: She wasn't raped.

P: She wasn't?

K: Did something else though.

P: What?

K: Well, I want you to tell me, Peter. By me telling you I'm just putting words in your mouth, which is foolish.

P: But, I told you everything I can remember.

K: Well, we talked about her legs and stuff, you were going to get sick. Why?

P: I don't know. Just the blood and everything, and thinking that I'd done it.

K: There's some reason why you said that to me before. But, I don't want to tell you. The reason I don't want to tell you, I don't want to put words in your mouth. All right? But, I'd rather have you tell me and then by you telling me this verifies what I already know and we also know you're trying to help yourself.

P: Well, I am trying to help myself, and I'm gonna give it every effort to help you.

K: All right.

P: The things that I said in the statement are the things I'm sure I did.

K: OK. What else did you do to hurt her?

P: I don't know.

K: Well, what do you think you might have done?

P: I thought I might have raped her.

K: Mm. What else?

P: I don't know.

K: Can you picture yourself raping her?

P: No. I couldn't picture myself doing it.

K: OK. I don't think you did. All right? Something else happened,

120

Pete, and I think you might be trying to block it out of your mind. I'd rather hear it from you because if I tell you all I'm doing is putting words in your mouth and I'm not helping you. You see? Now, you tell me. 'Cause you've already told us the biggest part of it.

P: I can't think of anything else.

K: Well, any other little details aren't going to mean that much. They're things that are going to help you.

P: I can't think of anything else though, right at this moment.

K: What would be the worst way you could hurt your mother?

P: By raping her.

K: Mm. Why?

P: Because it would be immoral, I think.

K: But, as I said, Pete, I don't think you did.

P: Yes.

K: But, Pete, other things happened to your mother in that house than what you've told us. I think you know but I think you're ashamed to admit to them. I think you were in such a frenzy you did things that an average normal person wouldn't do. All right?

P: Right. I already figured that. Do you think when this comes to court it will be considered temporary insanity?

K: Oh, Pete, don't worry about courts. All right? Don't worry about things like that.

P: That's all I can think of.

K: If they present what they have right now, before a judge, there's no doubt in my mind that the judge is going to think he's got a coldblooded killer, instead of somebody who went off the deep end for a few minutes. And, this is why I'm trying to probe your mind right now and get all this other stuff out, so when we present it to the judge we can show him that at a particular time this guy wasn't in a normal state of mind.

P: Well, I wasn't.

K: This is what I'm saying. But, we have to have all the facts. And we're probing awful deep on you, Pete.

P: I know.

K: You know, Pete, personally I think you want us to beat this out of you. You want us to punish you. You want us to beat you. We're not going to do it. We don't do things like that.

P: I know it.

K: And I think if we did this you would then tell us the whole story.

P: Can I put in that statement that I possibly could have done anything because I didn't have control of my senses?

K: Oh, there's no doubt in my mind there. But . . .

P: Well, that's what I mean because I don't remember details of what I did. That's what is messing me up. If I did I'd say 'em.

K: Mm. I wonder if you would. As I say, there are things there, but I don't want to put words in your mouth. Everything you've said to me so far you've told me. Now, you said something to me when we were together about kicking her. What do you recall about that?

P: I just may have used the phrase, not realizing what I was saying. I may have kicked her in the side or something, I don't know.

K: Well, this is what you asked me: Did she have any broken ribs?

P: Yes, because I may have kicked her in the side.

K: Well, she had three broken ribs.

P: She did?

K: Yes. That's another little point you thought of.

P: Has anything else come up on—on her that they—

K: Right. There's something else but this is the part that I want you to tell me about just like you told me about the rest of the stuff. There's one other detail that we need.

P: And that'll be the end of it?

K: Yep.

P: About washing her?

K: No. About something you did to her.

P: I don't know. Could I have punched her, or kicked her in the head possibly? I don't know.

K: Something other than that. Most likely it happened when she was flat on the floor.

P: Raping her.

K: No.

P: Anything like that? Sexual assault?

K: In a way.

P: I don't know. Could I have stuck it in her mouth or something? I don't know.

K: No, no. Did you?

P: No. Here I'm hung up. I don't know.

K: I don't think you did that. I don't think you raped her either. All right?

P: Yeah, neither do I.

K: What would be the most horrible thing you could think of right now that would really make you upset?

P: I think strangling her.

K: No. You didn't strangle her. You thought her throat was cut so I don't think you strangled her. Or did you strangle her before you cut her?

P: I don't remember anything like that.

K: About raping—why does that stick in your mind?

P: It looked like she had been raped and when Geoff looked, he says, "Pete, I think somebody raped her," by the looks of it.

K: Oh, I see. OK. Because of the way she was lying with no pants on.

P: Yes.

K: All right. But, there was no evidence of male semen. So, we know that rules that out.

P: Someone wouldn't try to cut out her sex organs, would they? or——

K: Possible.

P: 'Cause she had had a hysterectomy.

K: Possible.

P: I don't know. I'm just taking guesses now at what might have been found.

K: Well, could you have been that mad at her to want to do something like that?

P: No.

K: Seeing that's where you came from.

P: Yes, I bet I could.

K: Assuming this happened, what would you have done? How would you have done it?

P: I don't know. I wouldn't know how. If I was that mad I would have tried anything, right? . . . Mutilate or damage her.

123

K: Right, right . . . your mother was cut up a little bit, you know?

P: Was it a straight razor that was used?

K: I don't know that.

P: I'm pretty sure it was a straight razor. Now, it seems to me it's a straight razor. It may have been a knife. I don't know. I'm not too clear on that, so the straight razor seems clear to me.

By now, the knives the police had found in Barbara's house were being catalogued and tagged, destined for the police crime lab at Bethany. The razor was going there too. The straight razor Peter was talking about. The razor that hadn't been found behind the barn, or behind the gas station, but on the third shelf in the living room, the usual place.

K: OK. The one part when—what you said to me—cut out her sexual organs. What made you think of something like that?

P: That's all I could think of left.

K: Why?

P: I don't know why but that's what came out. So, if you want to use that as something I said, you know . . .

K: Oh no, no, no. I'm just wondering—I'm just curious why—why did you say something like that? This could be important.

P: I don't know. It was just something that all of a sudden came out of nowhere, in my head.

K: Did one of those other fellows mention that?

P: Nope. Just something that was there. It could be possibly something from what actually happened.

K: As I say, they don't know for sure yet, you know?

P: Yes.

K: But, I mean, that was an interesting statement.

A: Was that up to what you expected? There wasn't anything wrong with the statement?

K: Oh, no, no, no. It was just sort of interesting the way you said that, that's all.

P: Said what?

K: About raping her.

P: I didn't say it in the statement.

K: I know you didn't say it in the statement. I said about the way you said it to me.

P: Do you have a coat or something?

K: Why, are you cold?

P: Yes.

K: I can shut this window. You don't have a coat?

P: No.

K: Shut the window down for you, how's that?

P: I'm warm-blooded. I can't stand it if it's ninety degrees or more.

K: Why don't I get a hold of these fellows and we'll—what's this, your wallet?

P: Yes.

K: You haven't got much in it, huh?

P: No money.

K: Who's this, your girl friend?

P: Oh, it's just a girl I really liked once and since I had the picture I didn't want to get rid of it.

K: Whose Ford is that?

P: I cut that out of a magazine. It's a thirty-nine.

K: I was gonna say it was a thirty-nine. I had a thirty-seven.

P: Did you? I had a thirty-six.

K: I had a four-door station.

P: Did you? I had one of the first vee-eights. There should be a girl's phone number in there too.

K: Well, I don't want to see it. I don't want to pry. I'm going to see if I can get hold of these fellows. As I say, I'm looking at you here and you really look like you're exhausted.

P: What fellows?

K: Fellows who brought you here. So, relax for a minute.

P: You don't think I can lie there on the couch . . .

K: Well, Jesus, if you do we'll never get you up, Pete.

Mulhern came back.

M: Hey, Pete, I got one thing I want you to clear. You told me you remembered slashing at your mother's throat.

P: Mm-hm.

M: Did you cut her throat when you slashed at her?

125

P: Yes.

M: You did cut her. How far did you cut her?

P: I don't—let's see—it wasn't that large—that much. Something like that.

M: OK. Well, I have to take a short statement from you that you did cut her. OK?
Let me have your pen back again.

P: Thank God for high school students.

M: You're not kidding. When I changed out of my uniform to this suit again I must have grabbed my pen and I took it out with my pencil and threw it up by my wallet and forgot to take the damned thing.

P: Where's your uniform?

M: At home. I went home and—I've been up since you were up last night.

P: I've been up since seven to seven-thirty Friday morning, except for that sleep I got this morning.

M: How come you spell your name R-E-I-L-L-Y? Why do you do that? Why not R-I-E?

P: 'Cause that's the way I always spell it.

M: When you slashed at her, how did you do it?

P: Like that.

M: You went from left to right?

P: Yeah.

M: Just like that?

P: Only I used my right hand and I came across backwards.

M: So you used your right hand, you came from the right side.

P: Well, I came like that. From the left side to the right.

M: From your left shoulder to your right shoulder?

P: Uh-huh.

M: Did you draw blood?

P: That I don't remember. I don't remember anything about blood, until I get to where I'm back at a normal state again. This is when I called the ambulance.

M: You saw the razor cut, though?

P: I'm pretty sure. It's almost like in a dream. You know what I mean?

M: OK, sign.

P: Here?

M: Mm-hm.

P: And, here? Corner?

M: No, not there.

P: Are you proud of me?

M: Yeah. You want a jacket? Here, try this on, and I'll be right back. Peter, here's what I'm gonna do. I'm going to tape these two together, all right? Do me a favor on this one here. I put in August. I want you to cross it out where we're into September and have you initial it so we got the right one. I'm gonna take these two pages and combine them into one. By August twenty-eighth, that should be September.

P: Yes.

M: I want you to draw a line through all of it.

P: Why? So they'll know I corrected it when I read it?

M: Yes. It shows that . . . that I didn't change it later. That when it was shown to you, you changed it to September, the correct month. All right, now put your initials. As I say, what I'm gonna do is take these two and combine them into one, all one page.

P: OK. Can I have another one of your cigarettes?

M: I left them there so you can smoke them.

P: I shouldn't smoke other people's cigarettes, it bothers me.

M: Why?

P: I feel guilty about it. You must have given a pack and a half already.

Any particular degree of murder? Like murder one?

M: No, there's no premeditation. What's the show you watch that you got that out of? *Dragnet,* huh?

P: No, *Adam-12.* . . . This won't mess up my records for the rest of my life, will it? I got a lot off my chest in the last thirty-six hours. You know what I mean?

M: Well, like I told you coming up here, all you have to do is tell the truth. Then you feel better . . .

P: When I get it straightened out will you get me the help that I need?

M: . . . and everybody comes out a little better off.

127

P: Do you feel bad about knowing me, now that you know what I've done?

M: No, why should I feel bad? Hey, you know these things—everybody blows up once in awhile.

P: But this is pretty serious, isn't it?

M: So, that makes you a lesser man, you lost your temper at one particular time? Huh?

P: Well . . .

M: Do you think it's really that terrible?

P: Yes.

M: Well, it sounds terrible, murder and all that, and your mother's being involved, and yourself killing her, yes. But, I'm not a guy to sit here and judge you on something that you did. I may— five years from now—I may do the same thing. Nobody knows what goes on inside your mind, what goes on inside my mind.

P: I'm not being punished for what I did, I'm being helped. Right?

M: Yeah.

P: It's not a case where I need punishment. Correct? Whereas going to jail will punish me. Getting the help is something that I need.

M: Just don't interrupt me.

P: I'm sorry.

M: I keep losing my place.

OK, Pete, read that one over. Do that. This and this go together like this.

P: I gotta what? Read them all?

M: No, just the two that I combined into the one there.

P: I'd like to certify one—

M: Clarify.

P: —clarify one point which I changed. Where do I sign?

M: Right here. And right there.

Now, getting back to what we were saying before, you will be charged with murder. All right?

P: Will I need a lawyer?

M: I can't advise you one way or the other. You have a right to have a lawyer.

P: Yeah, but, I mean—the statement.

M: Doesn't matter. You can have an attorney at any time you want.

P: Yeah, but I mean, everything I said I mean, I mean it is the truth.

M: If you want to have an attorney, you have the right to have an attorney. If you can't afford one the court will appoint an attorney for you. But, this is a determination that you have to make.

P: Um, could I have any particular person advise me besides an attorney if I want to choose one?

M: Who do you have in mind?

P: Well, I meant Lieutenant Craig.

M: Lieutenant Shay? He cannot do it.

P: He can't advise me?

M: Pete, he's working on the investigation. The same way I couldn't advise——

P: What am I gonna do? Am I gonna end up answering all my questions myself?

M: Well, this is what I say. If you want to have an attorney, hire an attorney. I can't go out and hire you an attorney. At the same time I can't act as a legal adviser for you.

P: Do I have to have a licensed attorney?

M: He has to be licensed in the state of Connecticut.

P: What's going to happen to my things back in the house? I have a whole house full of stuff and the rent to pay and stuff like that.

M: Right now that house is in our possession. Nothing can be done to that house at this particular time.

P: Well, will they keep pets in there? There's a parrakeet in a cage and there's also a cat there.

M: Well, how about Geoffrey or Arthur? Won't they feed the cat or take care of the place?

P: Yeah, I guess. Also, if I'm going to be in a hospital, can I take my guitar with me?

M: Now, that I honestly don't know. I don't see why they would object, and again maybe they will.

P: What about the motor vehicle—the car? Will it be impounded by the state police, or——

M: No, see, we can't impound anything unless it has something to do with the crime.

P: I locked it up and left it in the yard there. Could the state police keep an eye on it and make sure no one tampers with it?

M: You don't have any family at all do you, Peter?

P: I just got my godmother who right now is in Canada. She doesn't know anything about this. Well, I don't care, if someone wants the pets they can have them. No, I don't want them to die. I want someone to take care of them. If someone will take them.

M: Well, I don't think there's any problem. If worse comes to worse we can leave the pets to the SPCA.

P: Yes. I don't think worse is gonna come to worse though.

M: I know you would be disappointed if you came home and they were dead.

P: Oh, I figured out where I got that murder one and murder two bit.

M: Where?

P: From *Hawaii Five-O*. The man there, every time, he goes, "Book him for murder one."
Do they have that anywhere? Or is that just something they made up for television?

M: Oh, I think New York State used to have different degrees of murder.

P: What I did is gonna be—not—I mean it's gonna be murder but it's not—it's not like premeditated because I didn't plan. You know what I mean?

M: I really don't know. We'll turn it over to the State's Attorney. You will be charged with murder. Now, it's up to him if he wants to drop it down to something lower.

P: What would he drop it down to?

M: There's murder and there's manslaughter. And, there's homicide with a motor vehicle. . . . They're a form of murder but they're not murder.

P: What is manslaughter?

M: I still get a little bit confused now. I worked under the old general statute which was different. It takes awhile, Pete . . .
Aren't you going to eat your sandwich?

P: I've just been nibbling at it, you know? Every time I eat something, you know, it fills me a little bit but then I lose my appetite just like that.

M: Well, let me go give this to the lieutenant and I'll be back.

Jim Mulhern left the room with the signed statement. In the other room, Corporal Schneider turned off the tape recorder. After twenty-five hours, they were finished with Peter Reilly at last. Corporal Schneider took the last reel of tape off the machine. Altogether there were five reels of tape, ninety minutes on each side. Corporal Schneider put the boxes of tapes on top of the file cabinet in Sergeant Kelly's office and left them there.

6

Peter was riding in a police car again, in the deep of the night. Again they were on Route 7, down the long straight stretch of road, past the swamp and the dark mountain. Only now he was going in the opposite direction. He was going to jail.

After Peter was photographed and fingerprinted at Hartford, Jim Mulhern had brought him back to the Canaan barracks and turned him over to Trooper Calkins. Mulhern went home to bed at last, and Calkins wasted no time. Within ten minutes, they were on their way. It was nearly 1 A.M. when they drove past the little house, roped off now, policemen standing guard. Peter looked at the house as they drove by.

"What happened to the car?" Peter asked.

"It's in a safe place," the policeman told him. "It was put in a safe place because it has a lot of expensive accessories on it."

Peter seemed satisfied, even pleased, at this attention from the state police.

"What's your name?" he said to the trooper, who identified himself as Trooper Calkins. He and Peter had once talked on the phone, when Calkins was gathering information on a girl who had run away from home. Peter remembered the conversation.

"Did I help you out?" he asked Calkins, and the trooper said yes, he had.

Trooper Calkins was a small, slim man, with a short dark crew cut and sad dark eyes. He had been on the force for eleven years. He thought Peter seemed relaxed and friendly, and they chatted during the half-hour ride. They were driving to Litchfield, the county seat, home of the courthouse and the Litchfield Correctional Center, more familiarly known as the county jail.

"Lieutenant Shay is a very nice man," Peter told Calkins. "Do you think this thing will interfere with my becoming a policeman, or with my driver's license?"

"I don't know," Calkins said. "What thing?"

"You know, killing my mother," Peter said.

"How did it happen?" Calkins asked.

"I looked to my right," Peter said, "and my mother was in bed. And the next thing I knew, she was on the floor of the bedroom, and I was standing over her and she was lying on the floor with blood on her. In between, there's a blank."

"Why did it happen?" Calkins asked.

"Oh, my mother was always on my back, for about the past four months," Peter said. "I know it was wrong, but in a way, I'm not sorry."

Trooper Calkins was very interested in the conversation, so when he had dropped Peter off at the jail, he sat in his cruiser and made some notes for a report. Later he destroyed the notes.

Litchfield is a historical gem, a classic New England town, a picture-postcard town. In fact, the jail itself is on a picture postcard, available at the pharmacy on the opposite corner, across the village green. And it is a handsome jail—red brick, substantial but not formidable. The entrance is around the side, at the end of a little sidewalk lined by a small white picket fence. A friendly sign hangs above the door. THROUGH THESE PORTALS PASS THE FINEST CORRECTIONAL OFFICERS IN THE WORLD.

The desk officer took Peter into a small room and told him to strip. Peter took off his clothes—brown shirt, Landlubber bell-bottoms, brown braided belt, the Converse sneakers. They asked him his weight and his height. "Five seven, one hundred twenty-one pounds," Peter said. It didn't seem to matter, though. They didn't have anything small enough, and the clothes they gave him were far too big. The khaki shirt hung loosely on his thin, narrow chest, and the trousers were baggy. He heard someone say $100,000 bond.

When they put him in cell 32, and the door closed loudly, he had one thought: that nothing else was ever going to happen, that he would be there for the rest of his life. Then he lay down on the bunk and immediately fell asleep.

Daylight came. Someone came to his cell door, unlocked it, and put down a tray of food. When the tray was set down, the cup overturned, and the milk spilled. The door closed again. Peter sat alone and ate, then he lay down again, rolled over, and was asleep almost at once.

Once again Peter Reilly was falling asleep just around the time that people who knew him were beginning to wake. It was a marvelous autumn day. People were picking up their Sunday papers. WOMAN, 51, DEAD WITH THROAT CUT. Joe O'Brien, the *Courant* reporter who hadn't been able to get any information from the police, filled out the story with human details, such as Mr. Kruse's complaint that the police wouldn't let him into the house to get the cat's dish. He quoted the police that "no suspects were in custody Saturday night."

Early Sunday morning, Marion called the barracks again. "Peter Reilly has been arrested for murder," a trooper told her. Marion stood stunned and silent, holding the phone. She and Mickey went down to the barracks then; they were told that a public defender would see Peter, and that he'd be arraigned the next day. Then Corporal Logan took Mickey into a room, and Lieutenant Shay asked Marion to sit down. He asked her if she knew whose dungarees had been lying on the floor at Barbara's feet. Marion said they had to be Barbara's, because she always wore hers rolled up at the cuff, and Peter never did. Lieutenant Shay asked Marion to tell him all she knew about Barbara and Peter and their life together. She told him that Peter's godmother sent money and that the Corvette always needed repairs. There wasn't a great deal Marion could tell him, but what she knew, she told. "You sit across that desk from him, you want to tell him everything," Marion said later.

Back home, Mickey called John Bianchi, the State's Attorney, who had once been Mickey's lawyer, and Barbara's lawyer, too. He was out, and Mickey asked that he call back.

Conrad King, a junior at Regional, had driven home from school with Peter and Geoff on Friday afternoon. "This just can't be true about

Peter," he told his mother. "He doesn't have any family. Isn't there something we can do?"

Beverly King already had her hands full, raising four children. Her husband was a telephone lineman in Falls Village, and besides keeping house for a family of six, Beverly worked part-time as a practical nurse.

But she told Conrad she'd see what she could do. Not long before, Beverly and a handful of people in town had joined, in an informal way, to help a boy from the Methodist Church who had been accused of arson. It had been a small but effective effort. They'd raised $1,000 bail and helped him get his job back. The little group was just about to disband when Barbara died.

Beverly had never met Peter Reilly, but Conrad told her that Peter had often stayed over at the Belignis'. Beverly called Jean Beligni and asked whether Peter needed help. "Oh no," Jean told Beverly. "Peter's Auntie B. will pay for everything. Thanks anyway."

In cell 32 at the Litchfield Correctional Center, Peter Reilly was awakened by a guard. "Come on," the guard said. "Pack up. You're going to boundover." There they locked him in again and gave him a pack of cigarettes, a ball-point pen, and a piece of stationery, in case he wanted to write a letter. Some of the other prisoners—like those in work-release programs—were not locked up, and some of them crowded around his cell door, asked who he was and what he was in for. There was a small kitchen, and one of the inmates who was talking to Peter, a thin, middle-aged man named Bob Erhardt, made Peter a cup of cocoa.

"What have they got you for?" Bob Erhardt asked.

"I feel too ashamed to tell anyone," Peter said.

"Hell, there's nothing to be ashamed of in here," Bob Erhardt said cheerfully. "We all did something to get here, so what can be so bad you can't talk about it?"

"Well, I'm so confused at this point, I don't know what to say, I'm very shy," Peter said. "My name is Peter Reilly, I live in Sharon. I've been at the Canaan state police barracks for hours and hours . . . I'm really a very shy person, I wouldn't fight back with anyone, I'm good in school, I have a good record, I'm very shy, I'm not very strong, I don't bother anybody."

He seemed rambling and incoherent, "talking in circles," Bob Erhardt said later. "Go ahead," he urged. "Get whatever it is off your chest."

"They are charging me with murdering my mother," Peter said.

Bob Erhardt was speechless for a moment.

"Come on now, you got to be kidding," he said finally. "Do you know what you're saying? Did you admit to it?"

"I think I did," Peter said. "I really don't know what I said, but I know I gave them a statement, and I'm not even sure what happened. All I can remember is that I came home and Mom was laying on the floor, and I called for an ambulance and they came, and then I was brought to the police barracks and questioned."

"Did you make a phone call to anyone?" Bob Erhardt asked. "Have you called a lawyer?"

"No," Peter said. "I haven't made any calls, I haven't seen anyone but the police."

"Well, I'll give you some good advice," Bob Erhardt said. "Get a lawyer, because you are going to need one."

One of the other men asked a guard for a phone book, and they looked under "Attorneys" in the *Yellow Pages*. One name they came to was Roraback, and that name rang a bell with Peter. Once he had heard Jean Beligni talking with admiration of a lawyer named Catherine Roraback, in Canaan, and he told the men now that he wanted her. They laughed. "You probably can't afford her," they said, but Peter was insistent. "That's who I want," he said.

Earlier Sunday morning, around 2 A.M., after Peter had been taken to jail, someone from Canaan barracks had called his cousin June to say that Peter had been arrested on a murder charge and that a public defender would be appointed to represent him. Sometime after eleven o'clock Sunday morning, a public defender, Henry Campbell, came to see Peter. He was a tall, stooped man with a gentle face. Peter still said he didn't need a lawyer.

Late in the afternoon, Peter called Jean Beligni.

"Are you all right, Peter?" she exclaimed. "Do you need anything? Where are you? Are you in jail?"

"I'm at, I think, the Litchfield Community Institution," he said vaguely. 'Wait a minute, I'll ask." He was away from the phone for a moment, then he came back. "Yes, it's the jail," he said. Geoff and Art Madow were down at the Belignis, with Paul, when Peter called, and they talked with him too. Peter asked Jean to please call Catherine Roraback.

All evening, Jean called Miss Roraback, hoping the phone would ring in her home as well as in her office. But late that evening, when she still hadn't got an answer, she called John Bianchi, the State's Attorney for Litchfield County.

"We're concerned for Peter," she told him, and asked for Catherine's home phone number. "We're all concerned for Peter," Mr. Bianchi told her. He said that Peter's arraignment the next morning would be "just a formality," but if she still wanted Catherine Roraback, he suggested that Jean try calling her secretary. "You can't afford Catherine," he warned Jean.

Miss Roraback's secretary told Jean that the lawyer was in New York, at a weekend meeting of the American Civil Liberties Union. Catherine Roraback had founded the New Haven chapter, and was on the national board. She would be back, the secretary said, on Monday morning, and Jean left an urgent message.

Sometime that evening, John Bianchi called the Madows. "I'm sorry to be so long in returning your call, Mick," he said. "I was away for the weekend." John Bianchi said he hadn't known that the Madows were waiting for Peter. "That's funny," Mickey said. "All the troopers knew."

On Monday morning, the first day of October, Peter was arraigned in the Eighteenth Circuit Court in Torrington. He looked pale and tired when he arrived, his hands clasped behind his back, handcuffed. Dorothy Madow, Mickey's sister-in-law, who had driven to the Litchfield jail with cigarettes and candy for him, drove over to Torrington. She was shocked, she thought he looked awful, and the jailhouse khakis didn't help. Even the article in the Winsted paper that afternoon mentioned Peter's baggy trousers. He was wearing unmatched boots, too.

When Catherine Roraback got to her office on Main Street, she heard that Peter Reilly had asked for her. She drove quickly to Torrington, arriving at court forty-five minutes late.

Catherine Roraback walked into the law library, where Peter was sitting at a table. Peter stood up when Miss Roraback walked in.

"Did you do it, Peter?" she asked.

"No," Peter said.

Barbara's cousin Vicky and her husband had driven over from New York and had seen Peter in the law library, too. Vicky and Barbara had been close, as children, more than forty years before, but as they grew up they drifted apart. In 1951, when Vicky's twin boys were born, Barbara and Hilda came to her house one evening, walked in, looked at the babies, and walked out again, without saying a word. A few years later, Barbara telephoned, asking whether Vicky had any baby things left; Barbara said a friend of hers was going to have a baby. But Vicky felt sure it was Barbara herself who was expecting.

Vicky had never met Peter, and when she came out of the library it was plain she had been crying. Her husband, a big man who looked like John Wayne, had been crying, too.

On Thursday morning, Peter stood up in Litchfield Superior Court, where his case had been transferred. He was still handcuffed when he came in, but he was much better dressed, in some of his own clothes that Jean Beligni had brought over to Litchfield. At the hearing, Miss Roraback asked that Peter's bond be reduced from $100,000 to $5,000, a more feasible sum for his friends to come up with. Mickey and Marion Madow told the court that Peter could have a home with them. Father Paul Halovatch asked that the bail be reduced, and so did the principal of the high school. So did Peter himself. "I know I would show up in court," he said. "I don't feel I have anything to run from." Finally, Judge Anthony Armentano cut the bond in half, from $100,000 to $50,000. He seemed affected by the turnout. "I am reducing the bond only because of strong community backing," he said. Nobody had $50,000, though, so Peter went back to jail in handcuffs.

Slowly, softly at first, then louder, voices began to speak out. At the town meeting in Falls Village, the Tuesday after Barbara died, Elizabeth Mansfield, who ran the general store, spoke for Peter. "Let's face it," Mrs. Mansfield said, "he's in a lot of trouble, and he has no one but the townspeople in this world." They talked about writing letters to Peter, and taking him clothes and cigarettes, but they didn't talk then about money. They all counted on Auntie B.

Then, pretty soon, Jean Beligni was back on the phone to Beverly King. "You asked if we needed help," Jean said, a little sheepishly. "Well: Help!" Jean hadn't been able to reach Auntie B. by phone, and an eight-page letter she wrote went unanswered. In the letter, Jean explained in detail what had happened to Peter the night Barbara died. "Peter had no blood on him and was not messed up in any way," Jean assured her, on Aldo's well-drilling letterhead.

"This is a quiet, gentle, sensitive, nonviolent boy," Jean wrote. "I am sure it was shock, confusion, and questioning under extreme duress that made him say whatever he said that caused them to arrest him. They apparently have no weapon, as they are still combing the woods and surrounding areas of the house."

Jean told Auntie B. about the weekend Peter was taken away, when so many people had tried to find him. "I guess for a while he felt everyone had deserted him. No one was allowed to see him, and he was never told that we were calling and were concerned about him."

Jean said that when Peter got out of jail, the plan was for him to stay with the Madows until the trial was over, in order to spare Gina Beligni, who had just turned seven, the daily ordeal of a murder trial. "After the trial," Jean wrote, "when Peter is found to be innocent, as I am sure he will be, he can decide whether he wants to stay with the Madows or with us.

"If you choose to help us in our attempts to raise Peter's bond, we would all be very grateful. If you choose not to help us, you alone know the reason."

Beverly King called her little fund-raising committee back together, and in a few days, they all met at the Methodist Church meeting room, upstairs from the room where Peter had gone to the Teen Center meeting. It was the beginning of an astonishing exercise in community concern that was to spread far beyond this tiny village. It would spread beyond Canaan and Falls Village, beyond Litchfield County, far beyond the state of Connecticut.

But in the beginning, in October 1973, it was a small struggle. It was sad too. Not only was a young boy accused of the murder of his mother, but so much was at stake, so much that was subtle and painful. This was not New York or Chicago, or even Hartford, where things could be done in anonymity. This was Falls Village, Connecticut, voting population 575, minus one. This was Canaan, where people knew where you parted your hair. This was where people led their lives.

In his bowling league one season, Mickey Madow had been voted

"Best Sport," and the police in town had finally begun to call him "Mick." Now they went back to saying "Mr. Madow."

Father Paul was a young priest, ordained just three years. He thought Peter was innocent and he was having his coin collection appraised, to help raise bail. But his pastor was an older, more conservative priest who disapproved of controversy. The parishioners at St. Joseph's included John Bianchi and Jim Mulhern.

Jean Beligni's aunt worked as recording secretary at the Canaan barracks. Trooper Don Moran used to come by and help Aldo move the rig. Gina Beligni shared crayons in her second-grade classroom with Michael Mulhern. Some people told Jean that for these reasons, especially because of the children, she shouldn't get involved.

She did, though. They all did. And by establishing the Peter Reilly Defense Committee, they involved themselves in certain relationships, some rewarding, some intricate and difficult, with the other members of the committee and the police. And with Peter. And Barbara.

Peter told Jean, one Saturday afternoon at the jail, that he had asked for permission to attend his mother's funeral. The funeral had been on his mind for a long time; he had mentioned it to Lieutenant Shay that night in Hartford. In all the hectic worry about Peter, Jean hadn't thought much about burying Barbara, but she called Newkirk's Funeral Home the following week. Her uncle worked there.

"When will Barbara Gibbons be buried?" Jean asked.

"She was buried today," her uncle said.

"Was it a service?" Jean demanded. "Who was there?"

It turned out that it wasn't a service, and nobody was there, although Mr. Pond from Newkirk's had read a few words when they put Barbara in the ground. It was just another piece of unfinished police business. There were no gravediggers; they used a backhoe instead, a kind of tractor with a scoop to dig out a place.

Right after Jean hung up, Peter called her from jail. "I got permission from the warden to come to my mother's funeral," he said. Jean said she'd call him back, then she called Mickey Madow. "I didn't have the heart to tell him his mother was already buried," Jean said. "He has permission to come to the service. What'll we do?"

"We'll have a service," Mickey said emphatically.

They called everybody they could think of, and a week later, at two o'clock on the afternoon of Friday, November 2, a graveside memorial service was held at Grassy Hill Cemetery on Sand Road in Falls Village for Barbara Valerie Consuelo Gibbons, 1921–1973. Thirty people attended, most of them teen-agers.

Barbara wasn't buried in the main part of the old cemetery, near the historic Civil War graves. They had laid her on the side of a hill, against the little building where they stored the winter bodies, people who died when the ground was frozen hard and couldn't be buried till spring thaw.

When the car pulled up in front of the black iron gates at the cemetery, Peter and an Officer Murphy walked up the hill together. Officer Murphy wasn't wearing a uniform. He was in a dark suit, with his dark topcoat draped widely over his right arm.

He and Peter stood very close together, at the head of the little grave. There were flowers on the grave, a spray of orange and yellow mums. Jean figured that because Barbara and Mr. Kruse had planted some mums in front of the little house, they must have been Barbara's favorite flower.

There was no eulogy. Father Paul read a prayer. Everyone bowed his head and said the Lord's Prayer.

Officer Murphy let Peter talk to people for a little while. Peter met Beverly King, who had started the committee, for the first time. His cousin June had come from New Jersey, and his school friends were there. Officer Murphy was very nice. Jean noticed that he never pulled or jerked Peter in any way, as they walked, and because of the way he held his topcoat, some people at the service never even realized that he and Peter were handcuffed together.

The sun was still bright and warm as Peter walked away from the grave. Five days later, he was indicted by a grand jury. He would have to stand trial, now, charged with the murder of the woman who was buried on the hillside, up by the storage house. No gravestone was ever put up. As Mickey Madow said, "When this happened, nobody said, 'Poor Barbara.' Everybody said, 'Poor Peter.' "

PART TWO

7

I was having a drink by the fire when Barbara died.

My husband and I had bought our first house a few months earlier. It was a stone-and-frame cottage at the top of a steep, winding driveway, ten minutes from the courthouse in Litchfield, half an hour from Canaan. The house was chilly, and the roof leaked, but the living room had a fireplace with a brick mantel and a brick wall, nicely smoked by the fires of past years. A trail stretched behind the house into woods of birch and pine, and there was a red playhouse for our daughter Anne, who was three years old. We all had time to spend together. Jim had quit his job as a financial analyst in New York that year. The job was steady but dull, and he wanted to work as a free-lance photographer. He'd decided to make the move, drastic as it was, before he turned forty, before it was too late.

I was free-lancing, too. At *Life* magazine, I had been a staff writer for three years, until it folded, and I had signed on as a contributing editor to a new magazine, *New Times*. Jim and I were beginning to suspect that two free-lancers in a family was too many, with a city apartment to keep up and the monthly mortgage on the house. Still, our first autumn in Connecticut was all we had ever wished. The colors

145

surged around us, and I was discovering narrow roads and church suppers and country journals to read by the fire, especially *Yankee* magazine and the weekly *Lakeville Journal.*

I first read about Barbara, and about the people who were trying to help Peter, in the *Journal.* I telephoned my editor, who said it sounded interesting as a story for *New Times.* On a Sunday afternoon in October 1973, I called Father Paul, who was mentioned in the *Journal* piece. "It's very bizarre," he told me, and took my phone number. Within an hour, Jean Beligni called. "This kid has just inherited about six mothers and fathers," she said. I asked to come to the next committee meeting and, because I'd never been in Canaan, we arranged to meet in the parking lot behind St. Joseph's. She said she'd be driving a white Mercury station wagon.

That is how it began for me, and for Jim, and even for Anne, as a story I read and a story I expected to write. For Anne, whose memories were just beginning to set, Peter Reilly became a natural fact of life. For nearly the next three years, Peter Reilly was a fact of all our lives. It made me happier sometimes, and sometimes more miserable, than any story I had ever done. It is hard to explain why, and perhaps it can't be entirely explained. Like birthdays, and earaches, and the weather, Peter Reilly was just something that happened.

"The most important thing you can do for Peter now is get him out of jail," Catherine Roraback had said to Mickey, and he passed the word along at the committee meeting. But it seemed impossible, although a few people had given $1,000 each toward the bond fund, and an ad asking for pledges had run in the *Lakeville Journal:* GET A BOY BACK INTO THE MAINSTREAM OF LIFE.

Most of the original members of the Peter Reilly Defense Committee were people who knew him well: the three families who had permission to visit him each Saturday in jail—the Madows, the Belignis, and the Dickinsons. Priscilla Belcher had lived in Falls Village when Peter was a toddler; she'd been his baby-sitter. Beverly King had rounded up two members of her original committee, Norma Hawver and Bea Keith. As the weeks and months wore on, new people came and old ones went, but at the first meeting Jim and I went to, these were the people we met. I had brought a stack of *New Times,* the magazine that was going

146

to run my article about Peter. Nobody had ever heard of it, but they were polite about it and seemed interested.

Two topics were discussed and dissected, hashed and rehashed, at the early meetings. How could they get Peter out of jail, and how in the world could this ever have happened?

None of us knew then all the details of the day and the night when Peter was out of sight—only that he had been taken from the house a few hours after Barbara died and had never come back; only that when different people tried to find him, they were told different things; only that Jim Mulhern had been with him, and that at some point, Peter had signed a statement saying he'd murdered his mother. He'd retracted the statement the next day, but, of course, it was too late.

"I asked him why he signed," Jean Beligni said. "And he told me, 'I got so tired, and it got so confusing.'"

She shook her head. "Jim Mulhern did his job," she said vehemently, "but his job could have been tempered with a little bit of humanity. He should have said to Peter, 'you're in serious trouble. You ought to get a lawyer.'"

"The police don't want people to have a lawyer," Bill Dickinson said. "They figure with a lawyer around, people won't talk. The police say their hands are tied."

"The thing about Peter," Jean said, "he's eighteen, and legally a man, but he's still oriented as a child. He's oriented to school, to doing what grown-ups tell him to do."

"Listen, I was talking to Catherine," Mickey Madow said. Most people called her Miss Roraback, but Mickey, in his breezy, salesman-like way, used first names. "She told me she's going to file a motion that the confession, or whatever it is, be thrown out, on the grounds that it wasn't voluntary, that it was coerced."

"Well, it's not believable," Jean said. "Peter dropped John Sochocki off at a quarter to ten. Then he had to drive seven or eight miles home. How he could have had time, in just a few minutes, to make all those calls, change his clothes, throw away the bloody clothes, get rid of the weapon, turn the 'vette around . . ."

"And they were grappling in the lake," Bill added. Marie Dickinson said nothing, but her hand shook a little as she reached for a cigarette. Barbara had told Marie someone was stealing gas from her car, and

147

there had been other strange goings-on in the neighborhood. Marie knew the police had found obscene scrawls on the wall at the empty house on Route 63, and she had asked Bill not to go out at night for a while.

"My girl friend thinks the police are covering up for somebody important," Jean said. "But I don't think so. They just walked in and saw the place and thought, 'Look at these odd people, look at the way they live, he must have a problem, he must have done it.' I guess they never thought we all were going to scream."

"It had to be somebody who knew the house," Geoff Madow said. "The back door was open. And it was never open. It had five or six locks. That door was *locked*."

"I got home at two-thirty or so," Mickey recalled. "And just then they called and said we should come down Saturday to give our statements. I said we were still up and would come down right away. But they said not to come. They said tomorrow would be soon enough."

Marion turned to Jim and me, at the end of a semicircle of metal folding chairs. "We're not asking people to decide whether he's innocent or guilty," she said. "It's the treatment we're protesting, the treatment he got, the treatment we all got."

"I'll say this," Bill Dickinson said. "If he did it, he had his reasons, and he should have taken off right away."

"He didn't do it," Jean said swiftly.

"I know, I know," Bill said. "I'm only saying, if."

"Peter doesn't have a mean bone in his body," Cilla Belcher said. "Barbara was a pain in the ass, and Peter didn't always get along with her, but they liked one another." Mrs. Belcher was the only member of the committee who'd ever seen Auntie B.

"Should some of us go down to New York to see Auntie B.?" Mickey wondered. "Confront her in person?"

"She's got a brother who's a lawyer," Jean said. "He probably told her not to get involved."

Although Jean talked the most, Mickey was the chairman of the Peter Reilly Defense Committee. Beverly King was secretary. She took notes, and she had begun to keep a scrapbook of clippings, pasting them neatly in a loose-leaf binder and dating them. The other officer was Bea Keith, treasurer. Bea had short, shaggy grayish hair, big round glasses, and a breathless manner. She had been a ballet dancer in New York before she came to Canaan to live with her mother, Florence Tompkins. Both of them were widowed now, and they lived in a big old house on the edge of town, once a country inn. Mrs. Tompkins couldn't get to the meetings, but she wrote letters at home, beginning with a "Dear Neighbor" letter to everybody in the Canaan phone book.

Bea had demonstrated in favor of Richard Nixon's impeachment and had been standing on the village green in Sharon for an hour a week, every week, for the past three years, in a silent vigil for peace. One or two people teased her gently about this, but most of the committee ignored it. Politics was not one of the common denominators of the Peter Reilly Defense Committee members, who had only Peter Reilly himself in common. Even that bond would wear thin as time went on, as tensions accumulated, as the worry became sustained. The members of the Peter Reilly Defense Committee would never be as united as they were in the first weeks after Barbara died.

At that point, their main worry was financial. Peter's bond had to be a cash bond, not a property bond and they couldn't afford several thousand dollars for a professional bail bondsman. They talked about tag sales and bake sales; they still needed $44,000. "That's a lotta brownies, honey," Jean said, to no one in particular.

Besides the bond fund, Bea was keeping a separate account called the defense fund. They had $378.95 in that fund so far.

"I put a canister at the Falls Village market," Marie reported. "And there was thirty dollars in it over the weekend."

"I tried to put one at Leader's," Jean said. "But they wouldn't take it. They said, 'It's too controversial. You know how it is.' I said, 'No, I don't know how it is. You tell me how it is.'"

Partly it was controversial because of the police. Lieutenant Shay, aware of the attitudes toward the police that were crystallizing in town, had told the *Lakeville Journal* that people must trust the police, and that the problem in this instance was that the local people didn't understand how a big-time murder investigation was carried out. "He made us sound like a bunch of hicks," Marion said indignantly. Marion was careful with her makeup; she wore wigs when her hair was messy, never a scarf over rollers, and she considered herself every bit as sophisticated as Lieutenant Shay.

And partly it was controversial because of Peter. When reporters roamed the streets of Canaan the weekend Barbara died, asking people outside Bob's Clothing Store, and the Rexall store, and Collins' diner what they thought, some people had said they didn't know, or didn't want to say. Many people had said, "They've got the wrong guy." But someone who knew a trooper at the barracks pointed out that all that Friday night, and all day Saturday, Peter had never shed a tear.

When the meeting broke up, Mickey Madow asked us to come by for coffee. In the dinette, with the dark blue and red poppy wallpaper that Jim Mulhern had helped hang two months before Barbara died, we sat around the table. Nanny sat in a chair by the window. She was petite and white-haired; she wore a lime green pants suit and shocking-pink lipstick. We talked about Peter and Barbara.

"Barbara was always watching the Watergate hearings," Geoff recalled. "We'd come home from school, she'd be yelling at the TV set, 'You damn fools!' She had an old marine band radio, more than thirty years old, but it worked fine until they broadcast something she didn't like, and she threw the radio right out the window."

"Peter came here a lot," Marion said. "Sometimes he'd wait in the car while we were eating, and when we'd ask him to come in and join us, he'd say, 'Are you sure you have enough?' He'd keep standing until somebody told him to sit down, and after he ate, he'd take his dishes off the table."

Nanny nodded. "He was a good boy," she said softly. "He still is. That's why we want him back."

In jail, Peter spent the time in a kind of uneasy limbo, as he waited for a hearing on the motion to suppress his confession.

Sometimes he watched TV. He listened to the radio Jean had brought him, using the earplugs. He went to a couple of AA meetings, just to pass the time. Jean had brought him books and homework, too, but he wasn't particularly interested. He preferred playing cards, and he once won a watch in a card game, then lost it in another game the next night. When Marion visited, Peter bragged to her about his new gambling skills. That dismayed her, and so did his new cynical attitude, which she felt he'd never had before. But Marion didn't know what to do about it. He wasn't always cynical, just for the first fifteen minutes

150

or so of the two-hour visiting period. "It takes him a while to become Peter again," Marion would report sadly when she got home.

No one under eighteen could visit Peter in jail, so a spirited letter-writing campaign began. Altogether he got 143 letters, mostly from teen-agers, although Joanne Mulhern wrote, and so did the Marine Corps, trying to recruit him. Auntie B. wrote an encouraging letter, telling him to keep his chin up.

Except for reading, and writing, and waiting, the only other thing Peter did one day was to walk across the Litchfield green to the courthouse. As he stood there, handcuffed, in the second-floor office of the State's Attorney, a state trooper took out a pair of scissors and cut off three thick strands of his hair. "Man, they must have found something," an inmate told him later, "or they wouldn't need a piece of your hair." Peter seemed worried then.

One rainy, cold morning in November, I went back to Canaan and drove around for a while with Jean Beligni. We drove past the little white house where Barbara died, with the mountain skimming up behind it. Now there was a sign out front saying WARNING! KEEP AWAY! Jean pointed out the Dickinsons' neat red house, and the Parmalees' house beyond it, a frame house in a cluttered yard. In Falls Village we stopped at Peter's high school, where Jean had graduated and where her boys now went. We took Sand Road, past the cemetery where Barbara was buried, back into town. Jean pointed out Bob's Clothing Store, where Barbara had shopped the day she died.

In Jean's kitchen, we talked a little more about Peter. She remembered a picture, the last picture of Barbara and Peter together, taken in the spring. Father Paul was allowed to see Peter in jail any day, not just on Saturday, and Jean said she'd ask him to get the picture for me from Peter. Then she showed me some of the letters he'd written to her and Aldo from jail, letters that started out "Dear Mom and Dad . . ." He was usually in good spirits on visiting days, Jean said, except for one Saturday when he'd seemed depressed, really down in the dumps. When she left, Jean noticed tears in his eyes. She thought about it all the way home, and by the time she got home, she was so upset that she sat down and wrote to Auntie B. "There are people on our committee who have worked so hard to help Peter who don't even know him," Jean wrote. "They are doing it because he is alone, and in the name of justice. Many are doing it out of Christian decency and in God's name, because they believe they are their brother's keeper. In God's name, why aren't you?"

Auntie B. called Jean when she got the letter. "I just can't get involved," she said. Jean thought Auntie B.'s voice was trembling. "I can't explain it to you," Auntie B. said. "You just don't understand the situation."

It wasn't easy to write about Peter Reilly without meeting him, so I wrote to Warden Brownell, asking if I could visit. The warden said no, but he said it nicely. He added that I was free to correspond with Peter, and he with me. So I wrote, telling him who I was, and he wrote back. Altogether he wrote me four letters from cell 4. The stationery was standard jail paper, and the spelling was standard Peter.

"I am very happy that your magazine is writing the story," Peter wrote. "My personal opinion about the situation is, The enterigation prosedures are, Mind boggeling and upsetting. . . ." He said he had been questioned by a guy who looked like Dick Tracy.

I'd asked Peter to tell me about himself, and he answered in terms of music and cars. He said that although he'd gotten his first guitar when he was only six or seven, he didn't learn to play until several years later, after he'd taken lessons from a farmer up the road. "Music is a part of my life," Peter wrote, "and these last ten weeks without a guitar has been absolutely dreadful. . . .

"I also am a nut about cars and I have a 1968 Corvette that I am going to have to sell. I think I'll buy a used V.W. Square back. . . ."

He said he wished they would catch the person responsible for killing his mom. He wished that eventually he would become very wealthy. He wished me a Merry Christmas and a Happy New Year.

8

On a cold December morning, Peter walked from the jail to the court-house, still in handcuffs, for his pretrial hearing. Catherine Roraback was asking that the confession he'd signed be suppressed as evidence, claiming that it was "involuntary and coerced" and had been obtained "in violation of his constitutional rights, including the right to have a lawyer present during questioning." The prosecution claimed that Peter had been informed of his constitutional rights—more than once, in fact —and that not only had he been aware of his rights but he'd also signed a waiver.

The elms were bare as Peter walked across the village green. They stood proud and rigid, as they were intended to. "We have the people and the houses and the elms and the hills," says an old history of Litch-field.

The first courthouse in Litchfield was a temporary affair, erected quickly in 1751 when the town was chosen as the county seat, over the ferocious protests of Goshen, Cornwall, and Canaan. The second court-house was more impressive, a picturesque oak building, painted white, with a red roof and a picket fence and windows of English crown glass, twelve squares to a window. It burned down in the fire of 1886, and its replacement burned two years later. Then the community, finally wiser, built a courthouse of granite, which is the one standing today.

Peter had been in this gray granite building before, on the day of his bail hearing, and on the day they cut off a lock of his hair, so it wasn't totally unfamiliar. I'd never been in the courthouse before, but I felt more or less at home, there was such an aura of friendliness about the place. Most of the courtroom staff had been around for years, notably Phil Plumb, a wiry, white-haired fellow who, as court messenger, filled the water carafes, did other odd jobs, and kept everyone entertained with yarns from his years as a sports reporter, when he wrote about the Gashouse Gang and Dizzy Dean.

In his courthouse career, Phil had worked both upstairs and down. On the first floor was the Court of Common Pleas, used for civil cases, along with clerks' offices, rest rooms, and the jury waiting room. Everything else went on upstairs, in Superior Court. Divorces were granted on Friday, which Phil, who liked to view life in terms of sports writing, called "Ladies Day."

The court on the second floor could be reached by two flights of stairs —one for the press and the public, for the witnesses and for people on trial, and the back stairs for the judge, the attorneys, and the courthouse staff. The courtroom itself was considerably less charming than country courtrooms are generally thought to be. The walls were painted an uneasy green, and fluorescent lights glared on the dingy carpet. The jury box, two rows of wooden chairs with arms and a thin brown cushion on each chair, lay to the right of the courtroom, just to the right of the witness stand. The sheriffs' chairs, also cushioned, ranged along the walls, and the thickest cushion of all was on the chair used by the official court reporter, Arthur Roberts.

Mr. Roberts was tall but a trifle hunched in the shoulders from so much sitting and bending over the stenotype machine. He wore gold-rimmed glasses and suspenders. His hobby was reading reference books. Mr. Roberts had been in the courtroom for twenty-six years, but there was a gleam of humor in his eye, in spite of it. He could take down three hundred words a minute on his machine and read them back instantly in precise diction, near-Shakespearean with a Massachusetts flavor. When Mr. Roberts pronounced the word *defendant,* as he often did, the last syllable rhymed with "can't." "Whatever would we do without Mr. Roberts?" a judge once mused aloud, during a hearing, and everybody smiled, including Mr. Roberts who, as a reflex, took down the phrase on his machine.

Two tall, high windows, the old schoolroom kind that are opened and closed from the top with a long hooked pole, were set into the west wall of the courtroom. Right next door was the Marden Coffee Shop, the only quick eating place on the block. It was run by a man who was also a guard at the jail; his wife worked at the counter, serving mostly pies and coffee and grinders. She had a brusque air and went about her business of serving in a hard-boiled way, like the waitresses Hollywood has always believed in.

Opposite the windows in the courtroom was a large institutional clock, with big black letters on a white circle and a sweeping second hand. At one side of the courtroom was the jury room, where jurors were sent when they weren't supposed to hear something said in court, or when they were deliberating. To reach the jury room, the jurors had to file out of the jury box and walk all the way across the center of the courtroom, very much as though they were crossing center stage. Behind the witness stand, just next to the judge's bench, there was a chalkboard and a tall gray steel locker, a regular gymnasium locker with a padlock. A deputy sheriff told me there was a skeleton in the locker, but I never looked.

Altogether, the nicest thing about the courtroom was the wood—dark and old, deep with the patina of the years. A broad wooden railing, hip-high—literally, the bar—separated the people in the spectators' gallery from the central well of the court. The judge's bench was handsome—as imposing, perhaps, as the bench in the grandly designed oak courthouse of old Litchfield, which one town historian described as "a raised dais with a broad pulpitlike desk [lifting] the judges to an almost ecclesiastical height."

Catherine Roraback smiled when Peter was brought into the courtroom, and she walked back to the rear of the room to meet him. She put her hand on his shoulder, and he smiled then, too. His face looked thin and somewhat hollowed, his nose sharp in the thin face. His hair was still long. Marion had brought over some of his clothes that the police had returned to her, and he was wearing plain brown slacks and a raspberry shirt, a ribbed knit that clung tightly to his chest. He was very slender. I remember Marion saying, "He's gaining weight at the jail, with all the potatoes and bread," and I wondered what on earth he'd looked like before.

155

Catherine Roraback was one of the best-known lawyers in Connecticut, and her family was one of the oldest, its roots running deep and tangled. Her grandfather and two of her uncles had been lawyers. They were all dead, but she still carried their names on her letterhead, the dates spreading back as far as 1872. One uncle, J. Clinton Roraback, had been a defense lawyer too, a big, portly man who carried a cane and lived most of his life in court, which is where he died, too, in the arms of the court reporter, eighteen years before the Reilly trial. "Good morning, Mr. Roberts," the attorney boomed, then crashed to the floor. Mr. Roberts knelt quickly, cradled Mr. Roraback's head in his lap, and called for a sheriff. Later, when the body had been taken away, the judge asked Mr. Roberts whether he should adjourn court. "No, I think Clint would prefer that court go on as usual," Mr. Roberts said. And it did.

Catherine's father had not chosen the law. He had been a minister at a church in Brooklyn, where Catherine grew up, only a few blocks from the Kasper family. One of the Kasper girls, Charlotte, who knew Catherine, married John Bianchi, the state's attorney, who was the Rorabacks' neighbor in Canaan. It was a small, complicated world.

Catherine had gone to Mount Holyoke, then Yale Law. She still kept an office in New Haven, though her main office was a little white-frame building on Main Street in Canaan, which she kept just as her uncle had kept it, with rolltop desks and wooden coat racks, left from olden days. Her mother had died, and her father was retired, a patient at Geer Memorial, where the VFW ambulance was kept.

Although her life was so deeply rooted in Canaan, Catherine Roraback was, in a way, more at home in New Haven. She fit in better there. She had been one of the defense lawyers at the Black Panther trial, and her work for liberal causes was well known, especially the legal work she'd done for Planned Parenthood, helping to get the state's ancient ban on contraceptives reversed. She'd gone into that project, which some doctors and lawyers were running as a test case in the courts, at the invitation of a doctor she knew from Yale. When he called and asked her to join the contraception crusade, she pretended not to understand. "Do you want me as a lawyer, or as a single woman?" she asked.

But for all her humor and candor, Catherine Roraback was not popular at Litchfield Superior Court. Partly because she was blunt and outspoken and liberal, involved in controversial causes, partly because of some of her family history, and partly because she was a woman, and a smart one at that, Catherine Roraback seemed to rub some people the wrong way. She was strong-looking, with a chunky figure and short, choppily cut hair that often fell into her eyes. She wore sensible shoes and had a habit of whipping off her glasses, nibbling thoughtfully at them, gazing at the ceiling with great interest, then turning sharply back toward a witness and hurling a question. Her nickname wasn't Cathy, but Kate.

Catherine and Peter walked to the center of the courtroom, to the long rectangular table where her assistant, Peter Herbst, was peering at papers. This was Peter Herbst's first job as a lawyer. He had a long, handlebar moustache and an air of dignified innocence, rather like a law clerk in Dickens.

Catherine and the two Peters and the lawyers at the opposite table and the handful of spectators in the courtroom all stood as Judge Anthony Armentano swept in. He was presiding over this pretrial hearing, which was an important step for Peter Reilly. Though the language was often intensely legal and hard to understand, the issue was vividly clear: If Peter Reilly's confession were squashed, the state would have a far flimsier case against him, and he would be likely to go free. If the confession he'd signed, and later recanted, was allowed to stand, obviously he was in far greater jeopardy. Everyone in the courtroom understood this, including Peter himself. He looked pale and tense as Catherine Roraback rose to ask that Peter's $50,000 bail be reduced. "His friends in the community have engaged in an extensive campaign to raise money for him," she said. "Mr. and Mrs. Madow have been anxious to have Peter come to live with them, and I know that Peter is anxious to do so."

Judge Armentano peered over the bench at Peter Reilly, standing beside his lawyer, gazing at the judge with a serious, tense expression. The judge looked cross, almost waspish, as though he had a touch of heartburn. "The bond remains at fifty thousand dollars," the judge said in a husky voice. "The crime is a serious crime. A man may be tempted to flight." Peter sat down then, his expression unchanged, and it didn't change many times during the next two days. The hearing lasted that long because, after a good deal of argument, Miss Roraback was allowed to play the tapes of Peter Reilly's polygraph test in Hartford.

"Pete, how are you?"

"OK. And you?"

"Good. Tim Kelly is my name. Sergeant of the state police."

"Pleased to meet you."

"Know why you're here, Pete?"

"Well, I guess, to determine whether the things in my statement are true."

"Right."

I was taking notes in shorthand, my own brand of shorthand, evolved over the years from classic Gregg into a personal system that went beyond classicism into more creative realms of abbreviations and spontaneous scrawls. But when I typed up my notes that night, I understood them very well.

"Do you know for sure who hurt your mother?"

"No."

"Did you hurt your mother?"

"No."

Here was Barbara, here in our winter courtroom, lying among us, naked and bloody on the floor, her T-shirt pushed up to *here*. I could see Peter making the gesture. Pushed up to here. Blood all over the place, on the chin and the throat and the carpet. Here was Peter, rubber-cuffed and connected, sitting in the seat of honor. Talking about Barbara.

"Does that read my brain for me?"

"Definitely. Definitely. And if you've told me the truth, this is what your brain is going to tell me."

"I just want to understand how it works."

"It works on your heart. That's your conscience. All we're trying to do is arrive at the truth. And the truth will be on that tape."

Sergeant Kelly had come to court to testify and to play the tapes. He looked big and strong, a striking figure, every inch a brown belt in judo. He had a round, full face with a round, full smile.

"Did any of these questions bother you?"

"Well, whether I harmed my mother or not."

"Why?"

"Well, that question . . . they told me up at the barracks yesterday that—how some people don't realize—all of a sudden, fly off the handle for a split second . . ."

"Right."

". . . and it leaves a blank spot in their memory."

"Right. This will help bring it out."

"Well, I thought about that last night, and I thought and I thought and I thought, and I said no, I couldn't have done it, I couldn't have done it, you know. And now, when you ask me the question . . . that's what I think of."

"Do you have a clear recollection of what happened last night?"

"Yes."

"Is there any doubt in your mind, Pete?"

"I didn't understand that last question."

"I was just trying to probe your subconscious."

"But I wasn't sure whether you meant what happened to her, or whether I knew who did it to her and everything."

"Well, I think we got a little problem here, Pete."

I smiled at Peter when he was taken out of the courtroom—one guard at his side, one behind him—and he smiled back at me. We still hadn't met, but he guessed who I was, there were so few people in court. I met Barbara's cousin June for the first time.

In the front row, the press row, there were just four of us. Two of the newspaper reporters looked incredibly young, just out of college: Stan Moulton of the *Berkshire Eagle,* and Greg Erbstoesser, who wrote for the *Lakeville Journal.*

The only veteran in the press row was Joe O'Brien, who had written the first *Courant* story. WOMAN, 51, DEAD WITH THROAT CUT. He had covered murder cases before and he looked hardened, at least in comparison with Stan and Greg and, I hope, with me. But Joe O'Brien was less cynical than he appeared. He was a family man, with five children, including two teen-aged sons. At the end of the second day

159

of Peter Reilly's pretrial hearing, after he'd heard the tapes, Joe O'Brien went home and told his boys that if they were ever arrested, they should say nothing.

"About hurting my mother. We went over and over and over it, you know what I mean? When he told me I could have flown off the handle, I gave it a lot of consideration. But I don't think I did."
"But you're not sure, are you?"
"That's right. Well, I could have."
"I think you possibly did."

Man and boy, talking man to man. Even smoking in the polygraph room.

"Is there any doubt in your mind, right now, that you hurt your mother last night?"
"The test is giving me doubt right now. Disregarding the test, I still don't think I hurt my mother."
"But you have a doubt, don't you?"
"Yes. I've been drilled and drilled and drilled. . . . I'm trying to think of what he did say. I know he told me something. I'm losing all memory now because I'm getting tired. But he did tell me that I could have forgotten. That really shook me."

Lieutenant Shay was in court. He was big too, but not as burly as Sergeant Kelly. He was in plainclothes, a chocolate-colored suit with a vest. Looking at his craggy, handsome face and square jaw, with his thick black hair and intense eyes, I could see what Peter meant about Dick Tracy.

Although there were just four people in the press row, John Bianchi thought that was four too many, and he asked Judge Armentano to bar us from the hearing. Mr. Bianchi declared that press coverage might create "an inflammatory situation" and he complained especially about the *Lakeville Journal,* which he pointed out had "headlines every week."

That was true. Even before the Reilly case, Mr. Bianchi had not been on the best of terms with the *Journal,* which had opposed him on various community issues. And then came the big headlines. SECRECY SHROUDS MURDER CASE IN FALLS VILLAGE was one of the first, then

160

FRIENDS SAY POLICE KEPT THEM FROM PETER REILLY. In that piece, Greg Erbstoesser had recreated the attempts by Peter's friends to find out what was going on, in the long hours after Barbara died. The article didn't mention Mr. Bianchi by name, but since he was the prosecutor in the case, whatever went on seemed to have had something, at least vaguely, to do with him.

Miss Roraback objected to Mr. Bianchi's motion. She wanted the press to stay. Judge Armentano peered out at us thoughtfully, and for a moment I expected he actually would throw us out. But he turned to Mr. Bianchi. "Can't we give credit to the rights of a free press?" he asked, in that slightly waspish way.

Then, however, he peered out into the courtroom again, studying us. I couldn't blame him. We were a motley quartet—two shaggy haired boys, who must have looked like children to the judge; Joe O'Brien, a character straight from *The Front Page,* and me, somewhere between Nancy Drew and Dorothy Kilgallen, a woman no one knew who wrote for a magazine no one had ever read. The judge asked us to come see him in his chambers, and we trooped across the thin green carpet, single file.

I sat at the end of the couch in the little study. Now that I was in the judge's chamber, I was ready for an argument on the First Amendment, but the judge didn't even sit down. He leaned against his desk in a casual way, and said a few words about the responsibilities of the press. Then he nodded. "Use your own judgment," he said.

Even though he felt as he did about the press, Mr. Bianchi seemed generally friendly with everyone. He was a remarkably affable man. Some people swore up and down that they'd never seen John Bianchi without a smile on his face. He was dapper and ruddy, with a haircut that always seemed fresh. His shoes gleamed, and he had a well-fed, prosperous look.

He was a hometown boy from Main Street in Canaan, where he lived in a creamy yellow Victorian house garnished with curly white woodwork and a wraparound porch, across the street from the Methodist Church. John's father owned a clothing store in Canaan, but the boy didn't want to go into that business. His mother had her heart set on John becoming a priest; instead, he married the girl from Brooklyn who knew Catherine Roraback. Then he began to study law, mostly because he wasn't sure what he wanted to do when he came back from

World War II. He went to Fordham, a Catholic school in New York City, although he'd first applied to Yale, where all the Rorabacks had gone.

It was more complicated than that, of course. It was more than the aristocrat's daughter against the haberdasher's son, more than the landed gentry against the immigrant family. And the prestige was not all on Catherine's side: A State's Attorney often went on to become a judge. "John isn't a simple person," Catherine Roraback once said to me. "But the least of my problems is whether John is a simple person." Still, one of the most fascinating aspects of the Reilly case was always the confrontation of Catherine Roraback and John Bianchi. They even shared a birthday: September 17. It was a classic confrontation involving antagonisms, ambitions and pride.

John Bianchi had been the prosecutor for Litchfield County about a year when Barbara was killed. Three judges had recommended him for the job, including Superior Court Judge John Speziale, Jean Beligni's cousin.

"As a prosecutor, I present the facts," Mr. Bianchi said. "I present the facts as I know them. As I got them. As I interpret them."

When the tapes of Peter Reilly's polygraph test were played in court, two and a half months after Barbara died, Mr. Bianchi hadn't sat down and listened to them all the way through. Just parts of them.

"I'm trying to figure this out. . . . a Corvette is a car you go like hell with. . . . You come flying in with that damned thing, and you went over her with the car, and you panicked."

"I didn't, though."

"Then why does the lie chart say you did?"

"I don't know."

"You don't know for sure if you did this thing, do you?"

"No, I don't."

"Why?"

"Well, your chart says I did."

"Would it definitely be me? Could it have been someone else?"

"No way."

"Now I'm afraid, because I was so sure I didn't do it, you know what I mean? I want to go back to school. I don't have any place to go."

"I think you want to tell me, but you're ashamed to tell me."

"But do I realize I'm ashamed?"

"Gotta keep digging. Gotta dig. Gotta keep pushing. I believe I did it."

"I *know* you did it."

Along with the words, there were sounds—a cough, a yawn, a tab top can opening. The sounds of life in a room so isolated, so removed, so thickly quiet. And beyond the sounds, there were the silences.

"You're right. Something's coming."

A long silence.

"Come on, Pete. Tell me."

A long silence.

"I told you the truth. Now I want to hear the truth from you."

"Somewhere in my head a straight razor sticks in."

"So where did you cut her with this razor?"

A helpless silence.

"The throat is the only thing I can think of."

After three and a half hours:

"Do you think we could quit now? . . . I think I'm saying things that I don't mean to say."

"Oh no. You're telling me the truth now."

And the end:

"Do you have any records of this? Have you been tape recording me?"

"No. I got my tape right here. That's all I need. That's you. That's your conscience."

Mr. Roberts sighed and smiled and flexed his fingers, flaring them straight out in front of him, like a fan, then squeezing them into fists, and flaring them out again. Transcribing the tapes had been a demanding job, and Mr. Roberts was glad it was over. When I'd chatted with him, before court started, he had explained his method. "I go into a trance," Mr. Roberts said. "I just take down the words. I hear them, but I don't listen or I'd be a nervous wreck." When I typed my own notes that night, typing so compulsively that I was still there, alone in the freezing room when the darkness in the pines faded to pearl gray, I knew what Mr. Roberts meant. You couldn't stop to listen. You had to wait till afterward, to try to understand.

Lieutenant Shay shook hands with Mickey and wished him a Merry Christmas. Catherine Roraback shook hands with Sergeant Kelly. Nobody shook hands with Peter, who was handcuffed and then hurried back across the green. I shook hands with June, and with her son, and said I'd see them in Hartford, where the hearings would resume after the holidays. Judge Armentano said he couldn't possibly make it before then. "I've got nineteen sentences to hand down tomorrow," he complained.

Christmas was a good day, even in jail. There was sirloin steak for dinner, and Warden Brownell let Peter's friends visit, even those who were under eighteen. Paul Beligni drove out and put a wreath on Barbara's grave before he came to see Peter with the rest of the Belignis. In the jail cafeteria, tables and chairs were moved around, and everybody sat in a big, laughing group.

Peter was allowed to play his guitar, another concession to the holiday, and the other band members brought their instruments and played with him. Some of the parents had been dreading the moment of reunion, but the meeting went easily. When Peter was brought down from his cell into the community room, he grinned at them. "What took you so long?" he demanded. "I got here three months ago."

The courthouse in Hartford reminded me of a Vatican palace gone to seed—an echoing, cavernous palace of justice, with vending machines and cuspidors standing incongruous in its pale marble halls. The pretrial hearing on Miss Roraback's motion to suppress the confession was continued in Hartford instead of Litchfield because of Judge Armentano. He had begun the hearing, so he would see it through, and it was now his turn to sit in Hartford Superior Court. Back in the press row, also seeing it through, were Joe O'Brien, Greg Erbstoesser, and myself, along with a new reporter, Charles Kochakian of the *Hartford Times*. Charles had bright dark eyes, a beard, and a wry manner.

The hearing resumed four months after Barbara died, on one of the coldest days of January. Again, only a few people had come to court— Mickey and Marion Madow, Peter's cousin June, with her husband and her son, and a handful of policemen, including Lieutenant Shay, Sergeant Kelly, and Trooper Mulhern.

Miss Roraback immediately asked that the tapes of the evening questioning be played, the recording of Peter's interrogation by Shay and Mulhern after the polygraph test. Judge Armentano seemed disinclined to play them, but Catherine Roraback insisted. She had heard the tapes herself and knew what they revealed. "The total context is relevant," she said. The judge said he'd reserve decision, and Jim Mulhern took the stand. With his blue eyes and brown wavy hair, he looked Irish, and he talked Irish, referring to Peter as "the lad," telling how he'd brought Peter his dinner, around 7:00 or 7:15 as Peter sat in the interview room in Hartford. The food had come from the vending machine downstairs: ham and cheese on a roll; a package of chocolate cupcakes, two in a package; a can of Coke.

John Bianchi looked directly at Mulhern, then at the judge, and spoke very loudly. "Upon entering the room, Trooper Mulhern, was anything said by you or by Peter Reilly?"

"I said, 'Hello, Pete,' and he said hello back," Mulhern said. "He said, 'Are you ashamed to know me now?' I said, 'Why should I be ashamed to know you?' He said, 'Well, because I did it. I killed her.'"

"Did you respond to that?" John Bianchi asked.

"Not right away, sir," Mulhern said. "He had kind of taken me by surprise. Then I asked him why."

"Did you get a reply?" Mr. Bianchi asked.

"Only that he was confused, and he didn't know. He said, 'We're going into it now, and it seems to be coming back to me.'"

"Did you at some time that day take a written statement from Peter Reilly?" the prosecutor asked.

"Yes," Mulhern said.

"Was this conversation before or after the written statement?"

"This was before the written statement," Mulhern said.

Catherine Roraback stared at Jim Mulhern, and he stared back. Of all the policemen she confronted in court, Jim Mulhern seemed the most hostile. His round, handsome face was sullen, like an altar boy trying to hold his ground against a crochety pastor.

"Does the statement, 'Are you ashamed of me now?' appear on the tapes?" she asked. She knew it did not.

"No," Mulhern said.

"But the statement about killing his mother *does* appear on the tapes?"

"I believe so, yes," Mulhern said.

"You did not question him at that time?" Miss Roraback asked.

Mulhern shook his head. "Only to ask him why," he said.

"But when did the recording begin?" Miss Roraback asked.

"I think it started after the door had been shut," Mulhern said.

Miss Roraback stared at him, then walked back to the table and picked up a yellow legal pad. She flipped pages, reading. Peter Reilly looked at Jim Mulhern with detached interest, but Mulhern looked straight ahead. His square Irish jaw stuck out a bit, tightly.

Crossing the soiled blue carpet, back to the witness stand, she twirled her glasses and they dropped to the floor. She picked them up, a dirty Band-Aid showing on her left index finger, and as Peter Reilly's glance followed her, Jim Mulhern looked quickly at Peter for a moment. Then he looked away again.

"Do you recall Peter saying to you, 'I don't know what to do, Jim. I'm still not sure of what happened. The only thing I'm sure of, she was on the floor.' "

"I don't recall," Mulhern said.

"Do you remember him saying to you, 'I'm being pushed into things. They won't allow me to say what I think'?"

"He may have said that. I don't recall," Mulhern said.

"Do you remember him saying, 'I'm not sure'?" Catherine Roraback asked.

"Yes," Mulhern said.

"Did that get put in the statement?" she asked.

"Yes," Mulhern said.

Catherine Roraback looked scornful and handed him a handful of white ruled paper. This was the statement Peter Reilly had given Jim Mulhern—the confession.

166

"Can you tell me where it appears in there?" she asked.

Mulhern took the statement and read it through. The courtroom was very quiet. At last Mulhern looked up.

"It isn't in the statement," he said.

Lieutenant Shay, in the front row of the spectators' section, gazed at the ceiling with interest, and I gazed with interest at Lieutenant Shay. Jim Mulhern and Catherine Roraback continued to stare at one another, as she asked about the different pages of the four-page statement.

"The statement was dictated by Peter to me," Mulhern said flatly. "He had been speaking with the lieutenant, and corrections had been made." He said that he had begun taking Peter's statement at 8:30 P.M. and had gone back in to take a further statement, "to clarify points that had been made," around ten o'clock.

"Does that further statement refer to how Peter Reilly was supposed to have cut his mother's throat?" Miss Roraback asked.

"Yes, ma'am," Mulhern said.

"When you were questioning Peter Reilly about that, do you remember him talking about how tired he was?"

"I believe he mentioned he was tired," Mulhern said.

"Do you remember him saying to you, 'It's almost like a dream'?"

"He may have," Mulhern said.

"Do you remember, after he had signed that statement, he then said to you, 'Do you feel bad about knowing me now, knowing what I've done?' "

"I believe he did say that," Mulhern replied.

"The same thing you say he said when you first came in?"

"No," Mulhern replied. "When I first came in, he asked me if I was ashamed to know him."

"After he completed that statement, did you leave the room?"

"No, I believe I stayed," Mulhern said.

"When did you finally leave Peter Reilly's presence?" Catherine Roraback asked.

"At that point, I think I stayed there and placed him under arrest," Jim Mulhern said.

John Bianchi took the statement and read it with what seemed to be a good deal of interest. Then he looked at Trooper Mulhern.

167

"It says, 'When I slashed at my mother's throat with a straight razor, I cut her throat,' " Bianchi said. "Is there anything in that statement that would indicate what, if anything, Peter Reilly did with the razor?"

"Yes, sir," Mulhern said.

Bianchi looked startled. "I mean, *after* cutting her throat," he said. "Is there a statement relative to the final disposition of the razor?"

Mulhern looked uncertain, and Bianchi looked tense. "Read it over carefully first," he urged.

Mulhern read the statement again.

"There's no disposition mentioned," he said finally.

"What did he say to you about the disposition of the razor that he used to cut his mother's throat?" Bianchi asked.

"He said, 'I could have thrown it over the barn roof, or over the gas station across the street," Mulhern answered.

Catherine Roraback got to her feet once more.

"Isn't it true, trooper, that when he said, 'I think I threw it,' he said, '*if* I used the razor'?"

Mulhern looked darkly at her.

"Possibly," he said.

Lieutenant Shay wore a lavender shirt with a lavender patterned tie, a watch with a wide band, and a confident smile. He confirmed that he had spoken with Peter early Saturday morning, at the Canaan barracks, before sending Peter into a bedroom to get some rest; that he'd gone to Hartford later in the day, arriving around 2:00 or 2:30, and he'd talked with Peter after the polygraph test.

"Did you listen to the questioning of Peter Reilly by Trooper Mulhern?" Catherine Roraback asked.

"Yes, I did," Shay said.

"Did you make any comments regarding what should or should not be in that statement?" she asked.

"I took Trooper Mulhern aside and I told him what points should be in the statement," Lieutenant Shay said. He said he knew that the evening questioning had been recorded.

"Have you listened to that recording since that time?" Miss Roraback asked.

"Yes I have," he said.

"Lieutenant Shay, did you at any time alter the tapes?" she asked.

"No, ma'am," he said.

Again Catherine Roraback asked that the evening tapes be played in court. "Is it important that we hear them?" Judge Armentano asked wearily, sounding as if he hoped she'd say no, not really. But Miss Roraback said, emphatically, that it was important, and she talked of "the flavor, the background, the atmosphere" of the questioning that she wanted made known.

Mr. Bianchi objected vigorously. "The best evidence is the testimony of the people who were there and not reliance on an electronic gadget," he insisted. The judge thought about it. "What harm does it do to hear the tapes?" he mused aloud, not seeming to expect an answer, and he said then that he would hear the tapes in a private room at police headquarters, with the accused and counsel present, but with the public and press not invited. John Bianchi looked slightly mollified, and the rest of us looked disappointed.

After the decision to play the tapes, there were more bits and pieces of testimony. Altogether, there was a fragmentary, piecemeal quality about the hearing that Joe O'Brien, who had covered court cases for years, said wasn't at all unusual for this kind of thing. Mickey and Marion Madow testified, each telling what they'd said and done the night Barbara died, how they'd seen Peter and waited for him. Marion wore her best coat, a curly chinchilla, and when she stepped outside the courthouse into the frosty sunshine, carrying a book and a newspaper and a shoulder bag, she looked very chic and confident. Somebody said she must be Peter's lawyer.

Barbara's cousin June looked distraught and wan, too thin in her navy blue suit with pink piping around the collar. She testified that after the various calls during the day, she'd finally called Mrs. Kruse that Saturday night, around 8:30, thinking Peter might have gone next door. Sometime after that, June said, she'd called the barracks again, and when she asked whether Peter needed a lawyer, the trooper had said, "It wouldn't be a bad idea." Around 2 A.M. Sunday, someone from the barracks called her and told her Peter was under arrest and was getting a public defender.

In the marble hall outside the courtroom, I introduced myself to Lieutenant Shay. "I can't comment on the case," he said, "but I'm very impressed with Catherine Roraback." I told him about the piece I was doing and that I was interested in what the people in the community were doing for Peter. "Believe it or not, I think it's a nice gesture on the part of his friends," Lieutenant Shay said. I said I believed him.

Backstage, I asked to see Judge Armentano. He was leaning against a desk, smoking a cigar. I said I'd like to come back and hear the tapes on Monday. He said I couldn't, but he said it pleasantly, and we chatted for a few minutes. I told him what I was writing, and he said he thought there were more interesting cases to write about. He waved his hand vaguely in the direction of the courtroom. "A first offender, it's usually just a family thing," he said casually. I was appalled, and later on I described the incident to Don Jackson, a former *Life* writer who had written a book called *Judges*. Don didn't seem at all surprised. "The presumption of innocence is a charade," he said. "Most judges presume guilt."

Across the street at police headquarters, I tried to talk my way into the polygraph room, but Sergeant Kelly said the room was in use. I said I would come back tomorrow, but he said the room would be in use then, too. The day after that? I asked, and Sergeant Kelly laughed. He let Jim take his picture though. Jim had come up from New York to take pictures for my article. For a mild-mannered financial analyst, brand new to photojournalism, he had ambitious plans. He intended to get pictures of John Bianchi, Jim Mulhern, and Lieutenant Shay at his desk. He wanted pictures, inside and out, of the house where Barbara died. And, beginning at 6 A.M. Monday, he would be working on a picture of Peter in handcuffs, by staking out the entrance to the Litchfield jail.

I wished him luck, and took the train back to New York. I called my editor, Steve Gelman, and we talked about the story. When Judge Armentano had called all four members of the press corps back to his chamber that December day in Litchfield, to discuss how a reporter might properly report a pretrial hearing, he had said, "Use your own judgment." So I did.

The last two weeks of January dwindled away, a deceptive lull. Then two things happened, two very different things that were, in a way, equally astonishing.

When my article appeared in the February 8 issue of *New Times,* with large chunks of Peter Reilly's polygraph test, a woman named

Jacqueline Bernard called the magazine office in New York. Somebody there gave her Jean Beligni's number, so Mrs. Bernard, a stranger to all of us, called East Canaan. She told Jean she had read the piece and would like to bail Peter out of jail. "How much do you need?" she asked. "Oh my God," Jean said. "Forty-four thousand dollars." Mrs. Bernard said she didn't have the cash, but she had some stocks that she could use as collateral for a bank loan. She said she'd send the check as soon as she could. Jean called me with the news. "Oh my God," I said. Then Jean called Father Paul. He said, "Holy mackerel."

Almost simultaneously, word came from Judge Anthony Armentano, down in Hartford, that Peter Reilly's confession was admissible evidence in court. "There may have been some repetitive, suggestive questioning, or the planting of ideas, by the state police," he wrote. "If such existed, and the court does not so find, such questioning, planting, or circumstance did not deprive the defendant of due process." He pointed out that Peter had been given a chance to sleep and had been given dinner. And he said that the tapes he'd heard—the polygraph tapes and the later tapes—depicted Peter as "a very intelligent, articulate, calm, alert individual who displayed no emotional anxiety, distress, or despondency during his interrogation."

It was like two halves of a good news/bad news joke. Peter was getting out of jail, but he was about to be tried for murder, and his confession would be used against him in court, where it would be heard by the jury and by the new judge, John Speziale, Jean Beligni's cousin.

9

Peter came out of jail by the side door, carrying a big cardboard box labeled COFFEE CAKE. All his belongings were in it, his clothes, a few books, and his radio.

He put the box in the trunk of our car and turned to Catherine Roraback. "So long, Peter," she said. She shook his hand and put her other hand on his shoulder. "Have a good weekend, and stay out of trouble." She smiled at him, and Peter grinned. Geoff Madow, who was carrying Miss Roraback's briefcase, grinned too.

"So long, Pete," a voice called from a barred window, and Peter looked up. He squinted in the sun and waved, but he could see nothing, because the jail windows had the kind of glass that let people see out, but not in. "That sounds like Merv," Peter said, and waved again. He had shaken hands with everybody in the jail when he left and had even found a certain pain in this departure. In the nearly five months he'd spent in jail, Peter had made friends. There were two men, especially, whom he'd liked: a drummer who had taught him something about music theory and an accountant, accused of embezzling, who had helped Peter with his bookkeeping homework.

A few reporters clustered near the car. One of them asked Peter how he felt. "It's a good feeling to be out of jail," Peter said, "but I won't be happy until they catch the right person."

"It was unbelievable," Peter said in the car, shaking his head. "It was just unbelievable to be able to step out of the courtroom and not have some clown with me. To be able to say, 'Tell Miss Roraback I'm out in the hall, having a cigarette.'" He shook his head again. "I can't believe I'm out."

"How the heck did you stand it?" asked Geoff.

Peter shrugged. "You just get up, and sit around, and sit around some more," he said.

It was a marvelous feeling to be driving Peter home. Mickey and Marion had been at court in the morning, for all the talking and the signing and the assorted paperwork that accompanied the release of a prisoner on bond. Then Catherine Roraback and Peter Reilly and Peter Herbst came out of the courtroom, and everybody seemed to be shaking hands with everybody else. The judge came out and took the bench.

"What are the plans of the accused?" he asked Miss Roraback.

"He'll be residing with the family of Mr. and Mrs. Meyer Madow in East Canaan, Connecticut," Miss Roraback said. Peter stood next to her, tense and pale.

"Is there any doubt in your mind about his appearance in court?" the judge asked.

"No, your honor," Catherine Roraback said.

John Bianchi looked reluctant. "He doesn't have the family roots that we would be most happy with," he said, "but I know the Madows to be good, solid citizens."

The judge asked Marion, in the spectators' gallery, to stand up. He looked earnestly at her.

"Is there any doubt in your mind about his appearance in court?" the judge asked.

"None whatsoever," Marion said, very firmly, and smiled a little.

I half-expected that court would be called off for the rest of the day then, as we used to get surprise holidays in grade school once in a while. But something important—the questioning of prospective jurors—had begun, and the voir dire continued all afternoon, as though nothing extraordinary had occurred.

Even Anne knew something had. She knelt between Jim and me in the front seat of the car and regarded Peter in the back with considerable interest. I was absolutely elated, but now that he was in the car, I didn't have much to say. It seemed wrong, and somehow in poor

173

taste—if there was such a thing as bad or good taste in murder—to start flinging questions at him. I thought there'd be time for that later, so I looked out the window and occasionally half-turned my head to watch him looking out the window.

He had a remote, detached expression on his face, which people who knew him well seemed accustomed to. His eyes were a clear hazel, and sometimes it was difficult to detect what he was thinking, or feeling, by looking into them. He seemed very cool, very contained. "He was always an odd child," Mrs. Kester, the Falls Village librarian, said. "I've known Peter since he was six, and he was not given to talking, *ever*."

We stopped by our house first, before going to the Madows', so I could change Anne's clothes. Jim opened Cokes, and Peter and Geoff followed me into the living room. Jim's guitar was on the far side of the room, behind the sofa, leaning against the wall in its dark blue fabric case, but Peter picked it out at once. "Is that a guitar?" he asked, only it wasn't a question.

I don't remember what he played, but I remember standing in the doorway between the living room and the hall, watching him from the back. His head was bent over the guitar, the light from the glass bottle lamp behind the sofa shining on his hair, long and silky, with bright highlights in it. I remembered what he'd said on the tapes, when I'd first heard them in December—about his music, his band. "Music's my life." I was suddenly struck with amazement, as I stood there watching him, Geoffrey looking at me from across the room. He's here. He's really here. Peter Reilly is out of jail.

He could have played all night, but people were waiting, so we piled back into the car again. We skimmed along Route 63, heading for East Canaan. A washline was strung across the back in the Parmalees' yard, with some tires lying up against the small front porch. The Dickinson house looked closed and quiet, and in a moment we were speeding past the Kruses' place. There were no more warning signs around the little white house, and the ropes were down. The house was silent, its small windows glinting with dirt in the late afternoon sun. There was no sign of life. Peter glanced at the house. "I wonder who lives there now?" he said.

"Nobody," I told Peter, but I didn't say anything more. I'd been inside the house, and I didn't know what else to say to him about it.

When I was working on the article, interviewing the Kruses, Mr. Kruse had taken down the house key from its hook in the kitchen and we'd gone next door. It was an awful place, smaller, dirtier, more depressing than I had imagined. I stood in the living room, looking into the bedroom, and I couldn't help looking up at where the top bunk would have been. The bunk was gone, of course. Everything was gone, except for a space heater in the corner of the living room, the old two-burner stove in the kitchen, next to the small basin that Barbara had used as the sink. I walked through the bedroom where Barbara died and looked into the dark little bathroom and the rear room with the door leading out. There was very little to see in the house, but there was much to feel and imagine. I didn't stay long; the house had a cold, sour smell, and although it had been a bitter January day outside, I was glad to be out. In the several years he'd lived there, though, none of Peter's friends had heard him complain about the place. He just seemed to accept it as home, as he had accepted so much about his life, including his name and the fact that he had no father.

Soon we were in Canaan, at the four-way stop at the Arco station, across from St. Joseph's, turning onto Route 44, to Locust Hill Way. The car turned up the hill and pulled into the driveway.

Nanny was standing at the dinette window, watching, holding back one corner of the white organdy curtain. She opened the door and held it as Peter came in. He smiled shyly.

"You've grown, Peter," Nanny said in a slightly shaky voice. Her dachshund Natasha darted around her feet, barking as she always did at strangers, with a shrill, furious bark. Peter reached down to the dog, but she skittered away. Peter and Geoff headed into the den, and Nan went to the phone to call Mickey's office.

Peter was showing Geoffrey a card trick when Arthur came in. "Hey, man," Art said to Peter. "How you doin'?" Peter grinned.

"You got to go to court every day?" Arthur asked.

"Yeah," Peter said, and shuffled the cards again.

A car pulled into the drive, and Nan went to the window. There was a rustle at the back door, and Marion came in. "I'm home," she called. "I need some help with the groceries." Arthur just kept talking, and Marion stood in the doorway of the living room, her hands on her hips.

"All right, guys," she said. "Move it!" Peter grinned widely as he and Geoff went out to get the groceries. Jamie Madow, just coming up the hill, picked up one of the bags.

Marion had brought boxes of Kentucky fried chicken, cole slaw, and loaves of French bread. "This isn't Peter's homecoming dinner," she explained. "This is just nourishment." Nanny spread a cloth and got down the plates, and the boys pulled up chairs.

"How was the food at jail?" Geoff asked.

"Geoffrey, it was like eating the hot lunch at school three times a day," Peter said, and all the boys groaned.

"I only had one fight in jail," Peter said. "Some clown was wisin' off about my case. But I didn't cause any trouble. If somebody said to me, jump! I'd say, how high?"

Then suddenly, it seemed, the house was jammed with people— Father Paul and the Belignis, the Dickinsons, and more—a joyous crush, with a good deal of laughing and talking, hardly any crying. A newsman from CBS in New York, who had been in court that day, came in. His name was Rick Kaplan, and he said he might come back with a camera crew to do a segment for the network news.

The phone was always busy. Marion made Peter call Mrs. Bernard in New York, though he felt shy; he called the Kruses, who had written to him in jail and enclosed a $5 bill. Bea Keith, who had never met Peter, was calling, in tears. "I'm just fine," Peter told her. Beverly King came by with two of her children. "I know I'm going to embarrass you," she said, then she leaned over and quickly kissed him on the cheek. "God love you," she said.

Ricky Beligni wore an ear-to-ear grin when he saw Peter and slapped him hard on the back. "How ya' doin', you ol' goldern houn'dog, you!" Ricky was a year younger than his brother Paul, but Ricky and Peter were friends, too. They'd played in the band together, and once, when Ricky and another boy were lost overnight on Canaan Mountain, Peter had joined a search party. Barbara had come over to wait at the Belignis' house while Peter helped look. It was a chilly night in November, the year before Barbara died. In the living room, little Gina was crying because Ricky was lost. "I'll take care of Gina," Barbara said, and she'd told her stories, wonderful stories of knights in armor and beautiful ladies, stories of Arthur and Guinevere. Jean Beligni was very impressed. "She didn't read Gina those stories, she *remembered*

176

them," Jean said. Long before the boys were found, Barbara had soothed Gina to sleep.

Now Peter and his friends all went downstairs, where the guitars and drums were.

Upstairs, in the dinette and living room, the parents laughed too and talked about how difficult it would be to meet the interest payments, nearly $400 a month, on the bank loan that was keeping Peter out of jail. They were worried about paying Catherine Roraback, too, though she hadn't set a fee.

"Aldo drilled a well for Arthur Penn once," Jean reported. "So I wrote him a letter. He directed *Bonnie and Clyde,* so I thought he might be interested."

Marion held up a torn bumper sticker: SUPPORT YOUR LOCAL POLICE in Day-Glow letters, bright orange on a black ground. Somebody had plastered the bumper of her car when it was parked at Mickey's office; Marion peeled it off. Dorothy Madow said a telephone man had come to her house to make repairs and had said to her, "Boy, your brother-in-law is in big trouble." Dorothy asked him why.

"Because people should support the police, no matter what," the phone man said.

Everyone wanted to know more about Jacqueline Bernard, the woman who'd bailed Peter out of jail. It was an amazing gesture from a stranger, and I'd have liked to know more myself, but there wasn't much I could tell them. She had asked that her name not be used because she didn't want to be known as a Lady Bountiful. When I talked with her, she mentioned that her son Joel had taken a year out of college in the early 1960s to do civil rights work in Mississippi, so she knew exactly what it was like to have an eighteen-year-old in jail and to want to get him out.

Late into the night, there was laughter and talk. Gina and Anne were playing in the den, little girls then. At the dinette table, Marion had piled some of the mail that had come in since the *New Times* piece. The magazine had run a box, asking for contributions to the Reilly Fund, so many of the letters had brought checks, too, some of them from well-known people. Beatrice Straight, an actress who had a house in Norfolk, had sent a large check and had persuaded a friend of hers to send one, too. Brendan Gill of *The New Yorker* sent a nice check

177

to Peter and a nice letter to me. He said he liked my article, and he'd sent copies to some lawyers he knew.

Most of the letters were from ordinary people. One retired couple sent part of their Social Security check. An anonymous note, with a dollar bill enclosed, said, "I am a law student, and this abuse of our legal system must be stopped." A prison officer in Louisiana sent $5 and a sad note, wondering how many of the young people he saw had doubts about what had happened. From places as distant as Deadwood, Oregon, Pineville, Louisiana, and Ann Arbor, Michigan, the letters came; already the Peter Reilly affair seemed to be touching a sensitive nerve somewhere in the national consciousness. A psychiatric nurse who had worked in New York prisons thanked the committee for what it was doing. "You are all bright lights in a dark world," she wrote.

I thought so too, not only that night, when Peter got out of jail and we were all so happy, but even afterward, when so much of the happiness had drained away, when some minor tensions, then some real grievances, had developed between members of the committee, and between some of them and me. I always thought so.

It was a wonderful night, but from time to time, in the midst of the laughter, somebody would say something serious, something that would recollect for everyone what might lie ahead. With several jurors already chosen, Peter's trial was not far off. The charge was murder, a Class A felony in Connecticut. In Peter's case, the state was asking for a penalty of ten years to life.

"The judge told the jurors not to think of the penalty," Jean exclaimed. "How could they *not* think of the penalty? They might be putting this boy away till he's fifty years old."

Meantime, the boy was downstairs with his friends, playing his guitar. It seemed so unbelievable. How could it have happened? And who had let it happen? Whose fault was it, anyway? Was it Lieutenant Shay, telling Peter he was a suspect but not telling him he should get a lawyer? Was it Sergeant Kelly, telling Peter the truth was on his tape? Was it the prosecutor who'd pressed for an indictment before he'd heard all the tapes? Was it the other policemen, too, or some of them? Were there several villains, or just one nameless, faceless villain, the System? Because the people here knew Jim Mulhern best, and because he'd known Peter, they talked of him more, and thought he should be given the button that a *New Times* reader had sent in. The button had

a picture of Adolf Eichmann and the caption read: I WAS ONLY FOLLOW-
ING ORDERS.

John Bianchi looked disgusted as he picked up the newspaper and
read the quotation out loud: "It's a good feeling to be out of jail, but
I won't be happy until they catch the right person."

He threw the paper down onto the counsel table and gestured
toward other papers in a small stack. The prosecutor was angry about
articles that had quoted Peter the day he was freed on bond. Peter
talked about the mail he'd got from people who read his story in
New Times, and he'd quoted someone as writing "We couldn't believe
the police worked that way." Mr. Bianchi also complained about a
New York Times story in which Catherine Roraback had talked about
the case, referring to Peter's interrogation by the state police as "a
grilling . . . they planted in his mind that he must have done it," and
describing Barbara Gibbons, whom she'd known, as a kind of "rural
Bohemian." Mr. Bianchi said he was very upset by these articles; he
felt they were prejudicial, and he said he felt very close to asking for
a mistrial.

Judge Speziale peered over the bench.

"Do you care to respond, Miss Roraback?" he asked.

Catherine Roraback sighed a little as she stood up; she had known
this was coming. She said she would address herself to two separate
issues. As for the *Times* piece, she said, she had already complained
to the newspaper, because her telephone talk with their reporter was
off the record. Miss Roraback said she was as upset about the article as
Mr. Bianchi—in fact, more so.

She defended the other articles, though. "Whether Peter Reilly's
statements are wise or not, whether they help or hinder is quite another
matter. But I think he has the right to make these statements," she
declared. "I feel strongly that Mr. Reilly has the right of free speech."

Thus in a small way, and in a small place, in an out-of-the-way
courtroom tucked into a corner of Litchfield County, Connecticut, an
argument continued, one that stretched back over many years, many
centuries. In general, the question was how free a person was to speak,
and under what circumstances, or whether any qualifiers ought to apply.
Those who opposed restriction leaned heavily on the First Amendment
to the Constitution, which guaranteed freedom of speech and press,

and those who were in favor of various restrictions leaned just as heavily on the Sixth Amendment, which guaranteed a fair trial. In the courts, restrictions on the press were popularly, or not so popularly, called gag orders, and in the case of Peter Reilly, one had already been handed down. "It's like Grand Central Station in this courtroom," the judge had complained on the morning of February 19, when the jury panel crowded into the room, and he spent his lunch hour that day dictating the gag order to his secretary. The defendant and the witnesses were prohibited from making "extrajudicial statements that might be reasonably calculated to affect the outcome of the trial." Besides the ban on interviews and extrajudicial statements, there were to be no tape recorders, no cameras in or around the court, not even any sketching.

Now, a week after that order, the judge was hearing from the prosecutor that perhaps his order had been violated. Judge Speziale frowned deeply, and said he would call a recess so that he could read the articles Mr. Bianchi had complained about.

"The car's gone," Peter said casually, as we stood in the hall. "The state of Connecticut put a lien on the 'vette. But I'm better off without it." He lighted a cigarette and leaned against the wall in the hall outside the courtroom. He still looked thin, but he looked far less tense, far more rested than he'd looked the week before. He'd had a good weekend, playing guitar with the boys, going to McDonald's. On Sunday he had gone to the 7:30 mass at St. Joseph's with Aldo and Paul, and at the Madows' he'd slept well. One morning, when Marion and Mickey passed by the den where Peter was sleeping, Marion had whispered, "Mickey, do you think he knows he's here and not in jail?" Peter had heard her, lifted his head from the pillow, and grinned. "I know I'm here," he said. "This is too soft for jail."

Aldo Beligni had picked up Peter at the Madows and brought him into Litchfield. All the grown-ups planned to take turns driving Peter to court; they felt that in this precarious period, he should have older people around, and indeed, this morning he seemed to be the youngest person in the room. Miss Roraback had even challenged the validity of the process by which a jury pool was drawn, on the grounds that it excluded persons from eighteen to twenty-one, but her motion had been denied. As the trial progressed, more young people began coming to court—Geoff Madow and the Belignis, Art Madow, and occasionally Wayne Collier and the Parmalee brothers, Tim and Mike. Groups of young people eventually showed up, too, often led by their teachers, to watch the proceedings as a kind of living lesson in sociology, psychology, criminology, even social studies; the criminal trial of an eighteen-year-old male accused of murdering his mother clearly fit into all sorts of interesting curriculum categories.

Meantime, however, Peter had only grown-ups to talk to. Legally, of course, he was a grown-up himself, as Sergeant Kelly had pointed out to him in Hartford. But emotionally and psychologically he was not. As Jean Beligni had pointed out earlier, he was still in school, accustomed to taking orders. "Making the legal age eighteen instead of twenty-one is the best thing that ever happened to the police around here," another committee member once said, with a trace of anger. Peter himself had underlined the point when he talked on the phone to a reporter the night he got out of jail. "I'm eating and sleeping and playing my guitar," Peter said, "but I'm staying close to home. I don't go anywhere unless I have an adult with me." He said it casually, not sarcastically; apparently he found no irony in what he said, and neither did the reporter.

As the recess dragged on, Chief Deputy Sheriff Pat Alfano stood in the doorway of the courtroom and mused on what Judge Speziale might do about the publicity. "He's tough," said Sheriff Alfano, a tall, curly haired, affable Italian whom nearly everybody called Patsy. "Some judges, you can get away with anything, but Speziale will cream you for doing the slightest thing."

Although a lot of people said a lot of things about other people in Litchfield Superior Court, not all of them well-founded, Patsy Alfano knew what he was talking about, because he and John Speziale had been schoolmates once, with a lot in common. The parents of both boys were Italian immigrants, hardworking and ambitious for their children, and the boys were high school classmates.

John Speziale was born in Winsted, Connecticut. His birthday was November 21, just one day after Barbara Gibbons' birthday. His father worked for the railroad, and his mother worked in a needle factory to help her children get through school. John always knew he wanted to be a lawyer, but there were five children in the family; never enough money, never enough new clothes. "Look at you," a girl in his class used to jeer. "Just look at you. Patches on your knee and on your fanny. How can *you* ever be a lawyer?"

In high school, John was known as a brain. He carried a briefcase to school. But he had other interests, especially music and tennis, and he was so cheerful and resourceful that he was voted the "Most Optimistic" member of the Class of 1940. At Duke University, he waited on tables, played in the marching band, and graduated Phi Beta Kappa in 1943. He went right into the navy, serving in the Pacific, and he was one of the first men to go ashore at Nagasaki after the bomb.

When he returned from the war he went back to law school at Duke. He passed the Connecticut bar on his first try and almost immediately became a Municipal Court judge. He ran for state treasurer in 1958 and won, with a little campaign jingle: "Don't dilly-dally; vote for Spez-ee-alley."

In 1961 he became a judge in the Court of Common Pleas, and four years later was appointed to the Superior Court. In spite of his success, he and his wife, Mary, did not move to one of the big old houses in Litchfield. They stayed on in Torrington, where he was a member of the Elks, the Knights of Columbus, and the Sons of Italy, and he dressed in plain black or brown suits, with a soft tweedy country-style hat to add a little dash.

When Peter Reilly was brought into his courtroom, Judge Speziale was only fifty-one—just as old as Barbara was when she died—but because he'd been a judge at twenty-six, he always seemed older than he was. He was stern, strict, and, as Pat Alfano said, he was tough. He wasn't what they called a hanging judge; he was considered fair and honest, and he had an old-fashioned, courtly air about him. On the street he invariably tipped his hat to women, even women reporters.

He had a round face and a soft smile that he didn't use much in court; usually he wore a serious, semifrowning look, his forehead creased, rather like a worried monsignor continually fretting about the parish debt. Sometimes, in court, the afternoon sun glinted off the rims of his glasses, and as he bent over the notes he was writing, with the desk light beaming down onto the pages, he looked as he must have looked thirty years before, when he studied so intently to make Phi Beta Kappa and to live up to his parents' dreams. The law was not only his life, but also his lifeline; his work, which was so burdensome, which involved the handling of the lives of other people, was made easier by his absolute reliance on the law. The law was written down in books, and life was always easier when a man went by the book.

He wore that worried look when he swept back into court after the recess, his full black robe making a definitive swish as he turned the corner of the doorway from chambers back into court. He said he had read the articles and felt they might indeed have created "a clear and present danger" to the fairness of this trial. He then read the entire text of the order he'd written during the recess. It threatened to use the contempt power of the court against any person who (a) "disseminates by any means of public communication an extrajudicial statement relating to the defendant or to the issues in the case that goes beyond the public record of this court, if the statement is reasonably calculated to affect the outcome of the trial and seriously threatens to have such an effect; or (b) makes such a statement with the expectation that it will be so disseminated." Regarding Peter Reilly, the order said, "The defendant is forbidden from participating in interviews for publicity and from making extrajudicial statements about this case from this date and until such time as a verdict in this case is returned in open court. Any violation of this order by the defendant may well lead to a revocation of his release on bail."

The language was legal and formal, but the message couldn't be missed. Peter Reilly wasn't nearly as free as he'd thought nor, for that matter, was anyone else.

None of the jurors, as it turned out, had seen any of the articles, but Mr. Bianchi moved for a mistrial, anyway. "Litchfield County has been inundated with publicity," he declared, and he asked for a two-month continuance, "so that the publicity will have been tempered by time."

Miss Roraback opposed it. "I'm as concerned as Mr. Bianchi that we have a fair trial," she said. "But we have seven good jurors already, none of whom has seen or heard this . . ." She motioned to the newspapers on the prosecution table, and smiled a little. "In my experience, I was always shocked to discover how few people read the newspapers," she said. Mr. Bianchi, who didn't have an office near Yale, and who had never taken part in a nationally known trial, flushed

183

a little. "I am likewise impressed with the jury, your honor," he said hastily. Miss Roraback laughed a little, Mr. Bianchi laughed too, and Judge Speziale said they'd go on with the voir dire.

John Bianchi, impeccable in a pearl gray suit with a powder blue shirt, looked at the latest panel of prospective jurors.

"We are here to determine who caused the death of Barbara Gibbons on September 28, 1973, in the town of Canaan, Connecticut," he told them solemnly. "This town is much more commonly referred to as Falls Village, Connecticut. Barbara Gibbons was murdered on the twenty-eighth day of September 1973, sometime between nine and ten o'clock that night." Then he read off the names of some of the witnesses the state intended to call.

Catherine Roraback stood up, dressed in pale blue, with a string of pearls, and about a quarter of an inch of her slip showing.

"Ladies and gentlemen of the panel, I am representing Peter," she said, and she half-turned and smiled at him. "Will you stand up, Peter?"

The jurors stared. They saw a pale young man, skinny and tense-looking with long, slender hands and large hazel eyes, his skin a little broken out, and his teeth a little crooked, his hair long and falling over his right eye. Miss Roraback paused, taking advantage of the stillness of the moment, then she said quietly that she wanted to correct something Mr. Bianchi had said.

"We're not here to determine who caused the death of Barbara Gibbons," she said, "but whether Peter Reilly caused it."

One by one, the jurors came out to be questioned, to take the oath of the voir dire—"to speak the truth." Some of them were clutching *A Handbook for Jurors,* the sixteen-page blue booklet each of them had been given in the jury waiting room. The style of the booklet was both pedantic and vivid, as though it were written for Boy Scouts who liked to read James Bond under the covers at night. Some of the text was lecturing ("The juror must be diligent and conscientious, patient and trustworthy . . . a juror must be courageous") and some of it was blunt and graphic ("What is evidence? . . . the evidence is what the judge lets the jury hear and consider. . . . Evidence may take the form of photographs, bullets, or a scarred face . . ."). But the booklet also promised, "You will witness a real life drama in every case that you sit on." I was fascinated by the drama of the voir dire itself, as these people came out of the jury room, trailing their ordinary sense of the serious, the tragic, the absurd. When Mr. Bianchi asked a woman from Winchester, who had two teen-age sons of her own, whether she would therefore feel sympathy for the accused, she shook her head. "I'm not really a sympathetic person," she said.

A juror could be challenged for cause, such as an occupation that made him unsuitable, or an attitude, a bias, that made him unsuitable. When capital punishment was a factor in jury selection, a common challenge for cause was to a juror who didn't believe in it. In this voir dire, a clear challenge for cause was to a man who said he was a social worker in the welfare department, employed by the state of Connecticut. "Would that make it difficult for you to be objective in this case?" Mr. Bianchi asked. "I think so," the juror replied mildly. "The Gibbons' case was part of my caseload."

Beyond challenge for cause was the peremptory challenge, less formally known as the hunch. Miss Roraback and Peter, on one side, and Mr. Bianchi, on the other, might excuse as many as eighteen people each because they didn't like the way the juror looked, or talked, or something the juror said, or didn't say, or just because they felt like it. Often the reason for a peremptory challenge was hard to pin down, but one thing was usually very plain: A juror excused by one side was usually a juror whom the other side liked a lot.

"As you look at my client," Catherine Roraback asked a woman in a purple pants suit, "is he innocent or guilty?"

"Why, I don't know," the woman said. "I'd have to hear his case first." She looked annoyed, as though a lawyer ought to know that already. Miss Roraback sighed a little.

"But he's innocent until proved guilty, isn't he?"

The woman looked startled. "Oh, yes," she said.

It wasn't a trick question. It was the presumption of innocence, a concept every citizen in the voir dire had probably recited in school, one that nearly every citizen now forgot. "I don't know," they said to Miss Roraback, or, "I can't say. I don't know the facts yet."

Once she phrased it differently. "What does presumption of innocence mean to you?" she asked a factory worker from Bristol.

"It would be like he and I would be in the same boat right now, you know what I mean? Can you figure that one out?" the man replied, and Miss Roraback smiled.

"You mean, you're innocent too?" she asked.

Another of the defense questions was whether a juror thought that just because Peter was in court, he had done something wrong. "Well, I assume he's here for *some* reason," a woman replied uncertainly. That sort of question, whether Peter's very indictment would weigh against him, led naturally into the question of whether a juror would tend to believe a police officer more readily than a civilian witness. "I honestly don't believe I would," said a breezy looking woman in gold and black bell-bottoms and a chartreuse blouse. She was married to a policeman in Hartford. But another woman said she certainly would consider a policeman more credible. "I've been brought up in a society where the police are always right," she said.

Just as presumption of innocence was a stumbling block for the defense, so for the prosecution was the concept of reasonable doubt. Judge Speziale had told the pool that "the state must prove its case in a criminal prosecution beyond a reasonable doubt," and said that when the time came for the jury to be charged, he would explain further.

Meantime, however, Mr. Bianchi had to find out a juror's ideas much earlier.

"Do you feel you would have to remove *all* doubt from your mind?" Mr. Bianchi asked a middle-aged woman on the stand.

"Yes," she said, as so many jurors before her had said, and Judge Speziale intervened.

"Maybe you don't really understand that question, because it's not that easy to understand," he said. "It would be your solemn duty to accept the law as I give it to you."

"I'd have to be sure in my own mind," she insisted. "I've got to be satisfied." The judge looked his sternest. "You mean, satisfied beyond the law as I explain it to you?"

She looked back at him seriously. "I don't know where that fine line is," she said.

The jury selection took several days. It was a delicate, difficult process, requiring experience, psychology, instinct, and lots of luck. In some courtrooms, scientific jury selection was popular, a process by which prospective jurors were compared with profiles of the population from which the jury pool was drawn.

The new science was expensive and comprehensive. Besides the usual questions about income, occupation, and hobbies, people might be asked about their TV-viewing habits and their feelings on a variety of topics from women's lib to the grain deal with Russia. Out of all this came certain answers. "If the juror is a fifty-four-year-old registered Republican who is the proprietor of a sporting goods store, computer printouts will tell you what he is likely to believe, even if he won't," said an article in *Psychology Today*. But a sizable study made in California, also reported in the magazine, found that the significant variance between jurors who voted guilty and those who voted not guilty was how much they liked the prosecutor. Those who liked the prosecutor voted guilty; those who didn't voted to acquit. Maybe jury selection wasn't a science, after all. Just chemistry.

At 3:10 P.M. on Thursday, February 28, 1974, the last juror was chosen in Docket #5285, *State of Connecticut* v. *Peter A. Reilly.* The jurors were:

Paul Travaglin, sixty-six years old, a bachelor from New Milford who still lived there with his mother. He said he had never been involved in politics.

Edward Ives of Litchfield, fifty, a Boy Scout leader and pillar of the community. His three sons were nineteen, twenty-three, and twenty-five.

William Jennings, twenty-seven, a tall, skinny redhead, father of two small children. He lived in Kent, but worked for the phone company in New Milford, and he read the Danbury papers.

John Wheeler, small and dapper, in a kelly green jacket, thirty years old. He lived in Harwinton but worked for the phone company in New Milford too. He was unmarried but had an eighteen-year-old brother.

Gary Lewis, twenty-nine, a tall, handsome man who looked a little like Richard Boone. He and his wife had two children, eleven and nine.

Helen Ayre, fifty-four, a minister's wife. Her children were seventeen, twenty-three, and twenty-four. She said she thought a lot about whether she could be fair and impartial, and decided she could. "I'm basically an honest person," she said. "I know myself."

Margaret Wald, sixty-one, a grandmother who spent the jury waiting time knitting for her grandchildren. Petite and cheerful, she dressed like a cheerleader in a full, swinging red skirt and a red-and-white striped blouse.

Gertrude Collins, sixty-three, short and plump, mother of children aged nineteen and twenty-seven, dressed mostly in red, including red shoes. She worked at the Becton-Dickinson factory in Canaan. She said she would feel some sympathy, and said a little later, "It might not be possible to remove every single doubt."

Raymond Ross of New Milford, sixty-three, tall, a little slump-shouldered, unsmiling. "I feel that young people are no worse off than we are, or no better off," he said, when he was asked about his feelings toward the younger generation. His sons were grown, twenty-eight and twenty-five.

Raymond Lind of Litchfield, fifty-one, a commercial artist, self-employed. He said he didn't think there was any such thing as a black-and-white situation. "I do very little talking," he said.

Sarah Waldron, thirty-six, mother of a two-year-old boy. She planned to drop him off at her sister-in-law's house every morning on her way to court and pick him up on her way home.

Carl Fabiaschi, twenty-eight, another snappy dresser, unmarried, with a gondolier's smile. He worked in Hartford for the state motor vehicle department. He knew some state police, he said, and said that might conceivably influence him, but when questioned further he said he thought he could keep an open mind.

Eleanor Novak, alternate, forty-one years old, mother of four children, ranging in age from nine to nineteen. Her husband worked at the Pratt-Whitney plant. Her hobby was making candles. She had bouffant blonde hair and a wide-eyed look.

Frank Sollitto, alternate, forty-five, manager of an insurance company, with the look of a Welsh poet. He had served on two grand juries in the past and said if he had to serve now, he would "do my duty."

Those were the jurors, and this was what they heard:

The Grand Jury of the County of Litchfield by this indictment accuses Peter A. Reilly of Canaan, Connecticut, of the crime of Murder and charges that at the Town of Canaan on the 28th day of September

1973 the said Peter A. Reilly, with intent to cause the death of Barbara Gibbons of Canaan, did cause the death of Barbara Gibbons, by slashing her throat, breaking bones in her body, and inflicting stab wounds, all in violation of Section 53a-54 of the General Statutes of Connecticut.

10

Mickey Madow kissed Marion. Patricia Alfano kissed her dad, Chief Deputy Sheriff Joe Battistoni's wife kissed him, and the first prosecution witness, Barbara Fenn, kissed Sergeant Chapman, the police photographer. Peter Reilly's trial was underway with a feeling of good will in the air. It was a rainy Friday, the first day of March 1974.

Bill Dickinson brought Peter to court and took a seat in the third row on the left side of the courtroom. The defense counsel table was on that side, the prosecution table on the right, near the jury box, so it became a habit for people who were friends of Peter, or who were at least favorably disposed toward him, to sit on the left. John Bianchi's people sat on the right, where he could greet them as he walked past the gallery on his way to his office, the State's Attorney's office, which opened directly off the courtroom. A center aisle separated these two groups of chairs in the spectators' section, so it was easy to choose one side or the other, just as people sat on either the bride's side or the groom's side at a church wedding.

There were six rows of seats in each section, six chairs to a row. The first row was still reserved for the press, a dozen seats in all. Although there were more reporters covering the trial than had covered the pretrial hearing, there still weren't enough to fill the entire row. Joe O'Brien of the *Courant,* Greg Erbstoesser of the *Lakeville Journal,* and Charles

Kochakian of the *Hartford Times* were familiar to me from the pretrial hearings. Now I met three new reporters.

George Judson was covering for the Waterbury paper. Two years out of Antioch, he wore Earth Shoes and had a lively humor, which helped.

Roger Cohn of the *Torrington Register,* who had studied writing with William Zinsser at Yale, was one of the best writers in the group. Roger had just graduated the year Barbara died; he was enthusiastic and ambitious, nice to be with. Farn Dupre was a small, shy-looking woman not long out of Beloit. She wrote part time for the *Winsted Citizen* and was being paid $12 a day for the Reilly trial. Farn thought it wasn't enough, and Roger advised her to ask for more.

There were no newspaper people from New York and no TV people anymore. Rick Kaplan of CBS wanted to film a segment for the network news and asked some of us to talk on camera about the case, but after the gag order, most of us were afraid to. In the long run we would probably be cleared of contempt-of-court charges. But in the short run we would be jailed, and while that might have been dramatic and interesting, meantime, I'd have missed the trial. John Bianchi had already moved for a mistrial, on the day the last juror was picked, citing "inflammatory" publicity. There was the chance, too, hinted in the gag order, that something we might say or write would lead to Peter's bond being revoked. Nothing at all seemed worth that, and when I went to the committee meeting the week Peter was out, I told them so. I said I would take notes, but the notes would be for a book someday, not for an article. The committee members were as chagrined about the gag order as the reporters were. "It didn't take them long how to figure out how to get to us, did it?" Jean Beligni asked bitterly. "All we have to do is say the wrong thing, or what somebody thinks is the wrong thing, and Peter's back in jail." Cilla Belcher agreed. "It's a form of blackmail," she said, "but we can't take the risk." I didn't think I could, either. I called Steve Gelman and *New Times*'s lawyer, and they didn't think so either. Later I was sorry, but at the time it seemed like the right thing to do, the only thing to do.

However, I wrote another article, one of the shortest, blandest stories I ever hope to write, two pages in *New Times* called "Peter Reilly Gets Ready for Trial." Jim said I'd never before written a piece in which I said so little so nicely. I couldn't say anything about the case, so I wrote about the people—the jurors, the sheriffs, the people

191

in the courtroom. They were nice people. Jim had taken a picture of Peter, sitting on our sofa the day we drove him home from jail, his head bent over the guitar, and that picture ran with the piece. It was a nice picture.

Mr. Bianchi was dressed in gray again, with a powder blue shirt and a fresh haircut. Catherine Roraback wore a two-piece dress in deep rose-pink with one strand of pearls. She and Peter Herbst and Peter Reilly gathered at the defense table, looking through some papers. John Bianchi had gone back behind the courtroom, then came out quickly, heading toward his own counsel table.

"He's coming out," Mr. Bianchi told Miss Roraback.

"Give me a minute," she said, without looking up, continuing to look through the papers on her table.

"I'll give you a minute, but I don't run the court, Catherine," Mr. Bianchi said tartly.

Everyone stood up as Judge Speziale swept through the doorway and stepped up onto his bench, the dais. "You may open court, Mr. Sheriff," he said.

The jury came out, filing solemnly across the dingy carpet to their boxed-in rows of wooden armchairs, the back row raised higher than the front so that all twelve jurors had an unobstructed view of the witness, the judge, the lawyers, and whatever else they were supposed to see. Edward Ives came first this morning, taking the first seat in the top row. On most days the jurors sat in various seats, except Gary Lewis. He would inevitably come out last, which meant he got to sit in the bottom row of the jury box, in the last seat, the seat nearest the spectators' gallery. If a juror were hanging behind, gathering a handbag or something, the people in the press row could see Gary Lewis waiting to fall in line behind that person. The two alternates, Frank Sollitto and Eleanor Novak, sat in wooden armchairs in front of the jury box, very close to the prosecution counsel table, not removed from the arena, as the other jurors were, but right there on the same level with everybody. On the first day Mr. Sollitto and Mrs. Novak looked a little uncomfortable sitting there, but by and by they forgot themselves and became engrossed in the drama the handbook had promised.

The first witness called by the state of Connecticut was Barbara

192

Fenn. She told John Bianchi that she was a registered nurse, employed at Sharon Hospital, and that on the night of September 28, 1973, she had been the evening supervisor in the emergency room. On the stand now, she wore a white pants uniform with a white jacket, and white shoes. She wore rimless glasses, with her grayish hair swept back plainly above her forehead, giving her a strict, serious, supervisory look.

She said she had been in the emergency room when Peter Reilly's call came through. "I said, 'This is Mrs. Fenn, the evening supervisor, may I help you?'" The person calling didn't give his name, but said he was at the house of Barbara Gibbons, and said, 'She's having difficulty breathing. There's blood all over the place.'" He sounded "a little apprehensive, a little excited." Mrs. Fenn said she told the caller she would dispatch the Falls Village ambulance and would notify the state police. She testified that she got the call "at approximately nine-forty P.M."

Trooper Calkins wasn't in uniform. He had a crew cut, though, and he wore a dark brown suit, as he identified the police log for the night of September 28, 1973. He explained that the Connecticut State Police operated on military time, and that 21:58, the time he'd received Mrs. Fenn's call from Sharon Hospital, meant 9:58 P.M. The log book became State's Exhibit A, the first in a long list of exhibits, and the call, and the time Trooper Calkins said she called him, became the first in a long list of topics that would be discussed, hashed over, and rehashed throughout the trial.

"Eighteen minutes!" exclaimed Charles Kochakian in the hall during a recess. "It took her eighteen minutes to call the police? Remind me not to go to Sharon Hospital if I'm in an emergency." We laughed; on the first day of the trial, the time element was still something to laugh about.

Trooper Calkins said he had radioed to Trooper McCafferty, who came to the stand next. Bruce McCafferty looked different, older than he had at the pretrial hearings, no longer the rookie. He had grown a thick moustache, which gave him an air of assurance, but as he told again how he'd arrived at Barbara's house and what he'd found, his eyes had a wide, apprehensive look. Miss Roraback talked about the time noted on the police report. "I have difficulty with military time," she said lightly. Judge Speziale looked up from his notes. "If it's more than twelve, just subtract twelve," he told her gravely.

John Bianchi walked back to the counsel table, picked up something, and walked back to the witness stand. "I show you a picture . . ." he began. From the press row, the picture showed as a flash of bright orange. Trooper McCafferty looked at it and nodded. The judge looked at it and handed it back to John Bianchi, who walked across to the counsel table and handed it to Catherine Roraback. She looked at it, her face angry. Peter Reilly looked at it and turned ashen. There was a tense silence in the courtroom as Mr. Bianchi handed the picture then to Mrs. Ayre, the first juror. She looked at it and passed it on. When it reached the end of the first row, Sheriff Battistoni, stationed next to the jury box, passed it from the front row to the back. Normally the sheriff didn't stand by the jury box, but he had been told that today and for the next several days of testimony, as these pictures and slides were shown, he was to stand there in case any of the jurors needed him. His hand was thrust casually into his pocket, holding a bottle of smelling salts.

The pictures were hideous. There was a full-length shot of Barbara, sprawled on her back, her naked body glossy, almost waxy-looking. The blood showed up as garish orange-red splashes on the color print. As the pictures came her way, Mrs. Collins put on her glasses, then took them off again and looked down, staring at the floor.

There were long shots, showing Barbara looking almost like a mannequin, remote and distant, and there were close-ups: the torso picture with the gaping, slashed stomach; the neck shot, showing Barbara's head nearly cut off; and the lower-body shot, with Barbara's pubic hair showing as a very black V-shape against the glaring whiteness of her thighs and lower body.

The jurors showed little emotion as they looked at the pictures. Some of them looked down, as Mrs. Collins had done, some looked at the judge or at Mr. Bianchi. Edward Ives nibbled thoughtfully at the end of the frame of his glasses. Sarah Waldron looked at the pictures and then looked across the room at Peter, keeping her eyes on him for a very long time.

Sgt. Richard Chapman, who had taken the pictures, was on the witness stand as the photographs were passed around. At one point, Catherine Roraback tried to stem the flow. "He's just trying to pile up the record with inflammatory material," she told the court, referring to the prosecutor. Mr. Bianchi looked solemn. "They show the crime scene, which I have a duty and obligation to show," he intoned, and her objection was overruled.

Sergeant Chapman had brought the slides of Barbara's autopsy, and Catherine Roraback objected to those too. There was considerable discussion as to whether they needed to be shown. "We can run through them quickly, like a movie, unless Catherine has some objections," Sergeant Chapman said helpfully. "Do you mean Miss Roraback?" asked the judge sternly. He spoke in a rebuking tone, but Sergeant Chapman looked unabashed. He had been a police photographer for more than two decades, and he knew the lawyers and the sheriffs very well. And he knew Barbara Fenn very well, whose husband was a state trooper.

Finally, after much discussion, the autopsy slides were shown. Judge Speziale called a recess while the screen was brought out, the shades drawn, and tables and chairs rearranged. The screen was set up facing the judge's bench, so that he and the lawyers might see the pictures. During the preview, the jury would be kept out while the judge decided whether or not the jurors would have a showing, too. Those of us in the gallery were not sent out, but since the screen was set up in front of us, facing the judge, we could only watch him watching the pictures.

"This is the face of the victim," Sergeant Chapman said in a detached, professional way, his own face faintly glowing in the light of the projector he was operating from the witness stand. The room was very still, very dark, and in the darkness, most of the sheriffs stationed around the courtroom, including some from downstairs, had moved quietly past the bar rail and lined up along the wall. Some secretaries had come from downstairs and were lined up along the wall, too.

The photographer went through the autopsy slides quickly, as he had said he could: the elbow; the abdomen; the right leg; the left leg; the vaginal region; the interior examination of stomach tissue; the vaginal region with surgical clips; a slide described as "an exploratory operation," with "the pathologist's right hand up in through the vaginal region." Then there was a slide showing "the vagina as exposed after resection."

Altogether, there were nineteen color slides. When the last slide was shown and the projector stopped humming, Robert Wall flicked on the bright overhead lights, and the secretaries and sheriffs standing along the wall quickly dispersed.

Miss Roraback objected, especially, to the interior pictures, pointing out that the vaginal injuries had not caused Barbara's death. "The picture of the so-called exploratory operation of the section of the vagina are highly inflammatory," she said, "especially for the women on the jury." But Mr. Bianchi called the slides "vital to the proof of this case."

The judge looked at Mr. Bianchi in a kind of stern appeal. "Is there a purpose for each one of the slides?" the judge asked, looking as though he hoped the answer would be no.

"Yes, there is," Mr. Bianchi insisted. "I claim them, your honor. Dr. Izumi informs me that the slides were taken for this particular purpose."

"I quite specifically object to the photographs relative to the vagina," Catherine Roraback persisted. "I am a woman, after all," she said, "and I must say that some of these pictures of the vagina and the so-called exploratory operation are the most disgusting and violative of my own sense of dignity as a woman as I can think of. That is not the area where the fatal injury occurred. These are additional injuries that were sustained, and I submit that they would be so inflammatory that it would be unfair, to put it mildly."

Mr. Bianchi took the floor then, his hands clasped behind his back, rocking back and forth slightly, in a classic orator's stance. He frowned. "Counsel is here as an attorney," he declared. "They are not very desirable for anyone to see," he said, and paused dramatically. "Murder never is."

Dr. Ernest Izumi had a gray, silvery crew cut and wore horn-rims. He was short, stocky, and prosperous looking, with bushy black eyebrows and bright eyes. He smiled at Mickey, and he blinked and smiled at the judge too.

"Are these slides essential?" Judge Speziale asked him, still seeming to look for an out.

"Yes, sir, your honor, they are," Dr. Izumi said, without hesitating. "I think the slides depict much more than I could present in writing."

"Do you need all the nineteen slides?" Judge Speziale asked, his voice sounding strained, almost desperate.

"If the sequence of the autopsy is to be asked for, I would say yes,"

Dr. Izumi replied. "For the sequence of the various factors to determine the cause of death, I would say yes."

Judge Speziale asked Catherine Roraback whether she wished to inquire again, and once more she brought up the interior body photographs. She looked hard at Dr. Izumi. "What is the purpose of these photographs?"

He looked back at her.

"The purpose is to show things as they were at the time the autopsy was done," he replied.

"Do I understand these photographs do not show the injury to the vagina?" she asked.

"There are multiple injuries to the vagina," Dr. Izumi said softly. "Two or more."

"But do the photographs refer to the injuries?" Catherine Roraback asked him, in a strong voice.

"Yes," he said.

"All of them do?"

"Yes," he said.

"Do all four show those injuries?" she repeated.

"Yes, ma'am, they do show the various injuries," he said again.

"All four?"

"Yes ma'am."

Catherine Roraback looked truly angry and asked Sergeant Chapman to show the slides again. Now it was Mr. Bianchi's turn to object. He said it was unnecessary. "Just the vaginal area," Catherine Roraback said briskly.

The lights were turned out again. Dr. Izumi leaned his elbow on the jury rail. Joe Battistoni moved up again, so he could see. The judge blinked sadly at the screen. "What does this depict?" he asked.

"This depicts the inner portion, as we are looking down into the pelvic area," Dr. Izumi said.

"Does this depict a specific injury?" Judge Speziale asked.

"Yes, sir, it does," the doctor said. "This would be very pertinent. I think this may be the picture that Attorney Roraback may question. I believe it's very pertinent."

"This is a specific injury?" the judge asked again.

"It is part of the injury," Dr. Izumi said.

197

"This has not been shown in great detail on the other slides?" the judge asked, almost hopefully.

"No, sir," said Dr. Izumi. There was a note of finality in his voice, and Judge Speziale gave in. The man who tipped his hat to women went by the book, too, and when he had to choose, the book came first. "Objection overruled," the judge said, and told Mr. Murdick to bring the jury back.

They filed back in, some of them smiling. They seemed to have got over the photographs. They seemed glad to be up and moving, even though in a minute they were seated again, three of the women bunched together in the top row. Mrs. Ayre was smiling.

Mr. Bianchi stood up and introduced the slides as evidence then, State's Exhibits 0-1 through 0-19. Now the jury knew what was coming, and Mrs. Ayre stopped smiling. Peter Reilly got up from the counsel table and moved behind the screen, where he could not see. The judge looked at the jury, then he looked at the clock. It was not yet five; there was time. He looked back at the jury again, his gaze seeming to linger on the women in the top row.

"I think we're going to wrap it up for the day," Judge Speziale said quietly, and some of the jurors smiled gratefully at him. Even people who went by the book could stretch a point and could give other people a little more time to prepare themselves. There was never a court session on Monday, so the jurors had a few more days.

"Have a good weekend," Judge Speziale said to them and to the courtroom in general, and quickly left the room.

The next day, Peter Reilly celebrated his nineteenth birthday. Beverly King baked him a cake and drove over to the Madows with it. She didn't completely understand the judge's order about "extrajudicial statements," but she was frightened by it, and she thought if she spoke to Peter she might somehow, someway, get him in trouble, so to be on the safe side she stayed in the car while her children took the cake in to Peter. There were a lot of people inside, the boys playing guitars, and the King children got so interested they stayed a while. They didn't tell anybody their mother was outside, so Beverly sat in the Madows' driveway for forty minutes. In the evening, the Madows and the Dickinsons took Peter out to dinner at the Blackberry River Inn.

Roger Cohn telephoned. "Did Peter have a happy birthday?" he asked Marion. "I'm not allowed to say," Marion told Roger, laughing a little, though she didn't mean it entirely as a joke.

"This is the face of the victim," Dr. Izumi said in a detached, professional way, as Sergeant Chapman had done. It was Tuesday, March 5. The jurors were in their box, and even though the spectators couldn't see the screen, the gallery was packed, with only a few scattered single seats empty here and there. Most of the secretaries and sheriffs were back.

Dr. Izumi took the wooden pointer Mr. Bianchi offered him and stepped up very close to the screen. "This is the lesion in the neck . . . this is more a front view, a remnant of skin." He pointed out what he termed "a defense wound," the hole in Barbara's hand. "This is a laceration or deep cut which penetrates through the palm of the hand, the exit point being the back of the hand," he said, very much as though he were giving a medical lesson. Several times he referred to "the patient."

Judge Speziale interrupted. "The two hands on either side of the screen, whose are those?" he asked.

"These are mine," Dr. Izumi said.

- "This is another view of the right hand, the same defense wound, with probe, to show the deep penetration," Dr. Izumi continued, and the slides clicked past. "This is the right elbow . . . this is a close-up view of a cut wound located in the left lower abdomen." Juror William Jennings puffed out his cheeks and blew out a breath, like a long, deep sigh.

Slide 10 was upside down, but nobody laughed or even smiled. Slide 11,. Dr. Izumi said, showed "in the region of the genital organs, outside of the vagina, a laceration here." Edward Ives glanced at Mrs. Wald, sitting beside him in the first row of the jury box. Sarah Waldron's face puckered slightly.

"This area depicts, from here to here, the deep pelvis." Dr. Izumi's pointer swung across the screen. "Inside the pelvis is the skin, and the soft tissues are open. These areas are shown to indicate the absence of the female genital organs because approximately one year before, these were removed, leaving an empty pelvis, but there are metallic sutures which remain after the operation." Slide 16 showed "external genitalia in the region of the vaginal opening where there are tears or lacerations in what is identified as the vestibule, that is, the opening areas."

Dr. Izumi asked for the next slide, 17. "This represents an inside view of the pelvis in the region where the genital organs had been removed. The purpose here is to demonstrate the penetration and breaking. . . . My finger had access into the pelvic cavity which normally is closed off."

The reporters, having nothing else to watch, watched the judge and the jury, and mostly the women on the jury. Even in the darkness, Mrs. Ayre's eyes looked pained. Of all the women on the jury, she was the closest to Barbara's age. She had a fixed half-smile on her face, a kind of grimace, as though she were commanding her face to stay in that position.

The last slide showed the neck again, "the voice box in the region of the deep cut wounds in the neck. The purpose here is to show that one of the bones in the left side of the neck has been either fractured or cut."

Altogether the slide showing took twenty-seven minutes. When the projector stopped whirring and the fluorescent light flashed whitely in the ceiling, Dr. Izumi smiled slightly and handed the pointer to Patsy Alfano. The jurors stared at the doctor as he went back to the witness stand, sat down, and looked at Mr. Bianchi. Mr. Ives looked at Mrs. Wald again, then looked back to the doctor. Gary Lewis, at the end of the row, suddenly turned to Mr. Murdick and gestured abruptly to him. Mr. Murdick obediently went over to the tall window nearest the jury box and opened it wide.

Before Dr. Izumi resumed his testimony, Catherine Roraback stood up and objected, this time in the presence of the jury, to the slides of the vaginal injuries. Her objection was overruled, once again, and Peter Reilly returned to his seat at the table.

Reading from notes he'd brought with him, Dr. Izumi described how he'd been called at home that Friday night, September 28, 1973, at 11:15. He arrived at Barbara's house and waited as long as he could for his boss, Dr. Elliott Gross, the Chief Medical Examiner. But Dr. Gross did not appear, and finally Dr. Izumi felt he should go in. "I didn't wait for Dr. Gross because as a medical examiner, I should go in and pronounce the patient dead," he explained.

"How did you determine that Barbara Gibbons was dead?" Mr. Bianchi asked. "Will you tell the ladies and gentlemen of the jury how you went about that?"

Dr. Izumi told, then, how he'd felt for Barbara's left pulse and had a hard time doing it, the room was so small. The wrist was cold. He said he'd taken off the white cotton blanket the man from the ambulance had used and felt Barbara's stomach. "There was very minimal heat, but the body was still warm."

"What was your determination after checking her life signs?" Mr. Bianchi asked. "Did you form an opinion at that time, doctor?"

"Yes," Dr. Izumi said.

"And what was that opinion?"

"The patient had expired," Dr. Izumi said. He caught himself, and smiled slightly. "The *victim* had expired, and at that time I had pronounced the patient dead."

At the counsel table, Peter Reilly calmly reached out and took a drink of water from his white styrofoam cup.

Dr. Izumi went on to describe the scene in general. He mentioned the coins and the ironed shirts on hangers on the curtain rods, Barbara's wet jeans and underpants. He said the rug was not wet.

Miss Roraback brought up the spurting of the blood.

"Would the person who inflicted those wounds have blood on him or her?" she asked.

"Not necessarily," Dr. Izumi replied. "It would depend on the position of the assailant. If the T-shirt were pushed up in this area, the spurting would be decreased."

When he felt the left pulse, Dr. Izumi said, rigor mortis was not present. "Rigor mortis is a medical term used to describe the stiffness of a body after death," he said, adding that rigor mortis usually set in about four hours after death. "It depends whether the patient is in good health or in a diseased state," the doctor said, and on such factors as the temperature, the time of day, the humidity. But in general, it took about four hours.

Then Dr. Izumi talked of livor mortis, which he explained as "the redness, the lividity, the color." "The blood will drain to these parts, with gravity," he said. "In a patient lying on her back, the blood would drain and leave the front pale."

"Did you at any time on September twenty-eight or twenty-nine observe livor mortis on the body of Barbara Gibbons?" John Bianchi asked.

"No, sir," the doctor said.

John Bianchi asked him to explain further.

"This is because of the deep penetrating wounds cutting the major vessels in the neck," the doctor said. "These are the main vessels that carry the blood from the heart to the brain. When these are cut, the blood, instead of being pumped to the head and to the brain, is pumped out, so there would be no redness."

John Bianchi looked thoughtful.

"Is it fair to say that livor mortis does not appear in a body that has lost all the blood that is normally in a human body?" he asked.

"Yes, sir, that is correct," Dr. Izumi said.

"How much blood does the human body contain?"

"In an average-size male, five quarts," said Dr. Izumi promptly, obviously prepared for the question. "In an average-size female, four quarts, approximately." He said that at five feet two, weighing 115 pounds, Barbara Gibbons could be considered average.

John Bianchi then asked how long it would take the heart to pump out four quarts of blood onto the floor.

Dr. Izumi looked at his notes. "They teach this in school: that a heart will pump five quarts of blood in sixty seconds. In one minute, that five quarts of blood can be pumped up."

Mr. Bianchi looked very serious.

"It would be less than a minute before all of the blood, or the majority of the blood, was pumped out of her body?"

"Yes," Dr. Izumi said.

"When that happens, Dr. Izumi, is the person dead?"

"No, sir," the doctor said.

John Bianchi did not look surprised. "Would you explain that?" he asked solemnly.

Dr. Izumi looked at his notes again and explained that there was a short period, four to six minutes, during which mouth-to-mouth resuscitation and cardiac resuscitation might be successfully applied, which is why medical people and ambulance drivers studied those techniques. After that period, though, biological death, real death, would occur. "If blood does not get to that brain within five to six minutes, this patient has died, biologically," the doctor said.

"Referring back to the body of Barbara Gibbons," the prosecutor said, "with the cuts that you saw around her throat, and the arteries you know were severed, and the blood that you observed on the floor, would you testify that for a person that size, blood would be pumped out of the body in less than six minutes? How long after receiving such lacerations would be the limit of her actual life?"

"Six minutes," Dr. Izumi said.

"One thing that was most important to us," he went on, "was that the gaping abdominal wound which revealed the yellow underlying fat had not oozed any blood out."

"Did that indicate anything to you?" Mr. Bianchi asked.

"Yes," said the doctor. "It meant that with those wounds, with very little blood, if any, it meant that the major incisions in the neck had been completely exsanguinated on the blood in the region of the neck."

"With that in mind," Mr. Bianchi continued, "do you have an opinion as to whether those other miscellaneous cuts, when they were inflicted, Doctor?"

"Yes," said Dr. Izumi. "It does mean that these wounds were inflicted after the patient had died."

At a recess, Marian Battistoni chatted with a neighbor. "I didn't know she was cut up so much," Marian said. Farn Dupre said she felt a little better, knowing Barbara had already been dead when most of the cutting was done. But I remembered what Mickey had said, as he recalled his own thoughts that night, when he walked into the house and saw Barbara dead on the floor. "She was hurtin' when she died," Mickey said.

Dr. Izumi's testimony lasted several days—long, wearying days that seemed to merge into one another in a murky, gray blur. Long recesses, often with the jury out, while the lawyers debated the law, dragged on too. Sheriff Battistoni never needed to bring out the smelling salts; the jurors had their own ways of coping. Mr. Collins usually took one quick look at the screen, whenever a slide came on, then looked down, not looking up again until the next picture was announced. The jurors looked numb, or just drained, most of the time. Sometimes one or the other would smile quickly, nervously, but nobody cried, although once Raymond Lind put his arm around Helen Ayre as they left the jury box.

The first days of March dragged on, too. The days were wet and windy. More than once, clinical and biological death was discussed. "Clinical death is described as how an individual or a doctor sees that patient," Dr. Izumi explained again. "In a period of one minute to five minutes there may be no pulse. It is during that time that the patient has no heartbeat. He appears dead, but he is really not, because it's only the clinical judgment of the observer during this time. It is during the zero to five minutes, when no oxygen is gotten to that brain, that death occurs, because there is cellular and tissue death. The patient is biologically dead at the end of five minutes."

John Bianchi looked thoughtful.

"So if a layman observed the body during this zero to five minute period, he might think the patient was dead?" he asked.

"Yes," the doctor said.

They discussed the rest of that night in the little house on Route 63, how they'd put plastic bags around Barbara's hands and rolled her in a sheet, to take her to Sharon Hospital.

"When did you next see that body?" Mr. Bianchi asked.

"At nine-thirty A.M.," Dr. Izumi said, "in the Sharon Hospital morgue, for the autospy."

Mr. Bianchi coughed slightly. "At this time, may we have the slides?" he asked.

There was another stir in the courtroom. "Oh my God," murmured Farn Dupre, to no one in particular. "Oh my God."

So the slides came again, seeming more horrible, somehow, than the first showing.

"What caused breakage of the nose?" Mr. Bianchi asked.

"This is a direct traumatic blow, most likely to occur prior to death because at this time blood was being pumped up to the head, brain, and face. Blood oozes out of the nostrils, as seen here, indicating that this had been done prior to death."

The first showing had been speedy, just twenty-seven minutes, but this time each gruesome slide was examined and discussed with agonizing slowness. Dr. Izumi asked for the next one, 2.

He described "a very deep wound to the left side of the neck here, extending across the midline of the neck, here where the voice box is, and extending beyond the midline to almost the right lower earlobe.

This is a gaping wound," the doctor said. "In the midline there is the larynx, or the voice box. The deep center wound was brought across the voice box someplace in this vicinity completely separating and opening the voice box so that the vocal cords could be exposed and closely seen."

"Are they visible in the slide, Doctor?" John Bianchi asked.

"Yes, they are," the doctor said, but to the spectators watching the jury, the answer was unnecessary. Helen Ayre grimaced at the screen, and Raymond Lind's eyes seem to have sunk deep into his head, as he watched.

"With such cuts, could a person speak before death?" Mr. Bianchi asked.

"No, sir," the doctor said softly but emphatically. "This victim could neither speak nor scream. There is no mouth, because these openings communicate directly with the outside."

Dr. Izumi talked about Barbara's hand then, and how he'd opened it so Sergeant Chapman could photograph the defense wound. "As a forensic pathologist, it's your experience that a wound such as that is incurred in defending oneself from an attacker?" "Yes, sir," Izumi said. Later, at the autopsy, when he took the bags off Barbara's hands, Dr. Izumi found, mixed with the dried clotted blood, four to six hairs. He picked them off her hand with forceps and put them in containers, which were sealed and witnessed.

There was the slight bruise on the right elbow, where Barbara must have raised her arm to ward off whatever blow she saw coming, and the deep wound in the abdomen, "one inch in length and gaping half an inch or more. It shows the underlying fat and the so-called soft tissue. This shows no oozing or clotted blood present. This occurred *after* death."

Dr. Izumi said her thighs had been broken after she died, too. He had cut into the leg and gone to the bone. "As I cut in and inserted my finger and brought out pieces of bone, there was absolutely no blood," he explained.

"If the broken legs had occurred before death, you would have found a large amount of blood?" Mr. Bianchi asked.

"Yes," Dr. Izumi said.

"And you did not find it?"

"I did not find it."

"Do you have an opinion as to how those legs could have been broken?"

"No, sir, I do not," Dr. Izumi said. "Except that we try, as pathologists, to reproduce a fracture, and it would take a large amount of force. A great deal of force."

There was a whisper, audible, in the courtroom, and Mr. Murdick, one of the sheriffs, whirled around. It was Marian Battistoni, but he frowned slightly at her anyway and put a finger to his lips.

"Can you tell me what you mean by a great deal of force?" Miss Roraback asked, when she cross-examined. "Are you referring to a swinging hit or a large object?"

"In the region of the head, this is a tremendous blow, the force of the blow being an object; I would say a soft object," Dr. Izumi said.

"Like a person's fist?"

"Yes ma'am."

"What caused the fracture of the legs?" she asked.

"A very forceful blow."

"Was there one blow or separate blows?"

"I don't know," he told her.

"It was a pretty powerful blow that broke those legs, wasn't it?" she asked.

"Yes," the doctor said.

"Could it have been caused by someone jumping on those legs?" the prosecutor asked.

"Yes, sir, it could," the doctor said, and even Gary Lewis looked shocked. Edward Ives took off his glasses and nibbled at one end thoughtfully.

There was the abdominal cut again, two to three inches long, one to two inches wide. Paul Travaglin rubbed the side of his head with the palm of his hand as he looked at the screen. Dr. Izumi said it would take some force to cause such a large tear, and that because there was no free or clotted blood around, he felt that that wound, too, had occurred after death.

There were the cut marks on the back, with no discoloration, also "produced after the victim was dead," and then the disputed slides again.

"Once more we are inside the body cavities," Dr. Izumi said. "Below and just to the right of the hysterectomy clips is a tear or cut wound. This is inside the pelvic cavity." He didn't speak with relish, exactly, but with interest and muted enthusiasm, as though he were onto an interesting case and wanted to be sure the class got the benefit of it.

"This is a one-and-a-half- to two-inch tear," he said. "No liquid or clotted blood, therefore, this occurred after death.

"This is the opening of the vaginal canal on the outside. This depicts cuts. These are a little deeper, a little further in. . . . This represents the inner portion here, within the pelvic cavity." He said he had found no male sperm present.

Finally, 0-19, the neck organs hanging outside, completely removed from Barbara's body.

"You testified that she could not talk or scream immediately after the neck cuts," Mr. Bianchi reminded him. "I would ask whether, during that period of time, would there be any indication of her breathing or gasping or any such activity as that?"

Dr. Izumi spoke carefully. "At the time the windpipe is cut, the air now comes out from these openings. The mouth plays no part in breathing at all. The victim would continue to breathe until the time of death. It would be labored or forced breathing."

"Would it continue to the time of biological death, Doctor?" Mr. Bianchi asked.

"Yes, sir, it would," Dr. Izumi said.

"Four to six minutes after this cutting, before the person was biologically dead?"

"Yes, sir."

"So there would be, during that span, some evidence of breathing, Doctor?"

"Yes, sir," Dr. Izumi said.

"You said that the biological death is the very, very end?" John Bianchi asked.

"That's correct," the doctor said. "Clinical death occurs from one to five minutes before biological death."

"Could a layman distinguish between clinical and biological death?" Mr. Bianchi asked. The doctor said yes, a layman could.

"So that this breathing, in a labored or gasping manner, could last from zero to four to six minutes?"

"Yes, sir," the doctor said.

The autopsy had lasted more than six hours, ending at 3:45 Saturday afternoon, while Peter Reilly was in the lie box at Hartford. Dr. Izumi's autopsy report became State's Exhibit Q, which John Bianchi read to the jury now, rocking a little on his heels, back and forth.

Most of the information was already known from the testimony, but there were odds and ends: Barbara's ulcer was 0.5 cm in diameter. Her liver was firm, yellow-brown, with extensive fatty degeneration and fibrosis. Her abdominal fat was one inch thick; several ribs were broken, too. In her stomach there were pieces of corn and small bits of meat from the TV dinner she was eating when Geoff and Peter left for the Teen Center meeting. The soles of both her feet were callused, with embedded dirt. She wore a denture plate.

But after all the testimony, one horror piled on another, what it came down to, simply, was that Barbara was dead because her throat had been cut, and then she had been mutilated and violated in the most hideous way. Was it any wonder that Helen Ayre slept badly? As Mr. Bianchi had pointed out, this information was "not desirable." Murder never was.

11

"I saw the jurors looking at my hands when Dr. Izumi talked about a great deal of force," Peter said. He sounded very calm as he said it, sitting at the table in the Madows' dinette. The late winter morning sunlight splashed through the small squares of windowpane and onto the oval cloth, as Peter read aloud from the morning paper. George Judson's article dealt with Dr. Izumi's testimony, so it was not pleasant reading, but Peter read it through, anyway, including a phrase about Barbara's "battered, bloody body."

Nanny sat on the high stool by the phone, where she had a good view out the dinette window, watching Peter. She looked worried, and after a moment, she spoke.

'You smoke too much, Peter," she said.

"Now that's funny," Peter said, almost absentmindedly, still looking at the paper, then he seemed to have caught what Nan said. "In jail I was smoking two and a half packs a day," he said, without looking up. "Now I'm down to a pack a day."

He put the paper down on the dining-room table, got up, and walked back into the den to watch TV. He was no longer calm but appeared restless, at loose ends this Friday, as he was on most Fridays, when there was rarely a criminal court session, and he had to stay around the house. Mickey and Marion had explained it was for his own good, and Peter not only accepted the restriction but said he agreed with it. Still, it left him with a lot of time on his hands, and on the days when there was no court, usually Mondays and Fridays, he sometimes stayed in bed much of the day, as he had done in jail.

Peter wandered out of the den again. "I've thought about doing professional car painting," he said. "There's gobs of money in it. I've sent away for a paint book. I might like to study law, but that seems kind of farfetched." Marion's sister was sending up from New York some information on getting a high school diploma at home, which Peter thought might help him make money. Perhaps because he had been dependent on so many people for so long, he didn't seem to want to have to depend on anybody else now. I remembered what he had written to me, from Litchfield jail: "My goal in life now is to become very welthy [sic] on my own."

A fat sparrow waddled across the yard now, in front of the dinette window. "Down where we used to live we used to get grosbeaks," Peter said suddenly. "Sometimes a purple finch. My mom was a fanatic about birds." He talked about jobs some more, and about jail, in his soft, rambling way. "All the cons took a liking to me," Peter said in a reminiscent tone. "One dude took me aside and said, 'It's a real compliment to you, what those people are doing for you.'"

Those people, the members of the Peter Reilly Defense Committee, had met regularly every week, going on six months now. Besides the original members, other people from Canaan now came regularly, including the other Madows, Dot and Murray, and Dick and Elaine Monty, whose son Matt was in the same class with Gina Beligni and Michael Mulhern. Only one member, Judy Liner, came from Litchfield. Except for a few people who dropped in to court some days, the citizens of Litchfield generally ignored the murder trial in their midst. Even the weekly paper generally ignored it, until the last week, when it ran a picture of the courthouse. But Litchfield had always held itself aloof. Two hundred years before the Reilly affair, a new settler in town, a Mrs. Davies, complained to a friend back in England, "There is nothing to associate with but Presbyterians and wolves."

The knife glinted through the plastic bag, tied with a green plastic twist tie. It lay on the prosecution table, along with the piles of books

210

and papers. Everybody in the courtroom gazed at it as John Bianchi picked it up casually and strolled over to the witness stand.

"I show you a knife with a wooden handle and ask if you can identify that," he asked Trooper Venclauscas, who nodded slightly.

"Yes, sir, I can."

"How can you identify it?" the prosecutor asked.

"This is a knife that I took into possession at the Gibbons home on September twenty-ninth," the policeman said. He was calm on the stand; as a trooper for eight years and member of the police crime lab at Bethany, he was at home in courtrooms, especially this one. He said he had put his initials on the knife, when he found it in a brown pouch on the side of a cabinet, around four in the morning, after Barbara died. There were two other knives in the pouch, but Trooper Venclauscas had taken this one, because it had blood on the blade. The blood had not been typed or identified, but it was human blood. The tip of the knife was broken off.

John Bianchi smiled slightly and walked across the courtroom to the defense table. "I have no more questions, your honor," he said, and handed it to Catherine Roraback. She studied it for a moment, and Peter looked at it too, his long hair falling over his right eye, shielding his face from the spectators. Then she walked over to the witness stand.

"At that time did you have a search warrant?" she asked.

"No, I did not," Trooper Venclauscas said. Miss Roraback turned to the judge. "This knife was seized during the course of a warrantless search," she said. "I submit that anything seized without a warrant is improperly seized." She objected to the knife being introduced, citing the Fourth Amendment, which provides for search by warrant. "It also includes the word 'unreasonable,' Miss Roraback," the judge reminded her.

"That's right, your honor," John Bianchi said quickly.

Catherine Roraback looked stubborn. "What the state police did is just go into that house with numerous people and rummage through the house, in flagrant violation of the United States Constitution and the constitution of the state of Connecticut," she said.

"Is this the first time you've seen the knife?" the judge asked her.

"Yes, your honor," Miss Roraback told him. Judge Speziale looked thoughtful. When John Bianchi's assistant, Corporal James Bausch, had brought the knife into the courtroom, and Mr. Bianchi had asked to introduce a new witness who would testify about a knife, Miss Roraback had asked whether the state considered the knife to be the murder weapon. "I don't know really how to answer that, your honor," Mr. Bianchi had replied cheerfully. "Whether it was actually the weapon that caused death—I don't think I could show that. But I can show through Dr. Izumi that this instrument will coincide with some of the markings on the body."

Judge Speziale said he would not rule on the matter just then. "I'll go back to it at some later date, your honor," John Bianchi said, and the jury was called out. During the long arguments as to whether something might or might not be introduced as evidence in court—a knife, a tape recording, whatever—the jury was kept out until the matter was decided. It was the right thing to do, the legal thing, but the recesses seemed to get longer and longer; this one had lasted an hour and fifteen minutes, and after a while, it got on the jurors' nerves.

Mine, too. This was my first criminal trial, and I needed a guidebook. What were the rules of evidence? What was hearsay? Could you introduce something and call it the murder weapon, *maybe?* Why couldn't you ask a leading question? Why was it all so complicated? As Jean Beligni said, "Why don't they just let you get up there and tell your story?"

Of all the lawbooks I consulted, only one really made some sense to me—*The Nature of the Judicial Process* by former Supreme Court Justice Benjamin Cardozo. "We like to picture to ourselves the field of the law as accurately mapped and plotted," he wrote. "We draw our little lines, and they are hardly down before we blur them." I understood him especially well when he talked about an element of chance. "Someone must be the loser," he wrote. "It is part of the game of life."

After Dr. Izumi's testimony, the parade of police officers resumed, as the state of Connecticut pressed its case against Peter Reilly.

I knew some of them by sight, and I'd talked with Lieutenant Shay and with Sergeant Kelly at the pretrial hearing. When the first piece came out in *New Times,* I'd sent them, and Jim Mulhern, a copy of the magazine. When my second piece appeared, the trial was already under way, so I didn't mail it. Instead, I just knocked at the door of the prosecutor's office and when Lieutenant Shay opened the door, I gave him a copy. He seemed friendly. But Sergeant Kelly turned away when he saw me in court. When I went next door to Marden's for coffee, Jim Mulhern was sitting on a stool at the counter. When I came up to the counter to order coffee to go, he swung his stool around, away from me, an unmistakable message.

The pictures my husband had taken for the second piece had turned out brilliantly. Jim Mulhern, looking proud and a little pugnacious, a good-looking Irish cop in full uniform, standing at his desk. Lieutenant Shay, rugged and handsome, working at his desk. John Bianchi in his office on Railroad Street, gazing thoughtfully out the window. Peter in handcuffs, coming out the jailhouse door. Later, in his darkroom, Jim made prints for everybody. I stopped by Mr. Bianchi's office one day and gave him his pictures, then I went by the barracks. Anne went with me for protection. When I said who I was, the officer at the desk, whom I'd never seen, looked furiously at me. He said that Lieutenant Shay and Trooper Mulhern weren't in and wouldn't be in. But another trooper smiled at Anne and even, a little weakly, at me. I had heard that there was some controversy among the police at the barracks, and among other segments of the Connecticut State Police, about the handling of the Reilly case. Apparently not all the policemen agreed that what had been done was what should have been done. I remembered that on the Saturday after Barbara died Sergeant Salley had told Mickey that Peter didn't need a lawyer then. But another trooper had told June, "It wouldn't be a bad idea." Several weeks after Barbara died, Mrs. Rose Ford, one of Peter's elementary school teachers, had written a letter to the *Lakeville Journal,* deploring the actions of the police, especially the "wall of silence" she said they had maintained since the beginning. "Somewhere between the terse 'no comment' and premature, irresponsible statements lies an area of suitable communication between the police and the public," she wrote. I agreed. I never understood why it had to be Them against Us.

When I was told at the barracks that nobody was in, I could have left the pictures, but I really wanted to see Lieutenant Shay and Trooper Mulhern again. I would have liked to talk with them. I know they wouldn't have discussed the case, but we could have talked about the law, and the system. We could have talked about Cardozo.

Sergeant Salley was on the stand again, the supervisor who'd first taken Peter away, the night Barbara died, to the barracks. Around 5:30 or 6:00 in the morning, Salley had got a call from Lieutenant Shay, still out at the murder house, telling him to read Peter Reilly his constitutional rights.

"Did you at any time tell Peter Reilly his mother was dead?" Catherine Roraback asked, in a very soft voice.

"I don't remember if I did or not," Sergeant Salley said. Miss Roraback asked him whether any other policeman had told him, and Sergeant Salley seemed to shake his head slightly. "I thought he understood," the policeman said.

At the defense table, Peter jotted down something on a pad of yellow legal-size paper. Catherine Roraback walked to the table, looked at the pad, then walked slowly, almost casually, back to the stand.

"Did he ask you to go to Mr. Madow's?" she asked.

"Yes," Sergeant Salley said. "I told him Lieutenant Shay wanted to speak to him before he went."

The civil rights card that Sergeant Salley had read to Peter used the phrase, "the offenses charged against you." But when Peter had asked Sergeant Salley if he was being charged, the policeman said he was not. In court now, Salley told Catherine Roraback that the phrase on the card was irrelevant.

Catherine Roraback looked at the card again, then at the trooper.

"You didn't volunteer any explanation?"

"No, I did not," Sergeant Salley said.

Mr. Bianchi leaned casually against the jury rail.

"Did you know this fella, Mr. Madow, at all?" he asked Salley.

"No, I did not," the policeman said.

"Other than the fact that he was connected with the Canaan ambulance corps, you didn't know what he did for a living or where he lived, did you?"

"No, I did not," Sergeant Salley replied. He went on to say that he had heard some conversations between Peter and Geoff Madow.

"Was it a tearful conversation?" Mr. Bianchi asked.

"No, it was not," Sergeant Salley said.

Peter usually had a grinder at Marden's for lunch, eating with whoever had brought him to court that day. Usually I had lunch with the rest of the press at Mitchell's, a restaurant down the street from the

214

courthouse. We had a good time together, trading gossip and opinions. There were black jokes passed around the table too, for that was one way to survive certain things. Farn Dupre said that when the AP wire carried Dr. Izumi's testimony, that Barbara might have been hit in the face with a fist, there'd been a typo in the copy, so that the doctor was quoted as saying that Barbara "could have been hit with a fish." At the *Winsted Citizen,* then, one of the reporters had set up a dummy headline that warned, "Killer Mackerel at Large."

Lieutenant Shay testified that when he'd arrived at the barracks, early that Saturday morning, he had advised Peter of his rights too, before Peter signed the waiver. "It is my custom to have a suspect sign two forms," Lieutenant Shay said, and Paula Wall, the law clerk's wife, sitting just behind the reporters, stirred restlessly. "A suspect," she murmured.

"WARNING" began the rights card Lieutenant Shay had read to Peter. "You have a right to remain silent. If you talk to any police officer, anything you say can and will be used against you in court. . . . You have the right to consult a lawyer before questioning and may have him with you during questioning." The waiver section read, "I do not want a lawyer. I know and understand what I am doing. I do this freely. No threats or promises have been made to me." It was signed Peter A. Reilly.

Sergeant Salley had not looked at the jury when he testified, but Lieutenant Shay looked directly at them, gruff but honest, the sort of person you could trust. On the stand, although Mr. Bianchi referred to Peter as "the accused" or, simply and coldly, "Reilly," Lieutenant Shay always called him "Peter."

"Did he at any time cry?" Mr. Bianchi asked the lieutenant.

"No, he did not," the officer said. "I was struck by the fact that he was very calm, very poised, and showed no emotion."

Lieutenant Shay had taken Peter to another room then, to talk with him privately. That was the talk that had lasted an hour or so, in a back room at the barracks. A quiet room, a quiet talk. That was the talk that had been recorded, and that was the talk that was too garbled, on the tape, for anyone to understand.

Now, on the stand, Lieutenant Shay told how Peter had gone to Hartford with Jim Mulhern. He mentioned a "conversation" with another police officer in Hartford. "Conversation" was the term that had to be used in the presence of the jury, at least for the time being, for the lie detector test.

Catherine Roraback again objected to Peter's statement as evidence, describing how he had found himself in a "coercive situation." She mentioned "prolonged interrogation, isolated from friends and relatives." Mr. Bianchi reminded the court that Peter Reilly had been given his rights four times and that Judge Armentano had reviewed "every bit of evidence regarding the interrogation." Mr. Bianchi looked at Judge Speziale now. "I don't know if your honor has had a chance to review the document," he began. The judge replied crisply. "I've got it right in my hands," he said.

Mr. Bianchi went on to quote from Judge Armentano's decision, though, as though Judge Speziale had never heard it. "He said it was freely given by an alert, knowledgeable young man, and he found no coercion, your honor," Mr. Bianchi said. The judge decided to confer with both lawyers in the back room and said he'd take a recess.

Joe Battistoni hit the gavel. "There'll be a short recess," he announced, and the judge smiled, ever so slightly. "I didn't say 'short,' sheriff," he said.

"What things did he tell you in Hartford that he had not told you before?" Mr. Bianchi asked Lieutenant Shay now, in an almost conversational tone. Shay said he remembered Peter saying he'd seen his mother in the top bunk and doing what Peter called "a double take." Then he said he'd seen his mother on the floor, with blood all around.

"He told me that he recalled picking up a straight razor and that he slashed his mother's throat," Lieutenant Shay said. "He told me that he remembered jumping on his mother's stomach, and he told me he may have washed his mother down."

The jury stared at Lieutenant Shay, seeming almost transfixed. Edward Ives leaned forward on his chair, the first seat of the second row, very close to the witness.

Lieutenant Shay said that Peter, during the Saturday night in Hartford, had looked "normal, calm, very poised." The evening session had followed the lie detector test, and during the course of the evening, Jim Mulhern had taken Peter's confession, which Peter then signed. Lieutenant Shay said he himself had been in the room at the beginning of the session. "Some of it came out with very little questioning," he said. "Some of it came out as a result of questions that I asked."

Catherine Roraback asked Lieutenant Shay what he meant by "normal," since he had never seen or spoken with Peter Reilly before the night Barbara died.

"What I meant by normal," said Lieutenant Shay, "was that I expected to find something different."

"Do you remember him saying, 'The blood scared the hell out of me'?" Miss Roraback asked.

"No, I don't," Lieutenant Shay said.

"Do you remember asking him, 'Why did you need an ambulance?'"

"No, I don't."

"Do you remember him saying, 'It looks like I did it'?"

"I think he did say that, yes."

"Do you remember his referring to a 'double take'?"

"He said that frequently," Lieutenant Shay said. "As a matter of fact, I think he used that term at six-thirty in the morning back at Canaan."

"Do you remember him saying, 'My mind went blank?' " Catherine Roraback asked.

"Yes, I remember him saying that a couple of times," Shay said.

"Isn't it true," Catherine Roraback asked, "that you suggested that Mr. Reilly needed some psychological help?"

"Yes, I did," Shay said.

"Did you tell him you'd try to help him get it?"

"Yes, I did," Shay said. "He said he needed somebody he could trust, somebody he could turn to. He said he didn't mean a lawyer; he needed somebody like a father."

"And then he began talking to you, is that right?" Catherine Roraback asked, her voice dark with irony. Lieutenant Shay looked her straight in the eye.

"Yes, ma'am," he said.

Bit by bit, line by line, Catherine Roraback was trying to draw out the dialogue in Hartford and to establish the atmosphere of that Saturday night, which seemed so long ago. Like the polygraph session, the evening questioning, which resulted in the signed confession, had been taped too, but Miss Roraback was not sure the jury would ever be allowed to hear those tapes, so she was trying to recreate the questioning now. Besides, even if the tapes could later be heard, there was a benefit, she felt, in having Lieutenant Shay say these things himself, things he remembered saying and things Peter had said to him.

I had not yet heard the evening tapes either. As this questioning emerged piecemeal in the course of a few days testimony, I was struck by the variety of its style and tone. At first, just after Sergeant Kelly brought Peter out of the polygraph room into the room across the hall, the talk was almost matter of fact. "One of the first things he said to me," Lieutenant Shay recalled, "was that he now was aware that he did do this thing that happened to his mother."

But when the questioning turned to details of the killing—the knife, the razor, the reason—the tone changed. Peter either said he wasn't sure, or else he would say he was sure and then change his mind and say he wasn't sure, and finally Lieutenant Shay had told Peter impatiently, warningly, "There are many things we can do to make this a difficult process for you." Sometimes the questioning was even briefly funny. When Peter asked for details on how Barbara had been killed and Lieutenant Shay declined to give them, Peter had pleaded, "Give me a hint."

Lieutenant Shay testified that he knew the autopsy details by the time he questioned Peter that Saturday night. He said he knew that Barbara's legs had been broken, and her stomach cut, and her throat slashed, and that there was a defense wound in her hand. He said he himself had brought up the legs and the stomach, when he talked with Peter, but that Peter himself had told Shay about the slashing of his mother's throat.

Once, in the course of the questioning, when Peter kept veering back and forth, especially as he continued to refer to "a double take," Lieutenant Shay had yelled at him, accusing him of playing "head-games" with the police and telling him the police had "proof positive" that Peter had done it. By that time, of course, fatigue was surely setting in. When Miss Roraback talked about the double take and about Peter's blanking-out, she asked Lieutenant Shay whether he thought Peter was tired. "I imagine he was," Lieutenant Shay said. "I know I was exhausted."

But then the mood had softened, and they had talked, Lieutenant Shay testified, "about life and death and God and so forth." They talked again of trust.

"Do you remember him saying, 'I've gotta trust someone'?" Catherine Roraback asked Shay.

"Yes, ma'am," he said.

"And do you remember a conversation after that about your family?" she asked.

"Yes, ma'am," he said.

"Did he at that point break down and begin to cry?" she asked.

"There was one point where his voice did falter," Lieutenant Shay said. "There was one point where we were talking about his life and his problems. I was trying to encourage him to cry."

"You said, 'Go ahead and cry'?" Catherine Roraback asked, disdain in her voice.

"Yes, ma'am," Shay said.

"Do you remember saying, 'I don't feel sorry for your mother, I feel sorry for you, because I think you've been a victim for years'?"

"Yes, ma'am," Shay said.

"Do you remember Peter then asking you where you lived?"

"He did ask me where I lived, yes."

When Miss Roraback asked Lieutenant Shay whether he'd had training in interrogation and who gave him that training, John Bianchi objected, but he was overruled.

"I've had the standard training at the police academy," Lieutenant Shay said, adding that he'd also attended a course given by Mr. Fred Inbau at the University of Maryland, a course that dealt with interrogation. "How do you spell that?" the judge asked, and there was a pause while he wrote it down.

"One of Mr. Inbau's principles is that you should establish trust with the person, is that right?" Catherine Roraback asked him.

"Yes, ma'am," he said.

Catherine Roraback leaned against the jury rail and studied the ceiling with infinite care.

"You should tend to get that individual to rely on you, is that right?"

"Yes, ma'am," he said. She flicked her eyes from the ceiling and stared at him.

"And that's what you did here, is that right?" she asked coldly. "You attempted to create yourself as a father figure, did you not?"

"That did cross my mind, yes," Lieutenant Shay said.

Except for the one outburst, Lieutenant Shay had apparently not yelled at Peter anymore, and, indeed, his part of the questioning seemed to have ended on a warm note. One of the last things Peter said to Lieutenant Shay, before the officer left the room and Jim Mulhern came in to finish taking down the confession, was to ask whether when they were finished, he could come to live with the Shay family, if they had room.

The weather was raw and cold, and when court convened at ten o'clock Tuesday morning, March 12, with the familiar clump of the gavel, Peter Reilly wasn't there. There was a brief buzz in the court-room, which subsided the minute Judge Speziale appeared, making the short sweeping turn around the corner into the courtroom. John Bianchi glanced at Catherine Roraback as she asked permission to approach the bench.

Miss Roraback handed the judge a note, signed by Dr. Roger Moore of Sharon, saying that Peter was sick and couldn't come to court. He had a high fever and had to stay in bed, because he had strep throat. The judge read the note, then said, for the record, that the trial would be postponed because the defendant could not be present. Mr. Bianchi rose. "The State would like to think about it just a bit," he said. The judge looked at him, then called a recess.

"Maybe they want to send out for a get-well card," Greg said, but George shook his head. "They're trying to arrange to have their own doctor look at Peter. Dr. Izumi." Charles Kochakian leaned over the rail and beckoned to Catherine Roraback, who came over to the group a little warily. "Is it over for the day?" Charles asked. "Is it safe to go back to Hartford?"

Miss Roraback grinned. "It's *never* safe to go back to Hartford," she said.

The knife was still in its plastic pouch, the jury still safe behind closed doors, as John Bianchi tried again, a week later when Peter Reilly was well and the trial was resumed, to get the knife introduced as evidence.

"I show you a knife," he said again, taking it out of the bag and handing it to Trooper Venclauscas on the stand. Again the trooper identified it by his initials. When Mr. Bianchi asked him to describe it, he said it was what he would call "a fish fillet knife, with a broken-off tip, with a six-inch blade and a four-inch handle."

Catherine Roraback brought up the Constitution again and talked of illegal search and seizure, but John Bianchi was well prepared. "The Fourth Amendment protects people, not places," he declared, and after some dialogue, Judge Speziale said the objection was overruled. The jury would be allowed to hear about the knife, and as they filed out of their room and took their places, they looked at it with interest.

Mr. Bianchi handed the knife to juror William Jennings, in the first seat of the first row, by the witness stand. Jennings took it gingerly, looked at it, and passed it down the row. When all the jurors had seen it, and the alternates had passed it to one another, the knife was introduced as evidence and given the suitably dramatic number of State's Exhibit X.

Miss Roraback only asked Trooper Venclauscas, then, whether he'd found the broken-off tip. He said he hadn't.

State Trooper James Mulhern took the stand and gave his address as Troop B, Canaan. According to the usual ritual, each witness was asked to point out the defendant in the courtroom, so that the identification could be on the record, and when Jim Mulhern was asked whether he saw Peter Reilly there now, he nodded slightly toward the defense table and looked at Peter for just a moment, as he had done at the pretrial hearings. Then he looked at Mr. Bianchi again.

Trooper Mulhern said he had been a trooper for six-and-a half years, stationed in Canaan nearly all that time, and that he'd known Peter Reilly for three or four years, calling him "an acquaintance of a mutual friend of ours." The mutual friend was Arthur Madow, and Mulhern remembered that "Peter and Arthur came down to shoot the breeze one evening." He added that another time, Peter and the Madow boys and Paul Beligni had come down to help him break up pieces of concrete in his yard. He told of driving Peter to Hartford early Saturday afternoon, the day after Barbara died. Lieutenant Shay had told Mulhern not to discuss the crime, so Peter and the policeman talked about TV commercials and motorcycles.

"At any time, did he cry?" John Bianchi asked.

"No, sir," Mulhern said. He described how, in between the lie detector test and the evening questioning, he'd brought Peter his dinner: "a ham and cheese sandwich on a roll, a package of chocolate cupcakes, and a can of Coca Cola."

During the polygraph test, Jim Mulhern had sometimes watched through the one-way mirror, but Peter hadn't seen him, so that when the trooper brought Peter his dinner, it was the first time Peter had seen him for about four hours, since they'd arrived in Hartford. Mr. Bianchi asked Jim Mulhern, on the stand, what Peter had said to him then.

"He asked me if I was ashamed to know him now," Mulhern said.

"I didn't hear that," Mr. Bianchi said.

"He asked me if I was ashamed to know him now," Mulhern said again, loudly. "I asked why. He said, 'Because I did it. I killed her.'"

John Bianchi looked quickly at the jury, then back to Jim Mulhern. "I didn't hear that again," he said, and leaning forward he cupped his ear with his right hand.

Mulhern looked at John Bianchi, speaking very loudly. "He said, 'Because I did it. I killed her.'"

John Bianchi walked to his table and came back to the witness stand with papers in his hand. "I show you four pieces of paper," he began, and Mulhern identified them as the statement he'd taken from Peter Reilly on the night of September 29, 1973. Each page was signed. Two of the pages were stapled together, and two were loose.

The statement was admitted as evidence in three parts: State's Exhibits Z, AA, and BB. It sounded complicated, but what it all seemed to mean was rather simple. Peter had confessed in segments, over a span of two hours and fifteen minutes. The first page of the statement was begun, according to the time Jim Mulhern had written in the margin, at 20:30 hours, the last at 22:45.

John Bianchi read the statement to the jury, rocking back and forth on his heels a little, in his familiar way. At first the statement sounded just like the one Peter had given to Trooper McCafferty, in the cruiser. It related how he'd gone to the Teen Center meeting, driven John Sochocki home, and then gone home himself. He got out of the car and went into the house. At that point, though, the Saturday night statement changed. It said:

> I entered the front door of the house and yelled, "Hey, Mom, I'm home!" There was no answer, so I looked to the right, into the bed-room. At first I thought I saw my mother, Barbara Gibbons, on the

top bunk, and then I saw her on the floor. I remember slashing once at my mother's throat with a straight razor I used for model airplanes. This was on the living room table.

I also remember jumping on my mother's legs. I am not sure about washing her off. Next I saw blood on her face and throat and I'm pretty sure on her T-shirt, which was rolled up to the bottom of her breasts . . .

The rest of the statement told how Peter had called the Madows, and Sharon Hospital, and gone outside to wait for somebody to come.

John Bianchi also read the loose pages. One of them read:

I, Peter A. Reilly, voluntarily make this statement to clarify an earlier statement. As I indicated in the previous statement, I slashed my mother's throat with a straight razor. I failed to mention that when I slashed at her with the razor, I swung with my right hand in an arc from right to left and I cut her throat. This is the only thing I wanted to clarify.

And, finally, the last page, timed at 10:45:

There is one statement I want to clarify: When I slashed my mother's throat with a straight razor, I cut her throat. This is all I wanted to clarify.

Now, in the courtroom, Peter Reilly bent his head, his hair falling over his face. The courtroom was very quiet as Catherine Roraback rose. She held one of the papers in her hand and showed it to Trooper Mulhern.

"Was it before or after he signed this page that Peter said to you, 'In the statement, can you say, I'm not sure?'"

"I don't know," Mulhern told her.

"But he did say that to you?" she asked.

"Yes," Mulhern said.

"But you don't remember if he said it before or after he signed?"

"I'd have to make a guess," Mulhern told her, and the judge turned to him. "We don't want you to guess," Judge Speziale said, not smiling as he said it.

Catherine Roraback looked at the pages again, then back to Mulhern.

"Page one started at eight-thirty P.M.," she said. "Is it fair to say that page two might have been started as much as two hours after page one?"

"Yes," Mulhern said.

Catherine Roraback then pointed out that Peter had asked again whether this statement could say he wasn't sure. "Did you tell him it would be included in the statement?" she asked Mulhern.

"I may have," Mulhern said.

"Is it *in* that statement?" she asked loudly.

"No, ma'am," Mulhern said, staring at her.

Catherine Roraback asked Mulhern about his presence in Hartford Saturday night.

"Did Lieutenant Shay suggest that you go in to see Mr. Reilly because you were close to him? Because you knew him best?"

"No, ma'am," Mulhern said.

"Do you remember asking him, 'Did you cut her throat?' "

"I believe so," Mulhern said.

"Do you remember asking him, 'What did you do with the razor?' "

"Yes, ma'am," Mulhern said.

"Did Mr. Reilly ever speak of a knife to you?" she asked.

"No, ma'am," Mulhern said.

She looked hard at him again. "Do you remember Peter saying to you, 'I don't know what to do, Jim. I'm still not positive any of it happened. The only things I am positive about are that she was on the floor, and I called the Madows, and what I had in my original statement.'"

Mulhern looked straight back at her.

"I believe he said something to that effect," the policeman said.

"Do you remember him saying, 'Everything I'm saying, it's like I'm making it up, I'm not sure about it'?"

"I believe so," Mulhern said.

"And this is not in the statement, is it?"

"No, ma'am," Mulhern said.

"Did you tell him his mother's throat had been cut before he told you he cut her throat?" the prosecutor asked.

"I had no knowledge," Mulhern said.

"Did you at this point know that her throat had been cut?"

"No, sir," Mulhern said.

Catherine Roraback seemed to find that hard to believe and tried to ask Mulhern about watching Peter, that afternoon, through the one-way mirror. The state objected, objection sustained, and she shook her head in a little angry movement.

"I'll start again, but I'll come back to that, I guarantee it," she said to the courtroom in general. Sarah Waldron and Margaret Wald smiled at her.

She didn't mention the mirror then, but simply asked the question: "Didn't you hear references during the questioning by Sergeant Kelly, references to the slashing of the throat?"

"I don't recall," Mulhern said.

"Let me show you copies of the report and see if that refreshes your memory," she said, smiling edgily, and handed the trooper a piece of paper, a report he'd written himself. Mulhern read it and handed it back to her.

"I must have heard it, then," he said.

"So you knew that Mrs. Gibbons's throat had been cut, is that correct?" Miss Roraback asked.

"Apparently yes," Mulhern said.

"And you knew at that point that Mr. Reilly had already been questioned about cutting his mother's throat?"

"Apparently yes," Mulhern said.

Mr. Bianchi brought out, in his questioning of Jim Mulhern, that Peter had said the razor was either behind the barn, or behind the gas station across the street, or still in the house. He was right the third time. Trooper Donald Moran later testified that he'd found the razor at 12:45 on Saturday, just about the time Peter and Mulhern were on their way to Hartford. Moran said he found the razor on the top bookshelf in the living room. The razor was closed.

John Bianchi had one more question.

"When you saw Reilly in Trooper McCafferty's cruiser, was he crying?" he asked.

"Not that I remember," Jim Mulhern said.

It was a long afternoon, and some of the jurors looked sleepy as they filed out of their room after the recess. But when the next witness for the state appeared, they suddenly revived. Here was a new face on the stand, a dark, slim man with a thin, almost gaunt look. When he was sworn in, he gave his name as John McAloon and his address as the Bridgeport Correctional Center.

225

"John McAloon, you are presently a prisoner of the state of Connecticut, is that correct?" John Bianchi asked in his most dramatic voice.

"Yes," McAloon said, going on to say that he was in prison for "theft of an automobile," and before that, he'd been in prison in Rhode Island for breaking and entering, and there were other charges he remembered, assault with a dangerous weapon . . . the list went on, going back a dozen years. The jury watched, not quite sure what to make of this witness, until he said that on the morning of September 30, 1973, he'd been an inmate at the Litchfield Correctional Center, when Peter Reilly was brought in.

"I was in cell C," McAloon recalled. "They put him in E. There was one empty cell between us."

"Did you thereafter speak directly to Peter Reilly?" the prosecutor asked.

"Yes, I did," McAloon said. "I asked him what he got busted for. He said, for killing his mother. At first I thought he said grandmother.

"I asked him what happened," McAloon went on. "He said that he had come home Friday night and that his mother was dead. At first he didn't know he did it, but after he was questioned, he realized he did it. He said his mother was drinking a lot and was making him stay home all the time, and that the night it happened he wanted to go out with some friends somewhere and she threatened to take the plates off the car, and that he just went crazy, went berserk, and the next thing he knew he had a knife in his hands and she was on the floor.

"He said he was illegitimate and didn't have a father," McAloon recalled. "He said his mother had been ashamed of him all his life. He said she had had an operation and was supposed to take some follow-up shots and didn't, and between not taking her shots, and the drinking, it was real bad."

He said that Peter had told him he'd got rid of the clothes he'd been wearing Friday night because he had been "all bloody in front." On the stand now, the witness recalled what Peter had said he'd done with those bloody clothes. "He rolled them in a ball, got into his car and drove somewhere, threw the clothes away, and came back to the house." As for the shoes, the witness said, Peter had "a pair of tan Hush Puppies."

226

"How did it come about that you gave this information to the state police?" Mr. Bianchi asked.

"I was talking to a trooper one day who was taking me to court," the witness said, "and I asked him, 'Do you think the kid really killed her?' He said he didn't know, because he wasn't involved in the case. And I said, 'I know he did it.' " And then, McAloon said, he'd told the trooper the story he'd just told here in court.

. John McAloon said nobody had made any promises, nobody had mentioned any rewards if he would testify, and, in fact, he couldn't even remember the name of the trooper he'd been riding with. "I wouldn't know the name if you said it," McAloon said. "A little short guy, smoking a pipe."

Catherine Roraback brought up names, too, asking the witness if he'd ever used an alias. At first he said no, then he reconsidered. "Excuse me, yes," he said.

"Was it Baker?" Miss Roraback asked him.

"Leroy Baker," the witness said, sounding faintly nostalgic. "I was in Miami at the time."

Catherine Roraback looked at her notes.

"Were you ever known as Richard Anderson?" she asked.

"I used that name one time to sign a book when I visited a friend," the witness said, and Miss Roraback turned away to the table where the exhibits were stacked.

"Were those the tan Hush Puppies?" she said, her voice ironical, and plopped the shoes on the table in front of him. He picked one up and looked at it, then the other.

"No," he said. "Those aren't Hush Puppies."

She asked him then about the clothes Peter said he'd discarded and about a weapon.

"Did he say razor or knife?" she asked.

"He said knife," John McAloon replied.

It seemed incredible. Was it a razor, or was it a knife? Or none of the above?

John McAloon didn't testify in the trial again, but when the Reilly trial was over, he did come back to Litchfield Superior Court. He came back to be sentenced, but at the recommendation of the State's Attorney, he got a suspended sentence.

Now, Judge Speziale looked at the jury with a weary little smile, as he told them again they were not to discuss the case with anyone, not even among themselves. "By now any one of you could give me the admonition," he said, "but I hope you hear it in your sleep, ladies and gentlemen. I *do* want you to obey this order."

As they put on their coats, the reporters talked with interest about John McAloon. "This is your basic bombshell," George Judson said.

12

The quality of justice in the Peter Reilly case was not diluted by haste. This was not ramshackle justice, pieced together, barely holding. The trial lasted seven weeks and, at least until the day of the verdict, no one seemed in a hurry, no one seemed to begrudge the time. As Sergeant Kelly had told Peter in the polygraph room, "We don't rush here. We take our time. We have no place to go."

What affected the quality of justice, it seemed to me, was its inconclusiveness, the element of contradiction. Perhaps there is often such an element in trial justice, but in the Peter Reilly trial, it seemed overwhelming. What mattered at one time to one person did not necessarily matter later to another.

What mattered most to Catherine Roraback was Peter's confession and the hours of interrogation that had led to it, even though Judge Armentano had allowed the confession, even though Peter Reilly had been read the Miranda warnings, the constitutional rights legally required by the Supreme Court decision. She was trying a criminal case, but within that framework she was raising constitutional issues.

But other things besides the confession mattered to other people. There was the knife, Exhibit X. The knife mattered to the jurors. When the time came for them to be shut up in the jury room, they took the knife along with them. They were interested in whether this knife, with the broken-off tip, could have made the cuts on Barbara's body. Two jurors brought in stopwatches, too, because they wanted to see how long such cutting, and such a killing, might take. There was the razor, which mattered to the police. Peter Reilly said in his statement that he had slashed his mother's throat with a razor. It was a straight razor made in Germany, inscribed with the number 7,000. The jurors handled it even more carefully than they'd handled the knife, and Frank Sollitto looked at it a long time, touching the blade thoughtfully.

There was a plastic bag of human hair, Peter's hair. Maybe it mattered, maybe not. Charles Kochakian, sitting next to me, groaned when an FBI agent began to testify about hair. Once Charles had sat through twelve hours of hair testimony, and he said he had learned one lesson from the ordeal. When it came to hair, they couldn't prove anything one way or the other. The police had sent Peter's hair to Washington, and, after making microscopic comparisons with the hairs found in Barbara's hands, the agency sent Peter's hair back by registered mail. The hairs in Barbara's hands, the FBI man said, were "brown head hairs, of Caucasian origin in one hand"; in the other, "one blond, several brown hairs, and one dark brown hair of Caucasian origin." He said Peter's hair had a streaky appearance, light brown to red-brown in color. He said two of the hairs found in Barbara's hand had the same characteristics as Peter's hair, and that they either came from Peter's head or from the head of somebody whose hair was like Peter's. Charles was right. These were either Peter's hairs or somebody else's.

There was an arbitrary element, it seemed, when another FBI man testified, a man who specialized in stains. He looked at the knife and said he had examined it for blood and semen. He found no semen, but he had found blood on the blade. It was human blood, but he couldn't tell whether it was male or female blood, or what type, or how long it had been there. He said he had used a sterile scalpel for scraping the knife and had found blood on both sides of the blade, but none on the handle. He said the police had sent three other knives to him for examination, but they hadn't sent any razor.

Besides the knife, the razor, and the hair, Peter's clothes were on exhibit, in a plastic bag. The FBI man said he had found no blood on the shirt, no blood on the left sneaker. The police hadn't sent the right sneaker. When he looked at the blue jeans, he said he couldn't find his initials on them, which was the way he marked things for identification.

This was the kind of thing that kept happening in the trial of Peter Reilly. Vague, unanswered questions, fragments of questions swooped through the courtroom like moths. There was, always, the question of the wallet, the money. Miss Roraback hoped to establish that Barbara had had a good sum of money in the house Friday, the night she died, although Lieutenant Shay had only found sixteen cents on the floor. Barbara's new wallet was never found. But when Catherine asked Jim Mulhern on the witness stand whether he had investigated a check cashed by Barbara the day she died, Mr. Bianchi objected that the question was immaterial. "I'm trying to establish that there was a large sum of money in the house," Miss Roraback said; nevertheless, the objection was sustained.

The clothes always mattered. Dr. Izumi had testified that Peter could have killed Barbara in the manner she was killed without getting bloody. Later in the trial, when he was recalled to the stand, he testified that the killer would have had to turn her over, or move her in some manner, in order to make the wounds on the back. The testimony seemed contradictory, or at least puzzling, and possibly very damaging.

Even Sergeant Kelly said he recalled the shirt and the dungarees. When he testified, he said that before he questioned Peter he had known there was "a good deal of blood around the neck and head area, and that Barbara's throat had been cut." But he said Peter had told him he thought he'd cut his mother's throat before Sergeant Kelly asked him about such cutting. But the autopsy on Barbara lasted most of the afternoon, and until it was over, the police apparently hadn't heard about the vaginal injuries. By the time they did, the polygraph test was over, and Peter was across the hall in the interview room.

"I went back in and asked Peter what was the worst thing he could have done to his mother last night," Sergeant Kelly said. "He said the only thing he could think of was that he raped his mother."

The jurors stared at Sergeant Kelly. A few of us had heard this testimony before at the pretrial hearings in January, but the jurors had not, and the shock of the statement was clearly traced now on most of their faces.

231

After Kelly told Peter that Barbara hadn't been raped, and after he'd declined to give Peter details, saying, "I want to hear it from you," Peter had told the officer, "I think I cut out her sex organs."

Sergeant Kelly testified he'd asked Peter then, "Why did you want to do something like this?" and Peter had replied that he didn't know. "Could it be because this is where you came from?" Sergeant Kelly had asked, and Peter had said yes.

Helen Ayre, mother of three, looked close to tears, then she arranged her face in that half-smile, half-grimace she'd worn during the autopsy slides.

Catherine Roraback looked sternly at Sergeant Kelly, but she didn't seem to be angry with him in the same way she'd been angry with Lieutenant Shay or, most of all, with Jim Mulhern.

"When you asked him, 'What was the worst thing you could have done to your mother last night?' " Miss Roraback said, "was that a question Lieutenant Shay asked you to ask him?" There was some exchange back and forth, then Tim Kelly said yes.

When Peter confessed to "rape," however, that was the wrong answer, so Sergeant Kelly had persisted. "What's the next worst thing . . . the next worst thing . . . ?" and Peter had answered "Jumping up and down on her" and "strangling her." As the testimony came out now in the courtroom, it sounded like a dreadful game of twenty questions, played for the highest stakes.

"Did you also ask him, 'What else did you do to hurt her?' " she asked Sergeant Kelly.

"Objection, your honor," Mr. Bianchi said again. "He's already answered that question." Catherine Roraback whirled angrily and looked at the prosecutor, then toward the bench. "He asked it sixteen times!" she said. Catherine Roraback knew precisely what was on the tapes. Mr. Bianchi, grinning angrily, moved that her comment be stricken.

"I don't remember the exact words," Sergeant Kelly said mildly.

"Do you remember asking that general question a number of times?" she asked. "Do you remember asking him, 'What else do you think you did?' Isn't it true that at least three times when you asked him what was the worst thing he could have done to his mother, he said, 'raping her'?"

"The number of times, I don't know," Sergeant Kelly said.

"You kept repeating that you needed one further detail, did you not?" Catherine Roraback asked.

Sergeant Kelly nodded slightly. "We talked about one further detail, yes."

"Didn't you suggest that it most likely happened when she was flat on the floor?"

"I don't know," Kelly said.

"And didn't Peter say, 'I think strangling her or something'?"

"I don't recall that," Kelly said.

"Didn't you go back to the question of, 'Why does rape stick in your mind?' Didn't you suggest to Peter that it was the way she was lying there that you were referring to?"

"I don't recall that, ma'am, no," Sergeant Kelly said.

"You don't recall?" she asked sarcastically.

"No," he said. Catherine Roraback shook her head briefly and looked down at her notes. She walked over to the defense table then and stood near Peter Reilly. The jurors turned to look at her, waiting for a question.

"Do you remember Peter saying, 'I'm just taking guesses now'?" she asked.

"I don't remember that," Sergeant Kelly said.

"Didn't you say, 'Assuming this happened, how would you have done it?'"

"I don't recall those words, no," Sergeant Kelly said.

"Do you remember Peter saying, 'I wouldn't know how to do it'?"

"I don't recall," Sergeant Kelly said.

At the recess, Con Hitchcock, a law student, chatted with me, advising me to notice the lawyers' techniques—how John Bianchi, in questioning a witness, often leaned against the jury rail, so the witness would look in his direction and thus would seem to be looking squarely and honestly at the jury. Catherine Roraback, on the other hand, often wandered away from the jury box and back to the defense table, sometimes standing behind Peter, her hand resting on the back of his chair, so that the witness would have to look at her and Peter, and the jury would tend to look that way too. Con Hitchcock said that shortly after the magazine article had appeared, he had been at a party in

233

Georgetown where two psychiatrists were discussing the article and the killing itself, in all its bizarre and gruesome aspects. One of the psychiatrists said there was no way in the world a son could have committed this kind of murder, and the other psychiatrist said only a son could have done it.

"Did he cry, trooper?" John Bianchi asked John Calkins. The trooper was back on the stand briefly, pleasant and a little sad-faced, with a soft voice.

"No," Trooper Calkins said quietly, telling again that when Peter had been returned to the Canaan barracks, Trooper Calkins had driven him to the Litchfield jail. When they passed the house where Barbara had been killed, Peter asked what happened to his car. He also told Trooper Calkins that Lieutenant Shay was a nice man, and Peter said he hoped his predicament wouldn't keep him from becoming a policeman, or somehow interfere with his driver's license. Trooper Calkins said that Peter told him he'd seen Barbara in bed, and the next thing he knew, he was standing over her, and she was lying on the floor with blood on her.

One man was missing when the jurors filed out on Tuesday morning, March 26, and took their seats in the jury box. Raymond Ross was sick with a high fever. Catherine Roraback had liked the serious-looking man with the two grown sons and had been pleased when he was accepted by the state as well. But after conferring with counsel, the court decided not to delay the trial, but to choose one of the alternates.

Frank Sollitto, as dapper and well-pressed as ever, and Eleanor Novak, still wide-eyed, stared at the clerk as he reached into the cardboard box to draw one of their numbers. He drew out number sixty-four, Mrs. Novak. She grinned and stood up, and the sheriff led her around the corner of the jury box, up into the top row, to the empty seat at the end. Some of the jurors in the box smiled at Mrs. Novak, who looked at the judge with an air of noticeable eagerness. Catherine Roraback smiled, too. During the voir dire, when Miss Roraback had asked Mrs. Novak what the presumption of innocence meant to her, Mrs. Novak had said simply that it meant he wasn't guilty.

Even Mr. Sollitto smiled when Mrs. Novak's number came up. "It's the only lottery I've ever won," he told me later.

With twelve jurors in the box, court proceeded again. Dr. Izumi made his last appearance, with two slides showing the cuts on Barbara's stomach and on her back.

"Did you come to an opinion with reasonable medical certainty as to what caused those wounds?" the prosecutor asked.

Dr. Izumi looked at the knife, State's Exhibit X, and said it would "match up with the wounds," pointing out that it was a "sharp cutting instrument," and that the tip of the knife was broken off, and that the wound was from one-fourth to one-half-inch wide. But when Dr. Izumi referred to it as "the weapon," Catherine Roraback scrambled to her feet.

"It's not a weapon, it's a knife," she said, and the prosecutor turned to her.

"It's a weapon," Mr. Bianchi said.

"It's a knife," Miss Roraback said.

"It's a question of semantics," the judge said. "Let's refer to it as a knife."

Dr. Izumi still held it in his hands. "My opinion would be that this knife is the instrument that caused this type of wound," he said carefully. He added that the same knife had been used on both the front and the back of Barbara's body. He said these wounds "were performed after death," and for a moment, the image of a killer standing over the dead woman, knifing and carving her, hovered in the courtroom. Dr. Izumi said the knife could also have caused the defense wound in Barbara's hand. He turned the knife over once or twice in his hands, in a thoughtful way. Catherine Roraback walked over to him, took the knife out of his hands, and walked away from the witness stand.

"Dr. Izumi," she said, with her back to him, "did you examine any other knives or instruments and compare them with these wounds?"

The doctor said he saw two other knives at the scene, but he "didn't have a chance to compare them" and hadn't compared them afterward, either.

Catherine Roraback said nothing, her back still turned to the witness, studying the ceiling again. A woman in the second row of the gallery stirred slightly. "She's taking her own sweet time, huh?" the spectator whispered to a man next to her.

Catherine Roraback turned back to Dr. Izumi, speaking quietly now. "If there were a knife on which the tip had not been broken off and that knife had the same width blade, could it have caused the defense wound you saw?"

"Yes, it could," Dr. Izumi said, adding that it would be unlikely, because of a "double scratch" shown on a slide.

"No more questions, your honor," both lawyers said, and Mr. Bianchi smiled. "May it please the court," he said, with a little bowing motion, "the state of Connecticut rests."

Miss Roraback stood then, looking vigorous, and immediately moved that the court dismiss the case entirely. The jury was sent out, while Miss Roraback argued that, basically, all that Mr. Bianchi had established was "a very gory and horrible murder was committed at the premises on Route sixty-three in Falls Village that were formerly occupied by the deceased and her son, Peter Reilly." She said that Peter's statements, his confession, came only after he had been "held in custody some twenty-four hours and given under highly questionable circumstances, at a time when he was extremely tired, at a time when he had not had sufficient food, at a time when he had gone through the extreme trauma of having found his mother in those circumstances," which she called "a horrible sight for anyone." She talked about the questioning. "Even at the end of it, as Trooper Mulhern indicated," she reminded the court, "Mr. Reilly was still saying, 'I still don't think I did it, I'm not sure of anything I'm saying.' "

She looked at the judge, speaking very earnestly, as though he were a one-man jury whom she had to persuade. "All of the facts seem consistent with a finding of innocence and not a finding of guilt," she said. "This defendant had clothing on which had no blood on it. He was subjected to a skin search. He had no indication on him that he had been involved in this horrendous crime. . . . Finally, your honor, I think there really is no prima facie case against my client."

John Bianchi's reply was swift. "In my opinion, there is overwhelming evidence in this case that is just the opposite," he said. "The evidence that Dr. Izumi just gave. Peter Reilly was there in the house when his mother was alive. She was gasping. It was clear that when he called, that Mrs. Gibbons was alive." Mr. Bianchi added, pointedly, that "it could only have been Peter Reilly who made the after-death wounds, because he was the only one there."

As for Miss Roraback's objections to the questioning, Mr. Bianchi reminded the court of Judge Armentano's earlier decision that "this is an alert, bright, able young man." Somehow, as Mr. Bianchi listed the adjectives, they did not sound entirely positive. "He was warned four times with much, much care," Mr. Bianchi declared. "The blurted-out, voluntary admissions that he made to Trooper Mulhern, who was his friend, when he brought him food . . . to John McAloon, who knew things only he would have known, that she wasn't taking her medicine, she wasn't taking her hormone injections . . . he told McAloon what he did with the clothing." Mr. Bianchi sat down, looking satisfied, as Catherine Roraback made her rebuttal.

"The gasping that Peter Reilly heard, if indeed he did, that could have been—as I understand Dr. Izumi's testimony—the body of Barbara Gibbons sucking in air after the trachea had been cut. That could go on for five minutes. The lungs taking in air could make a gasping sound.

"When you come to Mr. McAloon," Miss Roraback continued, her tone changing from serious to sarcastic, "I think you have to remember that Mr. McAloon said Peter had on tan Hush Puppies, which no one else has seen. Mr. McAloon, if that is his name, and I guess in this particular situation that *was* his name"—she glanced at Mr. Bianchi, who flushed and stared back at her—"Mr. McAloon said Peter Reilly told him he killed his grandmother."

Judge Speziale had listened carefully, even politely, as though he might indeed consider dismissing the whole thing. But it took him only a moment to deny the motion to dismiss, to glance at the clock, and to announce lunch.

"Is that all they got on this kid?" Roger Cohn asked incredulously at lunch at Mitchell's. "It's all over Torrington that Sam Holden keeps saying, 'We really got the goods on Reilly.' " Sam Holden was the County Detective.

Back in the courthouse hallway, Murray Madow was talking to Marie Dickinson. "I know a hunter who says gasping after death in an animal can go on for as long as half an hour, forty minutes," he said. "If Peter's mother could have been gasping for five minutes after she bled to death, why couldn't the killer have cut her up and Peter have gotten there in the last part of the gasping time?"

We didn't know it then, but the jurors wondered about that, too. Some of them thought that was a definite possibility. Others thought that if Peter had driven into the yard just as Barbara was being cut and had come into the house just at the end of the five minutes, it would have been too much of a coincidence.

Joe O'Brien had another question. "How could there have been blood on both sides of the blade and not on the handle?" he wondered.

Peter Reilly's defense began quietly, with no further preliminaries, just after lunch. A short, slim man with dark hair and a slightly abashed look took the stand. He wore two pins in his lapel, a white dove and a red ladybug, thus managing to symbolize the fight for peace and against aphids. It was a nice, homey touch, and in a way it symbolized a change of atmosphere in the courtroom, as the witnesses changed from the doctors and the policemen, the pros, to the housewives and schoolboys, the amateurs. They looked scared and unprofessional, most of them setting foot in a courtroom for the first time, witnesses for the defense.

The man with the dove and the ladybug was the Reverend Dakers, who said he had been at the Teen Center meeting that night and had gone, afterwards, to Johnny's for a cup of coffee with Father Paul "about nine-forty, nine-forty-five." He said it was hard to remember what Peter Reilly had been wearing, but he thought maybe it was a blue work shirt.

Barbara Curtis twisted a damp white handkerchief in her left hand and with her right hand held tightly to the side of the chair. She identified Peter's clothes, and she said she herself had been wearing a cranberry sweater and cranberry slacks, though when Mr. Bianchi asked her what other people at the Teen Center meeting had worn, she said she couldn't say.

"You are sure what Peter Reilly was wearing, even though you are unable to tell me what anybody else was wearing?" Mr. Bianchi asked.

"That's true," said Mrs. Curtis, who had given a statement about Peter's clothes to the police the day after Barbara died.

Sue Curtis, her daughter, looked at the shirt Mr. Bianchi held up and identified it as the one Peter Reilly had worn.

"It isn't any different from any other long-sleeved brown shirt with white buttons on it, is it?" Mr. Bianchi asked heavily.

"No," Sue Curtis admitted, and bit her nails. But Paul Beligni, behind the reporters, grumbled out loud. "That's no ordinary brown shirt," he said. "That's a fourteen ninety-five Van Heusen doubleknit."

John Sochocki, looking as though he had dressed in a grown-up's suit, the lapels wide over his narrow chest, the sleeves too long, hanging over his hands, said he had been given a ride home from the Teen Center by Peter Reilly. John Sochocki said he'd got to his house, not many blocks from the Methodist Church, at 9:45. He said Peter was wearing a brown plaid jacket.

"Are you married?" Catherine Roraback asked the witness.

"Yes," the woman on the stand said. She was wearing a rose-and-gray two-piece dress; she had fair skin and shinning red-blonde hair.

"What does your husband do?" Miss Roraback asked innocently.

"He's a Connecticut State police officer," Joanne Mulhern replied. The jury watched, entranced, as she related how, at the Teen Center meeting, both Peter and Geoff had said good-bye to her and had left about 9:30. She said she saw Peter again early the next afternoon, and he was wearing the same clothes he'd had on the night before.

Geoffrey Madow took the stand, and Marion looked worried. "John Bianchi really rips into kids," she had told me. At first it was easy for Geoff, as Catherine Roraback led him gently through the events of September 28, 1973. He told how, after the phone call from Peter, he'd raced back out to the car and had been the first person to get to Peter's house.

"And what did you see?" Miss Roraback asked softly.

"I saw Mrs. Gibbons lying on the floor in the bedroom . . . I said, 'Pete, I think she's been raped,' " Geoff said.

But John Bianchi took Geoff back to the living Barbara, the woman who drank so much and argued so much with Peter. At first Geoffrey held his own; when the prosecutor asked what Barbara and Peter had argued about, Geoff said "Watergate," and a ripple of laughter ran through the courtroom again. John Bianchi frowned.

"She was always picking on Peter, wasn't she?"

"Not all the time," Geoff said.

"They did use profanity when they would argue back and forth, didn't they?"

"Not all the time," Geoff said, looking uneasy.

"What did they say?" John Bianchi asked blandly.

Geoff murmured something and looked a little sick. Mr. Bianchi pressed hard.

"What did they say?" he said loudly.

"They might say, 'Fuck you,' " Geoff said, almost in a whisper.

John Bianchi looked solemn and spoke loudly.

"Isn't it true that they would use the term 'shit'?" he demanded.

"Yes," whispered Geoff. A woman behind the press row, a close friend of John Bianchi, gave a little snort. "Yes, *sir*," she said.

Art Madow, the Beligni boys, and Jim Holmes broke up at Geoffrey's answer, and Judge Speziale frowned at them. "Any more such outbursts from spectators and those spectators will be thrown out of this courtroom," he said. Coming from Judge Speziale, the vernacular was as surprising as it was refreshing; in a court of law, where people tend to say, "I utilized" instead of "I used," and "I observed" instead of "I saw," it was nice to hear "thrown out," instead of "eject."

Mr. Bianchi complained that he had lost the line of questioning and asked for the last exchange to be read back. Mr. Roberts lifted the white tape from his machine and read aloud in his most elegant and precise way.

"Question: Isn't it true that they would use the term 'shit?' " Mr. Roberts read carefully, with such beautiful diction that the term might as well have been "chrysanthemums." "Answer: Yes."

Mr. Roberts held his hands over his machine, poised for the next question, and John Bianchi nodded in a satisfied way.

"They would use such terms as 'bastard' and 'bitch,' didn't they?"

"Not to each other, no," Geoff said. He explained that they only used those terms about a third person, such as a teacher.

"In all the times you visited, what's your best estimate of the times Barbara Gibbons was drunk?" John Bianchi asked.

"Forty percent of the time," Geoff said. Mr. Bianchi showed him his statement, in which Geoff had said Barbara was drunk "about half the time," and Mr. Bianchi looked pleased.

"When she was sober, was she a nice person?"

"Yes," Geoff said clearly.

"What was she like when she was drinking?"

"Sometimes she was nice, sometimes she was bitchy. Depending on how she was feeling, I imagine," Geoff said, with a little smile.

240

Mr. Bianchi frowned again and showed Geoffrey the statement he'd signed, in which Geoff said he'd reached his own home around 9:30, though he'd just told Miss Roraback it was 9:40.

"What made you change your mind?" John Bianchi asked, with a definite sneer.

Geoff looked anguished. "It never *was* changed," he said. "It never *was* changed. I always meant, around nine-thirty to nine-forty-five."

"Were you subpoenaed?" John Bianchi asked suddenly.

"I don't know," Geoff said, and when the prosecutor pressed the point, as though to cast doubt on Geoff's friendship for Peter Reilly, Geoff suddenly looked over to the defense table. "Did you subpoena me, Miss Roraback?" he asked innocently. The judge looked up, startled, and Mr. Roberts stifled a smile as he took down the question.

John Bianchi then pulled out all the stops with Geoffrey, being harsh and ironic and florid, referring once to the house where Barbara died, as "the Reilly homestead," asking Geoff whether Peter had cried and how he had looked.

"What do you mean, he had a blank expression on his face?" the prosecutor asked scornfully.

"I don't know how to explain it," Geoff said helplessly, and Mr. Bianchi looked satisfied.

"Are you *sure* Peter Reilly was wearing the brown shirt we've been talking about?"

"Yes I am," Geoff said.

"He *does* have a brown plaid jacket, doesn't he?"

"Yes he does," Geoff said, and the prosecutor abruptly returned to Barbara's drinking.

"You visited Miss Gibbons's home about five or six times a week?"

"Yes."

"And about half the time she was drunk?"

"About that, yes," Geoff said.

Mr. Bianchi's last question was whether Peter was crying. "No," Geoff said, and the prosecutor thanked him. "No further questions," he said, turning aside.

Marion told about arriving that night and putting her arms around Peter. "I held him for a minute because I didn't know how to tell him what had happened. I just hugged him."

John Bianchi smiled widely at her, but she did not smile back.

"It was cold that night?" he asked Marion.

"It was cold, yes," she said, and the prosecutor asked whether Peter was shaking from the cold.

"It was not that kind of shaking," Marion said.

Mr. Bianchi widened his eyes.

"Oh, there are different kinds of shaking?" he asked.

"With children, yes," Marion said.

"He's eighteen," Mr. Bianchi told her. "The state of Connecticut says he's a man."

Marion looked at him. "But a mother says he's a child," she said. Helen Ayre smiled.

"Was he crying, Mrs. Madow?" the prosecutor asked.

"No," Marion said.

When Mickey Madow testified, there was a verbal scuffle, as John Bianchi tried to prevent the jury from learning that Mickey waited around that night, wanting to take Peter home. When Miss Roraback asked Mickey what he'd said to Sergeant Salley—that he would come down to the barracks and take Peter home when the police were through— the prosecutor jumped up and said it was immaterial. "It's highly material to the subsequent detention of Peter Reilly," Miss Roraback said dryly.

"Is it your testimony that you checked the pulse of the left wrist?" Mr. Bianchi asked when his turn came.

"Right," Mickey said.

"On the *left* wrist?"

"Right," Mickey said.

It was an Abbott and Costello bit, and the courtroom broke up. But the prosecutor's last question wasn't funny.

"Was he crying, Mr. Madow?"

"No, he wasn't," Mickey said.

The new witness had a faraway look in his eye. His name was Robert Erhardt, and his address was the State Prison at Somers, Connecticut. He said he'd first met Peter Reilly at eight o'clock in the morning, at Litchfield jail, the Sunday after Barbara died, and that at first Peter wouldn't say why he'd been arrested.

"I made him a cup of cocoa and gave him a pack of cigarettes, and he said, 'They're charging me with killing my mother.' I said, 'You got to be kidding.' I asked him if he had made a telephone call or talked to an attorney. He was talking in circles. He didn't know what to do . . . one minute he'd be talking about his school classes, then he'd leave it unfinished, and he'd talk about playing his guitar, then he'd say, 'What am I here for?' " Erhardt shook his head. "None of his statements were coherent," he recalled.

John Bianchi, who prosecuted this witness on a robbery charge, asked him whether he recalled saying to Sergeant Norman Soucie about Peter, "I don't think it was a planned thing."

"Definitely not," Robert Erhardt said.

"You don't remember saying it?" Mr. Bianchi asked.

"I didn't say it," the witness said firmly.

Instead of giving a statement to the police, Robert Erhardt had prepared his own statement, saying he'd been offered a "time cut" and a transfer if he would testify against Peter Reilly. "In my opinion," he wrote, "and I was asked for an opinion by Sergeant Soucie, I really feel that Peter Reilly is not guilty of the crime he is charged with." He sent copies of his statement to Catherine Roraback, to Peter Reilly, to me, and even to the state police.

John Bianchi asked Robert Erhardt whether he had refused to sign a statement for Sergeant Soucie because he was afraid some other inmate might hurt him.

Robert Erhardt was a wry, thin man with a glint of humor in his eyes, a man who, like Peter Reilly, had been put into Litchfield jail when he was eighteen. Now he was forty-five years old. He had been in various prisons, on serious charges—robberies, car thefts, intermittent escapes—off and on for sixteen years. So when John Bianchi asked whether he was afraid of another inmate, Erhardt smiled, a slight, wan smile. "I'm pretty well aware of how to carry myself in prison," he said. The wry remark had nothing to do with Peter Reilly but, in a way, it seemed the most important thing Robert Erhardt could say.

Of all the young people who took the stand, Paul Beligni seemed the most self-assured. Jean had given him a little lecture on how to handle himself. "Try to sound humble," she said, and she'd hoped

243

that as Paul sat facing the courtroom, her cousin John would notice the boy's profile and think, "Here is Sam's grandson, he's got the Speziale nose."

But as it turned out, it was neither Paul's humility nor his nose that seemed to matter most. After testifying, with a broad smile, that he and Peter Reilly were "the best of friends," and that he'd visited him "many, many times," Paul recalled the summer of 1973. The two boys were target shooting in the backyard, and Paul dug one bullet slug out of a tree on the side of the house, using the knife that was now Exhibit X.

"And what happened?" said Miss Roraback.

"I broke the point off," Paul said, smiling.

The calendar turned to April, but an ice storm came through, turning the branches of the elms on Litchfield green into sheaths of brittle diamonds. Charles said the sheriffs were keeping winter going so we wouldn't find out it was spring. There was, indeed, an air of unreality about all this, a sense of time suspended, as though we were Sartre characters, forever sipping lukewarm coffee from our paper cups, grouped around the water cooler in futile debate, doomed to roam restlessly, endlessly through the corridors at Litchfield Superior Court.

In fact, though, the trial was nearly over. Only a few more witnesses were called for the defense, most of them professionals.

Dr. Abraham Stolman, chief toxicologist for the Connecticut State Department of Health, said he had examined the razor and had found no blood on it. On cross-examination, Dr. Stolman said he found 22 percent alcohol in Barbara's blood, the equivalent of ten ounces of 86-proof whiskey or ten 12-ounce bottles of beer. He couldn't tell whether she'd been drinking whiskey, beer or wine, but she was "definitely under the influence of intoxicating liquor."

Trooper Walter Anderson looked at a sketch of the inside of the house and said he had marked "a bloody footprint" on the carpet, pointed out to him by Lieutenant Shay, near Barbara's left foot. But when the section of carpet was sent to the FBI lab, they sent back word that it was not a discernible footprint.

It had always been a puzzle that the razor that Peter said he used to slash Barbara's throat had been found closed and clean on the living-room shelf, where it was always kept. Obviously the police thought he might have washed it and dried it and put it away. So they had taken the kitchen sink trap and its contents, the bathroom sink trap and its contents, and the bathtub drain trap and assembly and contents, and sent everything down to the state police lab. No blood was found.

Sergeant Gerald Pennington of the police lab at Bethany testified that he'd compared fingerprints found on the door with prints of the victim, with prints of the officers at the scene, and with prints of the defendant. Two of the prints belonged to an auxiliary trooper, he said, but there was a partial palm print on the inside of the front screen door and a partial fingerprint on the rear screen door that were not identified, though identifiable. He said he couldn't tell how long the prints had been there, but they were definitely not Peter's.

There were only a few nonprofessional witnesses in the last days of the trial. There was Vicky, Barbara's childhood companion, all grown up now, plump and matronly, with gray in her hair and grown sons of her own. "His mother was my cousin," she said softly. She had never met Peter Reilly, until she saw him at his arraignment, but she said she'd held him in her arms that autumn morning, and he'd cried and cried. Vicky's husband, John, a large, ruddy-faced man, also testified. He waved toward Peter Reilly and toward his wife in the gallery. "He was crying—she was crying—I was crying!!" he boomed, throwing his hands into the air. Helen Ayre smiled broadly. Margaret Wald and Raymond Lind whispered together, but Gary Lewis merely looked bored.

The other nonprofessional witness took the stand late on a Thursday afternoon. The court had been recessed most of the day, and a number of people, to their everlasting regret, had already decided nothing would happen anymore that day and were not there when the jury was called back, after four o'clock, and the judge told Miss Roraback she could resume.

The witness gave his name, Peter Anthony Reilly, and said that he lived on Locust Hill Road in East Canaan, "at the moment."

His appearance on the stand, so late in the day, seemed a carefully planned move by Miss Roraback, who knew that she had to get to the language matter first, before John Bianchi did, to take the sting out of the words. So she asked Peter, right away, about the sort of language he and Barbara had used.

"Well, we did use bad language," Peter said, managing to look both a little abashed and a little pleased at his daring, an accused murderer in the role of Peck's Bad Boy. "I guess you would call it profanity." And when Miss Roraback asked him for an illustration, Peter smiled sheepishly. "We used terms such as 'fuck you,' 'bastard,' and 'bitch,'" He added that they didn't talk that way "on all occasions," only when they were arguing—sometimes about the car, sometimes about other things, "anything that happened to be of interest at the moment."

After only twenty minutes of testimony, court was adjourned for a long weekend. It seemed to have been a slow day, but there had been interesting activity backstage. The state had offered to plea bargain with Peter, promising a light sentence—three to five years—if he would plead guilty to manslaughter.

He turned it down.

Over the weekend, the word was out that Peter Reilly had been on the stand, like a Preview of a Coming Attraction, and on Tuesday morning, April 2, the courtroom was packed. Pat Alfano's hand-lettered sign had gone up on the door: COURT FULL. NO SEATS. Dot Madow said she thought she was more nervous than Peter himself, and he certainly looked relaxed, not tense at all, as he took the stand. He sipped water from a styrofoam cup that Phil Plumb had filled, and he smiled a little as he looked around, glancing briefly at the jury, then toward his friends in the spectators' rows.

"Do you recognize it?" Miss Roraback asked, holding up the knife, State's Exhibit X.

"Yes, I do," Peter said. He explained that his friend Wayne Collier had given Barbara the knife about a year and a half before, when she had complained that she didn't have a really good meat-cutting knife. "Wayne said that he had one that was old, but he gave it to her," Peter said, adding that Barbara kept it in a pouch on the side of the cabinet in the kitchen.

Miss Roraback held up the razor, State's Exhibit CC. "Do you recognize it?" she asked.

"Yes, I do," Peter said. He explained that Barbara had got it for him from Mario's Barber Shop in Canaan because it had a handle on it, and "I could work on balsa models without carving up my fingers." He said Barbara usually kept the razor on a shelf in the living room, on the shelf where they kept odds and ends, with two rows of books below it and one row above. That was the usual place.

"Do you know a lady by the name of [Auntie B.'s name]?" John Bianchi asked abruptly.

"Yes, I do," Peter said.

"Is she related to you?"

"No, she is not related," Peter said. Judge Speziale looked up from his notes and asked him to spell that name.

"Does she hold some standing in relationship with you, though?" Mr. Bianchi asked.

"I would say she is my godmother," Peter said. He said that she had bought them the car and had sent money regularly.

"Was your mother a welfare recipient?" the prosecutor asked.

"I believe so, yes," Peter said.

"And on September twenty-eight, do you know whether or not a letter was received at your home from [Auntie B.]?"

"I don't think so," Peter said. "All I know is, my mother cashed a check that day, that she received in the mail."

"Who did she receive the check from?" the prosecutor asked.

"It may have been from my godmother," Peter said. "I don't know."

"You don't *know?*" the prosecutor asked scornfully.

"Mm-hm, right," Peter said, very casually, perhaps a little too casually.

"Have you seen [her] since September twenty-eight until today?" Mr. Bianchi asked.

"No, I haven't," Peter said.

Mr. Bianchi asked him about the arguments he and Barbara had had, and about the "extremely rude and crude language" they'd used, and about Barbara's drinking.

"She drank wine," Peter said. "Every day, she drank wine. It was just something that she always did." When the prosecutor pressed, Peter said yes, that Barbara had had a drinking problem, but that he hadn't realized it until now.

247

"Do you remember when you left your grandmother's and your grandfather's house on Johnson Road?" Mr. Bianchi asked.

"Yes, I remember," Peter said.

"Weren't there serious arguments between your grandparents and your mother over such things as that?" Mr. Bianchi asked.

"I don't remember the arguments that well," Peter said. "There were arguments, but I don't remember specifically what they were about."

Peter was only ten when he and Barbara left Johnson Road. By then the arguments had become so serious, the atmosphere so hateful, that Hilda had had her daughter arrested for breach of peace. Now Peter looked directly at Mr. Bianchi, for a moment seeming remote, very much like someone who could take his fishing pole and go off to spend the day alone, leaving all the grown-ups behind.

At lunch two questions circled the press table. "How can you not know if your mother has a drinking problem?"

"How can you have a godmother if you aren't baptized?"

On the way back into the courtroom, Peter stopped me in the hall. "I am scared to death," he said. "How does it look?"

"Fine," I said. "You don't look scared at all. You look very cool." Why do people always say fine? He looked so cool that it bothered me, and I thought it might be bothering the jury. I should have told him so.

Peter testified about the wallet.

Altogether, there were three wallets in question. When the police searched the house, the night Barbara died, they found one wallet in a drawer, an old one with some old pictures and papers in it. It had not been used for a long time.

A second wallet in question was one that had been stolen from Barbara a couple of weeks before she died. It had more than a hundred dollars in it when it was stolen. Peter testified that Barbara had reported it to the police. When she died, it was still missing. Later, it was found.

A third wallet was brand-new, the wallet Barbara had bought at Bob's Clothing Store the day she died. When Peter came home from school that afternoon, Barbara had pulled it out of the right rear pocket of her jeans and showed it to him. Bob Drucker at Bob's

Clothing Store remembered selling it to her. When Barbara died, that wallet was missing. It was never found.

But when Peter Reilly was on the stand, brightly—even gaily—dressed in red bell-bottoms and a red sweater, it wasn't the wallet, or the drinking, or the arguing, that lay at the heart of it all. It was his confession, and his confession was written down.

"I signed several different sheets, but it's very vague to me," Peter told Miss Roraback. He said that before he had heard the tapes played back at the pretrial hearings, he hadn't remembered much of what had gone on. "A little bit, yes, but not hardly anything." He said he remembered "being interviewed by Sergeant Kelly and I remember being questioned by Trooper Mulhern, and I remembered signing a statement."

Miss Roraback showed him State's Exhibit Z. He recognized his signature, he said, but other than that, he wasn't sure if it was the statement he signed. She showed him Exhibit AA, and Peter said it was "something added to the statement after it was made," and although he recognized his signature, he said he didn't remember signing it. On Exhibit BB, he recognized his signature and his initials at dfferent places around the page.

Miss Roraback read from the statement now, as Mr. Bianchi stared at her. "I remember slashing at my mother's throat with a straight razor used for my model airplanes. This was on the living-room table. I also remember jumping on my mother's legs. I am not sure about washing her off." The statement went on, with the account of the phone calls, throwing the hibachi out of the way, Geoff's arrival, then the police. And the last addition: "When I slashed at my mother's throat with a straight razor, I cut her throat. This is all I wanted to clarify."

Miss Roraback put the statement aside and stood in front of the witness stand, looking at Peter.

"I ask you, Mr. Reilly, is that statement your best memory of what happened that night?"

"No, it isn't," Peter said.

"Did you in fact slash at your mother's throat?"

"No, I did not," Peter said.

"Did you in fact kill your mother, Mr. Reilly?"

"No, I didn't," Peter said.

Miss Roraback turned toward the jury. "I have no other questions," she said.

The prosecutor planted himself squarely in front of Peter, his legs spread apart a little.

"You have known Trooper Jim Mulhern quite well, haven't you?" he began.

"Yes, I have," Peter said.

"And he is a friend of yours, isn't he?"

"Yes," Peter said.

"You ever go to his home . . . you helped him do some work on his property . . . you know Mrs. Mulhern?"

"Yes," Peter said.

"And with this background, Mr. Reilly," the prosecutor said, "with the friendship of Jim Mulhern, showing you State's Exhibits AA, Z, and BB, it's your testimony that your friend Jim Mulhern wrote down something that wasn't true? or something that you didn't say?" The prosecutor made a little bow in the direction of the jury and looked shocked. "Is *that* what you are telling these ladies and gentlemen?"

"No, I never said that," Peter replied. "I said that I wasn't sure if I said this or not, that my signature was on this paper."

"Did you read it at the time Trooper Mulhern wrote it down for you?"

"I don't remember," Peter said. "I don't remember if I did or not."

"Were you sick, Mr. Reilly?" the prosecutor asked. It was one of the few times he had called the defendant "Mr.," and it did not sound natural.

"I wasn't sick, I don't think," Peter said.

Mr. Bianchi looked scornful. "Were you suffering from a lapse of memory or something during that time?"

"No," Peter said. "I was just totally exhausted."

"When did things start to go blank?" Mr. Bianchi asked.

"It's just the basic conversation," Peter said. "I don't remember it."

John Bianchi looked disbelieving. "But this good friend, Jim Mulhern, as he knew you, wrote this down and asked you to sign it, right?"

"Yes, he did," Peter said.

Mr. Bianchi raised his voice.

"When he walked through that door, with that sandwich and those two cupcakes and that Coke for you, Peter Reilly, and you looked up at him, and he hadn't been interrogating you at all, and you said to him, words to this effect, 'I suppose you are ashamed of me, Jim?' "

"I may have," Peter said.

"And he said, 'Huh?' or, 'Why, Peter?' And you said to him, 'Because I did it. I killed her.' "

"I may have said that, yes," Peter said.

Mr. Bianchi asked how John McAloon had known about Barbara's operation and that she wouldn't take her medicine.

"Will you explain to me, Mr. Reilly, how John McAloon could have known that without speaking with you?" the prosecutor demanded.

"Well, if he had been in that area, maybe I could have said it to somebody else," Peter said.

"Did you?" Mr. Bianchi asked, and Peter smiled slightly.

"I don't know," he said. "I could have."

"Since you didn't talk to John McAloon," Mr. Bianchi continued, "he just made up the testimony that he gave on the stand, that you told him you threw your clothes away?"

"He very easily could have," Peter said, and reached out casually to take a sip of water.

As he recalled that Sunday morning at Litchfield jail, he said he had talked with many inmates, including Robert Erhardt, crowding around the newcomer's cell door. They told him he needed a lawyer, and one of them got the Litchfield phone book from a guard.

"The name Roraback rang a bell," Peter said, on the stand, "and I said I would like Catherine Roraback. They told me I probably couldn't afford her." Mr. Roberts smiled quickly as he took down the testimony, and most people in the gallery, and in the jury box, laughed out loud.

"Your mother was breathing and gasping at the time you called Sharon Hospital?"

"I think she was breathing," Peter said. "She was making sounds or something. I thought she was breathing."

Mr. Bianchi waved the statement under Peter's nose. "You didn't say in here 'I think she was.' "

"Well, that's what I felt," Peter said. "I heard sounds. I thought she was breathing. So I said——"

Mr. Bianchi interrupted. "You said she was having problems breathing?"

"Well, she was making sounds, and I thought they were sounds of having problems breathing, so I thought she was breathing," Peter said. The prosecutor paused slightly, then swung back to face the witness.

"And there was nobody there but you?"

"Mm-hm," Peter said.

"And you heard Dr. Izumi say that the cuts on her abdomen and on her back and in her vagina area were all done after death?"

"I heard him say that, yes," Peter said calmly.

"And there was nobody there but you?"

Catherine Roraback objected and brought up the question of clinical and biological death, but she was overruled.

Now the prosecutor's voice dropped as he asked about a man Barbara had known. "In 1969 or 70, did he come to live at your house?" Peter said he had.

"And was he black?" the prosecutor asked softly. Peter said he was.

"And did he live with you and your mother in the same house?" the prosecutor asked again.

"Mm-hm," Peter said.

"And this was a pretty trying thing for you, was it not? Living with [the man], who was of another race, in your house—in that tiny little house with your mother and you—that had to be a pretty sad thing, wasn't it?"

"I guess," Peter said quietly. The courtroom was quiet too, seeing the couple in one bunk and a teen-aged boy in the other, as vividly as though they had been photographed.

"Could you tell me what you thought your relationship was with your mother?" Miss Roraback asked. It was her last question.

"She was my mother. I loved her," Peter Reilly said.

With the jury out, the complicated matter of the tape recordings was argued. The crucial issue was the polygraph test, inadmissible evidence in a Connecticut courtroom. "If he had been successful and passed it, he probably would not be sitting here today," John Bianchi argued. "The fact is, he didn't pass it, and this led to his confession."

"I take exception to Mr. Bianchi saying that Mr. Reilly did not pass the lie detector test," Catherine Roraback replied. "There is a very sophisticated question of whether or not an individual passes or flunks a test of this sort."

Judge Speziale sighed. "We've reached the point where the tapes have become deeply enmeshed in this entire trial," he said. Finally, with the jurors in their seats, he told them the polygraph "is simply too unreliable for you to give any consideration at all to the test results." But he said that if the court edited the tapes, to remove any reference to the lie detector test, the tapes might be misleading, so the court had decided the jury might hear them all. Then Mr. Roberts seemed to sigh a little, too.

Once the jury knew that "the interview" and "the conversation" were actually a lie detector test, they seemed fascinated by Sergeant Tim Kelly, as neat and robust as ever, not at all frightening, out of uniform, casually dressed in a plaid jacket and beige slacks. Sergeant Kelly faced the jurors across the table, with Mr. Roberts at an angle, his hands poised.

These were the tapes of the afternoon session at Hartford, which had so startled and affected—in so many different ways—those of us who had heard them then, for the first time, on that December day. They had been new then; even John Bianchi said that before the pretrial hearings, he'd heard only portions of the tapes.

As the tapes began, all of us in the courtroom went back in time, to an autumn Saturday afternoon when, across the country, millions of people were cheering from football bleachers, or washing their cars, and one young man was sitting in a small, soundproof room, in what he was told was the seat of honor. I had time, on this second hearing, to muse on what I heard, and I found the questions to be as interesting, in a way, as the answers, as Sergeant Schneider and Peter discussed the Corvette, spending money, and God. On the polygraph, I wondered, are an atheist's answers suspect?

The voice of Sergeant Kelly came through clearly, as it had in December. "I think we've got a little problem here." They did. And finally Peter again, at the end, asking whether the session had been tape recorded. There was an image of Sergeant Kelly pointing to the tape as he replied. "There's my tape. Right here. That's all I need. That's you." And Peter, perhaps nodding a little, as he agreed. "That's me."

The polygraph test was over. Then, at last, we heard them. We heard the evening tapes. We heard what had happened that Saturday night in Hartford. We heard all four hours.

We heard Peter in the beginning. "Well, it really looks like I did it. The thing is, I must have flown off the handle . . ."

We heard Lieutenant Shay. "Trust me. Tell me what happened."

We heard Peter in the middle. "Can you say I'm not sure, Jim? Everything that I say, the entire statement, I'm not sure of."

We heard Jim Mulhern: "Well, it sounds terrible, murder and all that . . . but I'm not a guy to sit here and judge you . . . Five years from now, I may do the same thing."

We heard Peter at the end. "Will I need a lawyer?"

On April 11, Catherine Roraback and John Bianchi summed up their cases in Docket #5285, *State of Connecticut* v. *Peter A. Reilly,* and the jury retired to try to reach a verdict.

13

Long afterward, people remembered that time with an intensity that seemed, at first, to be out of proportion to the number of hours and days involved. There was a weight, an emphasis, to the end of the trial and its aftermath that affected not only Peter Reilly and others most closely concerned, including the judge and the jurors, but also some of the reporters and spectators, too. Even some people who had never come to court, but knew only what they heard on the news or read in the papers, seemed to sense that what happened to Peter Reilly had something to do with them all.

Partly it was a feeling of involvement, a simple caring what happened, but beyond that, it was a process of perception, a process that had begun when Barbara died and Peter was taken away in a police car. It had been reflected in the confused, angry, bewildered voices at the early gatherings of the Peter Reilly Defense Committee, and it had deepened in the months since. Not everyone's perceptions were identical, of course, and they did not always lead to consensus, let alone to change. Still, the process had begun, and it would not be ended when the jurors reached a verdict.

April 11 was a chilly day, Geoffrey Madow's birthday. Chunks of muddy ice were clumped at the curbs on West Street, in front of the courthouse, and the village was scattered with patches of old snow.

Inside the courtroom, with its NO ADMITTANCE sign on the door, John Bianchi thanked the jurors for paying such close attention to the case and reminded them that the state did not have to prove Peter Reilly guilty beyond all doubt, but beyond a reasonable doubt. "My argument to you will be based on direct evidence, and on circumstantial evidence," he said. "Direct evidence is anything that comes through our senses." To explain circumstantial evidence, Mr. Bianchi described a winter scene. "If you came upon a house with your car one snowy evening, just as it started to snow, and you saw some footprints coming from the front porch, and you followed them around the house . . . and inside the door was a pair of wet rubbers, and a person came to the door, and the rubbers fit his feet, and the treads were the same . . . and he says he hasn't been out, the circumstances show the man isn't telling the truth." He looked at the jury and gestured toward Peter Reilly. "There is direct evidence that this young man committed this murder. There is overwhelming circumstantial evidence that he did so," Mr. Bianchi said, and sat down.

Catherine Roraback wore a pretty dress, a powder blue, with a silver pin and a string of pearls. Her hair was freshly washed and shone. But she looked wan. She had just learned that morning that her only brother Albert had terminal cancer. She had told Mickey Madow the bad news when she came in, and she'd told John Bianchi, too.

Still, when she faced the jury for the last time, she managed to smile at them. "This isn't like TV," she said. "I won't be able to point to somebody back in the spectators' section and say, 'That's the person who did it.'" Most of the jurors smiled at that, too, and some people in the gallery laughed.

"Mr. Reilly is charged with a very gruesome crime," she said. She stood behind Peter, her hand on the back of his chair, and spoke softly. "Mr. Reilly, who discovered his mother, knows that far better than any of us."

She walked slowly over to the evidence table in front of Mr. Roberts and picked up a paper with a bright red label, State's Exhibit C, the first statement Peter had given to Trooper Bruce McCafferty, as they sat outside the house that Friday night, only an hour or so after Barbara died. It all seemed long ago, another time, another world, as she read how Peter and Geoff had gone up to the Shopwell, after school, to see if they needed Geoff on the weekend; how they bought a dollar's worth of gas at the Arco station; how they'd left Barbara watching TV around 7:20, and how when Peter came home and found his mother, he'd called the Madows, and had gone outside to wait for help.

"I have read the above, and it's the truth," Miss Roraback finished quietly, and put the statement back down on the table. Slowly, as though she had all the time in the world, she took out each item of clothing from the plastic bag, looked at it with great care, and showed them again to the jury. She reminded them that even Joanne Mulhern, "the wife of Trooper Mulhern," had testified that these were the clothes Peter had been wearing. She reminded them that Lieutenant Shay, in the skin search in the Kruses' kitchen, had found "no blood, no bruises, no scratches," nothing but one red knuckle. She pointed out that although "everybody's memory of time is elastic," there was a general consistency, and that sometime between 9:45 and 9:50, Peter Reilly got home, and that, in just a few minutes, "he is supposed to have done this awful thing."

She shook her head slowly and walked back around the courtroom, standing behind Peter's chair. The hush in the courtroom was thick and tangible.

"You know what the questioning was like in Hartford," she said, in an almost gentle voice. "First it was Sergeant Kelly for three and a half or four hours. Next it was Lieutenant Shay. Then Trooper Mulhern came in. Then we had Lieutenant Shay and Sergeant Kelly again. And out of it all, as I understand the state's claim, Mr. Reilly made certain admissions. After he'd been told that they had him cold, after he'd been told that it really wasn't so bad to kill his mother—after all, he was *her* victim, she was not his—after he'd been told that anybody can fly off the handle—after he had been told and drilled that he had a mental problem, that he needed help, that he could turn to his great friends, Kelly, Shay, and Mulhern, and get it from them." She paused, and shook her head slightly, in that angry little way she had.

"He was not told that the Madows were trying to reach him. He was there in isolation, and in a topsy-turvy way, his world got turned upside down. Most shocking to me, the state police of Connecticut created in Mr. Reilly's mind the fact that it wasn't so bad to have killed his mother, and that, in fact, he had killed her, although Peter

257

Reilly, right up to the end, says, 'I still don't think I did it. I'm not sure. It's like I'm dreaming.' "

Again she walked over to the exhibit table and picked up a paper. "I remember slashing with the razor I used for model airplanes," she read, and looked at the jury. "You will remember that that razor had no blood on it whatsoever," she told them.

"I also remember jumping on my mother's legs." Again she looked up at the jury. "You will recall that that derived from the first questioning by Sergeant Kelly," she said, thus reminding the jury that it was the officer who had first suggested to Peter that he might have "jumped up and down."

She looked at the statement, then back at the jury. "On the tape, Peter said he swung from left to right. Trooper Mulhern wrote 'I swung at her from right to left.' What Trooper Mulhern wrote down was a little more consistent with where the cuts occurred," she said dryly.

"The last sentence on the final statement: 'I want to clarify one point: When I slashed at my mother with a straight razor, I cut her throat.' " She shook her head again. "I would raise a serious question as to where page one of that original statement may be," she said softly, "and whether perhaps . . ." her voice trailed off, "but that's really neither here nor there. By the time they got through with him at Hartford, I think he would have signed a statement saying he had tried to cut out her sex organs. I think they could have had Peter Reilly sign a statement that after he committed this horrible crime he had turned his mother over and inflicted those wounds on her back." She shrugged a little, with a half-smile. "Maybe they didn't know about them.

"I think they could have had Peter Reilly say almost anything by the end of that time," she said, her voice stronger now, "and I think the tapes bear that out.

"I ask you to consider whether it makes sense that when an individual says, 'I did it, I killed my mother,' you would say, 'Here's a ham and cheese sandwich.' Peter Reilly says, 'Thank you very much,' and Trooper Mulhern says, 'What's happening?' It hardly seems consistent with what Peter Reilly is supposed to have said before."

Then she came to John McAloon. "A man of many names, many crimes," she said dryly, glancing at John Bianchi, who flushed and stared at her. "If Peter Reilly said something to him about throwing away his clothes, it wouldn't surprise me. It's part of the same old pattern. It's not surprising that after that brainwashing in Hartford, he'd still be saying things of that sort. It's almost hardly necessary to talk about. I would submit that the Madows and Mrs. Mulhern are far better witnesses."

She walked around the defense table and came closer to the jury, reminding them that Barbara had complained about a theft, and that she had told Peter, the day she died, that she'd bought a brand-new wallet and had cashed a check for $100.

"What was found in the house?" Miss Roraback asked now. "Sixteen cents. The back door ordinarily was never open, but that night it was open, and it was on that back door there was an unidentified, but identifiable, fingerprint."

She paused again, in a thoughtful way. Altogether, her summation had a slow, deliberate, sometimes rambling quality, as though she was trying to anticipate every possible thing the prosecutor might say, knowing that once she stopped, she could not refute anything, ever again.

She walked back to Peter's chair again and put her hands on his shoulders. "He's a young man who's lived in Falls Village about all his life," she said. "He's gone to school here; he's been active in the Teen Center. . . . Few of us have ever been submitted to such shock. And after that traumatic moment in his life he was placed in isolation, away from his friends, held by the police and not given sleep or food. And he came out with these statements, which I submit should not be given any weight at all.

"How, if Peter came home and indeed committed this awful offense, do you think that he could have gotten so angry over what I consider to be a rather petty issue, the car? An issue we've all probably had with our own parents or our children. I submit that's probably the most common argument in the American household." Peter smiled slightly, and Helen Ayre smiled at them both.

"Would he have had time," Miss Roraback asked, in an almost musing way, "to clean himself up? And what about those clothes?" She looked at the jury, speaking in a louder, more definite tone now. "I submit that that's impossible . . . There's certainly reasonable doubt . . . I would submit that there is no verdict you can return other than one of not guilty," she said slowly, and sat down.

Judge Speziale looked at the clock. "Short recess, Mr. Sheriff," he called out, and the jury looked relieved, seeming to draw a sort of collective breath.

None of the spectators talked much. Beverly King had come, Marion and Dot Madow and Geoff, Paul Beligni and Pam Belcher. Bill and Marie Dickinson stood quietly together, and in the hallway, Peter and his girl held hands.

George Judson leaned against the bar rail, watching Peter in the hall with speculative interest. "I've been wondering," George said, deadpan. "If Peter had gone home to live with Lieutenant Shay, do you think he would have been happy?"

"There she was!" John Bianchi told the jury, and gestured toward the floor with a flourish. He clenched his fist and made a smashing motion toward his own face. "That happened before death, and there's no evidence that anyone else was there. We find cuts on her stomach"— Mr. Bianchi slashed across his own middle, with the side of his hand —"when there was nobody in that house but Peter Reilly!" He turned to the defense table and shook his finger at Peter, "when there was nobody in that house but Peter Reilly!" Peter stared at him. As I watched, Peter's profile from the spectators' gallery looked sharply, bleakly outlined.

Mr. Bianchi stalked over to the exhibit table and picked up the knife, waving it at the jury. "This was covered with a thin layer of blood, on both sides and on the cutting edge," he said forcefully. Miss Roraback rose quickly to object, admitting that it was an unusual thing to do during a summation, but she pointed out that this was not the evidence that had been given.

Mr. Bianchi just looked at her and shrugged a little. But it was an eloquent gesture, seeming to say that what he'd just said about the knife was now part of the script. And this was, in a way, a performance, well-rehearsed and effective. Earlier Mr. Bianchi had set the stage, in a melancholy and evocative word-picture of Peter's life and times.

"A dirty house . . . a mother who had clearly turned into an alcoholic," he said in a grave voice. "When she was murdered, she had a blood alcohol reading of point twenty-two and was under the influence at the time of her death.

"Recall the tapes, where he indicated that she was on his back constantly . . . that she harassed him about the car, the one real item that they owned . . .

"This had to be a very, very unhappy arrangement for Peter Reilly," the prosecutor said gloomily. "And thus it's not strange to me that when he finally began to tell what had happened in Hartford, he felt 'free at last.' His burden was gone."

The prosecutor stood close by the jury rail. "Would it surprise you, ladies and gentlemen, that he had difficulty in remembering each and every detail? It doesn't surprise me at all. He was finally free of this horrible life he'd been living." In the second spectators' row, Paul Beligni, who had spent so much time with Barbara and Peter, often sleeping overnight on the roll of foam rubber in the living room, sneered audibly. Sheriff Battistoni frowned at him.

Mr. Bianchi backed away from the jury rail. "The circumstantial evidence is *overwhelming*," he repeated. "If there was nothing else, no statements, do the circumstances lead you to believe that somebody else did this?" He gestured toward Miss Roraback. "She has *hinted* that this might be a robber." His voice dripped scorn. "Miss Roraback says there was sixteen cents in the house. Think about it. Is a robber going to take the time to mutilate her body after she's dead? Does it make sense to you that this is what a robber would do?" He paused dramatically and shook his head. "It sure doesn't to me.

"Now let's go to the direct side of the case, besides the circumstantial," he said briskly. "Miss Roraback has pooh-poohed—has told you not to give one iota of weight—to anything this young man said. I submit his honor will charge you differently on this. He will tell you that those confessions and admissions were voluntary, that they were not in violation of Peter Reilly's constitutional rights.

"Miss Roraback would have you believe that he was held in isolation. Nothing could be further from the truth . . .

"If he said, 'Get me an attorney,' that would have been done. But he said he wanted to go to Hartford, and he went, driven by his friend, Jim Mulhern."

As for Sergeant Kelly, the prosecutor continued, "he sat right here in front of you for two days, ladies and gentlemen, and you had an opportunity to view this man and to come to a conclusion as to what kind of an individual Tim Kelly is. You heard them discuss model airplanes and model boat building." Mr. Bianchi looked indignant. "Did he use a rubber hose to beat it out of him? He tried, in good police procedure, to do it gently.

"Then we come to Lieutenant Shay. He obviously was a bit angry. He got rather perturbed, I thought. But what did that mean to this young man? He wanted to go home with him! Is that the response of somebody who has been in anguish?

"And then we come to the other 'inquisitor,' "—Mr. Bianchi's voice was thick with sarcasm. "They would have the utmost *gall* to say that he altered that statement. But Jimmy Mulhern couldn't care less. He only wanted the truth." Mr. Bianchi repeated how Peter had asked Mulhern, "Are you ashamed to know me now?" and when Mulhern asked why, Peter said, "Because I did it, I killed her."

"If there was ever a confession, ladies and gentlemen, that was it!" John Bianchi declared, close up to the jury rail now, almost breathing into the jurors' faces. "Right then and there. To his good friend, Jim Mulhern."

As for John McAloon, Mr. Bianchi admitted, "he certainly is a man of many crimes." He turned to the defense table, with a slight smirk. "He's got almost as bad a record as Mr. Erhardt. Not *quite,* but almost." The prosecutor turned back to the jury, then, speaking in a low, conversational tone, as though he were confiding in them.

"You know what convinced me of the truth of John McAloon's statement?" he asked them. "When he said that the kid told him his mother had had an operation and wouldn't take her medicine. How in the world did John McAloon know that if Peter Reilly hadn't told him?"

He shook his head, backed away from the jury rail, and stood in the middle of the floor. The jury and the spectators watched, fascinated. The difference in the lawyers' styles had never been more evident than they were today. This could have been a scene from a theater workshop. Here was a woman who appeared to be something of a loner, intellectual, complicated, and subtle, given to philosophical musings; she had begun her summation with a remark about the judicial system in Scotland, which allowed a jury to reach a verdict somewhere between guilty and not guilty, the verdict, "not proven."

And opposite her was a prosecutor who was jovial and folksy, portraying a man of plain old common sense. And he was theatrical—he dramatically waved a knife, made mock slashes against his own stomach, and clutched the lapels of his chocolate-colored suit as he addressed the jury. He had begun his summation by declaring that he had been trying criminal cases for twenty years.

"This case, like all criminal cases, is a difficult case," he declared. "But I submit to you that the state of Connecticut has carried forth its burden. The statements that this youngster made to the police—are they liars? Recall the tapes. He said, 'Everything I said I mean. And it's the *truth.*' "

The courtroom door was locked, nobody could go in or out while Judge Speziale charged the jury. Peter Reilly, in a bright yellow shirt with a burgundy V-necked sweater over it, stared at him. The judge talked about the law, which he said made no distinction between direct evidence and circumstantial evidence. "It is your duty to consider circumstantial evidence in the same way as direct evidence . . ." In the voir dire, he had said he would explain reasonable doubt when the time came, and now he did. He said it meant "doubt which is something more than a guess or surmise . . . not a captious or fanciful doubt, nor a doubt suggested by the ingenuity of counsel or a juror." Reasonable doubt, he declared, was "a real doubt, an honest doubt, which has its foundation in the evidence or lack of evidence."

He pulled out a big white handkerchief and wiped his nose. It suited the occasion, just as John Bianchi's wiping his face with a white handkerchief, near the end of his summation, had been an appropriate flourish; Kleenex would have been entirely out of place.

Regarding the testimony of Peter Reilly, the judge said, the jurors were to remember "his obvious interest in the verdict which you ladies and gentlemen are about to render." Speaking of interests, he reminded them, too, that John McAloon's case was still pending, and "he may in his own mind be looking for some favors."

At the heart of the criminal matter, the confession, the statements of Peter Reilly, "This court says that they are voluntary. . . . the defendant was not denied due process under the Fourteenth Amendment." On the matter of the polygraph test, though, he said sternly, "You may not consider the polygraph test to have any bearing on the credibility, guilt, or innocence of the accused."

He told them their decision must be unanimous and that they must have "no concern whatever with the punishment to be inflicted in the

263

case of conviction," and, like Catherine Roraback, he mentioned three possible verdicts. The jury could find Peter Reilly guilty as charged, guilty of murder. Or they could find him not guilty. But whereas Miss Roraback had talked, rather wistfully, of the Scottish alternative, "not proven," the court's third option was different.

"If not guilty as charged, consider manslaughter in the first degree," the judge said. He explained that manslaughter meant causing a person's death "with intent to cause serious physical injury . . . intent is a mental process . . . ordinarily, intent can be proved only by circumstantial evidence." In the language of the lawbooks he knew so well, Judge Speziale explained that a person who committed manslaughter acted "under the influence of severe emotional disturbance: a sudden frenzy, or passion, of the slayer . . . what he does under the first hot spur of impulse."

He ended his charge, as he had begun it, by relying on the law. "The law does not require that the state must prove a motive. If no motive can be inferred or found, it may raise a reasonable doubt." He paused slightly. "Or it may not raise a reasonable doubt." The jurors walked across the courtroom then to the jury room. Their hard work was starting now. Eleanor Novak was smiling to herself. It was her wedding anniversary, and her husband had promised to take her down to Washington for the weekend to see the cherry blossoms.

"That car's worth money!" Peter exclaimed. He watched as the automobile, a black and white Thunderbird, turned the corner at the Stop sign, went past the Congregational Church, and rolled out of sight. He seemed relaxed, though he smoked constantly. The night before, Mickey had taken him and Geoff to see *Magnum Force,* to get their minds off things.

It was midafternoon. The jury had gone to lunch, not in a group, but in whatever arrangements they chose, just as they had during the trial. Miss Roraback objected that the jurors ought to be sequestered, but she was overruled.

Only an hour or so after lunch, a knock came from inside the jury room, and a vibration, a kind of electric shock, ran through the courtroom. Geoff Madow, who had gone back upstairs briefly, raced down the stairs to the courthouse door. "Pete!" he called. "Pete! They're coming out!" Peter raced up the stairs. John Bianchi came out of his office, looking very serious.

It was generally felt that the longer a jury stayed out, the more likely they were to find a person guilty. A verdict reached so quickly probably meant an acquittal, and John Bianchi looked tense as he stood near the counsel table.

The sheriff took the note from the hand that reached out from the jury room and gave it to the clerk, who took it back to Judge Speziale's chambers. In a few minutes, the judge swept out around the corner and stepped up to the bench. He told the sheriff to bring the jury out, and in a few minutes all the jurors were back in their seats, watching him.

It was not a verdict, but a question, and Judge Speziale did not look pleased as he read it aloud. "The plaid jacket—where is it?"

The judge looked at the jurors, who stared back at him, looking a little guilty. He reminded them, not smiling, that the jacket was not part of the evidence. "You are not to surmise or conjecture as to its whereabouts," he told them sternly, and sent them back to their little room.

As the jurors' handbook had said: The law was what the judge said it was, and the evidence was what the judge let the jury hear and consider.

Outside the jury room, the rest of the afternoon passed easily. With the trial over, some barriers were down, and conversation among sheriffs and spectators flowed freely. Phil Plumb knew a lot about juries. "If you hear a toilet flush, they're ready to come out," he said. "A little rap at the door means more questions. A loud rap means a verdict." A sheriff's wife, Marian Battistoni, said she'd read in the *New York Daily News* that a baby born in 1974 had a two percent chance of being murdered and was therefore more likely to be slain than an American soldier in World War II had been likely to die in combat.

Dinnertime came, without a verdict. Judge Speziale drove away with his wife and his daughter in his burgundy Fleetwood, smiling and tipping his hat as he came out of the courthouse. Marion and Mickey, Dot and Murray, Bill and Marie Dickinson, Beverly King, and a bunch of the boys went to the Village Restaurant. Peter hadn't had lunch, only a Coke, but now he was hungry, and he asked for a steak.

265

The night session had a strange eerie quality. The fluorescent lights turned the courtroom a garish white, with blackness pressing against the tall schoolroom windows. People came and went, in and out of the courtroom. Jacqui Bernard, the woman who had put up most of the bail, had come up from New York to hear the summations. She was a striking woman, with big, quizzical eyes and close-cropped, almost white hair, and she was noticed in the court when she showed up. She was spending the night at our house, and when Joe O'Brien saw us chatting together in the courtroom, he asked me who she was. But Jacqui had asked to remain unknown. She had done some writing for a neighborhood weekly in New York, so I told Joe she was a reporter for the *West Side News*. It was a limited truth, and Joe O'Brien, after fourteen years as a newspaperman, knew all about limited truths. "The *West Side News,* you say?" Joe grunted, halfway between a laugh and a scoff, not bothering to ask the west side of where.

Mr. Roberts leaned over the bar rail and chatted about other trials, other transcripts. He said once a man was on trial for armed robbery, and the lawyer was questioning a friendly witness who was supposed to testify to the accused man's character as an upstanding citizen. "Do you know this man?" the lawyer began. "Yes," the witness said. "Do you know his reputation?" "Yes," the witness said. "And what is his reputation?" "He's known as a straight shooter," the witness replied.

None of us talked about Barbara. When I thought about it later, it seemed natural that we didn't. Tony Cookson, a college senior who wrote a thesis on the case, explained why. "In court, it's just a terrifying game," Tony said. "You lose track of the person who got killed."

While we were milling around the courthouse, however, sipping coffee and telling jokes, the jurors were talking about Barbara. They had stopwatches in the jury room, the knife, and the razor. They scraped the knife on the table in the jury room and found that it made marks on the table similar to the marks on Barbara's back. Although in Peter's confession he said he'd used a straight razor, the jurors were much more interested in the knife. They were interested, too, in the psychological overtones of the killing, especially the vaginal cutting.

They generally agreed that Peter didn't know what he was saying on the tapes, that he was just saying what people were saying to him. But the jurors were aware how important the tapes were, and during the

266

late evening, they asked to hear part of the tapes again. They'd have preferred to listen in the privacy of their little room, but the judge made them come out and take their seats in the box again. He sat on the bench in his black robe, and the courtroom was still filled with spectators, even at this hour, as the last portions of the tapes played again in the courtroom.

They sounded different now. They probably sounded clearer because of the nighttime hush, but besides the clarity there was a new—or at least a different—reality. I thought Peter's words might be sounding very different to us now, in this courtroom context, than they had sounded when he was actually being questioned in Hartford. The jurors' handbook had promised "a real life drama" in the courtroom, but real life wasn't always the clearest reality.

Here was Peter's voice again, gravelly and low, as Mulhern got to the slashing of the throat.

"Did you draw blood?"

"That I don't remember."

"You saw the razor cut, though?"

"I'm pretty sure. It's almost like in a dream."

"OK, sign."

"Are you proud of me?"

"Will I need a lawyer?"

"I can't advise you one way or the other. You have a right to have a lawyer."

"Yeah, but, I mean—the statement—"

"Doesn't matter. You can have an attorney at any time you want."

"Yeah, but I mean, everything I said I mean, I mean it is the truth."

The jurors went home that night. They were still about evenly divided, as they had been at the outset: five voting guilty, four not guilty, three undecided. All together they took six ballots before they reached their verdict Friday afternoon.

I went over to the courthouse that morning. Time dragged. Hardly anyone had anything to say anymore, and I sat for an hour on the grass across from the courthouse, where I could see people coming and going,

267

but wouldn't have to make conversation. The jurors asked to go to lunch early, and this time they went in a group to a private room that had been reserved for them in the back of Mitchell's.

From the phone booth on the stairway landing, I called Jean Beligni, who was waiting it out at home. She said that the night before, on the eleven o'clock news, she'd heard the newscaster begin, "A jury today reached a guilty verdict . . ." and had felt so faint she had to put her head in her lap. A friend who was with her went into the bathroom and threw up. As it turned out, the item was about the Yablonski murders, and the newscaster went on to say that, closer to home, in the Peter Reilly case, the jury has not reached a verdict.

"I am absolutely going bananas," Jean said. "I just can't understand it. There's no weapon! There's no blood! And what about the other fingerprint? But Paul said to me, after he heard John Bianchi's summation, that for the first time during the trial, he was worried and thought it might go the wrong way."

I was trying to read *Yankee* magazine when the word spread in mid-afternoon that the judge had asked the jury be brought out. Charles had been expecting this; he took a typed piece of paper from his note-pad and followed along as the judge read the jurors a modified version of the famous "Chip Smith" charge, a little lecture that was considered by some lawyers to be both necessary and discreetly persuasive, by others to be nothing less than judicial arm-twisting.

"All right, ladies and gentlemen," the judge said, smiling a little wearily at them, "you have been deliberating for some time in this case. I have no criticism to make of the length of time you have been in conference . . . however, I feel it is my duty to give you whatever aid I can in arriving at a verdict, if you are having a problem.

"Although the verdict to which each juror agrees must, of course, be his own conclusion and not a mere acquiescence in the conclusions of his fellows, and although each juror has the right and duty to retain his own opinion, yet, in order to bring twelve minds to a unanimous result, each juror should examine with candor the questions submitted to them, with due regard and deference to the opinions of each other . . ."

Miss Roraback protested that she had never heard the Chip Smith charge used until a jury announced it was deadlocked, which this jury had not done. But the jurors had gone back into the little room, Helen

Ayre looking surprised and somewhat chagrined. Mr. Roberts was leaning over the bar rail, telling me about Chip Smith, also accused of murder, back in the 1800s, and the first use of the charge. "As a result, Chip Smith was hanged," Mr. Roberts said dryly. The rap at the door came then, twenty-six minutes after the jury had gone to their room. It was a loud rap. It was loud as thunder.

The jury filed back into their places. Most of them looked at the judge, although Gary Lewis looked right at Peter, and Helen Ayre looked straight ahead of her, at some point on the opposite wall. When the jury came out, she had noticed Peter cross his fingers, and after that she didn't look at him again. Not even when the jury foreman, Edward Ives, gave the verdict: guilty of manslaughter in the first degree. Not even when the clerk, at Miss Roraback's request, polled the jury, in the formal, rather frightening language of the law: "Helen Ayre, look upon the accused. What say you, is he guilty or not guilty of the crime with which he stands accused?" "Guilty," Mrs. Ayre had said, as each juror had done. Her voice sounded low and strained. Catherine Roraback never took her eyes off Mrs. Ayre, watching her even as the jury was dismissed and filed out of the courtroom in a single, silent file, in a courtroom so hushed that the quiet itself was obtrusive.

Judge Speziale set May 14 for sentencing and said the bond would be continued. But Peter hardly seemed to hear, as he stood at the defense table, his shoulders sagging, his face ashy white, his mouth hanging open. The judge said he wanted to commend the attorneys and to give them "the thanks of the state of Connecticut, and my individual thanks." He looked at the reporters in the first row and said he wanted to thank us, too, because he knew that CBS had wanted us to talk in defiance of the gag order, and he knew that we had declined. He said he appreciated that. "It has been a long road for all of us," Judge Speziale said. "We've all left a little bit of ourselves here."

He left the bench quickly then, and in a few minutes the courtroom was nearly cleared. Geoff Madow sat in the middle of the third row, his head buried in his hands. The prosecutor and his assistants went back into their offices; Miss Roraback put her hand on Peter's shoulder and said something to him, before she and Peter Herbst went back toward the judge's chambers. Marion Madow sat in the second row of the courtroom, nearly empty now, just looking at Peter, who still stood by himself at the defense table, his hand covering his mouth, staring at the floor. Bill and Marie Dickinson sat in the row behind her, watching Marion. Then Eddie Dickinson came over to Marion to give her Peter's coat. She looked at the coat, then she looked at Eddie, and then Marion burst into tears—loud, gasping sobs that caused her to bend over and cross her arms in front of her stomach. Mickey put his arms around Marion and helped her get up. "Come on," Mickey said gently. "Come on now. Let's go home."

I had been on my way out of the courtroom, following the other reporters, but I stopped at the door. Farn put her hand on my arm quickly, as she hurried past. "I'm sorry," she whispered. I was staring at Peter and the Dickinsons and at Marion, and when Marion cried, like one domino toppling another, I began to cry too, in the same loud, gulping way. Mickey hurried over to me and put his arm around me. "Do you want to come home with us?" he asked, and I said yes.

Going down the courthouse steps, Murray Madow spoke loudly, not caring who heard. "Now all we have to do is find the killer," he said angrily. A crowd had gathered on the sidewalk and across the street, on the green, watching people come out. A TV crew from Hartford had tried to interview the jurors, but they were escorted out of the courthouse by deputies. A woman standing in the door of the coffee shop said: "He was such an arrogant kid. He thought he could get away with it."

John Bianchi was smiling when Roger took his picture, and he paused for a comment. "That's all it was, manslaughter," Mr. Bianchi told Roger. "I believed that from the day it happened." Not far behind him, Joe O'Brien approached Catherine Roraback, but she shook her head. "I haven't got a goddamn comment," she said.

Peter Reilly came down the steps, flanked by a sheriff and two deputies, with Mickey Madow leading the way. Peter's hair was streaming in the wind, and he still had that ashen, sick look, his hands thrust into his pockets. Mickey looked bad, too. He was carrying Miss Roraback's briefcase. It was always heavy, filled with papers and bulging folders. Sometimes she had so much to bring to court that everything wouldn't fit into the case, and she had to use a tote bag or a satchel. Even a paper bag. Peter's plaid jacket had been in a paper bag—the jacket John Sochocki had mentioned, the jacket the jurors had asked about. When the police returned it to Marion Madow, along with the rest of Peter's and Barbara's things, the jacket had a red stain in front. Miss Roraback thought either it was wine, or the residue of a lab test the police had done, and twice she had brought the jacket into court, to show the jury the jacket wasn't missing. But each time she had changed her mind.

All evening, people came by to see Peter, very much as they'd done the night he got out of jail. Marion and Nan put out cold meat loaf, rice, and salad, and made pots of coffee. Marie Dickinson sat at the dinette counter, smoking. "The way I feel tonight reminds me of the weekend they took Peter," Marie said. "I keep asking myself, 'What happened?' "

Reporters kept calling up, but nobody was quite sure what Peter should say. Everybody remembered what had happened when he'd talked the day he got out of jail, and with the sentencing now hanging over his head, the fear remained. We called Catherine Roraback to ask her advice. "I think it's healthy for him to do it himself," she said. "He could just say, 'I'm innocent, and I hope someday I'll be able to prove it.' "

I didn't take many notes on what Peter said that night, or on what other people said. One reason was that I was in and out of the den, trying to get to the phone. The other reason was that I didn't feel like taking notes. I remember Peter sitting on the floor in the living room, looking up at Elaine Monty, telling her about the day. "John Bianchi came over to me afterwards and wished me good luck," Peter said.

I remember Marion's sister Vicky. She had sometimes been at the Madows' when Jim Mulhern came by. "He used to tease me and say, 'Aren't you afraid to live in New York City?' " Vicky recalled bitterly. "Well, I'll take my chances with the New York cops any day."

Late that night, the phone was still busy, and I slipped out and drove over to the Belignis'. The Belignis and the Madows were not nearly as friendly as they'd been, and although Aldo had gone over to the Madows' after the verdict, Jean, who was more outspoken, had decided to stay home. Jean was the first person I'd met when I first heard about Peter Reilly, and I wanted to see her tonight. We sat in her kitchen for a while, just the two of us.

Then I got back in my car. The night was dark, without stars, and I drove for hours. I drove like a fugitive through the night, with a crackling feeling inside my head, angry and guilty. Angry at myself for not having spoken out before. I wished I had tried to attract more attention, that I'd talked on Rick Kaplan's TV news, that I'd said, "Look at this. See what is happening here." But I hadn't wanted to miss the trial, which I enjoyed enormously; its marvelous characters with their marvelous lines, so tragic and funny, so much better than lines I could make up. I'd attended the trial as theater, a suspense drama with a happy ending, for not since the day I heard the tapes at the pretrial hearings had it occurred to me that Peter would be found guilty. At the trial, when I'd heard him say, "I'm not sure. Can you say I'm not sure?" that seemed to create plenty of doubt, and I'd written fancifully in my notes that I saw "reasonable doubt strewn over the dingy green carpet like rotting leaves."

I was stunned, too, by the freakish nature of all this, by the sheer chance that had brought me to the courtroom that December day, by the chance that had determined that it would be Judge Armentano who would hear the tapes; Judge Wall, they said around court, would probably have thrown the confession out. It was chance, too, almost a whim, that Judge Armentano had had some of the tapes played in open court. It seemed so random, and random was frightening.

The law had never caused much stir in my life. I had served on a jury once, a ridiculous episode in a New York City Civil Court with me and eleven other unqualified people attempting to unravel a complicated insurance claim, involving holding companies, real estate, mortgages, and liens. The verdict didn't have to be unanimous, just ten out of twelve, and after a few miserable hours, enough of us voted one way or the other to make a verdict, just to get it over with. As we were being polled in the jury box, one man changed his vote.

When my magazine piece appeared, a letter came from a man in Indianapolis, a social worker. "Too often I have seen the law is a club, used to break open the lives of people," he wrote. Now I had seen that too, and I ran from the sight.

It was after midnight when I drove through Litchfield, past the jail, past the courthouse with the clock tower, a town at rest. I drove up our driveway, went into the house, turned on all the lights, and made a gin and tonic. I called Jim in New York and I made some other calls, but I was still restless, angry, bursting to talk. I got back in the car, leaving my drink melting on the slate counter by the sink. I turned the car radio to a crazy level and drove south, looking for Tarrytown, where a birthday party for a friend from my *Life* magazine days was going on. I got lost several times, and it was about four in the morning when I got there. But there was still a remnant of a party going on, a good audience. I began to talk about Peter Reilly and what had happened to him. Daylight came, and I talked on and on, insisting, like the crazed old mariner, that everyone pay attention to what I had to say.

14

Eddie Houston at the Shell Station had told Peter he could have a job anytime, so in the weeks between the verdict and the sentencing, Peter pumped gas a mile or so from the little house where Barbara died. At home, at the Madows, he seemed unworried, even content, as he played his guitar and worked on an old car he was rebuilding in the driveway. He watched *Ben Hur* on television and rode his bike. When Roger came by to interview him, he took a charming and most uncharacteristic picture of Peter, standing by his bike in front of ·the house. "The thought of returning to jail scares me," Peter told Roger. "Someday I want to hold a job, own my own home, and raise a family. This whole thing is just throwing a wrench into all my plans."

My own plans hadn't been devastated, but they had gone astray. As the end of the trial approached, I had accepted an assignment from *The New York Times Magazine* to do a piece on Robert Redford. After a courthouse winter, surrounded by autopsy slides and sheriffs, I was ready for a little glitter in my life. I told the *Times* I'd be free the week after Easter.

Besides needing a professional change of scene, I needed psychological distance. Free-lance photography clearly was a dream we couldn't afford; Jim had begun looking for a regular job again. It was sad to have our hopes collapse, Everyman's dream of getting out of the rat race; it was even sadder to have so much trouble trying to get back in. Unemployment was a national epidemic in 1974; we began to borrow money, and our tempers began to shred.

But Peter wasn't free the week after Easter, so neither was I. I called the *Times Magazine* and explained why I couldn't do the Redford piece. My editor said all right, but later he grumbled good-naturdly to my sister, who worked there, that he didn't really understand my reasons. I couldn't blame him. But Peter Reilly had occurred in obscurity, and it seemed urgent, now, that the discussion of what had happened, and why, and what might be done about it, spread beyond the silent Litchfield hills.

I didn't write an article, because we thought the publicity might hurt Peter, who was more than ever at the mercy of the courts. Partly it was the shadow of the gag order, and partly it was the shadow of self-censorship, the eeriest shadow of all.

Bea Keith and her mother were writing letters. So was Jacqui Bernard. So I began writing letters, too. In my letters I asked for "legal, moral, or financial help," asking for anything a person might be able to give or do. Along with each letter, I sent some stories Roger had written; my *New Times* piece, with the tapes; and an editorial from the *Lakeville Journal,* "The Issues in the Reilly Case." The editorial, written by Robert Estabrook, pointed out that while a jury's judgment had to be respected, the police methods used in the case might make a verdict questionable. The editorial also called Judge Armentano's decision to allow the confession "appalling." Altogether, it was a kind of amateur crusader's kit, and Bill Dickinson made dozens of copies down at his shop. "If you need more, just holler," he said. When Peter came over to our house one warm afternoon, he helped collate the pages of the piece.

"Attention should be paid," Arthur Miller had once written about obscure people, so I wrote to him. I wrote to Philip Roth and Martin Segal, Paul Newman and Joanne Woodward, William Styron and William Buckley. I didn't know these people, but I knew they lived in Connecticut and thought they might care. At least, in my button-holing fervor, I thought they ought to. I wrote to Mike Nichols, who had a house in Bridgewater. Somebody forwarded my letter to him in California, and late one night he called me from there. We talked a long time, then Mike Nichols began writing letters too.

I sent a kit to Auntie B. by registered mail, but it came back marked "Addressee Unknown."

Peter sat at one end of our sofa, plucking little white feathers from the seat cushion. Dot Madow had driven him down to New Haven that day and he'd seen a car he liked, a silver and black 1934 Plymouth with a 318-cubic-inch engine. "It was beautiful," Peter said softly. "It shone like a new diamond."

The tape recorder lay on a table behind the sofa, the microphone between us on the pillows. There was so much I wanted to know about this young man with the shy smile, who looked at me, sometimes, as though I were miles away. We hadn't talked much during the trial, and now the day of sentencing was looming. I was afraid to think of what might lie ahead, but Peter didn't seem afraid at all.

"Did you know that I'm engaged?" he asked. "When Aunt Dot took us down to the car show at the Naugatuck Valley Mall, I saw a jewelry store. I went in and saw a one-third-carat diamond ring that I liked, but I'm going to need a bank loan." I couldn't think of anything to say to that. So I said that I had seen the girl at the trial a couple of times. She had an oval face, large dark eyes, and long, dark, straight hair. I said she was very beautiful. "She is," Peter agreed.

"When are you getting married, Peter?" I asked, finally.

"It's a long way off," he assured me. "July or August of next year, nineteen seventy-five. We'll both be out of school then, and I'll be working. I'll be on my feet financially."

"Where will you be working?" I asked.

"It's still up in the air," he told me, "but I'm thinking of the Southern New England Telephone Company. They pay four dollars and sixty-five cents an hour, with all the medical." I thought of the two jurors who worked at the phone company.

"I'm going to buy back the Triumph too," Peter was saying. "The body doesn't have much rust on it at all. The drive line is in rotten shape, but I'm going to put in a new motor, a new transmission, put a new rear end on it. I'm going to use foam mufflers, a three hundred horsepower Chevy V-8 engine. It's going to be quite the little racing car."

He smiled, and I smiled back. I didn't have any idea how to handle this. In a few days he would stand up in court to be sentenced for

276

manslaughter. I hadn't expected him to weep and wail, but I wasn't prepared for this. He was making plans. He was making so *many* plans.

Anne came in from the kitchen with a cup of apple juice, and sat in the window seat, watching us.

"Has she been baptized?" Peter asked suddenly, just as he'd been asked in Hartford, so long ago: "Have you been baptized? Do you believe in a Supreme Being?" Barbara had brought Peter up in a religious void, but apparently he hadn't stopped wondering. I said Anne was baptized Catholic, and we'd bring her up that way, so that later she'd have a basis for her own decision. Peter agreed. "I'm studying the Catechism myself now," he said. "You have to start someplace."

"I'd like to know a little more about your mother, Peter," I said. "I'm going to have to talk about her in the book, and make her seem real. That'll be hard, because I never knew her."

Peter nodded. "I wish you could have met her," he said. "You'd have liked her. She was something else. She was terrific." He laughed, a soft laugh with a crinkly tone. "When I was about eight or nine, when we still lived with my grandparents, my mom built a treehouse and she gave a cocktail party there. I remember stealing all the little olives and onions. Somebody who was running for office—I think it was Tom Meskill, before he became such a big wheel in this state —came over, and everybody sat around in a little circle twenty feet in the air.

"Then we decided to leave my grandparents' house," he said. He said it easily, with no hint at all of the hostility between the women.

"We lived on Music Mountain for about a year," Peter continued. "Then we moved back to Johnson Road with my grandmother until we decided to leave again."

"Do you know why your mother stopped working?" I asked. I had heard the other rumors of trouble surrounding Barbara, that she'd been fired because of an affair she'd had, a scandal involving blackmail. Barbara herself, in a letter to her Uncle Jim, had complained that Hilda had caused her to lose jobs, by writing "poisonous letters" to Barbara's employers.

But Peter didn't mention any of these things, so I didn't press him. "I remember when she worked at the Cole Insurance Company in

Cornwall Bridge," he said. "Now it's a real estate office. She worked there ever since I could remember. The Dickinsons used to baby-sit for me. I met Eddie when I was only four or five. Say, have you seen Eddie's car since he got it painted? It's candy apple red and gold, with swirls in back. It's really nice." I said I hadn't seen it.

"Then around 1965 or 1966 we went on welfare," Peter went on. "I was getting older, and I didn't have my grandparents to take care of me after school, and my mom couldn't have kept house and looked after me too. It was such a hassle," he said vaguely. "So she just decided: me, not the job.

"She used to write, I know," he said. "But I never saw any manuscripts." I said if there were any, I could show them to somebody in New York, and perhaps they could be published. "I could use two thousand, eight hundred dollars to get that car I saw this afternoon," Peter said thoughtfully. "But I wonder if the state of Connecticut would take the money."

We talked about Auntie B. "I don't know that much about her," Peter said. "She was just always called my godmother. I wrote her quite a sarcastic letter. I said, I'm out on bond, with no help from you. Where were you when I needed you? I haven't heard from her since. Where is she? It just totally baffles me. There are so many things that don't make sense to me."

Anne had left the window seat, and now she popped up behind the sofa, wearing a witch's mask from last Halloween. Peter smiled at her.

"I *see* you," Peter said.

"I *see* you," Anne echoed. We laughed, then Anne wandered away.

"I just think the cops were too darn gung-ho to grab someone," Peter went on, "and in the time they spent, whoever did it just got away." He said he wasn't bitter. "Just leery, now. I don't trust them anymore." But he said it casually. Something else he had learned from Barbara.

"She was a very nonchalant person," Peter said. "Didn't get uptight about anything. I'm not so used to my new surroundings. Dad goes by the rules, you know? I'm used to playing everything by ear, you know what I mean? I think things work out best that way, myself. Just give it time, and it'll work out. Things work out. They always do." He smiled at me, as though he didn't have a care in the world. And in a way he didn't. He seemed shielded—insulated, isolated from whatever was happening to him, even while it was happening. And so much had happened, not just on the murder night but in the time since. In the past eight months he had called three different women "Mom."

Peter was not sentenced on May 14. Albert Roraback died that day in Amsterdam. Judge Speziale had already postponed sentencing for one week, when Miss Roraback sent word that she wanted to stay with her brother a while longer. The judge had not been in touch with her directly, but he had called Peter Herbst and told him to telephone her over there and put a stop to the petitions he'd heard were being passed around in support of Peter Reilly.

Along with the petitions, buttons were being sold for $1, to help the Reilly Fund. Nearly everybody liked the idea, although not everybody had agreed on what the buttons should say. Some people had favored JUSTICE FOR REILLY, but others felt that that might upset the judge, who presumably felt Reilly had had his dose of justice already. Finally, PEOPLE BEHIND REILLY won by a show of hands. "But don't wear them in court," Mickey warned. "No buttons, no chewing gum, no posters." Bea Keith suggested a silent vigil, and Elaine Monty agreed. "We won't need posters," Elaine said. "They'll know why we're there."

Money was still a problem, although there had been a small increase in checks after the verdict, and only one, for $5, had bounced. The committee had sent checks to Catherine Roraback whenever it could, but in May, after eight months on the case, she had only been paid $3,500, not enough for her to pay Peter Herbst's salary. The committee held a coffee hour at which Murray Madow auctioned baked goods. The coffee hour was successful, in spite of the controversy over its location. The committee had hoped to hold it in one of the halls or parish houses connected with one of the churches in Torrington. But eight churches turned them down, and after some discussion of what Christianity was all about, or ought to be all about, anyway, they ended up having their coffee hour at a cocktail lounge, the Starlite Room of the Sky-Top Bowling Lanes, on a Sunday afternoon, when the lounge was closed.

Mickey and Father Paul asked the police commissioner to reopen the investigation into Barbara's death. There were several things they still wondered about, including the fact that Barbara's clothes were wet; the time sequence; the unidentified fingerprint; and, then, the wallets.

One old wallet of Barbara's had been found in the house when she died. But two wallets were missing then: the new one she'd bought that day, and the wallet she'd reported stolen, with more than a hundred dollars in it, not long before she died. On the Monday after Peter was found guilty, Elizabeth Mansfield, who ran a general store in Falls Village, called the *Hartford Courant*. She said that on November 15, 1973, she had found a wallet near the driveway of the vacant house she owned, just down the road from Barbara's place. There was no money in the wallet, only identifying papers of Barbara's. Mrs. Mansfield had taken the wallet to show to the defense lawyer, and then she'd turned it over to the state police.

The theft of Barbara's wallet always seemed part of an ominous pattern in the weeks before she died. She'd had harassing phone calls; obscene scrawls had been found on the walls in the vacant house nearby. Lieutenant Shay himself, in a news story shortly after Barbara died, had confirmed that the police were still investigating a reported break-in and theft. Jim Mulhern had testified about the phone calls, and Peter had testified about the stolen wallet. But the wallet that Mrs. Mansfield found wasn't produced at the trial. One more ambiguity; one more unanswered, or half-answered, question.

Peter was sentenced on Friday, May 24.

In the courtroom, the atmosphere was tight and tense. Marion sat with her chin in her hands, staring straight ahead. Peter's girl sat next to the bar rail, and alongside her, Peter was kneeling on one knee so they could talk quietly. Her long hair was spilling down onto the rail. Miss Roraback came over to get Peter, and took him into the little room that the jury had used. Miss Roraback closed the door behind her. A few minutes later, when Father Paul arrived, he walked over to the jury room and knocked. He was carrying his brown leather Bible, and, except that he was a little too young, it was like a scene from an old prison movie—Jimmy Cagney, or Mickey Rooney, on Death Row, and the padre coming to say a prayer. Mr. Roberts was as crisp and sprightly as ever, with an American Legion poppy in his lapel.

The judge came out. "Good morning, your honor," John Bianchi said loudly. "We are here this morning for sentencing, your honor, in *State of Connecticut* versus *Peter Reilly*. On Good Friday, April twelve, a jury of twelve found Peter Reilly guilty of manslaughter in the first degree after a seven-week trial. Since your honor presided at that trial, it seems unnecessary for me to review the facts of the case. . . .

"I did know the victim for twenty years, and I do know that she had certain problems, your honor. She was under the influence of alcohol at the time of her death. It is clear to the state, from the evidence, that when Peter Reilly got to his home, there was an explosion that resulted in the death of his mother. It is clear to the state from the evidence, from the interrogation of Peter Reilly in Hartford by the Connecticut State Police, from what he said there, that a sense of relief had come over him, that something had gone off his back at long last."

Mr. Bianchi looked very grave. "Now, there are some things the state knew also that did not come into evidence, your honor." He picked up a white envelope from the counsel table. "A benefactor of this family—a letter from her had been received by the family just that day, indicating that her assistance was finished, that the family was going to have to go it by themselves. And the benefactor has been completely out of this matter since that very day." Mr. Bianchi put the envelope down, glanced briefly at Miss Roraback, then looked back at the judge.

"I have always felt that this was a matter of manslaughter, not murder," the prosecutor said. "The end results took just seconds to accomplish. But Barbara Gibbons had a right to live. I would conclude by recommending a minimum of seven years to a maximum of sixteen."

There was a kind of rushing sound, a rustle in the courtroom. Then Catherine Roraback stood up. She was wearing the same salmon-colored two-piece dress she'd worn the first time I saw her, at the pretrial hearing.

"The defendant has denied his guilt of these charges," she said. "I would urge your honor to consider the total background of Mr. Reilly. He has lived here in the hills of Litchfield County. He has grown up here—gone to school here—had his friends here—had his roots here." She spoke slowly and with what seemed a tinge of sadness. "He has always enjoyed a very good reputation within this community. He is polite—responsible—respectful—sincere. He has a sense of humor. He enjoys the outdoors. He enjoys the company of his friends. He has been an adequate student." She smiled slightly. "Not an outstanding student, but an adequate student. He has worked for various people, who have submitted letters to your honor, including Aldo Beligni, who talks of Peter's desire to make something of himself.

"The other aspect of this case is the strength of community support," Miss Roraback said. "Some of it may seem excessive in your honor's eyes, but it seems to be a sincere expression of real support for a young man in trouble. The purpose of our criminal system, as I understand the theory, is rehabilitation, and I submit that however important the correctional aspects, they fall a good deal short of an ideal situation for a young man such as Mr. Reilly who has no prior criminal record.

"I myself observed Peter when he was in jail," Miss Roraback said, as though she were confiding in a friend, "and I watched a continuing period of what I can only characterize as a withdrawal from society, being skeptical of it; a slight cynicism."

Judge Speziale had alternated between watching Miss Roraback and looking at the letters and petitions he had with him. Now he frowned and interrupted her.

"I spent a good deal of time last evening over these letters," he said. "I do not find any remorse. I don't see remorse anywhere here at all, Miss Roraback."

Miss Roraback stared at him for a moment. "I think remorse is not the word to apply," she said. "He has stated that he is, in fact, innocent. I would not think that remorse is going to be created in Peter Reilly by incarceration. I do not think that Peter Reilly is going to turn into a better man in the length of time Mr. Bianchi is talking about. Peter Reilly, being the young man he is, highly impressionable, young, still in his very formative years, might indeed be made into a good and functioning member of our society if he were able to do so in a loving, warm family situation.

"In prison, he would be destroyed as a person," Miss Roraback said bluntly. "I don't think that's the intention of our law, but I think that's the result. I ask for the imposition of a suspended sentence. I realize it would be an unusual step, but this is an unusual case."

Now the judge stared back at Catherine Roraback. He stared and blinked, as though he could not comprehend what she had asked. Mr. Bianchi stared at her too, as one by one, people stood to speak in Peter's behalf. One by one they came up from the gallery, through the little wooden gate, and stood next to Peter at the counsel table, facing the judge. Barbara's cousins came first.

"I plead with you not to send him to jail," June said, clasping her hands in front of her tightly.

"We are the parents of three boys," Vicky said. "We have the room." Vicky began to cry.

Father Paul stood up. "Knowing his family background, and knowing Peter's personality, that he is so easily influenced, it would be best for him to be in a good family situation. There is no substitute for a good home."

Judge Speziale looked more and more worried as more and more people stood up. The frown lines on his forehead seemed to burrow into his skin, even as we watched.

Mickey stood up. "Your honor mentioned the word 'remorse,' " he said. "Peter has lived with us since—since this situation arose, and I have seen his sorrow. My wife has seen his sorrow. I have heard him say, 'My mom did this,' or, 'She used to do that.' " Sitting at the counsel table now, Peter began to cry. Watching him, Marion began to cry too. Mickey looked at Peter, then he looked at the judge. "A boy like this deserves a real good break," Mickey said.

When Marion stood up, she told how, when Peter was in jail, she had noticed his cynical attitude. "He was guarded and suspicious and was not sure of anything we said," Marion told the judge. "If he goes to jail, he's going to go deeper into himself. He *does* listen, and he's a very good boy." Marion reached out, right there in the courtroom, and stroked Peter's hair.

John Bianchi stood up once more. "The duties of the state are sometimes very heavy," he said solemnly. "This was a horrible homicide. There have been thousands of words written about this case. But I have not heard one word of Barbara Gibbons, who lies dead in her grave."

The judge looked at Peter. "Peter Reilly, do you have anything to say before sentence is imposed?"

Peter stood up. His hands were clasped behind his back again. "I will not be a threat to society," Peter said in a very low voice. "I just want a chance to live a decent life." Then he bent his head and cried.

"This is the longest trial I've had in my whole judicial career," Judge

283

Speziale said. "This is an extremely difficult case. This court is impressed by the outpouring of the defendant's friends in the community. But a human being has been killed, as a result of a very vicious and horrible homicide . . ." I wasn't crying, but I felt strange. The judge's voice seemed very faraway, and I seemed to hear only in snatches. "Court . . . sentences you, Peter Reilly . . . six to sixteen years."

Then there was another rush, another flurry in court. People were crying all around me. A woman on the aisle seat in the front row was crying so hard it was mentioned in some news stories. The troopers walked quickly over and stood behind Peter. John Bianchi asked that Peter's bail be raised to $100,000 now, and Judge Speziale, looking anguished, changed it to $60,000 instead. He said he would be ready to help counsel find the proper facility for Peter to serve his sentence, and then very quickly, court was adjourned. It was over.

We milled around on the green, in the chilly drizzle, watching for Peter. Raymond Lind, one of the jurors, was standing further down the green; he had come back to watch, too. A small crowd on the sidewalk was held back by policemen, and the way was clear. But we never saw Peter. As we watched the front door, a police cruiser backed into the little driveway alongside the courthouse. There was a slamming door, then the cruiser shot out of the driveway and made a fast right turn, speeding past us. "There he goes!" somebody shouted. Peter was off to the penitentiary, taken there under maximum security. There were two sheriffs in the back seat, one on either side of him, and two policemen in the front. He was shackled in leg irons, and handcuffed to a restraining band around his waist.

Peter had been convicted on a Friday, at the start of a holiday weekend. Now he had been sentenced on a Friday and was being driven off to Somers at the start of another busy, festive weekend. That night was Prom Night at Regional, and on Monday, the Memorial Day parade was held in Canaan, down West Main Street and out to the ballfield for the official opening of the Little League season.

John Bianchi, dressed in snow-white slacks like a yachtsman, spoke at the ceremony. Standing at home plate, he looked around the field, at the family groups sitting in the bleachers, at the children hanging out of the back of pickup trucks, at the clumps of people standing around on the wet grass of the outfield.

He stood with his hands clasped behind his back, very much as Peter Reilly had stood in court. "I want to tell you boys that the object of the game is to win," he said. "There is no substitute for winning."

The bond for an appeal had been raised from $50,000 to $60,000, and the extra $10,000 had to be raised at once, to save Peter from a prison weekend. Everyone had vivid pictures of gun towers and electric fences and men hanging around the shower room, just waiting for Peter Reilly.

We stood on the green while people scurried around, trying to raise the cash. Altogether, with the tears and the running around, and the people clustered in the rain, having been run out of the courthouse by Sheriff Menser, it was an absurdly theatrical scene, and it had an appreciative audience. In the State's Attorney's office overlooking West Street and the green, there were faces at the window all the time. Sam Holden was watching, and so was a blonde woman in a pink suit. She was laughing.

As it got chillier, some of the crowd came to my house and milled around my living room, sipping coffee Judy Liner had made. Nobody was crying anymore, but after a while some of us got nervous, just waiting around, and we drove back into town. Mickey was standing on the courthouse steps, looking worried. He said they had $7,000, but he couldn't figure out what was keeping Murray. At 1:48, Murray screeched around the corner of the jail. He had the rest of the money.

"Now will they bring Peter back?" Marie Dickinson asked. Bill shook his head. "Somebody has to go get him," he said. "When they take you to Somers, it's a one-way trip."

That night, for the third time in three months, there was open house on Locust Hill. The night Peter had got out of jail, the mood was buoyant; on the night of the verdict, it had been stunned and somber. Tonight the mood was somewhere in between: both down and up, and defiant. Marion told about getting Peter out of jail. A guard had talked with the Madows as they waited for Peter. "I'm glad you came for him," the guard told Marion. "That kid would have disappeared in here."

Peter showed off his souvenirs—two sets of white underwear with red stenciled numbers, a razor and five double-edged blades, a toothbrush, two big blue patterned handkerchiefs. "Very, very nice," Dick Monty said. "Just like home. All you needed was a bowl of milk and a cat."

Peter said he had only one major regret about the day. "I wish I hadn't gotten the haircut," he said. "The judge didn't even notice. It didn't help." Murray Madow looked annoyed. "But I'll tell you what *would* have helped," Murray said. "When you were on the witness stand, Peter Reilly, you should have cried and cried. You should have kept saying, I didn't do it, I didn't do it."

The Belignis didn't come that night, so I stopped by on my way home. I asked Aldo how he felt. "Disgusted," Aldo said. "We were like Chicken Little. We should have said what we thought a long time ago. Nobody's going to shut me up again."

"I've been thinking about the sentence," Jean said. "I don't think one man should have that kind of power. You know, I used to think the colored people were wrong when they said, 'Power to the people!' Now I think they were right."

Back in our living room, Jim and I talked about the trial, the verdict, the sentencing. Everything was over, yet it had just begun. Mickey warned the committee that they were settling down to "a long, steady grind." And the *Lakeville Journal* reported it that way. UNDAUNTED, REILLY FRIENDS PLAN LONG-TERM EFFORT. The *Journal* ran another editorial about the tapes, pointing out that Peter Reilly had been "almost pathetically eager" to cooperate with the police. And they published another letter from Bea Keith's mother, Mrs. Tompkins, a wry footnote to the past eight months. Since polygraph tests were inadmissible in court, she said, why were they given?

Arthur Miller called me the afternoon of the sentencing, and the next morning I drove down to Roxbury. I sat in his cluttered little studio in the back of a lovely old farmhouse with a view of the hills, faraway and serene. He was interested in Peter Reilly, and the next week he drove over to Canaan to meet Peter and the others. Roger described the famous playwright, attending a committee meeting, "dressed in a blue workshirt and tan chinos, cross-legged on a folding chair, puffing a pipe and listening."

Mike Nichols was back in town, too. He called his friend William Styron and suggested we all get together to talk about Peter Reilly.

"Why not?" Styron said, and suggested Sunday at his place. It sounded casual, but Styron already felt strongly about the Reilly affair. He said he had had his doubts about the tapes when he first read *New Times,* then he had put the matter aside. "Oh well," he said, "that's the way Connecticut justice goes." But he remembered it, and when Mike Nichols called, he was ready to get involved. William Styron, who had won a Pulitzer for *The Confessions of Nat Turner,* was not unfamiliar with the criminal justice system. He and Nichols, along with Philip Roth, had posted bond for a man who was finally cleared of a murder charge after three trials and seven years in New York prisons.

The group that Rose and Bill Styron had gathered in their Roxbury home more than made up in glamor for my loss of Robert Redford. Besides Mike Nichols and the Styrons, Jean Widmark was there, the producer Lewis Allen, and an array of writers, including Renata Adler and John Phillips. The months of the trial had been emotionally and financially draining for Catherine Roraback; there was talk of a new lawyer, and Arthur Miller stopped by to say he was working on that. We had drinks; we ate spaghetti carbonara, salad, and chocolate mousse; and I went on another talking jag. But the Styrons and their friends wanted to hear, and when Mike Nichols suggested that the group pledge a year's interest on the bail loan, some of them agreed to contribute. Bill Styron wrote a check that evening and handed it to me to carry back to Canaan.

Later—much later—as the Peter Reilly affair became well known, the involvement of these people was considered window dressing, an up-country version of radical chic. But it was never that. Peter Reilly wasn't lettuce, or grapes; he wasn't black or Chicano, or front-page in *The New York Times.* On the day after sentencing he was on the last page, near the TV listings.

Once in a while, word would leak out that one of the famous people to whom Mike Nichols had written had sent a check to the Reilly Fund, and a name might appear in the paper: Elizabeth Taylor, Candice Bergen, Art Garfunkel, Jack Nicholson, Dustin Hoffman. But mostly it was a very quiet, very backstage effort, which made it especially valid. When James Wechsler, the columnist for the *New York Post,* wanted to meet Peter in response to Jacqui Bernard's appeal, Mickey and Marion drove Peter down to Westport one Saturday. They spent the afternoon there, and Jimmy Wechsler wanted to write a column, but because we were afraid that publicity then would not help Peter, Jimmy Wechsler agreed not to write.

Police Commissioner Fussenich had announced he would not reopen the Reilly investigation, as the committee had petitioned him to do, so Roger Cohn did some legwork on his own, starting at Bob's Clothing Store. Bob told Roger about the wallet Barbara had bought on the morning of the day she died; he told Roger that he had been questioned by the police and had given them a signed statement. Roger talked with Lieutenant Shay, who told him that although the police had two wallets connected with the case—the old one found in the house, and the one found by Mrs. Mansfield—they'd never found the new one. Roger went out to Falls Village and talked with people around Barbara's neighborhood, including Tim and Mike Parmalee, teen-aged boys who lived just down the road.

Around that time, too, the Connecticut State Police announced that its troopers were switching from the standard .38 caliber pistol to the .357 Magnum, one of the deadliest handguns around, capable of blowing off an arm or a leg. They were switching to a new ammunition too, a hollow-nosed bullet that flattened out, then mushroomed, on impact. The switch was criticized in many places, including some newspapers and the civil liberties groups and the Episcopal Diocese of Connecticut, but Commissioner Fussenich seemed undisturbed. "We don't use a gun to slow a person down," he said. "We shoot to kill."

In other police news, there was a personnel change at Canaan Barracks, and Lieutenant Shay was transferred back to Hartford.

By the end of summer, Peter had a new lawyer. He was T. F. Gilroy Daly of Fairfield, recommended by Arthur Miller's law firm in New York. Roy Daly was tall and slim, with crinkly blue eyes and the smile of a matinee idol. Once he had been a prosecutor himself. From 1961 to 1964 he was assistant District Attorney under Bobby Kennedy and had been involved in prosecuting organized crime in New York. In 1970 he ran for Congress on the Democratic ticket, but lost, and in 1974, when he entered the Reilly case, he was practicing law in a quiet little office on a quiet road in Fairfield. He worked part of each week as deputy state treasurer in Hartford, so he did not take on many private cases. But when he and Arthur Miller and Murray Madow had lunch at the Fairfield Hunt Club, he seemed interested in taking this one.

I met Roy Daly soon afterward, at a meeting in his office. Aldo Beligni was there, and Father Paul, with Mickey, Murray, and Peter, and we talked all morning about the case. Mr. Daly said he would proceed on two levels—on a civil suit to appeal the verdict, step by step through the higher courts and, simultaneously, he would try to get a new trial.

It was a slim hope, the requirements for a new trial being so strict. There had to be "newly discovered evidence," evidence that would be judged admissible at a new trial and would be likely to produce a different result. New trials, therefore, were virtually unknown, and there was no compelling reason to think Peter Reilly would get one. We could only hope, and hope had never been nearly enough.

Still, Roy Daly said he would get going on it. There was no transcript of the long trial for him to work from yet. Mr. Roberts had to do that in his spare time, when he wasn't working in the courtroom, and it would be months before a transcript was ready. So I gave Roy Daly a copy of my notes to work with, in the meantime. I had taken the notes in shorthand, including the polygraph tapes, then typed them. Altogether, there were 182 single-spaced typed pages. They were not as official, nor as complete, as Mr. Roberts's pages, but I liked to think they were as interesting to read. The official version didn't mention rotting leaves.

Peter went back to school in the fall. His senior schedule was about the same as it had been in September 1973, except that in Contemporary Problems he was excused from the "Crime in Society" segment and assigned to examine the problems of the American Indian.

Another winter set in, and another character joined the ever-changing cast. It was a private detective, James Conway, who had followed the case in the papers throughout the trial. Once he had even written to Catherine Roraback. "A case isn't won in court," Conway said. "You need an investigator." He lived some distance away, near Hartford, yet he volunteered to come over to Canaan and help out. But Catherine Roraback was suspicious of the stranger's offer. She felt that many private detectives in Connecticut worked closely with the state police, too closely for comfort. "Why should we leak what little information we have to the prosecution?" she asked herself, and because she didn't have an answer to that question, she didn't answer the letter.

As it turned out, Jim Conway wasn't connected with the Connecticut police, although he had once been a policeman in New York City, walking a beat. After that, he'd been a bail bondsman for ten years, so he knew his way around the courts. He was a short, husky man with a fringe of short, white hair surrounding a bald spot, and a paunch surrounding his middle. His socks were often unravelling and falling down around his ankles. "I cultivate the hayseed look," he told Mickey Madow, the first time they met. It was not the way you would expect a detective to look, which is the way Jim Conway wanted it.

After the trial, when Roy Daly took the case, Jim Conway tried again. This time he didn't write a letter; he drove down to Fairfield, without even calling first, and introduced himself. The two men talked a long time, then Jim Conway entered the case. At first he worked on it part-time, on Saturdays and Sundays, whenever he was able to drive over to Canaan and poke around. But the more he saw and heard, the more he asked and listened, the more enmeshed he became, the more the case turned into a crusade. He even barreled up Canaan Mountain in a snowmobile one day, following the advice of a dowser who had poked around the area with a divining rod and told Jim about bloody clues that might be on the mountain. Another day, Conway tried to squeeze into the crawl space under the church near Barbara's house, but he didn't fit.

He asked questions. He went to some orthopedists and a pathologist he knew and asked them about the method of the killing; they thought Barbara might have been killed outside the house, perhaps hit by a car. Not long after Christmas, Jim Conway talked at a committee meeting. He said he did not think the knife introduced at the trial, Exhibit X, was the murder weapon. He thought a very sharp instrument had been used, a razor type, such as a sheetrock knife. As for the vaginal injuries, Jim Conway thought Barbara's body had been penetrated with an empty whiskey bottle.

Arthur Miller had stayed in close touch with Peter and the Madows, and he was a regular visitor in Canaan. The boys were accustomed to having him at the table now. That first night he'd come, not long after

Peter was sentenced, they'd felt shy. Nan served fried chicken, and the boys weren't sure whether, with Arthur Miller there, they should pick it up with their hands. Then Arthur Miller picked up a piece of chicken, and the boys grinned. "O-*kay*," Geoffrey said, and everybody picked up a piece of chicken, too.

Jim Conway and Arthur Miller hit it off right away. Miller liked the earthiness of the ex-flatfoot, and they spent a lot of time in the low-ceilinged living room of Miller's elegant old farmhouse, trying to figure it out.

They decided to give Peter another lie detector test; they thought he might have seen someone in the house and not said so because he was afraid. One Saturday a detective from Hartford, a friend of Conway's, came to East Canaan and gave Peter another polygraph test, right there in the Madows' living room. Timothy and Michael Parmalee were invited over to take the test. They came willingly, and Mickey Madow reported at the next committee meeting that all three boys had passed.

A couple of weeks after the test, Dr. Milton Helpern, the former Chief Medical Examiner for New York City, came into the case, at the request of Arthur Miller. Dr. Helpern was an expert on forensic pathology, the medical specialty that reconstructs how deaths may have occurred. Dr. Helpern came to Litchfield and looked at the slides and pictures.

Although Dr. Helpern didn't send anybody a bill, money was still a problem for the committee. The year's bond interest pledged at the Styrons was running out, and Mr. Roberts still hadn't been paid in full for the transcript of the trial. Many people, including me, were surprised that a defendant had to pay for the transcript of his own trial, but unless he had a public defender, he did. For months we had been making calls, and Marion and Bea Keith were writing letters to the IRS, trying to incorporate the committee as a tax-exempt group, the Legal Defense Fund of Litchfield County. In the long run, it would help anyone who needed legal aid and couldn't pay. In the short run, it would help Peter, because he was the first person who'd applied. But becoming a tax-exempt group was a discouraging process, as it was no doubt intended to be. I had spent days on a round of frustrating phone calls to the IRS office in Boston, but all I got sounded like a bureaucratic runaround. Later in the year, the incorporation was approved, but when Mickey talked with a reporter from the *Berkshire Eagle,* in late February, he sounded dejected. "We're at a low ebb," Mickey said.

Roy Daly had not yet been allowed to hear interrogation tapes, but Judge Speziale intervened, and finally Daly and Bob Hartwell heard them at the courthouse. After he heard the tapes, Roy Daly filed a motion asking that a panel of experts be appointed to try to interpret the tape that had been made by Peter and Lieutenant Shay at Canaan barracks early Saturday morning, about ten hours after Barbara died. That was the tape that had not been played at the trial, because it was too garbled. Roy Daly said somebody should try to ungarble the tapes "in the interest of justice," but nobody ever did.

On the thirty-first of March, the defense filed a motion, listing other things it wanted: lab reports on Barbara's clothes, any liquor bottles found at the scene, the unidentified fingerprint, and Barbara's eyeglasses. The next day, Mr. Daly filed another motion, asking for a new trial. He claimed new evidence—and he didn't even know, then, about Sandra Ashner. The phone calls had not yet begun, that remarkable chain of calls that pointed to a possible new suspect.

On a balmy summer night in June, Peter Reilly graduated from Housatonic Valley Regional High School. The ceremony was held outdoors, on the broad lawn. Gloria Schaffer, Connecticut's Secretary of State, petite and pretty, talked about the graduates "entering the world of adults," and she quoted Art Buchwald. "We, the older generation, have given you a perfect world, and we don't want you to mess it up." Diplomas were given in alphabetical order, so Ricky Beligni was way up front, Peter pretty far in the back, and John Sochocki six places behind Peter. John still had a scared look about him, as though he had not got over what had happened to him since his interrogation the night Barbara died.

Peter was in the paper the next day, with a picture and a headline: CONVICTED KILLER RECEIVES DIPLOMA. John Sochocki was in the paper again two days after that, when he drowned. John had gone to the Falls Village swimming pond Monday night with a group of friends. He couldn't swim, but he dived into eight feet of water, in the dark. Father Paul said the Requiem Mass for him on Thursday morning.

Elizabeth Mansfield died that same week, after a long illness. She had found Barbara's wallet. The funerals were held one hour apart and the burials were in the same cemetery, St. Joseph's.

By the time hearings on a new trial began, Peter Reilly had become a full-fledged celebrity.

Roger Cohn had noticed it beginning, not long after the verdict, even before the sentencing. One Saturday night in early May, Roger went to a dance in Cornwall, organized to benefit the Reilly Fund.

At the dance Roger saw how, when Peter walked in, people stood and applauded. There were whistles and cheers, Roger said, and something about it bothered him. It was the first sign of a celebrity aura beginning to swirl around Peter Reilly. At first it was thin and wispy, like the first threads of morning mist around Canaan Mountain. Eventually it would nearly envelop him.

Some of the attention was to be expected. In this rolling green corner of Connecticut, where the State Police Reports in the *Journal* tended to involve loose cows on Route 7, or complaints of deer-jacking, an accused killer was something to see. And the attention accelerated when well-known people were attracted to the cause. But a writer in the *Register* had complained about "the Peter Reilly cult" much earlier, just after the sentencing. It was a familiar American perspective: the victim as hero.

In December 1975, *The New York Times* ran two long articles on Peter Reilly. The stories began on the front page and continued inside, for several thousand words. Arthur Miller had gone to the *Times* for lunch that fall and had asked that John Corry write about the case. He and John Corry had gone to a Manhattan police precinct to visit some homicide detectives Corry knew and told them about the Reilly case. At first the New York policemen were inclined to be skeptical, inclined to believe their fellow policemen, but when they read the polygraph transcript, they changed their minds and said they'd help in any way they could. Later, John Corry went to Canaan, and Nan set another place at the table, as she had been doing for visitors for two years.

CBS came to Canaan to film Peter playing with his band for a segment on "Sixty Minutes." Three newspapers sent photographers to take pictures of the people taking pictures. "Cameras Whirr with Reilly in Star Role," said a headline.

Newsweek came, and *Time. Good Housekeeping* offered $300 for an interview with the committee. Peter was a property and everybody wanted a piece. Another writer began talking about a movie deal; Peter was told he would get rich.

"I think Peter's caught in a spider web," Jean Beligni said. It was a web we all had spun together, though, including Peter. For two years he had been a fixture—often the lead item—on the local six o'clock news, and sometimes again at eleven. Nanny would wring her hands in annoyance and dismay as her dinner cooled on the stove. "I'd kind of still like to think of myself as an unknown kid from northwestern Connecticut," he said, on a day in early spring, standing in the Madows' driveway. But the quote went out over the UPI wire, with a UPI picture of Peter; microphones from Channel 3 and Channel 8 draped around his neck.

Always—or almost always—people's intentions had been to help Peter. But somehow, in the helping, Peter acquired a dimension that exceeded the facts, perhaps even the implications, of the tragedy. When the *Torrington Register* printed "The Ballad of Peter Reilly," by George Cyr, Peter balanced on the brink of legend. And what better place could there be for a legend than a town called Canaan?

15

It was like the second act of a play. There had been an unusually long intermission, nearly two years, but now the curtain was going up again.

Once more the Litchfield green was covered with snow, and new flakes drifted heavily down past the tall schoolroom windows. Inside, there were some changes. At the threshold of the courtroom, a sheriff stood guard by a metal detector that had been there ever since Judge Speziale got a death threat. It wasn't connected with the Reilly case, but they had to take precautions. The call had come late at night. Mary Speziale had answered. "We're going to blow your husband's goddamn head off!" the caller had said, and hung up. A few minutes later, the phone rang again. It was the same voice. "And we're going to do it tonight!"

In the press row, Roger and George and Greg and Farn were replaced by other new young faces. Joe O'Brien was back, an entrenched courtroom veteran, and Charles Kochakian was back too.

Beyond the bar rail, most of the principal players were onstage again. Mr. Roberts set up his stenotype machine in the same efficient way. Judge Speziale, presiding, still looked studious, and when a courtroom artist sketched the judge, he caught the light from the desk lamp glinting on his steel-rimmed glasses, and my memories came rushing back.

John Bianchi looked a little more rumpled, a little less sleek, than he had at the first trial. There was more pressure on him now; in this suit for a new trial, Peter Reilly was the plaintiff, and John Bianchi referred to himself, and to the state, as "the defendant." But he was still the orator; he often referred to Roy Daly as "my brother" or "Brother Daly." Along with the prosecution assistant, Robert Beach, there was another attorney at Mr. Bianchi's table. He was Joseph Gallicchio, whose suits were beautifully tailored; his teeth very white. His voice came out dark and velvety, as though it were filtered through his sideburns.

Roy Daly, of course, was the major replacement in the cast. But his assistant, Bob Hartwell, had the same Dickensian appearance as Peter Herbst—moustache and glasses, and his hair had a rounded, old-fashioned look, as though it might have been cut around a bowl.

Even some of the witnesses were familiar, especially in the first part of the hearing. Roy Daly was basing his petition for a new trial on three major issues: a new time sequence; his charge that the state had withheld evidence that might have cleared Peter; and new evidence.

Time was truly of the essence. In the trial, Mr. Daly said the prosecution had fixed the time of Peter Reilly's arrival home at 9:30 to 9:40. Barbara Fenn, the night supervisor at Sharon Hospital, had testified that Peter's call came through at 9:40, and Marion Madow had said she got the call from Peter between 9:40 and 9:50.

Mr. Daly now asserted that Peter hadn't arrived home until 9:50 or a bit later, and he called witnesses to prove it.

Father Paul and the Reverend Dakers, who had seen Peter leave the Teen Center, testified that they'd reached Johnny's Restaurant, a few minutes away from the church, at 9:50 P.M. John Sochocki's aunt, Judy MacNeil, testified that John, whom Peter drove home that night, had arrived at exactly 9:45. She remembered the time because she hadn't expected him until eleven or so, and she was surprised to see him back so early. She said she had told the police this, and they had come back later to ask whether her clock agreed with the noonday siren in Canaan. She said it did.

Jim Mulhern testified that he'd timed the drive from John Sochocki's house, not far from the church, out to Peter's house. He said it had taken five minutes and twenty-nine seconds. After he testified, Jim

296

Mulhern glanced at Peter. The policeman's sideburns were longer now; he wore a yellow shirt, a rust-colored tie, and a plaid jacket.

Joanne Mulhern was back, as fresh and pretty as ever, to say she'd left the Teen Center at 9:45. She said when she got home, she had called Sharon Hospital to talk to a friend, and the switchboard operator told her she was very busy because an emergency call was coming in from the Barbara Gibbons place. Mrs. Mulhern said it was 9:51 or 9:52 P.M.

The switchboard operator, Elizabeth Swart, said she remembered Joanne Mulhern calling that night, and she remembered, too, that Peter had called.

Nurse Barbara Fenn had taken that emergency room call. She had been the first prosecution witness at Peter's trial, and although she had changed jobs since then her testimony had not changed. She said she still remembered the call coming in at approximately 9:40, and she stared hard at Mr. Daly as she said it.

He reminded her that the state police got the call at 9:58.

"I ask you: Did you wait eighteen minutes to call the police, from nine forty to nine fifty-eight?" Mr. Daly asked.

"I can't recall," Mrs. Fenn replied.

Mr. Daly produced an emergency room log sheet that the executive director of Sharon Hospital had brought in, along with a radio log showing ambulance calls.

"I ask you again: Did you wait eighteen minutes to notify the police?" Mr. Daly asked.

John Bianchi objected.

"I claim the question," Mr. Daly said sharply, "on the basis that her testimony in the earlier trial was false." The courtroom was suddenly very quiet, the harsh word *false* vibrating in the air. He turned back to the witness. "Do you know of any instances where you've waited eighteen minutes in an emergency situation to notify the state police?" he asked. "Could you have received the call later than nine forty?" Barbara Fenn, in a smaller voice now, said she could have.

At the original trial, Marion Madow had described the scene from the movie *Kelley's Heroes,* which she'd been watching when Peter called. Marion had estimated the time 9:40 to 9:50 P.M. Now, Roy Daly called Michael Marden, director of prime-time feature films for

CBS Television in New York. Mr. Marden testified that the scene Marion described, where the last soldier was boarding a tank to cross the river, had been transmitted by the network to its affiliated stations at precisely ten seconds past 9:50 P.M. on the night Barbara died. When Mr. Bianchi cross-examined, Mr. Marden said that a local station might have omitted that scene, or shown it later, but it could not possibly have shown it earlier.

Dr. Frank Lovallo said that Barbara had called him that night sometime between 9:20 and 9:40, to ask about some tests she'd had done. Dr. Bornemann's daughter-in-law, whom Peter had spoken to and had taken to be the doctor's wife, said his call came "between nine forty-five and ten."

"The case is surrounded by clocks," *The New York Times* story had said, and John Bianchi seemed to agree. "All these clocks and watches," he said with irony, "and none of them seem to match."

The testimony on the time sequence came early in the hearing, some of it vaguely familiar, even a little boring. Then, after court was adjoured one day, word came that the fingerprint on the back door of Barbara's house had been identified at last. It belonged to Tim Parmalee. His fingerprints had not been on file at the time of the trial. But in the spring of 1974 Tim was picked up for stealing a car. His fingerprints were taken, and now they were matched. It was an irony that Barbara, with her prankish sense of humor, would have relished. The car Tim was accused of stealing was taken from Jacobs Garage in Falls Village, the shop with which Barbara had had a long-running feud.

When the fingerprint match came in, a new reporter asked John Bianchi whether the Parmalee brothers would now be charged—word was out that the new evidence involved Michael Parmalee as well. Mr. Bianchi laughed. "Charge them with what?" he asked, and even the *Lakeville Journal,* in its next editorial, had a word of caution. "It does not necessarily follow that either of them committed the crime," the *Journal* declared. "To rush to such a conclusion without either indictment or trial would be to do to others the sort of injustice that some of Reilly's defenders contend was done to him." Around East Canaan, the subject was much discussed. "We're the Legal Defense Fund of Litchfield County," Jean said to Elaine Monty, when they talked on the phone. "What'll we do if the Parmalees come to us for help?"

Elaine gulped and said she guessed they'd have to help. Jean thought so too. "I'd feel like a hypocrite if we didn't," she said, and Marion agreed.

Our house was closed for the winter, no heat or water, so for most of the hearing, I stayed with the Madows, sleeping in the extra bed in Nan's room. The atmosphere was strained. Mickey had left his job after more than twenty years, and was trying free-lance as a salesman. Marion was working for an accountant in Salisbury during the day and doing bookeeping at the *Lakeville Journal* some nights. "It's hard," Marion said, simply, about their situation. She didn't complain, but she seemed depressed, even when things seemed to go well at the hearing. One night she and Nan and I were watching the Shirley MacLaine TV special, just the three of us. Mickey was on the road, and the boys were out. Marion said she enjoyed happy shows, and as much as she liked Arthur Miller, she didn't care for his plays, or for any play that wasn't happy. She remembered another play, *The Glass Menagerie,* that she hadn't liked. "I just walked out feeling sorry for her," Marion said. "I don't like sad endings. I have enough sad endings in my own life."

The committee meetings were different now, too. There were arguments. Some committee members were unhappy because on *Sixty Minutes,* Marion had told Mike Wallace that if it hadn't been for Mickey and herself, Peter would have had no place to go. And, at a committee meeting, she had told the others that she would do anything, walk over anybody, for Peter's sake. Some of the people on the committee said Marion was getting a swelled head from all the publicity; Marion replied that some of the people on the committee were small-minded and jealous. "I wish we could all go back to the way we felt in the beginning," Beverly King told me wistfully.

Sergeant Pennington was back, talking about fingerprints. He said that at the time of the trial, he'd had 325,000 fingerprint cards on file. Now he had 400,000. He recalled how he'd taken the picture of Barbara's back door, that night after midnight, after he'd dusted the door with a gray powder. Mr. Bianchi asked the sergeant whether he could determine the age of a print, and the sergeant said he couldn't. When shown the photograph of the print, he explained that through a color reverse process, the shades were the opposite from what they appeared.

299

Judge Speziale smiled gently. "So white is black, and black is white," he said.

Timothy Parmalee was clipped and trim in his dark green uniform, a marksman's medal on his jacket. He had enlisted in the Army in the spring of 1975 and had been called to active duty that fall, when he turned eighteen. When Roy Daly questioned him about his activities on the day Barbara died, Tim said he'd had dinner with his father at their house on Route 63. His sister, her husband and their six children lived there, too. His mother was working the evening shift at Wash 'n Dri, where one of Peter's jurors had worked.

Around 6 or 6:30, Tim continued, he went to the Falls Village market to buy diapers for his sister's baby. He went to the package store, too, along with his brother-in-law, and Wayne Collier, to buy beer. Timothy said he didn't go in, though. Then they went back to his father's house. It was around 7:30.

"And did you stay in your father's house for the rest of the evening?" Roy Daly asked.

"No," Tim said.

"Where did you go when you left?"

"Across the road to my uncle's house."

"Were you alone, or was someone else with you?"

"Wayne was with me. We just sat down and talked and drank beer," Tim said. "Till eight thirty, quarter to nine."

"And then what did you do?"

"Went over to my sister Marie's house . . . used the phone." Marie's house was next door. Tim said he had called a girl in Massachusetts and talked "twenty, twenty-five minutes."

"About what time did you place that call?" Mr. Daly asked.

"Five minutes to nine," Tim said.

"And the call lasted twenty, twenty-five minutes. Is that what you said a moment ago?"

"It was before quarter to nine I made the phone call," Tim said.

"Now, after you finished the call from your sister Marie's house, what, if anything, did you do?"

"Went back to my uncle's house," Tim said. "Drank more beer and talked until my sister Marie came home from work. She went to her own house. I went in after her."

300

"About what time was that?" Mr. Daly asked.

"Ten after nine, quarter after nine."

"What did you do after that?"

"I went home, said good-night and went to bed."

It may have sounded early for bed, but in a newspaper story during the hearing, Duke Moore, a reporter who lived in Falls Village, explained the neighborhood tempo. "Often Friday and Saturday nights consist of nothing more than hanging around, drinking beer, talking, finally going to bed, often early," he wrote.

Tim testified that he went to sleep at once, and slept until twenty past one in the morning, when his father woke him to say that a policeman wanted to talk to him. It was Jim Mulhern, sent out by Lieutenant Shay to make the house-to-house check.

Later in the hearing, Jim Mulhern confirmed Timothy's account. "He came out of the bedroom," Mulhern testified. "This was roughly 1:40, 1:45 A.M."

"The room Timothy Parmalee emerged from, if he did, was on the first floor of the house, is that correct?" Mr. Daly asked.

"Yes sir," Mulhern said. "First door to the left as you go in the front door."

John Bianchi's assistant, Robert Beach, asked a question.

"When Timothy Parmalee came into your presence, did you make any observations as to his physical appearance?"

"Yes sir," Mulhern said. "The only thing he had on was a pair of trousers. . . . He appeared as if he had been in bed, sleeping."

"Did you leave [your] bedroom until you were awakened sometime after one o'clock to talk to Trooper Mulhern?" John Bianchi asked Tim.

"No."

"How long have you known Peter Reilly, Mr. Parmalee?" John Bianchi asked Tim.

"Ever since he moved up to the corner," Tim said.

"Did you ever play with Peter Reilly at the house wherein his mother was murdered?"

"Yes," Tim said.

"Did you ever stay overnight at this same little house?"

"Yes," Tim said.

"Have you ever gone in or out of the side or back door?"

"Occasionally," Tim said.

"And is it true that you also went in the front door?"

"Yes," Tim said.

"Prior to September 28, 1973, can you recall the last time you were at the house?"

"Week and a half, two weeks and a half. Not really sure," Tim said.

"Going back for approximately one year, what is your best estimate of how many times you were at the house?"

"I am really not sure," Tim said. "Quite a few times."

Mr. Bianchi questioned two Parmalee sisters, both married. Marie Parmalee Ovitt said she got home from work at ten past nine, the night Barbara died.

"Did you see your brother Timothy between the time you got home at about nine-ten and before nine-thirty?" Mr. Bianchi asked.

"Yes, I did," she said.

"And how do you determine that that was the time you saw him?"

"Because I watched the last few minutes of 'Pins and Needles,' and that went off at nine-thirty," she replied.

Over at the Madows, I remembered, they'd begun watching *Kelley's Heroes* then. Mrs. Ovitt said that when Timothy came in, he stayed "not too long. Five minutes, at the most."

"And did you see him again that night?"

"No I didn't," she said.

But Tim's other sister testified that she had. From about twenty-five of ten, she said, she was sitting opposite Tim's bedroom door; the door was closed. Just after ten o'clock, her sister Marie came over, wanting Tim to baby-sit.

"I went in and tried to wake up Timmy in his bedroom," Judith Machia said. "He was sleeping, and I couldn't wake him up. It was about ten after ten."

"Between twenty-five minutes of ten, and the time that you went in—shortly after ten o'clock—to wake Timmy up, did anybody come in or out of his bedroom door?" Mr. Bianchi asked.

"No," she said.

I drove in to court with Peter, Art, and Geoff one morning, sandwiched in the middle of the front seat. Peter was driving. Arthur, in the back seat, was complaining that it was his turn to sit in front. Everybody was smoking except me, and I wished I were.

On the way to court, Peter pulled into the Texaco station across the road from the little white house. I looked over at the yard, and I asked them, for the last time, about that night.

"Why did we ever go to that Teen Center meeting?" Geoff asked. It was a melancholy question, but Peter answered lightly. "Because I thought Nancy was going to be there," he said.

"I sat over there in the chair," Geoff said, "with Schatzi in my lap, under the elm tree, watching the sun go down, and I was thinking, this is the end of something. I know it sounds weird now to say I thought that, but I really did. And I don't know why I did." Peter said nothing.

"I came home that night and everybody was gone," Arthur said. "I asked my grandmother, 'Where is everybody?' Nan said there was an ambulance call. 'Peter's mother's sick,' she said. So I boogied on over to Sharon Hospital, thinking they took her there."

Peter looked into the rear-view mirror. "When you got to the house, Art, did they say my mom was dead?"

"Nope," Arthur said. Peter seemed about to speak, but just then Geoff spoke. "Shay took me into that van, and he searched me, and he didn't even take off my socks. I said, 'Don't you want to look between my toes?' "

Peter didn't say anything more. He started the motor, and the radio came on again. It was tuned to Bob Steele, Barbara's favorite.

In the courthouse hallway, I saw Tim's wife and her parents. Tim and Chris Sager had been married the year before, and they had a baby girl. Mary Sager, Christine's mother, had just written a letter to the *Journal,* defending Tim, very much as her husband had written after Peter's conviction. I remembered Mr. Sager from a committee meeting, volunteering to make arrangements for the dance. Now he looked worn and strained, and the sum of the human factors, in all this, suddenly seemed overwhelming. We said hello, and I wanted to say something more— maybe that I was sorry, and I started to mumble some words, but then it just seemed too awkward, and I let it go.

Assisting Catherine Roraback on the Peter Reilly case had been Peter Herbst's first job after law school. Now, as he took the stand, Judge

Speziale looked a little concerned. "Rise, Peter Reilly," he said. Peter stood up, and the judge read the attorney-client privilege, which sounded rather like the seal of the confessional. The judge told Peter that if he waived that privilege, things he told Peter Herbst might now be disclosed. Peter Reilly said he understood, and he did waive it.

On the stand, Peter Herbst said there had been some problem getting some of the statements they wanted from the State's Attorney. He said John Bianchi had told him "it was such a hassle to go to the trouble of Xeroxing all the statements," so John Bianchi had said he himself would decide what was exculpatory, and pass it along to the defense. Peter Herbst said he'd never known that John Sochocki's aunt was interviewed by the police, that he hadn't got that statement or the statement from Dr. Bornemann's daughter-in-law, whom Peter had spoken to when he called for help the night Barbara died. He said he remembered Elizabeth Mansfield bringing in the wallet she'd found and now, in court, he looked at the wallet in the plastic bag and said yes, that was it.

Peter Herbst didn't finish testifying that day, and the next morning he took the stand again, first thing. The courtroom was settling down to a new round of legal arguments, when the witness's first statement startled everyone awake. He said that after court adjourned the day before, he'd been asked to stop by the State's Attorney's office before he left the courthouse. Inside the little office, Peter Herbst said, Mr. Bianchi had asked him a question. "Pete," he'd said, "your privilege is gone. At any time—before, after, or during the trial—did Peter Reilly admit his guilt to you?"

John Bianchi, at the counsel table, flushed, and Mr. Gallicchio stood up quickly. "Objection, your honor," he said. "The question is whether or not Peter Reilly is entitled to a new trial. It's not a question of his innocence or guilt." Mr. Gallicchio's voice faltered a little toward the end, as though what he was saying sounded as bizarre in his own ears as it did in mine.

"All I want is the answer to the question," Roy Daly said, and the judge looked at Mr. Gallicchio. "Do I hear a motion to strike?" he asked, and Mr. Gallicchio, still looking surprised, said yes. "Motion is granted," the judge said.

As interesting as that revelation was, the most fascinating part of Peter Herbst's testimony concerned the new evidence.

"Did you know of a woman named Sandra Ashner?" Mr. Daly asked.

"No, I did not," Peter Herbst said.

"Did you know whether Michael Parmalee had requested a separation from the United States Army based on alleged homosexuality?" Mr. Daly asked.

The collective noise in the courtroom wasn't a gasp, more of a shuffle. Homosexuality—the most dreaded, derided thing in a small New England town. Being a queer. When the citizens of nineteenth-century Canaan hanged Jeff Davis in effigy, they dressed him in petticoats first. Now the sound in the courtroom nearly drowned out the witness's answer.

"No, I did not," Peter Herbst said.

Mr. Roberts had taken Roy Daly aside and asked him to please speak a little more slowly. He sometimes spoke very quickly, especially when he seemed angry. After so many years in the courtroom, Mr. Roberts knew very well that a person's talking speed could affect what the person was trying to say. "By the time an attorney asks a question five times, he's lost sight of the subject, the predicate and the object," Mr. Roberts said, a little sadly.

So Roy Daly spoke very slowly and deliberately to the young woman wearing slacks and a pea coat. She had a small, pointed face, a sharp chin, and long, wavy black hair. Her big dark eyes had a sad, almost haunted look. As Sandra Ashner spoke, she created, in this familiar courtroom, a most unfamiliar world.

A country way called Undermountain Road ran behind the Kruses' place. There was a large dairy farm down that road, where the hired man, Sherwood Scanlon, lived in a trailer with a woman named Jacqueline Watson. Another couple was living in the trailer, too, Sandra Ashner and Michael Parmalee, whom Sandra called "Mick." Sandra had a little boy named Bobby.

Sandra Ashner and Michael Parmalee had not been living together long, and she had never met his family. In the middle of the afternoon on the day Barbara died, she testified, they walked from the trailer to the Parmalee place on Route 63. When they passed the Kruse property at the corner, Barbara was out in the yard, and Michael pointed her out to Sandra.

Back at the trailer that evening, Sandra said, she gave her son a shower and heard him say his prayers. She put him to bed. In the bedroom she shared with Michael, Sandra said, she was sitting on the bed. "Michael come in," she testified, "and he says something was wrong. He says, 'Well, something is wrong at home.'"

"Did he, thereafter, do anything?" Mr. Daly asked.

"I believe he left," Sandra Ashner said.

"He left the trailer?"

"Yes."

She said she went to bed and awoke around seven or seven-thirty the next morning.

"Did Michael Parmalee, after you got up, come back to the trailer?" Mr. Daly asked.

"Yes," she said. "About eight-thirty, nine o'clock."

For the next few weeks, then, Sandra said, Michael acted strangely.

"He woke up—one, two, three o'clock in the morning, we sit on the couch," she said. "He would be upset, shaking and nervous." After a while, Sandra moved out of the trailer. She and Bobby went to live with her mother, and although Michael came to see her a couple of times, they didn't live together any more.

When the police had questioned her on October 7, 1973, Sandra told them that Michael had spent the night with her in the trailer.

"Did there come a time when you decided to tell somebody what you have said here today?" Roy Daly asked.

Sandra Ashner said that, more than a year later, she had told the visiting nurse, thus setting off a chain of phone calls that resulted in the County Detective coming to see her, then the police, then Jim Conway. I stared at this young woman, so tough yet scared-looking, wondering where she had found the strength to stand up to the barrage of questions she must have faced. "What she went through for Peter, you can't imagine," Jim Conway told me later, but even when I saw her for the first time, on the stand, I had an inkling.

John Bianchi looked at her scornfully. "So you and Michael Parmalee occupied the same bedroom?"

"Yes," Sandra said.

"And you did, did you not, on September 28, 1973?"

"He was not there that night," she said.

"You didn't occupy the same bedroom on September 28, 1973?"

"No, he was not there," Sandra said. "He left."

"You went to bed by yourself?"

306

"Yes. When I woke up, he wasn't there."

"Did you wake up by means of an alarm clock?" Mr. Bianchi asked.

"No," she said. "Mr. Scanlon woke us up. He walked by the room and he would say, 'Get up.'"

"And when Mr. Scanlon woke you up, Michael Parmalee was not in bed with you at that very moment?"

"No, he wasn't," the witness said.

"When you went to sleep, it was about what time? Nine-thirty?"

"I went to bed about quarter to nine. I fell right to sleep. I was on medication, for my foot."

"What doctor treated you?" Mr. Bianchi asked.

"Dr. White at the Torrington Hospital."

"And you were taking . . ." Mr. Bianchi paused. "What day did you see Dr. White?"

"Oh my Lord, that was so long ago, I don't remember," Sandra Ashner said, and Mr. Bianchi smiled slightly.

"But you remembered in 1973 that Michael Parmalee left the trailer that night and didn't come back until the next morning and didn't sleep with you. You remember that pretty well, don't you?"

Sandra Ashner looked straight at the prosecutor.

"This is important," she said. "My foot wasn't."

Mr. Bianchi paused again.

"In October of 1973, you told the Connecticut State Police, 'We stayed in the trailer all night,' didn't you?"

"I said that because I didn't want to get involved," Sandra Ashner said. "I had a child."

"You didn't tell the truth in the statement that you made on October 7, 1973," Mr. Bianchi said, "and today, you are telling us the truth?"

"Yes," she said.

Judge Speziale had turned to watch the witness as she spoke. I thought, as I watched him watching her, that he must be looking down on her, this man who preferred his women on a pedestal, and tipped his hat to them with a shy flourish on the street. But, as had happened to me before in this case, I was wrong.

Paul Beligni spoke even more confidently than before, a college student now. He said that in early 1973, an Army investigator named Greg Harrop had visited him in East Canaan. They had sat at the kitchen table, the table I knew so well. Jean sat at the table with them.

"Did you tell Mr. Harrop about a telephone conversation you had with Michael Parmalee?" Roy Daly asked.

"Yes," Paul said. "I told him that Michael Parmalee had called me and asked me to lie for him about the fact that I knew he was a homosexual so he could get out of the Army."

"Did you know whether Michael Parmalee had called anyone else and asked anyone else to lie?" Mr. Daly asked.

"Yes," Paul said.

"And who was that person?"

"Objection, your honor," Mr. Bianchi said quickly, but Paul answered anyway.

"Peter Reilly," he said.

Mr. Daly looked grave. "Did you, in fact, ever have a homosexual relationship with Michael Parmalee?" he asked Paul.

"No, and not with anybody else," Paul said firmly.

Mr. Bianchi moved that the answer be stricken. "It was unresponsive," he complained. But the judge glanced at Paul. "In fairness to the young man," the judge said quietly, "I am going to let it stand."

Mr. Daly had another question. "After the visit by Mr. Harrop to the area, did you have occasion to observe the relationship between Barbara Gibbons and Michael Parmalee?"

"Many times," Paul said. "I observed Barbara Gibbons bad-mouthing Michael Parmalee about what he had said about Peter and I, calling him names and so forth. 'Hey queer, how is things in fairyville?' and so forth."

"And did Michael Parmalee react to Miss Gibbons's observations?" Mr. Daly asked. "What kind of a reaction did you observe?"

"Not too good a one," Paul said.

When the Army investigator came to see Peter, he didn't sit in Barbara's kitchen. The three of them—Barbara, Peter, and the investigator—stood at the edge of the road, by the Army car, as Peter answered the investigator's questions.

"I told him that I was not a homosexual," Peter said, now on the stand, "that I had never had any homosexual activities with Michael Parmalee, that Michael Parmalee had called me from the base and asked me to say that I knew that he was a homosexual."

308

"Did you, in fact, ever have a homosexual relationship with Michael Parmalee?" Mr. Daly asked.

"No, I didn't," Peter said.

"After that visit, did you observe your mother's action whenever she saw Michael Parmalee? . . . Did she taunt him?"

"Yes," Peter said.

"Was Michael Parmalee ever again allowed into your mother's house?" Mr. Daly asked.

"No," Peter said.

"Was Timothy Parmalee ever again allowed into that house?"

"No," Peter said.

"After that interview, did you see Timothy Parmalee in front of your mother's house?"

"Yes," Peter said. "Three or four weeks before the murder . . . outside the house, looking in the window." He told of an incident about a year and a half earlier than that. Michael Parmalee had been visiting Peter, and Peter accused Michael of stealing money from Barbara. "I confronted him with, 'Did you take money from my mother?' And he told me yes, he had. And he gave the money back to her."

Mr. Bianchi stared at Peter. "You palled around with the Parmalee boys?"

"At one time, yes," Peter said.

"And it's true, is it not, that you agreed with Michael Parmalee that you would lie on his behalf?"

"Yes I did," Peter said. "Because he wanted to get out of the Army so desperately."

"And it was because you were his friend that you were willing to lie for him, is that not so?"

"Yes," Peter said.

Michael Parmalee had long, straight hair parted in the middle, and a hollow-eyed look. He told Roy Daly he had been in the Army for about five weeks before he went AWOL, and he was eventually discharged.

"What was the basis of your discharge?" Mr. Daly asked.

"AWOL," Michael said.

"Did you attempt to get out for any other reason?"

"Yes," Michael said. "Grounds of being homosexual."

"Did you tell anybody connected with the Army with whom you had a homosexual relationship?"

"Yes," Michael replied. "Peter Reilly and Paul Beligni."

"In connection with your attempts to get out as a homosexual, did you speak with Peter Reilly?"

"Yes, over the phone."

"And did you ask him to do something?"

"Asked him to lie for me."

Then Mr. Bianchi had a question.

"Did Reilly and Beligni agree to lie for you?"

"Yes," Michael said.

Later in the hearing, Mr. Bianchi called Michael Parmalee as his own witness. Michael said that he and Sandra Ashner had indeed gone to visit his mother's house that day, but he said they went "in the morning hours, around nine, nine-thirty." He said his sister Marie drove them back to the trailer on her way to work.

"What is your testimony as to the time that you went into the trailer to spend the night?" Mr. Bianchi asked.

"Believe it was five-thirty," Michael said.

"What time did you retire?"

"Just about nine o'clock."

"And what time did you get up?"

"About seven, quarter after."

"And at any time from approximately nine o'clock until around seven on the morning of September 29, 1973, did you leave that trailer?"

"I did not," Michael Parmalee said.

Mr. Daly showed Michael a statement he'd given to the police on April 17, 1975, in which he said he went to bed at 9:30 that night, September 28, and woke up the next morning around 8:30. Michael Parmalee agreed that it was his signature on the statement. It was signed by Jim Mulhern, too.

"When you woke up, who was in the bedroom?" Mr. Daly asked.

"Myself," Michael said.

"Alone, right?"

"Yes."

"Did anybody awaken you?"

"I believe Sandra did."

"Did you ever tell the police that 'No one awakened me, I just woke up?' "

"Yes, I did," Michael said.

"Was that on April 17, 1975?"

"Yes."

"Were you telling the truth when you spoke to the police?"

"Yes," Michael said. "To the best of my recollection."

But this was Mr. Bianchi's witness, so he had the last question.

"Mr. Parmalee, no matter what your testimony is about the time you went to bed on September 28, 1973, and the time you got up in the morning of September 29, 1973, did you leave the trailer?"

"No I did not," Michael said.

Mr. Roberts said in all his experience, he'd never known anything like this hearing. It lasted five weeks, with more than three dozen witnesses, and thus was more like a trial than many actual trials. Like the original trial, it had its lighter moments, as when Thomas McAloon took the stand. He was the brother of John McAloon, who had testified that Peter told him he'd killed his mother and thrown away his bloody clothes. Thomas McAloon had come down from Warwick, Rhode Island, to testify about his brother John's honesty. The question, in the language of the law, was whether a person's "reputation for truth and veracity was on a par with mankind in general." Thomas McAloon said his brother's reputation wasn't on that level. Then he got entangled in cross-examination, and finally he shook his head stubbornly. "I was asked to tell the truth," Thomas McAloon said. "The truth is, he's a liar, and that's the truth."

The hearing was like Peter's trial in other ways, not only in its conflicting statements but in all its ambiguities and contradictions, its half-answered questions and fragmented answers. A bank teller testified that she had cashed a check for Barbara on the day she died, and the canceled check was introduced as evidence. Ruth Madow, Murray and Dot's daughter, testified that she'd seen Tim Parmalee several days after the murder with a large amount of money. Tim had testified that he had taken the money from his uncle. His uncle was sick during the hearing and couldn't testify.

Margaret Parmalee, the boys' mother, who had lived in the house on Route 63 for forty years, testified that the two windows in Tim's bedroom couldn't be opened because there was "paneling over the windows." Trooper Dean Hammond, who had examined the room, said there wasn't any paneling. He said they couldn't be opened from the inside, though, because the window sash had been painted, and the windows were stuck shut. Trooper Hammond had checked Tim's room on October 9, 1973, more than a week after Peter Reilly had been arrested and arraigned on a charge of murdering his mother.

Sherwood Scanlon, the hired man, said he got up at 4 A.M. to do the morning farm chores. Life in the trailer may have been casual, but it wasn't easy. Around 7 A.M., he said, he returned to the trailer and woke everybody up.

"Will you tell his honor where you found Michael Parmalee when you woke him at seven or a little after on September 29, 1973?" Mr. Bianchi asked.

"In bed," Mr. Scanlon said.

"And was he in bed alone, or was somebody in bed with him?"

"He wasn't alone," Mr. Scanlon said.

"Who was in bed with him?"

"Sandy Ashner."

Jackie Watson, who lived with Scanlon, testified that she'd been cooking breakfast for everybody, bacon and eggs, around 7.

"Did you see Michael Parmalee come out of the bedroom that morning?" Mr. Bianchi asked her.

"Yes," she said, and Mr. Bianchi looked pleased.

But then Roy Daly, in turn, asked the witness to draw a sketch of the trailer. She did, and he pointed to a rear door.

"Could someone enter through that outside door," he asked, "and proceed down the hallway, and you would not be able to see them from the stove area?"

"Not from the stove area," she agreed.

On February 13, 1976, Mr. Bianchi first called Michael Parmalee, then Timothy Parmalee, to the witness stand. He asked them four of the questions they'd been asked on the polygraph test they'd taken voluntarily at the Madows's on February 8, 1975.

"Did you ever have sexual relations with Barbara Gibbons?"

312

"Do you know for sure who killed Barbara Gibbons?"

"Did you have anything to do with the death of Barbara Gibbons?"

"Are you withholding any information concerning the death of Barbara Gibbons?"

Both Michael Parmalee and Timothy Parmalee testified that he'd answered no to each question at the time the test was given. Now, a year later, each of them answered no to each question again.

But this was not a criminal trial. The State of Connecticut was prosecuting no one. Judge Speziale had underlined the point when Timothy took the stand, after his fingerprint had been identified. "You have the right not to answer any questions, which you feel may incriminate you," he said, and he added: "This is a witness, and not an accused." Roy Daly acknowledged it. At one point, Mr. Beach, the prosecutor's assistant, motioned toward Mr. Daly. "He attempts to cast the wrath of God upon an entire family . . ." Mr. Beach said, "to say 'Well, one of the brothers did it.' "

Mr. Daly made a small bow toward the bench with a kind of injured elegance. "My only burden here," he said, "is to persuade the Court that if one juror heard what has been heard here, one juror would have a reasonable doubt."

Not all the people who were subpoenaed got around to testifying. One of Barbara's caseworkers, who came to the hearings with her own attorney, didn't testify, and neither did Wayne Collier. Wayne had told Jim Conway he had been drinking beer with Tim Parmalee and others the night Barbara died, and that his mother had dropped him off and picked him up later.

But the most tantalizing potential witness was John Bianchi. Roy Daly tried to make the prosecutor take the witness stand, but he was overruled. "There is no case of reasonable necessity here," Judge Speziale said, looking irritated, and calling it "a highly unorthodox and objectionable procedure." Mr. Daly then read into the record a list of questions he wanted to ask the prosecutor, including whether the state police had gone to Tim Parmalee, after the fingerprint was matched, and told him not to worry; whether Jim Conway had been harassed and threatened and told to mind his own business; and whether the state police had questioned Auntie B. for several hours at the Canaan barracks, not long after Barbara died, and had later threatened her with criminal prosecution if she came to Peter's aid. In the language of the law, Mr. Daly said he based these questions "upon information and belief."

Arthur Miller had brought two doctors into the case, both of them from New York. Their testimony came several days apart, but what they had to say seemed part of a piece. One of them talked about Barbara, the other about Peter. These were the threads that were woven together again, near the end, just as at the beginning they had been ripped apart. This was what it was all about and had always been about. Barbara and Peter. Peter and Barbara.

Dr. Herbert Spiegel spelled out his name. "S," he began. "P, as in Peter . . ."

Dr. Spiegel was a psychiatrist, on the teaching staff at Columbia University in New York, and had a private practice. Roy Daly had heard of the doctor's work in hypnosis and discussed it with Arthur Miller, who discussed it with another doctor he knew. Then Arthur Miller called Dr. Spiegel. "If Peter has amnesia, can you get it out under hypnosis?" Arthur Miller asked, and the doctor said yes, he could.

On January 6, 1976, Roy Daly and Arthur Miller drove Peter down to Dr. Spiegel's office in New York. The doctor tested Peter using a method called the Hypnotic Induction Profile, which he himself had developed over the past eight years. The test had just been recognized in the scientific literature in early 1975 and had not been available at the time of Peter Reilly's trial.

When Dr. Spiegel tested Peter, he found Peter had "a break in his concentration" and couldn't be hypnotized. Still, he told Peter that he was in a trance and that he should keep his eyes closed. Dr. Spiegel told Peter to imagine a movie screen and then describe what was happening on it. Peter accounted for every fifteen-second interval, from the time he walked into the little house. There was no amnesia, no lapse of memory, no "gray area."

Now, on the witness stand, Dr. Spiegel prepared to testify about Peter's personality.

Mr. Bianchi objected furiously. He said he wasn't sure what the definition of a personality was, and anyway, it was absolutely immaterial.

Peter Reilly had been a puzzle, and something of a problem, for Judge Speziale throughout the trial, and even afterward. Especially afterward. The judge had often wondered why an eighteen-year-old boy would say he killed his mother if he hadn't, and he had never been able to come up with a satisfactory answer. Here was a chance, perhaps, to find out. The objection was overruled.

I was not in court when Dr. Spiegel testified, but Carol Cioe, from the *Register,* said he looked like Groucho Marx. This is part of what he said:

> He was a somewhat immature young man who has a serious deficit in his ability to identify who he is as a person. He has difficulty in integrating his concept of self, and a poor ability to integrate his conceptions of others.
>
> Because he had such a low self-esteem, under conditions of interrogation he needs support, protection, and understanding of a question, and formulating an answer. Without that support and guidance, he can easily be confused, and he most certainly can easily accept as a fact something he knows nothing about. This is especially true because of his long-standing respect for authority, especially police authority.
>
> The word 'brainwash' is more of a journalistic phrase than it is a professional term. But it loosely relates to the way in which deception or coercion is used to evoke in a person a response that is consistent with a particular hypothesis that the interrogator imposes upon the subject.
>
> There is related to that the other phenomenon that is often called "amnesia," and this is where the deception takes place: that an event may not occur in the presence of an individual and, if it does not occur, he has no way of recalling that the event took place. If, in the context of a coercive brainwashing interrogation, or where deception was used, if a person with a low self-esteem is told that events happen that he does not remember, his shaky confidence in himself, combined with his respect for authority, may lead him to believe that perhaps the event did take place.
>
> Here is a young man who has a shaky sense of self in the first place—and now, awed by what he has just seen—when he returned and saw his mother's body—how does he perceive it? He has trouble perceiving others, anyhow. Under this startling new situation, he is now trying to integrate to the best of his ability. What is he perceiving here?
>
> He stated that he could not account for what happened. Then, under subsequent interrogation procedures, he was told that certain events took place. He is presented with questions about what happened, and he says he doesn't know. Then he is told that, although he doesn't

know, there are ways in which he can remember this event, and one of the devices used in trying to sharpen his recall was the use of the polygraph. He accepted the 'scientific' atmosphere of using the polygraph as a means of touching something within himself, as a means of accepting the proposition that, perhaps, he should confess because the police authority believed that he did it. He had no proof that he did *not* do it, and he accepted the notion that he must have had amnesia for an event that took place. He accepted in his unstable condition the notion that not knowing it took place would be accounted for by "amnesia." In deference to the police authority, he accepted the responsibility for the killing on the basis of their assertions.

The concept of his ego integrity is essential in withstanding the kind of interrogation he was put through. Somebody with a strong sense of self could very possibly have dealt with the nature of that interrogation. Somebody with such an immaturity and diffusion of self was helpless.

The New York Times said Peter listened to the testimony "with his usual impassive stare." But Carol Cioe said Peter had "blushed and stared at the floor" when he heard the doctor say he was so gullible.

Finally, Roy Daly asked the doctor if Peter Reilly was the type of person to cry in public, or to fly into a rage. John Bianchi, who had asked several witnesses about Peter's tears, called it "immaterial and irrelevant." But again, the judge wanted to know. Dr. Spiegel said a person whose self-esteem was as low as Peter's perceived emotions in a very shallow way, almost an alienated way, and the least likely thing such a person would do would be to cry. As for rage, he said, it wouldn't even occur to him that he had the right. Apparently it still didn't occur to him. When the doctor examined Peter, on January 6, 1976, Peter told him he wanted to become a policeman.

Dr. Milton Helpern had been the Chief Medical Examiner in New York City for twenty years. He had retired, but he was still considered to be as familiar with the anatomy of murder as a man could be. Arthur Miller had arranged for Dr. Helpern to come to the courthouse back in the spring of 1975 to see the pictures and the autopsy slides, and now Dr. Helpern was in the courthouse to testify. He took the stand, smiling a little boyishly, his white hair falling over his forehead, looking a little like Robert Frost. He had seen the pictures before, but he studied them again, looking at Barbara lying slashed and bloody on her bedroom floor, her torso so glaring white, the blood splotches around her head bright orange. Peter watched Dr. Helpern, and Mr. Gallicchio watched Peter.

Mr. Daly posed a long, hypothetical question.

"Let us assume, Dr. Helpern," the lawyer said, "that Peter Reilly departed a Teen Center meeting at nine thirty-five or nine forty P.M., drove to a friend's house, and arrived there at nine forty-five P.M.

"Assume that he then drove to his home, the driving taking five minutes and twenty-nine seconds, arrived at his home, locked the door of his car, found the body of his mother, called an ambulance, called the family doctor, and spoke to the doctor's daughter-in-law for two or three minutes.

"Assume that he called a nurse at Sharon Hospital, who asked several questions, and who then called another ambulance, and then the state police at nine fifty-eight P.M., and that the trooper arrived at ten-o-two P.M.

"Assume also that no trace of blood was found on Peter Reilly, and assume also that he was five feet seven inches tall and weighed one hundred and twenty-one pounds.

"And assume that the following wounds were inflicted: a stab wound in the hand; a blow to the elbow; a blow to the nose, breaking it; at least two severe slashes to the throat; three broken ribs; two broken thigh bones; a deep penetration of the vagina with an unknown object; a minor brain contusion; and multiple stab wounds of the back.

"Based on these assumptions, and on your qualifications and your experience, what is your professional opinion as to whether Peter Reilly killed his mother?"

Dr. Helpern said Peter couldn't have done it. He said he couldn't have, in that amount of time, in such close quarters, considering that the body was turned over, without getting some blood on him. He said that even if Peter had thrown away his clothes, there still would have been traces of blood under his fingernails. Even if Peter had not been alone, he said, he couldn't have done it. In fact, Dr. Helpern said, if he were asked that same question about any person, he would say that no one else could have done it, either.

It was the same question I'd been hearing since October 1973 when I first met the people in Canaan and heard about Peter Reilly. I had heard it throughout the trial, at the committee meetings, and in the

317

Belignis kitchen, sitting around the kitchen table, on a Sunday afternoon, near the end of the trial.

"How can you not get bloody, when you're in such a rage?" Jean had demanded. "They say he went berserk—but then, would he be so careful? So methodical? They charged him with a crime that didn't fit the temper."

Of all Peter's friends, the Belignis had known Barbara best. There was the night when Ricky Beligni was lost on Canaan Mountain, and Barbara had come and told stories to Gina. Another time, she came to pick up Peter, who was downstairs in the basement practicing with the band. Jean was out shopping, so Aldo sat in the living room with Barbara. "I tried to entertain her," Aldo said. "But she was very negative that night. She was criticizing the army, and I had been in the army. But you couldn't help liking her. She never put on airs. She was herself. Whatever she felt like saying or doing, she would." I said I wished I had known Barbara, and Aldo said he wished I had, too. "You missed something," he told me.

"You know," he continued, "I saw her that last afternoon. I was driving past the house, and she was asleep in the chair, sleeping in the sun. She had a book on her lap, and her head was tilted to one side, on her shoulder. She had a very serene look on her face. And you know what I thought? I thought, isn't she pretty?"

On the morning of March 25, 1976, five weeks after the end of the hearings, thirty reporters and photographers were jammed into the foyer of the Litchfield courthouse, wedged in the doorway, clustered around the water cooler, spilling out onto the steps. Barbara Bongiolatti, Judge Speziale's secretary, counted them. She had been up late the night before, making Xerox copies of Judge Speziale's decision.

She had known the decision even before she began typing it, and the judge knew she knew. When he handed her the manuscript, entitled "Memorandum of Decision," she smiled. "You guessed, didn't you?" he said. "Yes," she said. "I guessed." She had not worked for this man for nineteen years without learning something about him. She knew he was fair, and she knew, about halfway through the hearings, what a fair man would have to do.

The memorandum ran thirty-four pages, at fifty cents a page. But even the reporters for the smaller papers threw money wildly at the court clerk as he came down the stairs from the judge's chamber, carrying copies of the decision.

Judy Liner looked over Carol Cioe's shoulder. 'What does it say?" Judy demanded. "What's the outcome?" They thumbed through the pages quickly, wading through the background of the case, the careful legal language. They found what they were looking for, at the bottom of page nine.

"After a long and deliberate study of all of the transcripts of the original trial, and the instant proceeding, together with the pleadings and exhibits in both cases, this court concludes that an injustice has been done, and that the result of a new trial would probably be different."

The reporters and photographers were exclaiming, some even running for the phones, or looking for Peter. But Peter wasn't there. Neither was Marion, or Mickey, or Roy Daly, or Jim Conway, or Arthur Miller. Neither was I. John Bianchi was in San Maarten, and Peter Reilly had stayed home. He was drinking iced tea in the dinette, waiting for the phone to ring. Marion and Mickey were at work, but Nanny was with him, and so was Joe O'Brien.

Judy Liner called Peter from the phone at the grocery store, next to the courthouse.

"You got it, kid," she told him.

"I've got it! I've got it!" Peter yelled. Then he cried.

Meanwhile, back at the courthouse, some of the reporters, realizing that Judy Liner was their only link with Peter Reilly, asked if she knew where he lived. "Follow me," Judy said. "I'll be doing eighty all the way." So Judy led a convoy of cars, seven or eight of them, from the courthouse over to Canaan, doing eighty, easy, along Route 63, through Goshen, past Cornwall, past the Parmalees and the Dickinsons and the Kruses, past the little white house where Barbara died.

While the reporters were coming, Peter made some calls. He called Marion, then he called Catherine Roraback. He called Arthur Miller. Nan suggested that he call Auntie B. "I don't think so," Peter said.

Later, reporters talked with some of these people, too. Marion said she couldn't express her happiness. "It's like having a child with an incurable disease," she said, "and then you find out there's a cure." Arthur Miller said he was delighted. "Do you know what this shows?"

he asked the *Times* man. "It shows that if people don't simply accept what's handed down from above, and if they don't surrender to despair, they can change things. They can get justice."

Both lawyers were quoted. Roy Daly called the decision "a victory for justice," and Catherine Roraback said she was "very pleased for Peter." Although the new lawyer seemed the hero, a *Journal* editorial, "Debt to Miss Roraback," had pointed out during the hearing that she'd made an essential contribution to justice. "Whether someone else would have conducted the original defense in exactly the same way is not the issue," the paper said tartly. "No one else seemed interested at the time."

But there was enough glory to spare, glory to share. The judge's decision came just one year after Roy Daly had begun his quest for items of evidence from the state, including the unidentified print. Even after he got it, for months he couldn't find anybody to try to match it. The Federal agents wouldn't get involved without the consent of the state police, and the state police wouldn't consent until somebody Daly knew in Fairfield made an urgent personal request. When I asked Daly whether the delay could be called obstruction of justice, he smiled. "Let's just say this is a funny case," he said.

When the press got to Peter, he held a news conference in the driveway at the Madows's, the house on Locust Hill that had a $15,000 mortgage on it, to pay for part of Peter's bail. "I was hoping all the way," Peter told reporters, and some wrote later that there were tears in his eyes. But he didn't have much else to say. As Geoffrey Madow said, "We talk mostly about cars, and when we don't talk about cars, we don't talk very much." And *The New York Times* story the next day said that Peter seemed "as impassive as ever." The *Times* story was at the top of the front page, continued inside, with a map of Litchfield County, showing Canaan, Litchfield, and Roxbury, Arthur Miller's town, marked with black dots. There was a picture of Peter, grinning from ear to ear, on the front page of the *Times,* too. But Peter was accustomed to this kind of publicity, now.

I was at home in New York when Marion called me from her office, right after Peter called her. "Joan, Peter got a new trial!" she said.

"I knew it, Marion!" I shouted into the phone. "I knew it!"

Marion's sister Vicky mailed me a copy of the judge's opinion, copied from her copy of Joe O'Brien's copy. It was remarkable reading.

Judge Speziale said that although the petitioner hadn't proved that the state had withheld exculpatory material, and in fact, the State's Attorney "had made every effort to be fair," there certainly was newly discovered evidence. Most of it could not have been discovered, he said, "with due diligence," either before or during the trial. This included the identification of the fingerprint and the statement of Sandra Ashner. He noted that the state had claimed that Ashner was not a credible witness, but he pointed out that the issue was not whether her story was credible but whether it was admissible. He said it would be admissible if there were a new trial, and beyond that, it would be up to a new jury to decide whether or not to believe it.

He said that although "time was a key factor," he didn't blame Catherine Roraback for not calling in the film man from CBS. "The discovery of the actual broadcast time of a specifically identified scene in a television program goes beyond the scope of reasonable due diligence."

The judge didn't blame the police. "They were engaged in investigating a brutal and violent slaying. They were justified in considering the petitioner a suspect." He criticized Miss Roraback for not bringing in an expert to raise the issue of the reliability of Peter's confession, which, he said, "went totally unexplained."

He let the jury off the hook. "We must not lose sight of the fact that to convict Peter A. Reilly the jury had to believe and find that he was guilty beyond a reasonable doubt. The unusual circumstances of this complicated and bizarre case explain why the jury at the original trial must have had great difficulty in arriving at its verdict."

He had lived with this case, he said, for more than two years, and he had reached a conclusion. "It is readily apparent that a grave injustice has been done, and that upon a new trial it is more than likely that a different result will be reached."

I had lived with the case a little longer than Judge Speziale, but my own conclusions were not so apparent. I was disappointed in my vision. Here was a case of grave injustice. I'd had a front-row seat, yet I was able to make only vague discernments, as of shadowy shapes upon a stage.

Certainly I could see the painful connection between money and justice. Money would have helped so much to ease the burden and the threat from the beginning, sparing Peter his five months in jail. Beyond

321

that, my most obvious conclusion—and the most frightening—was the essential riskiness of justice.

In the nearly three years since I made that first call to Father Paul in Canaan, I had run many emotional lengths. When I first wrote about Peter Reilly, I had been a writer for ten years, but nothing I'd written ever had such a dramatic effect on other people's lives. When my article led to getting Peter out of jail, I felt enormous joy. It was more than pride, it was real joy, that something I might write could have such a direct and happy effect on somebody else. I remember that joy.

I remember the sorrow, too. I hear Edward Ives saying "Guilty." I see him blinking quickly as he looks at Peter. I see Peter, the color of ashes, staring at the floor, his hand covering his mouth. I see Marion doubled over in her chair.

Eventually I felt relief; it was over. Not that all the questions had been answered. Was the affair a cover-up of some kind or, as Peter had said, were the police just overzealous, "too gung-ho"? Among the throngs of witnesses at the trial and at the hearing—nearly ninety people altogether—who was right? Who was wrong? Who killed Barbara Gibbons?

The most resonant question in the case had always been answered, from the time that handful of housewives and working men got together in an upstairs room and became the Peter Reilly Defense Committee. As it once might have been phrased: When shall we achieve justice in Canaan? When those who are not injured are as indignant as those who are.

There were two postscripts to Judge Speziale's decision. The first was John Bianchi's announcement that he would proceed with another trial; but even if he did it was "more than likely," as the judge had said, that the result would be different. The other was that, of all things, Jim Conway was arrested. He was charged with illegally carrying a gun in Litchfield County, where his gun permit wasn't valid. Jim Conway said he had surrendered his gun voluntarily at the courthouse during the hearing and had been given a receipt; but the charge said he had refused to hand over the gun, which then had been seized from him. He was indicted. "When I came into this case," he told me later, "I used to feel like the Man of La Mancha, always falling off the rear end of a horse. Now I feel more like a character in *One Flew Over The Cuckoo's Nest*."

I knew what he meant. A death in Canaan had occupied my life and the lives of my husband and daughter to a degree that had strained us all. Anne was a toddler when it all began; now she was finishing first grade, old enough to sense how preoccupied I'd been. Jim and I still had drinks by the fire, and he was happily back at work as a financial manager, but sometimes we didn't seem to have much to talk about, other than Peter Reilly.

On the day before Easter 1976, Jim and Anne and I drove up from New York to Litchfield. It was past five in the afternoon when we reached our house, and I knew I had to hurry to get to the market before it closed. I looked in the refrigerator, then in the cupboard, clicking off in my mind what I could quickly get to tide us through the weekend. Milk, eggs, bread, butter, a canned ham. "It's nice to be back in the country, isn't it?" I asked Anne, who was standing in the doorway. "But where do you think I have to go now, right away?"

"To court," Anne said.

It was not a question, and I stared into the cupboard, not wanting to turn and look at her. "No," I said finally. "Oh no. I don't have to go to court anymore."

I did go back once more, though. One day during Easter week I drove into Litchfield and parked in the town lot, behind the county agent's office. There was plenty of room now. I walked up West Street to the courthouse, past the Marden Coffee Shop. Under New Management, it had become the Colonial Pizza. I wondered what had become of my crusty waitress.

After the scramble and the hubbub of the hearings, with the metal scanner and the network news, the courthouse now seemed hushed, the kind of country courthouse I had seen in the movies. As I walked down the first floor hall, my footsteps echoed. This is more like it, I thought.

There was no one to stop me, so I went up the back stairs, the stairs reserved for the judge and attorneys and courthouse staff. At the top, the door to the law library was open. I could see Catherine Roraback at the far end, near the window, talking to someone. She was free for lunch, so we walked down to the Village Restaurant and sat in the second-last booth. I was surprised and pleased to find her in the courthouse, and I asked what brought her back to Litchfield. It was something minor—a client accused of drunk driving, I think—and she didn't seem to want to talk about it. It occurred to me that these are hard times for constitutional lawyers.

"Do you feel you're a scapegoat in this case?" I asked her, and she said she did feel that way, more or less.

"I'm a Yankee, a WASP, and a Roraback," she mused. "There's always been some dislike—and I know enough about my family to think some of it has probably been justified. People have an idealized version of what goes on in a courtroom," she said, "and to deal with that illusion is something most people are not capable of doing. I have reached a certain level of cynicism, but I don't think I'm quite cynical enough." We each had another Bloody Mary.

I wandered back to the courthouse and went upstairs to Superior Court. A young man with lots of bushy black hair was up on a charge of third-degree burglary, accused of stealing a color TV set, some pieces of pewter, and an old Kodak. Bond was set at $3,500, and he was taken away in handcuffs. John Bianchi, representing the state of Connecticut, told Judge Bracken that was the end of the docket for the day, and court was adjourned.

I stayed in my seat until the others had left. Then I walked up to the bar rail and said hello to John Bianchi. He said hello, and I asked if we could talk a bit. He said yes, though he looked a little wary, and I was not surprised. We walked back to the law library and sat at the table near the window.

"I don't look on this as an unusual case," Mr. Bianchi said. "It was not a difficult case. It was relatively simple. The only unusual feature is that a lot of people became interested. I wish this happened more often." He said it with a perfectly straight face, and I felt obliged to remind him that he had tried to throw the press out at the very start, back at the pretrial hearings.

"I just felt, from the portions of the tape I heard, that it would damage him," Mr. Bianchi said. "Supposing that the only thing that was on that tape was just his admission and confession. How could you ever report it? With a headline that said, REILLY CONFESSES GUILT? We read your article, and we were wondering how he ever could get a fair trial. People were sending me that magazine from all over the country." I said I'd sent him one too. He said he remembered.

I was surprised that he hadn't bothered to hear all the tape before he pressed for an indictment, but I hadn't come to argue. I wanted to listen, and as we talked, he seemed relaxed. He put his feet up on the table. His dark gold loafers gleamed. He lighted a cigarette.

"You always have to ask yourself two questions," he said. " 'Have I got the right person?' and, 'Is there sufficient evidence for you to proceed?' 'Have I got the right person?' " he asked, rhetorically. "I couldn't prosecute somebody if I didn't think he was guilty. I couldn't sleep nights.

"I've never thought, 'This is the prosecution's verdict,' or, 'This is the defendant's verdict.' The way I look at it, the State's Attorney represents the people." I thought of Jean Beligni, repeating what Peter had said to her one Saturday, when he was still in jail. "Oh, Mrs. Beligni," he said, "it's the state of Connecticut versus Peter Reilly." And Jean had tried to comfort him. "Oh, Peter," she said. "Everybody isn't against you. *I* live in Connecticut."

When I asked John Bianchi about the jury verdict, he laughed.

"Long ago I stopped trying to figure out what a jury might do," he said. "It must be very hard for a jury. Reasonable doubt—not a surmise, not a conjecture, not a guess. You almost have to define it in the negative. Reasonable doubt," he said again, slowly. "Isn't that a corker?"

We walked out into the courtroom. It was empty, except for John Bianchi and me. The first time I'd heard of John Bianchi was when Jean Beligni told me that she'd called him the Sunday night after Barbara died. "I told him, we're concerned about Peter," Jean had said. "And John said, 'We're all concerned about Peter.' " Now, after all that had happened, I stood with him in the courtroom, and we looked at the picture of Judge Warner hanging crookedly over the jury box. "Judge Warner was State's Attorney for twenty-one years," he said, "before he became a judge." He went into his office then. He was whistling.

I went downstairs, using the back stairs again, to see Mr. Roberts. I knew I was being compulsive. Like some kind of amateur recording angel, I was making the rounds, jotting down the numbers, even though I might never know how they added up.

I knocked on Mr. Roberts's door, half wood, half frosted glass, just right for a country courthouse. Mr. Roberts had his sleeves rolled up and his jacket hanging on the back of his chair. He was wearing his suspenders and the rimless glasses and speaking into the Stenorette. I had never been inside his office before, and it was just about as I'd expected—neat, plain, tidy—except that on the wall behind him was an enormous colored poster, nearly a mural, of Cypress Gardens.

Mr. Roberts said he had learned a lot about people from where he sat. "The longer I sit in that court, the more I know things are not absolutely black and white," he said. "I used to know an awful lot, when I first got out of school, then out of the army. But I've been in that courtroom twenty-eight years, and I don't know quite so much anymore."

They locked the courthouse at five, and I didn't see Judge Speziale. He wasn't in that day, and he wasn't necessarily expected back. He had been named Chief Judge of the Superior Court, which meant he had a lot of other things to do, and within a year, he would probably be appointed to the State Supreme Court. Meantime, even if Peter Reilly were to be tried again, Judge Speziale would not be involved anymore. It was over for him too.

But we talked another day.

"If I seemed a little dour during the hearings," he said, "it was because of that death threat." I suggested he get an unlisted phone. He said listed was better, so people could call if they wanted to. Otherwise they might be more dangerous. But he said he could see that a listed phone had its drawbacks.

I had spent twenty-six months waiting to sit down and talk with this man, and now we were talking about telephones.

But we talked about other things, too. In real life, as opposed to life in court, he seemed an approachable man—pleasant, plain-spoken. We talked about his studies and his growing up, and he said he had never been able to figure out that yearbook label. He said he had never been optimistic. He had gone by the book, though, at least until now. With his decision, he had written new law. *State* v. *Reilly* would go down in the books, too, in the *Connecticut Law Journal* and other places. It would be cited and recited, the phrases of the decision studied and endlessly analyzed by all those law clerks out of Dickens.

"I could have ducked this hearing," he said. "I had already been named Chief Judge. I could have gotten out of it. The headaches, the anguish—who needs it?" I said I knew what he meant, and that what bothered me was the factor of chance.

He spread his hands apart, palms up, and shrugged expressively.

326

"Life is chancy," Judge Speziale said. "This is real life. You take a chance."

I said I had seen people take a chance with the law, and it was frightening. He threw up his hands again.

"*Life* is frightening," he said. "The law is imperfect. What's perfect? We're not robots, and as long as we're dealing with real people, we're dealing with imperfection."

I said I guessed so, but I know I sounded unconvinced.

"Listen!" he said. "This is not the best of all possible worlds. This is no Thomas More Utopia. The system works slowly, sometimes imperceptibly. But it *works*." He sounded a little impatient now, so I said I was certainly glad, after nearly three years, after all the drama and the trauma, that he had decided as he had.

Judge Speziale smiled. "It worked out," he said.

Peter Reilly spent Good Friday 1976, the second anniversary of his guilty verdict, working in the emergency room at Sharon Hospital. It was part of his training for the job of ambulance attendant. He and his girl had broken up, and his plans were vague. He would probably never get to be a policeman. "One of these days," Aldo Beligni once warned Jean, "Peter is going to walk away from us, and not look back."

On a Sunday afternoon, I sat at Jean Beligni's kitchen table. Beverly King came by. Anne played upstairs with Gina, who had turned nine. Big girls now.

"What an education this has been for all of us," Jean said. "For us, and for our kids. I can't watch *Petrocelli* anymore. *Petrocelli* is a big fairy tale." Beverly laughed softly. "We all learned," she said.

Most of the kids I knew had graduated and scattered. Eddie Dickinson was working at Eddie Houston's Shell station. Paul Beligni was going to college. His brother Ricky, who had told me the most terrible thing he was learning in Contemporary Problems was that his father was always right, was married now, and a father himself. Arthur and Geoffrey Madow were working as ambulance attendants in Hartford too. There was still very little for young people to do around town; after two years and all Joanne Mulhern's efforts, the Teen Center was never built.

Something had changed, though. "I think that because of what happened to Peter, it won't happen to anyone again," Jean said.

That didn't mean that Peter would not be tried again. The charge was reduced to manslaughter, but the state kept insisting there would be another trial. Later there would be some doubt as to who would prosecute. John Bianchi died on the Canaan golf course one hot August afternoon. He was fifty-four years old. His funeral mass was held at Father Paul's church, St. Joseph's. Fifty state troopers lined the sidewalk and saluted as the coffin was carried out.

In Jean Beligni's kitchen, Beverly King paged through the scrapbooks she'd kept, four bulky loose-leaf binders that told the long, astonishing story, beginning with the article in September 1973: WOMAN, 51, DEAD WITH THROAT CUT. Beverly said she intended to keep clipping, but for the moment, her collection stopped with the *Lakeville Journal* of April 1, 1976.

There was a long editorial that week entitled "A Grave Injustice," praising Judge Speziale's decision, and calling for "some soul-searching" on the part of the state police. The *Journal* also praised the American system, under which an injustice could be remedied. On the front page, a long story listed the characters and the chronology of the Reilly case— from September 28, 1973 to March 25, 1976; alphabetically, from John Bianchi to James Shay. The central characters appeared in a large front-page picture, captioned MOTHER AND SON. The two of them are standing against the barn, near the house, where Mr. Kruse kept tools and barbed wire and Peter kept parts for his car. Both Barbara and Peter are wearing dungarees and matching sweat shirts with striped sleeves. Barbara is rubbing her little finger and thumb together on her left hand, as she had a habit of doing. Peter is looking toward the house, and Barbara is looking at him. She is smiling.

Publisher's Note

In preparing this book on the trial of Peter Reilly and the subsequent judicial proceedings leading to the granting of his motion for a new trial, the author drew on her three years of direct involvement with the case. The text is based on the official court transcripts, the author's own notes on the trial and related court proceedings (which she attended almost continuously from start to finish), and extensive interviews with virtually all the principals in the case.

Author's Note

For her help with this manuscript I am grateful to my friend Terry Kuschill.

	DATE DUE